Wraiths and Wanderings

E.K Earle

MIDNIGHT
ATELIER
PRESS

Lottie —I hope my Charlotte grows to be half as brave as you.

Mum — I told you I'd write you something weird.

Sean — I love you.

There are some content warnings I wanted to mention in advance.

Self-harm/suicide

Gore

Substance abuse (alcohol)

Please keep safe as you journey.

CHAPTER ONE

T hunder crackled in the distance as the trees whipped back and forth, dancing to a secret rhythm only they could hear. Fat rivulets of rain traced patterns down the nouveau windows overlooking the darkness. This was one of the last sticky summer rains Massachusetts would see before autumn settled in, shrouding the world in a refreshing chill once more. Despite the depth of the night outside, the study remained dimly lit by a single desk lamp and the soft glow of computer screens.

Charlotte hunched over her desk, face tilted toward the microphone, her voice a papery whisper as she eyed the footage on the screen. Her script was displayed on the second monitor, the font size increased to accommodate her strained eyes in the late hour.

"In the years since its birth, Evermoor House has played host to many monstrosities." She paused to lick her lips, eyes darting to the amber-filled decanter by the window drapes. *Not yet.* She softly shook her head, returning her attention to her work. "One woman remains here now, playing guardian and mother to the restless spirits seeking refuge within."

Charlotte leaned back, waiting for the woman in question to come into frame on the first monitor. Atmospheric B-roll played, slow and eerie as the slightest hints of specters blurred in and out of shadowy corners, white faded orbs of light betraying their existence. She had edited the film from her stay already and created a thirty-minute episode, the last of ten similar videos. She had spent the summer on her most ambitious project as a vlogger and influencer yet--Summéance.

Not only a cute play on words, but also a video series exploring some of the weirder and more terrifying supernatural events and spaces she could find. She had encountered ghosts, banshees, and even what seemed like the telltale marks of a satanic cult in the area.

Charlotte had spent eleven weeks alone in her RV, constantly churning out content, refusing to stay still for too long. She had returned to her ancestral home, Winterbourne, earlier that night, as though the change in seasons had beckoned her home. Her gaze wandered as she half paid attention to the footage but quickly returned as the guest of that particular video swept on camera—Evermoor's current owner.

She sat frozen in silence, her microphone muted as she watched the video one final time. Her channel had received a lot of skepticism, predictably, but also a lot of fans. Charlotte cringed whenever a subscriber commented and called her a ghost hunter; she was *not* that sort of tacky. She fancied herself a historian, capturing and preserving the things that lurked in the foreboding folds of darkness. Her job was to unveil the gritty supernatural world to those unbelieving and unknowing, going against everything Charlotte had been told as one of the privileged few that knew the truth. That monsters lurked in the shadows—and that she knew how to find them.

Charlotte watched the rest of the footage with unseeing eyes, her thoughts elsewhere.

⤞⤝

The camera panned over the estate. It was charming in many ways, yet horrific in even more. The shot shifted—first, a sweeping view of the acres of dewy overgrown grass, mist rolling over it as wildflowers crept toward the sky. Next, a shot of a carriage house, the elegant but heavy doors banging open in an invisible breeze. A chapel, crooked tombstones littering the grounds beside it. Then finally, the house itself. The camera cut again, this time sliding through a series of footage traipsing through the inside of the rambling antebellum. It only captured brief glimpses—was that a woman falling from that balcony? What was that dark shadow, right before the kitchen cupboards seemed to slam open of their own accord? The faint sounds of childish giggles, the tinkling ivory keys of a piano, and the low, unsettling moans of suffering pervaded the otherwise haunting silence that enveloped the house. The sweeping shots cut to a woman in front of a camera, as otherworldly as any apparition as she settles against the crimson backdrop of her parlor, the room itself seeming to weep like a freshly cut wound.

Charlotte had chosen this home as the last for her video series for the nearly palpable darkness that seeped through every crack in its history. She had been nervous contacting Eleanor; she didn't want to come across as one of those two-bit ghost-hunting channels with their spirit boxes and flashing torches, scaring themselves for the sake of titillating their audience. Every video was a chance for her to expose the world to the truths they may not be able to see otherwise.

Evermoor House was once a plantation home with a horrible, violent history. It wasn't just about the ghosts or the other creatures that lurked in the darkness for Charlotte. This job, *her* job, was to expose the darkness and bring justice to light in whatever way she could. To preserve the truth in history where others might avert their gaze or even choose to rewrite the words. She wouldn't give them the chance. Charlotte believed people should be confronted with the truth—no matter how ugly it may be.

"Are you ready to begin?" Eleanor asked. She shifted in her high-backed chair, smoothing her gown with long delicate fingers. Eleanor's lips, stained with mauve, curled into a curious smile as she stared past the camera at Charlotte. With a nod, Charlotte scooted forward, her heart thrumming with excitement. Every ghost, every creature, every interaction—they still caused her stomach to flip, as though each was inching one step closer to a truth that evaded her.

Eleanor was not unlike an otherworldly spirit herself. Elegant and poised, her dark eyes pierced Charlotte. Soft golden embers crackling in the gaping maw of the mantelpiece illuminated her. Her angular face was youthful, yet there was a wisdom shadowing her eyes that betrayed her. Eleanor's dark tresses fell in waves around her, the white chiffon gown clinging to her body making her appear even more like a spirit.

"The Evermoor family kept this estate for, oh, approximately a hundred and fifty years, before they . . . abruptly departed about the same length of time ago." A ghost of a smile slipped across her face. "If you believe the words of the townsfolk during that time, they claimed that they never actually left. That driven to madness by the sins of their ancestors, they committed mass suicide in the great hall just through that archway over there"—Eleanor nodded her head toward the archway behind Charlotte—"the angry whispers of the spirits becoming too much. The spirits of the last of the Evermoors roam these halls now, too, trapped here as they continue to relive their own violent deaths."

"Would you say they're just rumors?"

Eleanor answered Charlotte's camera with a wink, eyes twinkling. "At the end of the day, everything has a whisper of truth to it. I could tell you my truth, but it might not be the same truth as you or anyone else."

"And can you elaborate on that?" Charlotte asked eagerly. Leaning forward, she braced her exposed forearms on her knees. The jagged gleaming white scar on her left arm glinted in the low lighting.

Eleanor paused for a moment, her pert nose scrunching ever so slightly. "I call myself the Warden of Evermoor. Do you know what that means to me, Miss Charlotte? It means that I am like a guardian to this place. All I can offer is a respite for the souls that congregate here to process and hopefully find inner peace. Though some have found what they need, whether it be on their own or through our communication"—Eleanor flourished a hand at the spirit board that sat on the low table before her—"restless souls from all over flock here, searching for something more. And that is alright, for this house should provide comfort to atone for the misery it has seen."

Charlotte wriggled forward further in her seat, taking care not to ruin the dramatic shot of Eleanor she had staged for the interview.

"May I ask, why *do* you stay on this property, welcoming the dead? What compels you? Why not live your life for yourself instead of for those that are gone?"

Eleanor's gaze pierced her again. "Tell me, why do any of us do anything? It is because we care about what we do. If not me, then who? Why wait for someone else to bear a burden that I can?"

A chill ran down Charlotte's spine at her words.

⤜⤙⤛⤚

Forty minutes later, they wrapped up the interview. A few spirits had decided to join in, flickering the lights and sending a breeze through to blow out the candles. It had filled Eleanor with mirth—and created some compelling content. Not that many on Charlotte's channel truly believed in spirits. They all thought it was a high-quality performance she orchestrated, no matter how real it got. Charlotte flicked off the camera, thanking Eleanor once again as the other woman removed the microphone clipped onto the neckline of her gown. As she pressed it into Charlotte's hand, the mirror above the fireplace shook ferociously, the rest of the candles around them blowing out.

"Oh, come now," Eleanor chastised lightly. "Miss Charlotte is a guest. Must you misbehave?"

The rattling stopped as two children appeared. For Charlotte, spirits always reminded her of looking at a blurred photo, as though the subject had started to move right as it was taken. They were solid enough save for the edges, blending and blurring into the background around them. They had stopped fooling her a long time ago, even when hidden amongst the living.

"Deidre, Annette, girls." Eleanor spoke to them as if she were their mother. "There's no need for any of that. What are you girls playing now?"

As Eleanor engaged with the blood-splattered ghost children, Charlotte's thoughts began to roam. She'd spent the last few days in the company of Evermoor House and its residents, capturing some astounding footage, but it had unsettled her. Not the ghosts, though. The séances they'd done were nothing new; she'd gone to her first as a preschooler. And Eleanor had reassured her, nothing malevolent resided there—at least not anymore. They *were* a bit gloomy and could catch you off guard, but that was no big deal.

No, it wasn't the dead that unsettled Charlotte. As always, it was the living, how they looked through her like the unobservant would a spirit. She thought Eleanor was the same, seeing Charlotte as the persona she had curated. She was the dauntless content creator with an insatiable need to uncover the deepest secrets of the occult . . . until Eleanor had managed to disturb Charlotte by seeing *within* her, glimpsing her very core rather than looking straight through.

"And why do *you* do this, Charlotte?" Eleanor's attention had returned to her guest as her ghostly children scampered off, apparently off on another game. They were the youngest children when the Evermoor family line had ended. Not realizing they had died, they were blissfully unaware of the atrocities of their lineage. Eleanor let them play and acted the part of their mother. It was, as she explained, the kindest thing she could do for them.

"Oh, you know, for that sweet partnership money," Charlotte joked halfheartedly, packing her gear. The interview was over—that meant she would be back on the road to her own family home shortly. She had promised she wouldn't stay away much longer; as August wound to an end, that time had come.

Eleanor arched an eyebrow. "You know that is not what I mean. I can see it, around your heart. It's fractured and dark. There is something you're holding on to, something making you the way you are. It's no different from the others here." She swept her arm in a broad arc, pointedly glancing to where the ghost twins had run off to. "You cannot let it consume you the way that it does them, or you'll create your own living purgatory. You must learn to be kinder to your soul."

Charlotte gave her a taut smile. "I'll be sure to take that on board."

"What is buried in you? Tell me, what burden puts you on this path?" As Eleanor asked, a cacophony of wails and cries rose around them. As if the spirits in this house could feel the pain inside of her.

"Well . . ." Charlotte hesitated, staring down at the camera in her hands. It felt heavier than normal. "I didn't have a conventional upbringing. I mean, that mustn't surprise you. It seems like yours was quite unusual, too." Eleanor gave a bemused huff. "Well, I feel compelled to do this. The world has so many secrets and mysteries to it, and I think people deserve the truth. There are too many unheard voices out there, and it's like you said—if not me, then who? I had about as much choice in this path as you had in yours." The tightness that had begun to coil in Charlotte's chest loosened slightly as she finished her rant. A calmness swept over her—an exhaustion, really. She shook away the familiar fuzziness clouding her thoughts; she couldn't afford to spend another night out on the road.

"Lottie, love." Eleanor used the same soothing tone she had with the ghostly children. Reaching for Charlotte's hands, she held them in her icy grip. "You need to make choices for yourself. Do not let yourself be consumed by the past." She paused, stiffening as her eyes bored into Charlotte's. "The ghosts whisper around you. Tread carefully."

Charlotte chuckled weakly, pulling her hands away. "Thank you for everything, truly. I better get on the road."

Half an hour later, Charlotte pulled her RV off the winding driveway from Evermoor House and onto the quiet little streets of the nondescript town it slumbered in. The light from the great hall faded away in the distance, plunging the estate into darkness amongst the pine trees. A thought occurred to Charlotte as she pulled onto the highway, sending a shiver down her spine. It could have just been a coincidence, as it *was* a common nickname, but she had a feeling that coincidences didn't simply *happen* around Eleanor.

She had called her Lottie, a nickname no one in her life had uttered since the incident.

Charlotte leaned back in the chair, sagging her shoulders as the screen rolled to footage of herself talking about the video's sponsor. She hated watching herself. Her dark too-wide eyes and pallid skin were washed out against the splash back of the RVs kitchen. She was confident in her edit, even as she listened to herself drone on about "how you, too, can learn to edit like a pro with this one easy course."

With several strokes of her keyboard and a few clicks of her mouse, she had the audio overlaid on the video. One more check to make sure it was synced up, and she would be done. She knew she didn't have to, but she was a perfectionist. And right now, anything that could keep her mind engaged was good.

Charlotte shivered, tugging her unbuttoned cardigan tighter. She hadn't brought a throw blanket with her to the study, having beelined up the stairs of the slumbering house sometime shortly before midnight. It was an unspoken promise to herself—if she didn't acknowledge the world outside of her bubble, it could not get her. That meant not even stopping, not even for a moment, to tell anyone she'd returned.

With one swift movement, Charlotte was on her feet and traipsing to the decanter that had been mocking her for the last hour and a half. With a practiced hand, she flipped a clean whiskey tumbler from the tray below and unstoppered the decanter, eyeballing the liquid she sloshed into her glass.

She had an *extremely* practiced hand.

With a sigh she leaned against the window frame, blinking away the feeling of grit and sandpaper in her eyes as she glanced about the darkened room.

It had been her mother's study, and her grandmother's before her, and her *grandmother's* mother's before even her. It'd continuously been passed down to the next generation of Blythe women since the house had been built. It had remained by and large untouched; the same deep mahogany and leather furniture, several centuries old, had been brought over from France, and still remained in the same positions across the hardwood floors. Occasionally a rug had been added or removed; perhaps the curtains had gone through a few iterations. Charlotte still hadn't even moved all of her gear in—she hadn't seen the point. And maybe, just maybe, some minuscule part of her didn't want to claim it for herself.

A sharp pain lanced her skull. Cracking her neck, Charlotte pulled the ribbon out of the end of her long chestnut braid. She ran her fingers through the twists, pulling them apart to fall down her back, hoping to relieve some of the pressure on her skull. She tucked the ribbon into her cardigan pocket, shuffling back over to her desk. Carefully placing her glass down, she slid back into the seat, determined to get the video up before dawn.

"One more watch," she sighed to herself, settling back down in the ancient leather seat.

CHAPTER TWO

Charlotte had just hit Upload when a streak of darkness sprang straight at her. She shrieked before realizing it was just her cat, who'd finally worked out she was home.

"Oh, Speckle, it's just you, you naughty boy," she huffed playfully, wrapping the large black void up into a cuddle. He mewled in her arms as he snuggled closely.

Specter Blythe, most affectionately referred to as Spec or Speckle, was Charlotte's beloved black kitty. He'd been with her since she was a small child. Admittedly, she'd wanted a black cat because of Salem the warlock—the television one, not the one who'd actually inspired the pop culture phenomenon whose gruesome tale her father had regaled her with as she clutched her new kitten. Sometimes the truth seeped out in the strangest ways. Much like the cat who'd inspired his companionship, Charlotte wondered if there were more to the cat than met the eye.

"This has been a hard summer indeed, kitty," Charlotte apologized, scratching his chin. He stared at her disdainfully. She knew it was because he'd missed her the last few months, not out of true malice.

"Oh, don't look at me that way," she complained. "You would have absolutely hated being on the road that long, trapped in the camper with me. And I met a lot of things that you and I both know you would have brawled with. At least you got some freedom here."

Her trip had taken her all over the place, and none of them would have been good for Specter. She had uncovered a lot of hoaxes and pure nonsense, though some of it had made for decent entertainment, much of which was her debunking the supernatural folklore that led to them becoming urban legends. There were a few occasions where she *had* found the real deal, such as with Eleanor. And the woman who'd been murdering people on the highway outside Scranton. Charlotte grimaced—putting *her* to rest had been quite a task. Same with convincing the faeries handing out changelings to stop, as they'd swapped out the president's grandkid, nearly causing a media ruckus.

She still wasn't sure what had compelled her to announce such a daunting vlog series to begin with. It wasn't as if her Boston views had been bad—her numbers were good, and so were the partnerships. She definitely didn't need the money, either. Perhaps it wasn't about either of those things. Maybe she just needed the illusion of choice, to get out of the manor home and pretend to be the Charlotte she showed the world.

A soft rap at the door dragged her away from her thoughts. Charlotte's grandmother poked her head in, silver locks pulled tight away from her lined face. Her eyes, as dark as Charlotte's own, were creased with worry. *Goodness, has she always looked so worn out?*

Edith Blythe, the matriarch of the Blythe family, glided in. Her nimble feet padded across the floor, her slight frame shrouded in a bathrobe.

"Is this where you came, Specter? I was wondering where you went when I found my biscuits and cream untouched." Edith wriggled her fingers at him, flicking a concerned glance at her only grandchild. "I didn't realize you had returned, lovey."

"I didn't want to disturb you, Grandmother. I had a lot of work to get through."

Charlotte tensed as Edith reached a hand over. Instead of touching Charlotte, though, her grandmother laid a hand on Spec, running it through his silky, soft fur. "Silly kitty," she murmured. "Always knowing before me."

"Sorry," Charlotte breathed. "I just know that you're sore when it storms, and thought it prudent to let you rest."

"Silly child, you know that I would rather know you were safe. These old bones are a lot less weary when they aren't heavy with worry." Her grandmother lifted her lightly wrinkled hand to Charlotte's chin, tilting her face upward. "The circles under your eyes have darkened. Have you rested at all? You can't be sleeping well in that dreadful vehicle. Why don't you stay in nicer places? It's not as though we can't afford it."

Charlotte gently swatted her hand away. She was well aware that the purple smudges under her eyes had begun to deepen, forming hollows under her eyes.

"It's the principle of it, grandmother. I built my career around a grungy, realistic exploration of the occult and its pervasiveness in history. I don't want to become one of those snobs that lives in luxury and can't authentically connect with their content." She didn't have to say that she didn't particularly relish spending Blythe money, either; she wanted to keep herself separated from it and what it meant for a while longer. Separated from the obligations it brought.

Her grandmother sighed, straightening up. Spec licked his paws as the two women spoke, meowing now as if in agreement with Charlotte.

"Oh, hush," Edith scolded him. He purred back, stretching out languidly on Charlotte's lap as they stared each other down. Sometimes she felt her grandmother could understand him on a whole other level.

"Anyway." Edith finally broke eye contact with the cat. "I hate to be the bearer of bad news—"

"Then don't be?"

"—but they've been contacting you again. There's only so long you can avoid them for, my lovey." Edith tapped a bundled pile of envelopes on the edge of the desk; Charlotte hadn't noticed them before. The younger woman was careful to touch only the paper, avoiding her grandmother's hand, as she reached for the envelopes. She scowled at the cursive script upon them: *To the Mistress of*

Winterbourne, Miss Charlotte Blythe. She had a feeling she already knew their contents, but she slid one out from the stack and opened it gingerly.

"If you continue to oust our community . . . consequences . . . blah blah. . . . Duty . . . making a mockery. . . . Absolutely rubbish."

Charlotte snatched the remaining pile, pushing back her seat in one fluid motion. A startled Specter hissed at her before leaping back onto the vacant seat. In several short steps, she crossed to the fireplace, throwing them in. She hesitated for a moment, her hand stretched out, wondering if she could conjure *that*, would it answer if she called? She hurriedly yanked her hand back, grabbing the matches from the mantle. Soon the papers curled up in a small flame.

"You can't just do that every time they try to contact you," Edith sighed.

Charlotte shrugged. "I'll do it as long as I can get away with it, that's for sure."

Her grandmother sighed once more, bidding her good night. Charlotte waited until well after the door had clicked shut before sinking onto the small sofa by the fire. Holding a seat cushion to her face, she let out a muffled scream. She hated that her grandmother was right, but it wasn't fair. She wanted nothing to do with them—why couldn't they feel the same way? Why couldn't they take the hint? She was making this content to piss them off, to show them that she didn't *care* about their stupid Society.

Casting the cushion aside, Charlotte scowled into the now empty room, push-ing to her feet to pace in silence. Specter appeared to have slunk off after her grandmother. She was well and truly alone once more. Passing by her desk, she snatched up her glass and chugged the remainder of her drink, wincing slightly as it burned her throat. Charlotte found herself back at her drink cart moments later, decanting the thirty-five-year-old scotch she had been favoring as of late. She sloshed some into her glass, raising it to admire its amber tint and to let its smoky aroma captivate her senses.

She wandered back over to the large windows and stared out beyond its panes, into the dark and stormy Boston night. For a moment, as she nursed her drink and let it dull the pains and aches in her body and heart, she wondered what it would be like to be an ordinary person. To be anyone other than Charlotte Blythe, the last surviving Blythe daughter and heiress to Winterbourne Manor, as well as the legacy set by her occult-ingrained family before her.

➤➤➤ ⋘⋘

Charlotte stayed up late in her study. She sought to soothe her soul with glasses of the sweet liquid ambrosia, losing count at some point of how many she had poured.

She was perturbed by the stack of letters. Not that she would ever let her grandmother know—no, she could never drop her bravado. She worried how they would escalate it. Would they come to her home? Grandmother didn't hold the grudge she did, didn't hate the Society for what they had done, so she wasn't entirely sure how the older woman would react to them. As the last twelve years had shown Charlotte, only time would tell.

Did she want them to come? To finally confront them for the blame she laid upon them and them, upon her? There would be a reckoning one day. It was merely a matter of time.

In the wee hours of the morning, Charlotte finally succumbed to her exhaustion and admitted defeat. She found herself staring up at the canopy of her bed, too tired to do anything yet too keyed up to sleep. It was the same most nights she had spent in that house since becoming the head of Winterbourne.

She tossed and turned, wiggling into every position she could think of to try and trick herself into comfort. While Charlotte dreaded sleep, not even she could run on none. Her lanky legs twisted in the sheets, the duvet swept to the floor in a dramatic fit of rage. Charlotte couldn't shake her feelings of foreboding, much as she tried.

"Screw it," she muttered, flinging back the sheets. She was going to need assistance resting that night, whether she liked it or not. She grumbled to herself as she shuffled over to the vanity by the window. The curtains were drawn, but she knew dawn would be coming soon. She was too deep in sleep debt to care. Being on the road so long had drained her.

With a grimace, Charlotte picked up the loathsome little bottle hidden behind her jewelry box and her perfumes. Her grandmother had dragged her to a doctor when she'd returned post-college and realized that Charlotte's sleep was erratic, to put it mildly. They'd prescribed sleeping pills. Charlotte typically refused to take them, holding out until desperation overwhelmed her. The pills had a heavy sedating effect and messed with her quite a bit. The last time she had taken one, about six months prior, she had slept for several days and awoken only to feel worse than she had before. Catching up on sleep reminded her of caffeine withdrawal. It made her feel ill, bringing on intense headaches, and though she knew it was good for her, she still disliked it.

Pouring out a powdery ivory tablet, Charlotte lifted the glass of water she kept on the vanity and drank deeply. She steeled herself before downing the tablet, shuddering as it slipped down her throat. She caught a glimpse of herself in the mirror as she returned the glass.

Her waist-length chestnut locks were in disarray, frazzled and knotted. She hadn't showered that day. She hadn't even used dry shampoo, opting instead to braid it. Nor had she redone said braid after releasing it earlier, and her tossing and turning had mussed it, giving it the appearance of a bird's nest. The purple bruises under her eyes accentuated how large and somber her dark eyes were, and her face was certainly looking thinner than normal. Her grandmother would be sure to notice *that* detail when she saw her in daylight. Scowling, she pinched the bridge of her nose. That was a problem for later. For now, she needed rest—rest that would hopefully stop the nightmares.

Drifting back to bed, she could already feel the drug beginning to work. *Too skinny*, her grandmother would tell her when she awoke. Charlotte didn't eat enough and that's why the medication always hit her so hard, Edith would scold her. Her head was beginning to swim as she made a note to actually eat something when she got up.

Sleep descended on her fast and rough like a tidal wave. As she drifted into a dreamless slumber, she felt a twinge, the strange feeling that something was wrong. As she wondered why, sleep finally found her and wrapped her in its embrace.

CHAPTER THREE

Grit filled her mouth, and her head throbbed like she'd been whacked with a mallet. Charlotte groaned as her stomach roiled. Either she was dying, or she was being hit with the worst combination of sleeping tablet aftereffects and hangover she had ever experienced.

She had no idea what time it was as she forced her eyes open. The drapes remained firmly shut—no hints of light. Had morning even come yet? Whimpering, Charlotte wiggled to the edge of the bed. It was some minutes later before she was able to worm her way out from beneath the sheets, fumbling her way across the room to her water. She chugged the water remaining in the glass, gagging slightly. It was stagnant. *Jesus.* She had to air her room out more, apparently.

Cursing and muttering to herself, vowing to never take a sleeping pill again—a lie—and that she would *never* drink again—an even more flagrant lie—Charlotte somehow managed to extract her velvet dressing robe from amongst the mass of clothes strewn over "the chair" in the corner. She called for Specter, "Here, puss puss," but got no response. He clearly hadn't wormed his way in. With a grunt, she mustered what little energy remained, dragging herself downstairs to the dining room.

It mustn't have been too late, as her grandmother was still in there, picking at scones with cream and jam as she pored over the paper. Charlotte sniffed appreciatively as the sweet scent of freshly ground coffee beans filled the air.

"Mornin', Grandmother." Charlotte stifled a yawn as she trudged across the long intimidating room. The dining room had once been the focal point of the family. It was where meetings had been had, fasts were broken, and merriment was had. On the far wall lined with windows, emerald-green velvet curtains rustled in the morning breeze. Opposite this wall, the one that let in sunshine and hope, was the dreaded wall. Charlotte kept her eyes roaming elsewhere whenever she came in here.

"You can't just drink coffee, young lady," Edith scowled as Charlotte poured herself a steaming mug. She sipped it, moaning satisfactorily as the flavor of the beans danced across her tongue. It was a Kona brew, her favorite.

"I could live off of coffee like this just fine," she murmured happily, headache subsiding with each sip. Edith pushed back from her chair, picking up a plate from the sideboard and loading it up with pastries and fruit.

"Sit," Edith demanded, pointing at the seat across from herself as she slid the plate onto the table. Rolling her eyes, Charlotte slid onto the seat, nursing her mug. Her grandmother gave her a look until she picked up a scone and took a bite.

Clearing her throat, Edith said, "It's nice to see you rest up. I was a little worried when you didn't wake up yesterday, but I assumed by the empty decanter that you'd had quite a party by yourself."

Charlotte choked on her scone, whacking her chest. "What do you mean, yesterday?"

"You slept through the day. *Again*." Her grandmother's slim shoulders rose a whisper, her tone nonchalant as she resumed picking at her own breakfast. "I imagined you needed the rest more than you pretend you do."

Charlotte cursed to herself, apologizing as Edith's eyes narrowed. "Sorry, Grandmother. I just have a lot of work on my plate with Summéance, is all."

"That's what you called your . . . video series?" Her grandmother frowned; she didn't quite understand Charlotte's job still, didn't appreciate Charlotte's "lack of respect" for the community.

"Yeah. It was a play on 'summer' and 'séance,' 'cause it was a two-month-long supernatural vlog—"

"I understand the wordplay, Lottie." Charlotte tensed. Grandmother hadn't called her that in years—and now, just a day after Eleanor had done the same? It couldn't have been a coincidence. She let it slide. "I was commenting on the vulgarity. I didn't realize being a video blogger had to be so lowbrow."

"Vlogger, Grandmother."

"Yes, that. Eat your food, please."

With that, they fell into silence. Unfortunately for Charlotte, with nothing else to focus on, her gaze wandered and soon fell on the one place she didn't want it to. The wall.

For the matriarchs of Winterbourne, it had always been important to signify strength. In taking their role in the Blythe family legacy, they must instill themselves in the community. For these women, one way of domineering attention had been through the use of portraiture. As the dining room of Winterbourne was commonly used for most dealings of political, occult, and social interactions, the main wall of the room was lined with portraits all done in the same dark gothic style. Upon the time they turned twenty-five, each woman had found their way onto the wall, the hauntingly lifelike portraits drilling their silent gaze into their descendants for lifetimes to come.

They dated back to 1885, when the first portrait was hung. Though it wasn't the first family matriarch, it was the one of Katherine Charlotte Blythe. Katherine—Kate, as she had been known—had settled the Blythe family in New England and helped to establish the New World occult branch. Her stern countenance had a confidence that seemed to seep from the portrait even now. The black backdrop contrasted with the intricate golden frame that held her, as did the snow-white dress that had her dark eyes sparkling. She had begotten a tradition, and thus every head of the family had her portrait done the same, creating an effect much like a darkened hallway lining the wall.

Six portraits along the wall remained uncovered, including Edith's. The portrait to the right was covered in a black crepe shroud, as it had been the last twelve years. Beside that was another golden frame, empty of a portrait. Charlotte's frame had been hung not long after that night, anticipating the day she would claim her role as the head of the family. The Blythe family matriarchs, heads of one of the wealthiest and most influential families in American occult society, stared down at her, their silent gazes judging her.

All save one.

"We need to get yours done, too, my lovey," Edith murmured.

Charlotte glanced away as her grandmother's voice dragged her from her reverie. "No thanks, Grandmother. It's too soon." She tore her scone apart, brow furrowed.

"I miss them, too," she said gently, "but we cannot let the future be held back by the past."

Charlotte was quick to retort, "If that were the case, then I wouldn't need a stupid portrait to begin with, or any of this other crap we've been doing for centuries now."

"Legacy and doing our job is different from letting the past drag us down." Hurt washed over Edith's face at Charlotte's snide remark. A pang shot through Charlotte's heart.

"I didn't mean to be so rude, Grandmother." Edith bowed her head in acknowledgment of Charlotte's apology. "But it's archaic. Why do I have to do it? You're still doing just fine."

"You and I both know I won't be here forever. And it's more than tradition. I know it may seem unfair to you that we have something we must do, but is that not the point of society? We all do our bit to keep things going. I've been patient and undertaken being the head of the family for you, lovey. You've gotten to go to college and have a different career without the weight of this all, which is more than most of us. All I ask is that you consider that it might just be your turn soon."

"It's the twenty-first century. We don't just have to do shit—sorry, I meant 'stuff'—just because we're told to." Charlotte continued tearing at her scone, glowering at the portraits surveying her. "We're free to make choices."

"That's true. You can make whatever choice you want—just as I am making the choice to remind you that being a member of the Society is about the greater protection of supernatural and ordinary communities alike. That there is a great responsibility that we would rather see not fall into the wrong hands."

An uncomfortable silence fell between them. Charlotte knew her grandmother was right. She'd done her post-graduate specializing in occult history, and how it all tied into the greatest and most turbulent points of history. How easily those with a taste for power could run rampant without watchful eyes upon them. The Society had even had to step in recently as members of the administration on the nonsupernatural side got a taste for the wrong kind of power. It had been ugly, and some of the cover-ups had even gotten onto conspiracy forums. Social media certainly hadn't helped with the spread of information.

Luckily for the Society, the president created such fantastical levels of news on his own that anything they'd had to smooth over was quickly forgotten with the next news cycle. Everyone soon forgot the shapeshifter, a rather bashful and recent Society recruit, apparently, that messed up the facial features of a rather prominent woman, or the ghoul that had been used to cover up the death of a senator at a demon summoning gone wrong.

It had been a weird year for the occult.

As Charlotte pondered over what to say, her phone let out a shrill ring like a tornado siren in the middle of a Texas storm. Charlotte apologized to her grandmother profusely, scrambling for her phone in her robe pockets. Grasping for it so hastily that she almost dropped it, she stammered out more apologies as she swiped the screen to unlock it.

It was an alert noise she had set up for a certain email account. Whenever this particular account emailed her anonymously, shit was usually about to go down.

Mass murder outside Salem, off the highway. Suspected mass murder for occult reasons. No Society or law enforcement on the scene. Dark magic seems involved. Museum—Umbra Hollow.

An image of a large home sprung into her head. Charlotte had actually visited there before. It was haunted; she knew that already. She'd seen some of the lost specters roaming during a school trip there as a kid. She didn't doubt that there might be a supernatural link. One final line finished off the email.

Same magical traces as the 2008 massacre.

Her blood froze as she read the line back over several times. It was the lead she had been looking for, but forever dreading. The dark magic that had killed her parents had left a distinct mark that no one ever found again. Each magical being had its own signature, and this one seemed to have disappeared from the face of the earth after that day. But if it were here again . . .

Charlotte pushed back her seat hurriedly, tripping over herself as she rushed from the room. She stopped at the doorway leading out of the dining room. "I'm truly sorry, Grandmother. I wouldn't leave unless it was crucial. I'll be back soon."

Edith Blythe smiled ruefully at her granddaughter, her sad gaze drifting back to the covered portrait. "Is that the only reason why? Or do you not want to be here?"

Charlotte tensed up, her heart rate spiking. "Because I have to," she said through gritted teeth. Edith shook her head ruefully.

"I think you may be searching for answers that might not exist, my dear. Hunting for retribution won't bring them back."

"I'll be home as soon as I can," Charlotte snapped, sprinting to her room.

She was dressed and on the road within three minutes and twenty-six seconds. This was a record, even for her. The GPS said it would take her approximately thirty-six minutes to get to Salem, Massachusetts, yet Charlotte managed it in twenty-three rather illegal minutes, according to the speedometer of her RV.

"Okay, Specter," Charlotte muttered to her kitty. He had meowed plaintively as she threw on the nearest clothes and grabbed her satchel. She didn't have time to reassure the cat that she would be back soon this time, so it was easier to throw him onto the shoulder of her white cotton shirt. He'd clung for dear life as she belted her brown linen trousers into place and shoved her feet into a pair of boots, almost forgetting her socks before dashing out. "We're almost there, kitty. It's not going to be pleasant, okay? You're probably going to want to stay in the RV."

He mewed again and Charlotte sighed. There was no way he was going to let her out of his sight again. *Just as well*, she supposed gloomily. He was pretty good at noticing things were awry before her. Maybe it wasn't the worst thing to have him watching her back.

As Charlotte pulled onto the highway into Salem, she cursed as an unmarked police car whizzed past her. They were already hot on it, then. This was going to be trickier than she thought.

CHAPTER FOUR

Umbra Hollow, once home to the Van Baird family, had been converted into a museum sometime in the last few decades. The house had been restored to its former glory and was now maintained by a heritage society, letting the privileged members of the current society wonder and marvel at the aesthetics of a bygone era, ignorant of its true past. The Van Bairds had disappeared suddenly over a hundred years prior, effectively ending their line. It was one of many unexplained mysteries surrounding this place that intrigued people. Even the Society was clueless, despite it being one of their own.

The sprawling estate was beginning to swarm with cops and media—exactly the people that Charlotte had hoped wouldn't be there, at least for a little bit. She had parked the RV down a dirt path away from the property; it would draw attention she didn't want or need. Instead, she'd made her way on foot, wriggling through broken fences on neighboring properties with her satchel jostling on her shoulder, Specter's head sticking out the top as he looked around with excitement.

The Queen Anne mansion, looking like something out of a fairytale, soon came into view. It sat on a small slope, looming over the scene below. The police had created a makeshift battering ram out of a cast-iron garden bench and were heatedly arguing if it was okay to smash in through the front door. Other officers tried to wrap crime scene tape around the porch while simultaneously ushering away the insatiable media.

Charlotte snorted in disgust, hidden in the shadows of a willow tree bordering the property. They were like vultures, looking for the next meaty story they could get their talons in. She thought of her own camera she had grabbed on the way out, a spur-of-the-moment decision to record what she saw for her channel.

She had a more noble purpose, though, she told herself, even as her face heated with shame. She was documenting history, preserving it to warn future generations of the folly of her times, to expose the inexcusable lengths the occult community went to cover and shift fault. Because she knew they were going to spin this, just like they did everything else.

As Charlotte glanced around furtively, Speckle cried and scurried out of the bag, leaping onto the grass and dashing forward. Biting back a curse, she raced after the cat, praying they wouldn't be caught. If the Society got wind of her being here, she wouldn't be able to keep dodging them. And they might try to connect her to that night *again*, if the email was true. She wouldn't get off so easily the next time.

Stupid cat. Oh, you foolish, stupid *kitty.* Charlotte's satchel bounced around on her shoulder as she awkwardly jogged across the lawns, dodging behind the trees and tripping over wildflowers as she struggled to keep Specter in sight. If just one person turned away from the gathering at the front of the house, they would notice this strange lanky girl rushing toward the house. For once, Lady Luck seemed to be on her side as she finally caught up to him. He'd gotten all the way to the side of the house before she had managed to, though.

"I guess we can look for a way in now," she muttered between wheezes, glaring at Specter. He gazed up at her, blinking slowly. "Doesn't mean I'm happy with you right now, though, mister."

Hoping no one had seen them or attempted to round the corner, Charlotte began rummaging through her bag. She had been in such a rush that morning that she hadn't replenished her full kit, now silently cursing herself for it. *Surely* she had some sort of potion or spell that could dispel the boundary that sealed off the house. She was certain it was magic keeping them out. She could feel it, as natural as breathing.

Charlotte reached up and grasped a window frame, the shock of dark magic piercing her palm like a needle. *Yep, definitely bad magic.* She winced. It had a familiar distinctly metallic feel.

Mewing impatiently, Spec wrapped around her legs, pulling at her shoelaces before strutting away, tail pointed skyward, as though on a fun afternoon jaunt. With another harried glance around, she followed him.

"Where are you going?" she hissed as he rounded the back side of the house. Her heart almost gave out as he turned the corner; she was certain the back would be as crowded as the front entrance. Thankfully, it was deserted; the back porch was under renovation and had been completely sealed off. She could see from some broken tape warning them to keep out that this way had already been tried and subsequently abandoned.

She glanced at the drainpipes and lattices, wondering if they might support her weight and allow her to get to an upper balcony. Two stories tall with a low attic, Umbra Hollow left little options on its porches for her to secure entrance. She climbed the steps, wondering how to skirt the giant hole in the porch center.

"Meooooow."

Charlotte's head snapped in the direction of Spec's excited mews. He was by the cellar entrance, one that opened up with two doors, pawing at it. With a sigh, she clambered after him.

"I think they would have already tried it, kitty," Charlotte told him. "Here, climb in my bag. We're going to have to go upwards, I'm afraid."

Spec narrowed his large topaz eyes, batting at the cellar door again. With a sigh, she reached out for the handle to show him it was locked. It creaked open, revealing a narrow set of stairs leading down into darkness.

"Well, crap, I guess you were right." Charlotte frowned as she stared down into the gaping darkness, uneasiness washing over her. Scooping Specter up in her free arm, she crept into the cellar, pulling the door shut firmly behind her.

⋙ ⋘

They were greeted by such a deep darkness that Charlotte couldn't see Specter's eyes at first. Taking deep steadying breaths to calm herself, she urged the cat onto her shoulder before groping around in her bag, hunched on the cellar steps still. Though it took her a moment, she eventually flicked her small flashlight on and readied a vial of salt in her other hand.

She couldn't tell if she was trembling or if Specter's purrs were vibrating throughout her entire body as she made one careful step after another to the bottom of the cellar. It fast became apparent that it was not a heavily used space. Clutter filled the room, from moth-eaten remnants of fabric to Civil War-era farming machinery. It was chaotic, and *extremely* dusty.

Carefully weaving through the crowded space, Charlotte spotted another set of stairs, presumably leading into the main house. However, as she passed a particularly dusty spot, both she and Specter began to sneeze.

"Bless you," she whispered to him before freezing. A moan began to emanate from somewhere within the cellar—as if something long dead had been awoken. She gripped her salt tighter and lowered the brightness of her torch before pointing it toward the ground. Specter jumped with ease from her shoulder and began winding his way through the chaos toward the stairs. Heart pounding, she crept after him, taking one cautious step after another, certain something would leap out and catch her unawares.

The bottom of the stairs leading into the house were in sight when she finally spotted the source of the horrific groans. Moping right by the foot of the stairs was a ghoul, an undead being with little thought beyond eating. It especially loved fresh, recently deceased people but would settle for a decaying corpse or two if it had no choice. She had no doubt it had slunk its way into the cellar at the start of the *feast* upstairs. The stench of such an abundance of fresh death would have had such an allure that even the smartest ghoul couldn't resist.

"You've got to be kidding me," Charlotte whined to herself. The pull of the dead above definitely had its attention, but the ghoul was too stupid to work out the stairs. It would absolutely notice if she tried to waltz by it, however, and with the jagged set of chompers on it—she could see the saliva dribbling from its crooked jaw—she wasn't getting past it with all her limbs intact in such tight quarters. None of the salt or crosses she had tucked away with her would work. It was a husk of a thing with no morals, no thoughts beyond its own gluttony. At the same time, it was too dark and risky for her to dig for her bag and see if she had something more potent to throw at it.

Charlotte didn't realize Specter had skulked off until it was too late. Her heart jumped to her throat as his hiss filled the air. Her brave, stupid cat was mere feet away from the ghoul, goading it, tail wriggling as he pranced. The ghoul lunged into action at the chance of a fresh cornered food source. Thankfully Specter was faster, skidding away from the ghoul as it slammed into a pile of steamer trunks. Specter continued yowling, skittering away somewhere in the darkness as the ghoul dove after him. Seizing her chance, Charlotte dropped everything but her flashlight into her bag and raced for the stairs, calling to Specter as she clattered up them. He was already looping back around as she called to him. Unfortunately, so was the ghoul.

Now that it had prey in its sights, the ghoul was able to navigate the stairs with an ability that frightened her. It was rapidly gaining on Specter as he bounded up after her. As she reached for the door, praying it was unlocked, Specter launched himself onto her shoulder. She winced as his claws dug into her flesh through the thin cotton. The ghoul was so close behind them on the stairs that its scent shrouded her, rotting flesh and decay, somehow sickly sweet and rancid all at once. Gagging, she twisted the handle frantically, almost falling through the door as it opened. She slammed it shut behind her as hard as she could, leaning her full weight against it as the ghoul smashed into it on the other side. She struggled against it, gasping for air as her lungs tightened, throwing herself into the door as she fought to secure the lock. After a few minutes of struggling, she finally managed to click the lock into place.

Leaning against the door as the ghoul thudded against it on the other side, Charlotte breathed a sigh of relief. They'd gotten into the house and escaped being eaten by what was essentially a sewer monster. They were getting there.

Still, she wasn't sure how long the door would hold. With a muttered curse, Lottie pricked her finger with a pin from her bag and drew several small runes near the hinges and doorknob, muttering an evocation over them, furrowing her brow as remembered how. Hopefully, whoever spotted her spell would assume it was part of the original one's cast. She stared at it doubtfully, wondering if it would even do anything. She hadn't tried anything like it in a long time.

"Come on, Spec," she murmured to her companion, still on her shoulder. "Let's see what's happened here."

Dropping the torch back into her satchel, she began to scope the place out. The cellar door had popped out onto the kitchen. Adjusting her bag, she strode toward the nearby saloon-style doors.

It was a larger home, overflowing with gilt and gaudiness. She wondered how much of it was the original work and what had been an update. White and gold cornices and detailing were contrasted by heavy wallpaper while expensive and loud vases nearby overflowed, full of bouquets. Her grandmother would call it tacky, and Charlotte was inclined to agree.

Dining trolleys and sideboards full of silverware lined the walls of the small room she'd slipped into. She spotted a drink cart with a hundred-year-old wine bottle and whistled. Whatever shindig had been going on, they'd gone all out.

She frowned. Where was the staff? She herself only had hazy memories of her trip there, but something was amiss. They wouldn't have had the service trolleys set up if it were an open museum day. This was a VIP service. Brandy and hors d'oeuvres of pâté and brie were set on trays, ready to be served. Her stomach growled as she remembered she hadn't eaten more than a few bites of scone that morning. Spec sniffed eagerly at the pate before she shooed him away.

Were the staff all dead? Had they gotten away?

Several doors led off of the room. The largest led into a dining room, whilst several smaller, more inconspicuous doors appeared to be servant exits. Charlotte poked her head into the servant doors but saw nothing of note—simply interconnecting hallways that would get the help through the house without them being noticed. *A good escape route for a murderer, perhaps*, she thought grimly.

"Alright, Spec, stick by me," Charlotte told him sternly. He licked a paw before stretching out, then bounced away toward the dining room door. Her bravado wavered slightly as she pushed through. It was laid out for an elaborate lunch. A banner suggested it might be some sort of anniversary, a party. She treaded fast and silently over the carpet, following Spec around the table and through another set of doors out into a hallway.

She heard the police still bashing the entrance from her left as she glanced about, looking for a hint of the supernatural. Nothing blocked the entrance door, yet it barely budged with their efforts, despite the fact that wood like that should have easily splintered. She briefly wondered why they hadn't smashed in a window, but of course, they would have tried that. Charlotte wondered how they would explain that to themselves later. A door not breaking, they could potentially explain. Glass not shattering, though? Perhaps they would tell themselves it was bulletproof. Or perhaps it would remain forgotten, depending on the scene they found inside.

Charlotte scoped out the rest of the hallway. A grandiose staircase to her right led upstairs, and the rest of the hallway was lined with identical doorways. Her stomach knotted with anxiety, but she scolded herself. She didn't have the luxury of time; whatever had been used to lock the house down would be broken soon enough. All she had to do was pick a door.

She spun in a wide circle, paralyzed in thought. Specter stared up at her expectantly.

"Where do we go, kitty?" she whispered. It was as if her center of gravity had shifted— one moment, she was questioning, wondering. The next, there was this inexplicable pull in her, as though the world was tugging her along. Without thinking, she followed the feeling to a door down the hallway, sucking in a deep breath as she pushed on it, Specter right on her heels.

CHAPTER FIVE

The door slammed shut behind her, narrowly missing Specter's tail as he hissed in reproach. Bookcases were filled to the brim from floor to ceiling, a beautiful green-leather-topped writing desk in the center of this room. Small decorative tables with flower vases littered the space, several ladened with empty champagne flutes.

As she rounded the open pocket doors that led out into the ballroom, cleverly hidden between some of those bookcases toward a corner, a scream caught in Charlotte's throat. She froze.

Bodies littered the floor. Blood pooled beneath them, staining their expensive dresses and suits. Many of their mouths were twisted in horror, an unspoken scream slashed across their faces. Their white unseeing eyes stared ahead vacantly. Like a war-torn battlefield, the dead were numerous, splayed out around and on top of one another. Ringing filled her ears as she drifted away from herself, an unwanted memory tearing through her mind.

Charlotte clamped her hands over her ears as she tried not to sob. She couldn't see what was happening, but she heard their screams, heard the tearing of clothes and flesh, and the thud of bodies against the ground. She was so scared. They were all dying out there, but she was hiding, she was pathetic, a coward—

She swayed, eyes unfocused as they skimmed over the scene in front of her. It was just like *that* night. The way they were sprawled there, broken and unfixable, their organs spilling out of them. So violent and senseless; pain for the sake of pain. Who, or what, would do this?

Anger pulsed through her veins, burning her from the inside. It tore up her forearms like strikes of lightning. Someone could have stopped this—should have. She could have *done* something this time if she had been here.

She wasn't a child anymore.

"Alright, I know you're in here." Charlotte's voice echoed. She spoke without thinking, letting her anger drive her. "Come on out, then. You're not scared of some little girl, huh?"

Even as the words flew from her mouth, Charlotte knew she should be terrified. But the fear wasn't there—nothing but rage burned within her. Charlotte didn't care. It was too much like last time. She was dimly aware of Specter, his meow distorting into a howl as he pranced away from her, beelining toward something glinting on the floor. She continued pacing.

"Whoever or whatever the hell you are, show yourself! What do you gain from doing this? You've still got this place locked down with magic, so that must mean you're in here somewhere, right? Come on, what are you waiting for? Don't be a little bitch."

Charlotte wove her way through the throng of bodies, searching as hot angry tears bit at the corners of her eyes, salt stinging against her tongue. She let out a frustrated scream once she reached the middle of the room, spinning around. Her foot slipped in a rapidly congealing pool of blood. Her lips parted in a silent *Oh* as she felt herself falling backward, the back of her head making contact with the floor below.

⟶⟩⟩⟩ ⟨⟨⟨⟵

They were gone. They were gone, and they were never coming back. They were gone, and she had done nothing.

These thoughts repeated through her mind, a broken record. Though she sat there, unable to move, those thoughts continued to whirl through her mind.

They were gone, and she had been too much of a coward to do anything.

Her grandmother was talking to a paramedic. They had called in their own people, working in all areas of the normal parts of the government, to come help clean up. They wouldn't be able to hide the evidence otherwise.

In the span of a few minutes, her parents had gone from being alive, living, breathing beings, to becoming evidence.

She'd been wrapped in a blanket after they'd found her on the floor, sobbing hysterically as she curled up beside her mother's cooling body. She wanted to scream when they pulled her away from her mom, but she didn't have the energy, didn't know how to use her body anymore. Lottie had stopped existing the moment her mother and father had stopped breathing. They took her away from them, and she would never see them again.

They were gone, and she was still there. They were gone, and she could still breathe. They were gone, and she wished she could be too.

". . . state of shock, understandably. She's going to need a lot of help after this level of trauma; it's going to affect her for life."

"My poor girl . . ." Edith murmured between her own tears. "My poor babies."

"She's the only lead we have, though. She's also our only suspect—"

"Goddamn it, Charlie, she's lost her parents! I lost my daughter *just minutes ago. Look at that face. You honestly believe one sixteen-year-old girl, who looks like she weighs as much as a feather, could have orchestrated and pulled off a mass murder?"*

"She could have had help. We still have to investigate."

"Lottie is just a child! Look at her—she's just a little girl still."

She could hear her grandmother sobbing, but it sounded so far away. Everything sounded so far away. Charlotte's head lolled forward—they had given her something to calm her, but it just made her feel heavy. The pain was still there, just muffled now. Her chin slumped against her chest.

Her eyelids fluttered as she looked down at her lap. She was still wearing her ivory satin kid gloves. They were now stained, leaving a bloody trail up to her forearms. Her mother's blood, the blood that had given her life, now stained her. She stared at the splatter. The skin that emerged from under it was clean, porcelain. Her arms burned as though they were being branded, and the urge to quell that pain rose within her. If she sliced away the tainted gloves, sliced away the flesh beneath, she could stop the pain.

She wasn't in control anymore. Some far away, deep part of her—it was gaining control now. She surrendered herself to it. Do whatever you need to do. Just make it stop hurting.

Her body began moving of its own accord.

Lottie was floating further away now, like a boat caught in a storm, the ocean sweeping her away from the shoreline. It was okay, though. She wanted her ship carried out to somewhere it could be lost, forgotten about.

"Lottie!"

Her grandmother's screams jolted Charlotte from her stupor. They had their arms around her, too tight, yelling at each other. It wasn't until one of them tore the dinner knife from her hand that her body processed the first tear of pain. Then it was on fire, screaming hot fire that twisted and bled and hurt but felt so good at the same time—

"How did she even get the knife? How bad is the damage?"

"It needs stitches; it's a pretty deep gash—"

"Tourniquet it first, cut off the blood flow. We need to get her to the hospital! Grab the wheel, Charlie. I'll ride back. Ms. Blythe, get in now, we aren't waiting for you."

Bright lights danced across her eyes as pain seared through her consciousness. It was a tether, bringing her back to the world from the haze. The irony of this was not lost on her as she smiled.

That tether would soon be torn, and she, too, would be gone.

Chapter Six

*T*here was nothing but darkness. No thoughts, no feelings. No pain. Just simple, blissful black. It stretched on forever, with no end and no beginning. What was time? It was finite and infinite there. Nothing mattered.

There was something in the dark. Something new, something different. It began to unravel, a slash of crimson that needed no illumination. It tugged and pulled, and there was no choice—just follow the red thread as it wove through.

The blackness lessened. It was now grey, muted. There was cold there, but there was also warmth beginning to creep in. It sped up, pulling faster, harder.

Then, suddenly, it wasn't dark at all. The gray disappeared and the world turned bright and chaotic. There was pain and heartache time and time again.

None of it made sense.

He remembered. He was himself. He had died. Then it went dark, and everything went away. He remembered, and it was too much to bear. Suddenly he was a drowning man, gasping for air, stuck between the dark and the light. There were people between; dark shadows dancing between the layers, waiting to escape, to do something. He saw the other people, then. Watched them fall to the floor. A man spoke—there was a wrongness to him. Something to fear. He retreated to the dark, the man's face burned in his mind.

He would stay in there once more, where they could not get him. Not again. But then a softness called to him, beckoning. The thread is connected to it, and he knew if he followed it, all would be well. It hummed with energy, with magic.

*Then he was there and not there at all. He could see, but they weren't his **own** eyes—were they?*

His home was different, changed, but somehow he was there and in the darkness no longer. There were bodies, scattered all about, but he could not scream. That was when he spotted him. *The golden-haired angel—or so he would seem on the outside. No. He was the golden-haired demon that had entrapped him so long ago, who didn't seem to notice him as he weaved his way through the room.*

The boy, demon, angel—his name was Atticus. He knew that. They were friends . . . used to be friends? He was jumbled, disoriented from the dark. Something was missing.

Atticus leaned over a girl sprawled on the ground. She wasn't like the bodies around them. There was still an aura of light to her. The boy's face contorted for a moment—was that disgust on his face? His gaze was drawn from the boy by a flash of color. He was shocked to see the red thread lead to her. There was a cat hissing beside her, hissing at Atticus, but the golden boy merely pet him, whispering softly. He slid something into a brown bag beside her. What is the demon boy doing? How is he here?

Why is he here?

Atticus stood once more. The boy's face conveyed nothing as he glanced over to him, then vanished into the shadows.

⟫⟫⟫ ⟪⟪⟪

"Meow!"

Charlotte's eyes fluttered open as the rough scrape of Spec's tongue licked at her cheeks. His breath washed over her face like a wave, the aroma not unlike hot, putrid seafood.

"Oh, that's feral," she murmured. "Stop, kitty, that's disgusting."

Her stomach roiled and her head swam as she pushed herself up into a sitting position. The back of her head throbbed with pain. Bright dots flashed before her eyes as the world came into focus once more.

She wasn't in the ambulance; she wasn't trapped in her memories. She had been knocked out. She reached a hand to touch the throbbing lump at the back of her head. She had slipped. That must be why her head stung like a bitch. Charlotte tentatively felt around her head through the strands of her braid, her fingers brushing over something warm and sticky. There was definitely blood back there, but she was fairly confident it wasn't her own. She wasn't sure if that was a good thing or not.

Spec crawled onto her lap, mewling plaintively as he kneaded her shirt. She dropped her hand from her head onto his, scratching his ears reassuringly. "I'm okay, Speckles, I promise. Just a bit sore. I wasn't out long, was I?"

Charlotte then remembered that they were in a ballroom full of the recently deceased. A ballroom full of people that had been slaughtered by some unknown entity that was probably still in there with her and could, theoretically, also kill her at any time. Scrambling to her feet, Charlotte grabbed Specter and held him under her left arm, digging through her satchel with her right hand. Her fingers grasped one of the vials clinking about and tugged it out, her thumb pushed against the cork, ready to unleash it as she spun on the spot, taking in the room. She wasn't sure she could do much against something that could do *this*—so similar to the unknown being that had massacred her own family, she thought again—but it might buy them time.

It was as deserted as it had been when she went down. She could hear the distant yells of the authorities trying to get in. Next to no time must have passed. There was, however, one rather dramatic change.

The spirits of the departed now milled around the room. Noncorporeal beings, ghosts were able to interact with the living plane of existence when they had control over themselves. However, in the same vein, ghosts experiencing violent enough feelings were also able to do so, their emotions overriding anything else with their pure, undiluted energy. That was how you got poltergeists and malevolent spirits. Given the day they'd had, she was pretty certain these spirits had every right to be angry and scared.

She gripped the vial tighter as she eased her way back toward an exit. Many of the ghosts were motionless, their spectral forms glitching between planes of existence. Some of them might pass on there and then, lacking any hold on their lives before. If they were confused enough, they might not remember anything at all and move on, or they'd be too confused to remember that they were dead and remain on this plane. With so many of them in one space, there was a good chance of at least one hostile ghost amongst the lot.

Charlotte held her breath as some of them faded away, hopeful that the others would follow. One or two looked down at their own bodies, faces contorted, unable to comprehend what they were seeing. Then there were others who began to drift away. She knew they would now haunt this place, reliving their last moments on some sort of instinctual level, their deaths hard-coded into the remnants they left behind in death. She pitied them worse than the ones that knew they were dead. At least they would get to move on.

As the crowd of the departed dissipated, Charlotte noticed a somber being that didn't quite fit in with the rest. She uncorked the vial, ready to fling it. It was some sort of potion; she wasn't sure what kind, exactly, but it would do *something*. The other spirits that had converged were from the bodies of those that had just passed. This one was in attire from another time—clearly not a recently dead.

"Shhhh, Spec," she warned him. He continued twisting in her grip, forcing her to drop him. She cursed as Specter paused in front of her, growling, hackles raised as he stood between herself and the unusual spirit. The ghost hadn't noticed them yet—or at the very least, he wasn't paying attention to them. His square jaw was downcast, lips twisted into a mournful expression. Unlike many of the recent ghosts that didn't have a great grasp on this plane and thus were different tones of grey, he had some color to him. The edges around him blurred just enough to reveal his true nature. His auburn hair was slicked back neatly from his face, a few tendrils loose at his temples as though his hair had been mussed. The cut of his black-and-white suit, along with his posture, led her to believe he might have been an upper-class gentleman. Either way, he clearly shouldn't have been there. She had never heard of or seen this ghost haunting here before.

"You can leave now," she called out to him. "The living will be in here soon to deal with what happened here. I'm sure you have some long-lost love to haunt or something; why don't you move along while I find out what happened?"

Specter continued spitting as Charlotte readied the vial. She finally saw the shimmering blue liquid within. *Ah, a banishing potion. Perfect.* "Move along, or I'll move you myself. This is not the place for your spooky ass."

The spirit lifted his head slowly, turning to look at Charlotte in surprise. "You can see me, miss?"

Charlotte winced at the hope blooming across his face. "Yes, I can, but I can assure you, whatever your deal is"—she gestured to his dinnerware—"is very different from what I'm here for, and quite honestly, I'm tight on time right now. I need to find someone that isn't too traumatized to tell me what happened here. So, off you go."

His dark eyes remained on her as he cocked his head slightly, gesturing with one gloved hand to the sprawling bodies. "Do you mean the murders?"

"Did you see it?" Charlotte's interest piqued. The gentlemanly ghost frowned in concentration, as if mulling something over. The front doors rattled loudly, a warning. If the dead were finally leaving their bodies, surely whatever spell or incantation that sealed the place would be broken soon. No spell at this scale would last. They'd be here in moments at the earliest, minutes at the latest.

"Look," she told him, impatience creeping into her voice. "If you're not going to talk to me, I need to find someone who will. Good day, best of luck, and all that jazz. See ya."

Charlotte tiptoed around the bodies, making her way toward another door coming off the room. She had seen a few ghosts float that way; hopefully, she'd be able to track one down with some useful information before it was too late.

"Wait!" he called out as she reached the door. She half turned toward him, hand on the door handle. Spec had trailed after her, keeping a few feet behind, and was already back in protector mode. "I would wish to talk to you. If that is amenable to you, that is, miss."

The repeated slamming of the front doors caused Charlotte's shoulders to tense. "Ugh, fine, yes. But we can't do it here—"

Even as she spoke, excited shouts came from the distance. The door was giving in. Then came a thunderous crack as the wood finally began to give way.

"Follow me," the ghost said, bowing courteously before strolling through the door that she hadn't yet opened. Rolling her eyes, Charlotte mumbled under her breath about the dead and their stupid walking-through-walls gimmick. A pang of guilt shot through her heart as she glanced back at the corpses left behind them, the sight of their unnaturally bent bodies searing into her vision as the door gently swung shut.

The ghost was waiting at the foot of another staircase for her, dark eyes wide.

"Forgive me, miss. I believe it has . . . it has been some time since I found it necessary to navigate obstacles in such a way. That was inconsiderate of me."

"Whatever," Charlotte muttered. She lifted her head, listening intently. "We gotta hurry. You might already be dead, but I'd rather not join you when they find me here in the middle of a mass homicide and hit me with the death penalty."

He tilted his head in acknowledgment. "Then let us make haste. I have a place where we can speak in absolute secrecy." He gestured to the cupboard under the stairs. "Please, head through here."

"Are you insane? Do you think they aren't going to check under the fucking stairs for the murderer? I might as well walk up to them right now and tell them I did this all, then." *This isn't happening.*

Flinching as Charlotte cursed, the ghost merely gestured to the cupboard once more. "Please, trust me. There is a secret passageway through here, I assure you." He slipped through the wall, leaving her and Spec on the other side. *I should just run for it*, she thought, *even if it means dealing with the ghoul again.* The front door smashed open with a thunderous roar—she was out of time and shit out of luck. She had to follow the emo ghost.

Opening her satchel, she urged Spec to get in and told him to be quiet as she yanked the cupboard open and stumbled in. It was pitch-black inside. Fumbling around Specter, she pulled her flashlight out again and flicked it on.

It was a normal linen press, all three sides filled with spare towels and miscellaneous bathroom products. The ghost was nowhere to be found. Charlotte bit back a shriek of anger, the nails on her free hand digging into her palm. She'd been hustled, and now she had no time to escape. She was *screwed*. They'd find her in here, and it wasn't just the police that was an issue. When the Society got word that she was the only remaining person alive in another massacre—

"She must have done it! There were over a hundred people there and she's the lone survivor. I don't buy her story—she just happened *to be under a table and didn't see who killed them all? Fallacy. She absolutely* is meddling in something forbidden and dark . . ."

". . . She's just a girl; she couldn't have done this all on her own. She must have accomplices."

". . . imprison her. It's the only way we can make sure she doesn't commit evil like this again . . ."

"Even if it wasn't her, I'd feel safer knowing that she was locked away . . ."

". . . locked out even the highest ranking among us with her dark magic . . ."

Charlotte began to hyperventilate, clutching her throat, chest tightening. It was all the same, except this time there would be no leniency, no grandmother to vouch for her. They wouldn't give her a fair trial. She would get the blame, and that would be that. She let out a sob and slipped to the ground. This was it.

"Miss? Are you alright? Why are you crying?"

The voice of the melancholy ghost cut through her anxiety like a searing blade as Charlotte grappled with her broken, distorted thoughts. She glanced around wildly, spotting his head as it poked through part of the wall.

"This is the secret panel, miss. You must knock here"—he pointed to the upper right corner of the bottom wall paneling—"seven times. A sharp rap, if you would. It will spring open and you can come through. You mustn't dally."

Charlotte's head swam as she followed the ghost's instructions. He smiled encouragingly, his head and part of his upper torso poking through the wall. Lo and behold, on the final tap, the panel swung inward, just large enough to allow a man to fit through. She stared at the ghost as he ducked back in, motioning for her to follow.

"This cannot be happening," she murmured, swiping at the tears that had welled up moments before. Spec shifted about in her bag as she crawled through on her hands and knees, wondering what she had gotten herself into by chasing the lead.

The panel closed behind her, sealing them both tight within.

Chapter Seven

"Now where have you taken me?" Charlotte groaned as she hunched down, rubbing her freshly hit head. She'd dropped her torch when she crawled into the space, having tried to stand and quickly realizing it was maybe three feet tall at most. Whoever had designed the tunnel hadn't thought it out too well. Spec scratched at the inside of her bag as she lifted the top for him to free himself. This way, if something happened, he could at least try to escape.

"I'm sorry for the close quarters, miss. It is a hidden passageway, you see. It's cut into the space under the stairs and slopes downward, leading away from the house. It was built into the home to provide safe passage, lest something go awry. It is so secretive that it is not even on the floor plans. I sincerely doubt they will find you, should we continue along."

Charlotte sighed and scrambled about for her flashlight; she had kicked it when trying to right herself, knocking it against one of the odd-sloping walls. Snatching it up, she tapped the flickering light, realizing with dismay it had gotten damaged. While it still shone, it was now a fractured, weaker light. It barely illuminated the foot of space in front of her. What she *could* see, though, was the spectral being who'd trapped her down there. He was crouched down as well, despite there being no need.

"Will you allow me to escort you, miss? I'm afraid they're getting rather close now, and I worry they may still hear us, if you fear such a thing."

"Of course I fear that, you impeccably mannered dick," she grumbled to herself. "Just lead us out of here, then."

With a nod, he turned around and started crawling. Charlotte stared after him in confusion before she began shuffling after him on her hands and knees.

"Why are you crawling? Can't you just float along? You're a *ghost*. Why bother?"

"I merely wanted to make you feel more comfortable, miss."

They shuffled along in darkened silence. Eventually, her torch completely gave out, forcing a frustrated Charlotte to cram it back into her bag. Specter took the lead in front of her, keeping his tail low so it would swish back and forth reassuringly over her hands as she crept through the darkness.

It was several long minutes before the quiet was broken.

"So, what's your deal?" Charlotte finally asked. She hadn't even asked this complete stranger—yes, he may have been dead, she told herself, but he was a stranger nonetheless—his name before following him into the bowels of a haunted murder house as she ran from the authorities. It hadn't been a high priority for her ten minutes before, but as the pressing need to escape lessened, her natural curiosity kicked in. "What's your name? Why are you haunting here? Like, you clearly know you're dead. So what's the deal?"

The ghost was silent as they crept along. Charlotte was beginning to get irked when he finally replied.

"Wade. Wade van Baird, miss."

She was stunned into silence. Van Baird, as in the missing Van Baird family. This had been *his* home. No one had seen hide nor hair of him or his family since they disappeared. Her heart raced, mind spinning as she wondered what had happened for the ghost to finally show up now.

"I know there is some impropriety to my request, miss, but may I ask your name?"

Wade's voice interrupted Charlotte's train of thought. "Oh, I'm Charlotte. Charlotte Blythe. The cat is Specter."

"Blythe? Of the Bostonian Blythes?"

That caught her attention. "Yeah. So you know us, then?"

"Of course, Miss Blythe. Through the Society. I imagine that was why you were here today?"

This dude was throwing her some serious curve balls. A morose ghost hanging around a massacre that had nothing to do with him after being missing for a hundred years? Charlotte was intrigued. There was a mystery afoot, and she wanted to get to the bottom of it.

". . . but that was how I realized you weren't here for the Society."

"Wait, what?" Charlotte had tuned him out as she mulled over her thoughts.

"You can't have been here because of the Order, I said, Miss Blythe. There is no dark magic on you."

"Wait, you can prove there was dark magic? And how does not having dark magic make you so sure I'm not here on behalf of the Society? What are you saying here, Wade?" She paused. "Wait, you said 'Order.' You mean Society, right?"

"My apologies, I was mistaken. You are correct." He sounded distracted. "Perhaps we could speak on this when we are in more comfortable accommodations? I fear that this may not be the most appropriate location for this particular conversation."

Charlotte muttered under her breath, "Yeah, I guess so, seeing as your ghostly butt is in my face right now."

"Pardon?"

"Nothing. Don't sweat it."

<hr />

It seemed like there was no end to the tunnel. There was a point just past the house where it turned into pure dirt with some beams scattered throughout, presumably to keep it from collapsing. It had set Charlotte on edge; she didn't want to die trapped underground, somewhere no one would even find her body.

The quiet between them was broken only by the sound of rocks shifting and her own breathing, and the occasional hiss from Spec as he caught a paw on a root. Was it five or twenty minutes that passed? She truly didn't know.

Finally, the tunnel began to widen and dim light began to filter in. She sighed in relief as she saw her hands in front of her once more. Her relief was short-lived, however, as the earth began to shake and rumble.

"Ghost, that better not be what I think it is." Charlotte's voice rose in pitch, dread rearing its ugly head. Spec hissed at Wade's backside as he continued crawling at an even pace. *Stupid ghost*—stupid, *stupid ghost.*

"I'll go check, Miss Blythe," he offered as she opened her mouth to snap at him. Without waiting for her to answer, he vanished. She despised ghosts doing that. Not only was it completely unsettling, but you couldn't be sure of what they were doing when they vanished. Were they plane jumping, or were they simply invisible to the human eye? He could still be lurking there. She didn't know him; what if he *were* a malevolent spirit and planned to bury her alive?

"Don't you dare think like that while you're trapped underground, you idiot," she whispered to herself as hot tears began to prick the corners of her eyes. "You're okay, everything is gonna be fine . . . you have to keep it together and not panic."

Drawing in a deep breath, she nudged Specter onward. The tendrils of light grew as Charlotte repeated to herself that she was going to be okay. Soon all her focus was on her words and not her thoughts, her body on autopilot as her knees bruised and her palms landed on small rocks. Eventually, her knee caught on a large mound of earth and she fell forward, slamming headfirst into the earth, her mantra finally broken.

"I hate this, I hate him, I hate everything—"

"Are you speaking to me, Miss Blythe?"

Charlotte shrieked as Wade's head burst forth from the wall in her periphery, heart racing as she flung her hands over her head. Her chin hit the ground, scraping over a stone. Wade hissed in sympathy.

"Warn me next time you're going to do that," Charlotte moaned as her entire being throbbed. It was shaping up to be a bad day for her. Wade's entire torso now hung through the passageway, guilt etched across his face.

"I'm truly sorry; I didn't mean to startle you. Can I be of assistance in any way?"

Pushing herself back up onto her hands and knees, Charlotte coughed and shook her head. She had eaten some dirt on her way down. "You've done plenty, thanks. Wanna catch me up?"

Charlotte startled crawling forward again, her eagerness to escape growing despite the pain wracking her. Wade's upper body bobbed alongside her, still sideways. Seeing him move like that made her shudder; it was unnatural.

"Part of the tunnel toward the house has appeared to have collapsed, possibly as a result of the number of people in the house. I apologize for taking so long; I took the liberty of popping back to see if the situation had changed. The local authorities seemed to have gained access, the Society mingled amongst them. They are surveying the scene and have sent search parties to ascertain the whereabouts of the culprit. I did not hang around long—some of those that perished were getting scared, I am afraid to say. I suspect that no one will have the time to find this tunnel or yourself, Miss Blythe."

Charlotte sighed with relief. "That's something, at least."

"This tunnel is also about to end, so please take care getting out, Miss Blythe."

He was right. Wade floated ahead of her, disappearing upward abruptly. Charlotte smacked into the end of the dirt wall, her attention focused on his vanishing form. Spec spat with rage as her hand landed on his tail.

"Sorry, kitty! I wasn't paying attention." Specter gave her a look that seemed to say yes, he could tell that much.

Above them was a wide square-shaped trapdoor. It appeared to be made of floorboards—that must have been how the light filtered in. She stood, reaching her arms up. The trapdoor was up fairly high, but her hands could reach it with her elbows bent. Already exhausted from crawling, Charlotte's muscles screamed in protest as she pushed, her palms flat against it, her heels digging into the dusty earth beneath her.

"Would you like me to try and pull?" Wade's voice floated down from above them.

"If you can get it, go ahead."

Pausing to take a deep breath, she told him they would go on the count of three. She could already feel the blisters forming on her palms as she steeled herself.

"Are you ready, Wade? Okay. Three, two, one—go!"

Charlotte began to push against the heavy trapdoor again but was met with much less resistance this time. Sweat began to trickle down the back of her neck; she had been too worried before to notice just how much the late summer day had begun to heat up. Every part of her body cried for relief. Time seemed to slow to a crawl as she fought the urge to scream and let her arms drop. Spec meowed encouragingly, his paws on her thighs as he pushed himself upward, evidently trying to help.

Then, ever so slowly, the trapdoor began to creak and rise away. Her forearms shook with the effort, vision swaying as she pushed with all the strength she had left. Wade started calling out words of encouragement as the wood splintered from years of disuse, and the entire world seemed to shift with her efforts.

"One last big push, miss. I think we have it!"

With a scream of rage and pain, Charlotte threw her weight into it, arms extended as far as they could. The trapdoor went from being raised a few inches to slamming open with extreme force. One second, she had her palms pressed against the aging wood; the next, she fell backward as her hands pushed against thin air, landing on her backside. Though a sharp stab shot up through her, Charlotte began to laugh. *What a stupid day.* She could see the roof of what appeared to be a cottage above, quickly blotted out by a concerned-looking Wade.

"Are you alright? I would reach down, but I'm afraid I've worn myself out grasping onto the handle."

Charlotte could see that Wade looked exhausted. He looked like a ghost more than ever now. He was faded, his color seeping away, as though he were struggling to maintain his form. He was blurring more around the edges now, too.

"It's fine. Thanks for your help."

⟩⟩⟩ ⟨⟨⟨

It took several uncomfortable and undignified minutes of throwing her satchel and Specter up before she could haul herself out. Once she was on solid floor, she rolled onto her back, eyes closed as her heart thrummed loudly. She couldn't remember the last time, if ever, that she had exerted herself like that. Even on the supernatural hunting front, she was ashamed to admit she didn't do a lot of physical stuff. Charlotte briefly wondered if she would ever move again and how she would manage to get back to the RV, let alone home, in one piece.

Then she remembered why she had even left the house that morning, and her eyes shot open, determination and adrenaline refueling her. She sat up too fast, causing her head to sway, dots appearing before her eyes. Shaking them away, she put her head forward between her legs, sucking in deep breaths. Her headache pounded away, an irritating reminder of her pain as she gritted out, "I need you to tell me what happened now, Wade. All of it. Make this worth my time and effort."

Wade edged toward her slowly. She could see his neatly polished black dress shoes stepping delicately across the floor, as though he were scared of it giving away beneath his weight. Despite being able to float and having no weight or corporeal form, he acted as human as she did. *Old habits die hard*. She suppressed a snort of laughter as Wade crouched beside her.

"Forgive me, but I worry about the state of these accommodations, Miss Charlotte." Her name rolled off his tongue, like he was savoring the sound of it. She was surprised to realize his accent was more polished than her own, distinctly not Bostonian—mid-Atlantic. He dropped his head. "I may be fine here, but you and Master Specter could be subject to more harm. Is there perhaps somewhere else we could relocate to for now? I would be most obliged to speak to you once I knew you were safe."

"You're being awfully considerate for a dead person."

Wade bristled. "Though I may lack certain functions, I can assure you I have not lost my sense of empathy and compassion. So, if you would, *please* allow me to escort you somewhere safer."

Charlotte cringed, cheeks heating. "Sorry. I guess I'm just a bit shaken. I have my RV parked somewhere nearby."

Wade bowed his head as she scrambled to her feet, double-checking her satchel as Spec wrapped himself between her legs. She sighed with relief to see her phone was undamaged, then pulled up her navigation app. The pin locator she had dropped on the van's location—a habit she had picked up amongst her adventures—was still there. It was a several-mile walk, a bit longer than she wanted, given they had to take a wide berth, but it was manageable.

As Charlotte straightened herself up, she noticed the state of the cottage. It was half burned away, the furniture that remained covered in mold. It didn't look as though it had seen anyone in some time, but you could never be too safe. She kicked the trapdoor shut and pulled a smoky moth-eaten blanket over it, mentally noting to douse herself in sanitizer later. She then shifted a small table over it for good measure, just in case anyone came looking.

"It's gonna be a bit of a hike, if you don't mind helping keep lookout, Wade."

"Not at all."

"Oh." She paused, taking a look around the one-room cottage. "What is this place, anyhow? And how did you know it was here?"

Wade shifted uncomfortably, setting her on edge once more. It was a few long moments before he answered her. "It was the caretaker's cottage. That's why the tunnel led here, as an escape route from the house."

Suddenly, his dark downcast eyes were soft and somber, somehow more than before.

"I had to use it the night my family perished."

CHAPTER EIGHT

Charlotte gulped. "I had . . . well, I had no idea. I can see you're haunting here, but I should have connected the dots, but—well, shit. I'm sorry." She hesitated before adding, "No one knew you or your family died here. You all just disappeared. Are they still here, too? What happened?"

Wade squeezed his eyes shut. "They . . . they did not remain with me. That is fine. I am fine. Please, let us continue. I worry for your health. I also worry that they will spread their search outward soon, so we must continue."

She paused for only a moment before deciding not to push the point. *Not yet.* They hurried out as Charlotte explained how her phone and the navigation application worked while they began the trek to her RV.

❧ ❧

"This is your automobile? Why, it is a hulking beast!"

It had taken them longer than Charlotte cared to limp back to the RV, choosing to cut through some fields out of caution instead of using the visible paths. She had chatted with Wade the entire time. Charlotte wasn't used to a ghost being so engaged, so . . . present. The mystery surrounding him deepened with every word that slipped from his lips.

Charlotte's face heated at Wade's amazement. "I take it you haven't spent a lot of time outside of the house?"

He remained enraptured by her RV, ignoring her question. "I fear I have missed out on a lifetime of wonders. Perhaps it is fate that had your path and mine crossed today."

Charlotte waved a nonchalant hand. "That, or mass murder. Come on, get in. We need to go."

Ushering him in, Charlotte hurriedly strapped in and made sure Specter was comfortably curled up in the small dining space before cranking the beast into gear. Slipping her phone into the holder, she pulled up the map on the touchscreen. She knew she should head back to Boston, but . . . what if they had seen her? Looking at her phone for a minute, she found somewhere she could take an RV without being suspicious before pulling back off onto the road and setting on her way.

⟫⟫ ⟪⟪

It took just over twenty minutes for her to pull up at a nearby state forest. With the way that Wade rambled and amazed at the passing world, it felt as though it had simultaneously taken forever yet no time at all. She had followed the highway the entire way, blending in with the traffic. If the invention of RVs had astounded Wade, it was nothing compared to seeing his first pickup truck waving a flag with the president's name and campaign slogan on it.

"Is this truly what the world is like now? Where is the eloquence, the sense of order, and propriety? The *dignity?*"

"Christ, you're a snob. Let people be people." She paused before muttering, "You're not wrong, though."

Charlotte pulled off the highway. Like a lot of state forests, it was popular for camping, hiking, and families. She actually saw several other RVs as she pulled up near the ranger's station.

"Stay put," she told Wade sternly. "I have to go pay for a spot for us. Specter, you watch him."

He sat beside the cat, unsure of what to do while alone. So much had occurred in the last hour or two, and experiencing time once more was jarring, unfamiliar. There were gaps, things he did not understand. Much he could not recall.

"What am I to do?" he asked Specter softly. The cat mewled in response, stretching out on the table. How undignified, *he thought.*

"You could come back with your friend."

Wade sprung to his feet at the all-too-familiar voice cutting through the silence. He glanced about, eventually landing on the blond prince sprawled across Miss Blythe's bed. He stiffened, intent on telling the boy that he should not *lie across a lady's bed, when the boy spoke again.*

"It's nice to see you out and about after all these many years, Wade." The boy smiled, his crystal blue eyes sparkling. "You had the humans worried there for a long time. You wouldn't even know these new ones, it's been so long since you've been out to play."

Wade didn't respond. Atticus pouted, slithering off the bed. Sauntering over to Wade, he leaned against the kitchenette, the playful smirk having returned. The boy acted with such . . . familiarity.

His friend. Atticus is—was—his friend. He tried to recall . . . his head ached. There had been ice when he met him. He had been there, for a long time. Always there. What happened?

"Don't stress yourself overthinking, it'll come back," the boy cooed. Dressed in a green velvet vest and black trousers, his cotton sleeves billowed in a rather unfashionable style as he leaned forward to look Wade in the face. Wade remembered—Atticus telling him he liked looking like an eighteenth-century French artist. They had argued over . . . over him not standing out.

Atticus was a demon. And Wade had made a pact with him.

*Wade stared, horrified. His body, though not truly there— was it?—felt **numb.** What had Wade done? What had happened to him?*

*The demon smiled widely at Wade, reaching over to pat his cheek. His hand tingled against Wade's skin. "You can call for me when the time is right. You'll **know** when, my friend."*

He vanished into the shadows, leaving Wade ever more bewildered.

⋙⋘

Wade was, as it turned out, not great at staying put. Charlotte slammed open the door to the RV after the most grueling twenty minutes of her year. A rather obnoxious family in front of her had the audacity to argue the out-of-state fee. By the time he had begrudgingly agreed to pay, Charlotte was at her wit's end. Finding out Wade was missing only compounded her frustration.

"Dude, you had one job!" she scolded Spec. If a cat could have looked taken aback, he did. Specter jumped down from the dining table and dashed to the bedroom.

"I'm sorry, I'm not mad at you, I'm mad at the stupid ghost," she called after Specter.

"Are you calling me stupid?"

"Holy shit!" Charlotte's heart leaped into her throat. Wade had popped up beside her again, a silent phantom. Charlotte grasped onto the amethyst suede of the dining booth to keep herself upright. She glared at Wade, who stared back, indignant.

"See any other stupid ghosts around here? 'Cause I sure don't."

Wade sniffed. "Perhaps it is I who should be angry. You do not see me insulting you."

"No, I'm definitely the angry one. I told you to stay put! But you didn't, and then you had to scare the hell out of me on top of it."

"I will have you know, I remained in your vehicle at all times. I was merely familiarizing myself with your moving home. There wasn't a lot to do when you alleged you wouldn't be more than a few minutes. The dead get bored, too, and your feline did not wish to engage with me."

Charlotte rubbed a hand against her face, weariness washing over her. "I guess you've got me there. Would have been nice if you called out or something so I wouldn't assume the worst. Next time, let me know you're here when I come in, alright?"

Charlotte slid around Wade, trying not to bump into him. It was awkward. She knew she could have just gone through him, but it didn't feel right.

Her RV wasn't the most luxurious, but it wasn't too shabby, either. It was one of the few purchases she had made with her inheritance. It was midrange with a functioning kitchen and entertaining area, a bathroom, and a bedroom toward the back. She had comfortably lived in it for months at a time. As soon as she had earned enough though, she paid it back. Accepting family money felt like accepting the life that had ruined hers. She wanted to be free, to be independent, with nothing holding her back or holding her accountable.

Turning on the coffee pot, Charlotte bustled about making herself a cup as Wade looked on, his brow furrowed again. *What is he thinking?* His intense gaze remained fixed on her as she slid into the dining booth, drink in hand. She gestured for him to take a seat opposite her.

"I miss it," he said quietly, watching her. Charlotte raised an eyebrow, and he sighed. "Coffee was such a joy. I did not overly care for brandy, unfortunately, so it was one of the things that I could partake in with my peers most oft. I wish I could embrace its bitter bite upon my tongue once more."

"Do you have to make everything so dramatic?"

Wade bowed his head. "My apologies."

Squirming uncomfortably, Charlotte took a sip of her coffee. Not a fan of sweetness, she drank it black. It used to be out of necessity—there were many a long night during her college years she wouldn't have made it through otherwise—but she had rather grown to enjoy it over the years. It had become familiar and reliable for her. She could see why he missed it.

"I'm sorry, I get it. I'd hate to not be able to have coffee, either." Getting up, Charlotte grabbed another full mug. She slid it in front of Wade before taking her seat again. "Look, I know you can't drink it, but you can pretend to nurse it like you would with your bros or whatever."

Wade smiled at her for the first time, eyes sparkling, a dimple forming in his right cheek. "I am unsure of what any of those words mean, but I appreciate the sentiment."

They sat there in silence for a long moment as Wade stared at the coffee with wonderment. His hair, slightly too long for the style he was trying to hold it in, curled around his ears in slight waves. He was clearer than he had been before, the edges of him more defined. She could see details of him now that they were sitting that she hadn't noticed earlier. His eyes were a dark grey, like a thunderstorm over the sea. His features seemed to be sharpening by the second, becoming less ghostlike as she stared.

"Are you alright?"

Wade's voice snapped Charlotte out of her thoughts. "Sorry. I'm not used to seeing ghosts so high-def, you know? You're usually a lot less visible. Or do I want to say they're usually more distorted? Anyway, you're looking more alive than dead, and that's fascinating. Can I ask what you're thinking? Maybe that's the key to your appearance."

His eyes darkened further, head tilting back so he could study the roof of the RV. Charlotte's eyes widened at the thick gash across his neck. It was like seeing a fake wound that kids asked their parents to paint on for Halloween. It didn't seem real. Running from ear to ear, it was as if a serrated blade had torn across his throat with an unsteady hand. Charlotte's entire body tingled, hot and cold at once, her hands trembling as they cupped her mug tightly.

"I was thinking about what I saw before you arrived. Is that not the reason you and I are here?"

Charlotte glanced away hastily, cheeks burning. Her eyes landed on her satchel, which she had tossed on the table earlier. "Yeah, that's true. Um, do you mind if I use my gear while we chat, actually?"

"Gear?" Wade looked back down at her, cocking his head slightly. "May I ask what you mean by that?"

Charlotte fished about in her satchel, pulling out her smaller camera and tripod. "It's for recording," she explained. "I can play this back later and it might help me remember certain details." Beads of sweat gathered at her hairline. She didn't have to tell him the whole truth: that she may end up broadcasting him on the internet. He wouldn't get it. He also might not be willing to talk if she did explain.

Wade straightened himself, staring ahead at the camera with a dignity and refinement that astounded her. "Tell me when you would like me to start, Miss Blythe."

With a nod, Charlotte flipped the screen around to watch him through it, fascinated by how *real* he appeared on it. She almost couldn't believe he wasn't alive. The bending of the light around him, though, that slight blur, was the only real giveaway. Not to mention the gaping gash that she couldn't see but knew to be there. Flicking the On button, she gave him a thumbs up. "Tell me why you're here, Wade."

"I had been condemned to darkness longer than I care to admit, my soul burdened by the weight of my own death. Death has never beckoned quite so many before me, however." Wade paused, frowning again, his eyes darting to the window contemplatively. "It was a normal event. I have seen many similar ones in my life. This was no different to any of those. It was a celebration, of life and of death.

"It happened all of a sudden. One moment, there was merriment. The next, the screams began. The doors slammed closed and this wave washed over the room. I have not felt the cold in many a year, yet I felt it then, this malevolence like ice water. They were not ordinary humans, the staff. No, they had been selected with purpose. They had dark magic within them, and they used it to seal those humans in like cattle. Then the slaughter began."

He shivered. "They were merciless, trained assassins. Without thought or mercy, they spilled the blood of innocents like a socialite spills wine. The way they moved, the way they harnessed magic . . . I have no doubt that they are part of the occult community. The way that they killed then vanished with a blink, as though they had never been there—it leads me to believe that a greater power within our community is orchestrating their movements. I also believe that there will be more murders just like this one." The brooding look on his face returned.

"What makes you say that, Wade?" Her voice was barely a whisper as his somber eyes locked with hers.

"Because this isn't the first time they've murdered like this, with this intention. There was purpose and meaning here, much like the night my own family died."

⟫ ⟪

Charlotte was shaking as she flicked off the camera. It felt like a private moment, too raw for film. "You mean, this is what happened to your family? This isn't the first time you've . . . experienced this?"

"I believe so." His eyebrows furrowed, his head tilted quizzically. "It is odd. I don't appear to remember as clearly as one might. It was a ball of some sort, I believe. Perhaps it was for my sister's coming of age? We called it a debutante ball then. If you are not familiar, it is when we welcome our young women into society as eligible—"

"I know," Charlotte snapped. "I had one. That was when *my* family and friends were slaughtered. It was a Society-held debut."

Wade bowed his head. "This leads me to believe my theory about a connection is true, then."

"Slow down a minute, buddy. I still haven't wrapped my head around what you've just said yet."

Charlotte closed her eyes, the dull memory of the screams of her friends and family echoing through her mind, thoughts racing. What if Wade was right? What if these weren't some one-off freak supernatural experiences? What if they were all connected, and her desire to know why her parents had died was finally leading her down a path to truth? What if, all along, the Society that had tried to indoctrinate her, tried to convince her that she was part of their effort to keep the world safe from the horrors and dangers of the supernatural and occult, was at the heart of the worst of these monstrosities?

"I'm sure you miss what life was like before everything was taken away from you as much as I do," Wade continued, keeping his voice low. "I would give anything to go back to it. I want to assist you however I can, Miss Blythe. There is a fury rising within me, and I believe I will finally be able to achieve my eternal rest if I am able to quell it. Please allow me to help you seek the truth amongst the darkness."

Her chest tightened, a pang shooting through her heart. His large dark eyes were so mournful as they gazed at her, his sculpted brows pulling together as he pleaded silently. Her breath caught as his long delicate lashes fluttered, naive innocence washing over his exquisite face. She was being drawn in by him, the anger that usually drove her being replaced with something else, something greater.

Compassion.

Charlotte wanted to help this strange, charming ghost and release him from the pain that kept him trapped in the past. The same pain that had her chained, it seemed. Perhaps together, they could unlock their shackles.

Instinctively, she reached a hand over to touch his. To let him know he wasn't alone anymore, and that she would help him. Her open palm passed through his hand, cold piercing her skin like a thousand knives that she couldn't make contact with. In that moment, she made up her mind. Neither of them would be alone anymore.

Charlotte said something to Wade that she hadn't to anyone in a long time.

"Let's do this together. And . . . please, call me Charlotte."

CHAPTER NINE

"**I**s this truly the plan, Miss Charlotte?"

"Do you have a better one? 'Cause I haven't seen you offer one."

Wade was perched on the passenger seat beside her, a snarling Specter wedged between them with his ocher eyes trained on the ghost. Charlotte had found a different path back on the off chance they had been followed somehow. The entire situation was a mess, and her head was still reeling. She had no choice in her involvement, though.

The scene she'd stumbled upon, her debut, Wade's own tale—there were too many coincidences for them *not* to be connected. That's what she told herself, anyway, as she fought the urge the yank the steering wheel, to drive away. The Society was sure to be crawling all over the place by now, looking for a way to cover it up. If they found out she'd been there earlier . . .

Her grandmother insisted otherwise, but she knew in her heart they still blamed Charlotte for that night.

"It's simple. You're a ghost. You can blend in and go invisible. Even Spec can go relatively unnoticed. I'll approach as though I've just gotten there, looking for content. While I create a distraction"—she glanced over at the ghost—"you and Specter can go on an information hunt. He's weirdly good at not being noticed. I swear he disappears."

"But what do we expect to accomplish, Miss Charlotte?"

"Just Charlotte," she corrected. "Drop the 'miss.' Oh, don't look at me like that. I haven't wounded your sensibilities that bad. This is how investigations *go*.

I'm sure even you've read a detective novel. Maybe even hired one yourself." A grin split across her face at his affronted expression.

Wade sighed, mouth tightening into a grimace as he glanced between her and Specter. "Alright, I will team up with your feline companion and ask if any of the other spirits saw anything or knew their assailants."

"That's the spirit."

Wade glowered at her joke as she parked down the road from Umbra Hollow.

⤜⤛⤜

Charlotte stood at the back of the gathered crowd with her camera in hand. It was as if the entire town had turned up in the hour she was gone. That could make things both easier and harder; she could blend in better, but would she be able to track down any useful information?

It didn't help that the second Specter had scampered around the side of the house with Wade in tow, the panic had set in. She'd warned Wade about the ghoul they had locked in the cellar and that it might have gotten out since. The idea of Spec running into it without her nauseated her. She'd also left most of her kit behind. Being busted armed wouldn't look good for her; she was certain the Society would use it against her.

Sucking in a deep breath, Charlotte steeled herself, ready to push her way through the crowd. She would begin interviewing random people, under the guise of recording for her channel. It should attract the attention of the people in charge fast enough. The regular police were dealing with the media, off to the side on the vast lawn. The Society, as incompetent as they were, would find her eventually if she made enough noise.

She was found before she even stepped forward.

"Charlotte Blythe."

An unknown feminine voice from behind Charlotte said her name with striking familiarity. "Fuck," Charlotte muttered under her breath before turning around.

The owner of the voice was slightly shorter than Charlotte, her bouncy jet-black curls making up for their several-inch difference in height. Wide-rimmed glasses framed her dark eyes, a perfectly arched eyebrow raised as though she had just asked a question. Jeans and combat boots clad her muscular legs, her leather jacket sleeves rolled up to reveal toned brown arms. The girl bounced on her heels, brows raised in question.

"I'm sorry, but who are you?" Charlotte shifted uncomfortably. There was an intensity to her that was alarming, shrieking at Charlotte to back away. She needed to put some space between them; it was obvious she wouldn't be able to take this girl in a fight.

"You *are* Charlotte, right? From Wraiths and Wanderings?"

She felt herself relaxing. It was just a fan from her channel.

"Yeah, that's me." She forced a grin to her face. "Did you want a selfie or something? I can even put you in my new video if you're interested—"

"Babes, I'm gonna stop you right there. I knew you'd turn up here. I know your videos cover up a lot of info you don't let slip, and I normally don't catch you at places when you're there, but even the normies are aware of this one. So, we gotta do something about it."

An icy wave washed over Charlotte. Should she know this woman? What did she mean by not catching her? Her chest tightened and she desperately wished she had a glass, a bottle, of something strong in hand.

"I don't know what you mean," Charlotte mumbled, looking for an escape. She could attempt to run, but the other woman would not only keep up easily—she'd absolutely be able to take her down. Her RV was also a bit down the road, away from the crowd.

She'd been cornered.

"Let's go for a walk and a chit-chat." The stranger grinned at Charlotte, a weird perkiness to her words that Charlotte didn't find comforting.

⤳ ⤳

The stranger may as well have been holding her at gunpoint. She corralled Charlotte away from the safety of the crowd to the opposite side of the house.

"Wanna tell me what this is about?" Charlotte couldn't help the sharp edge to her voice. The sound of the crowd was a distant din now, the shrubs and trees surrounding the stately home acting as a buffer. The strange girl leaned against the house, pulling a packet of cigarettes and a lighter from the inner pocket of the jacket. She held the smokes out toward Charlotte, who shook her head.

"Not my vice," Charlotte rasped, eyes darting around, looking for an escape. The stranger gave a one-shoulder shrug before lighting one up. Charlotte waited silently, her eyes flickering between the stranger's face and the billows of smoke she breathed out.

"I'm Hazel Williams."

A name, at least.

"I watch your channel. I just came down from Evermoor. Eleanor's real weird, but nice."

"So you're a subscriber?"

Hazel shrugged again, exuding detached coolness. "I *guess* you could say I'm a fan. I'm a Hunter. Your channel gets me a lot of leads."

Charlotte shuffled uncomfortably. She had never met a Hunter. The Society spoke of them in a condescending way; after all, *they* were the gifted families and could handle it. Hunters and the like were deigned riffraff.

"I've been doing this for a while, Charlotte, and so has the rest of my family. We clean up the scummy stuff that the Society sees as beneath them. They're always out for the glory shots, never the things that can help. Remember your werewolf lead? How you had that interview with him and he said he'd never done anything that the locals were accusing him of?" Charlotte nodded—the community had ousted him as a werewolf, alleged he'd been eating people when he turned. "Turns out the same couldn't be said for his secret pack. Don't you know? Wolves don't travel alone. His crew *was* eating little kids—and *not* in wolf form."

Charlotte's stomach roiled, and she couldn't stop it. She hurled in a bush beside her as Hazel continued smoking, unperturbed.

"You see why I smoke these devil sticks, Charlotte? You have to do something for your sanity when you clean up the ugly stuff in life." Hazel dropped the butt of her cigarette and squashed it into the dirt with the toe of her boot.

"I didn't say that stuff to make you feel bad or mess you up." Her tone was a lot gentler now, placing a hand on Charlotte's shoulder. "I said it because I see you as a valuable resource, even if you're still a bit posh and gloss over things like all the rest do. And I know you know something about whatever is going on here. Your channel is a message, right? Rich girl's way to get the grown-up's attention? That's why you try to expose fuck-ups and cover-ups right?"

Charlotte wiped her mouth on her sleeve. She felt oddly small and defensive as this cool, collected stranger listed off how much more *competent* she was. And she was right; Charlotte had started the channel to get them angry, a childish retaliation.

She was just a rich little girl trying to provoke people for attention.

"Anyway," Hazel continued, a gleam in her eye as she pushed her frames up her nose. "I think you and I can be an asset to one another in solving this, babes."

Charlotte froze as Hazel grinned widely. She'd planned to find Charlotte, had expected to win their confrontation. She was about to say something when a distinct yowl cut through the air, followed by a haughty "Unhand my companion, lest I fly into a fury!"

~~~>>> <<<~~

Despite the discomfort in her stomach, Charlotte shoved past Hazel and ran toward the rear of Umbra Hollow, toward Wade's indignant outcry. She heard Hazel racing behind her. Time slowed down as she pumped her legs, cursing internally. Specter had never gotten caught doing *anything* before; that cat could vanish if he wanted to. *What the fuck has this ghost done?*

They rounded the corner to find a drained-looking Wade, distress etched across his face. A cloaked group were gathered by him, a small carrier in the hands of one cloaked individual.

"Specter! Wade!" Charlotte called out. She made to race toward them, but Hazel snaked out a hand, grabbing the back of her cardigan. "Let me go! They have my cat!" Charlotte snarled, glaring over her shoulder at the Hunter.

"Don't be stupid," Hazel hissed as the group turned to look at the two girls. "Do you not see who they are?"

Charlotte's attention returned to the group. While many of them remained cloaked with their hoods drawn, she did recognize one person. With his walrus-like mustache and almost cartoonish features, Dirk Ashgarde stepped forward, his dark eyes full of mirth as he smoothed down the front of his wrinkle-free vest. *The Society.*

"Miss Blythe. I thought this was your familiar." His deep voice had the quality one would associate with a beloved grandfather—a little gravely but gentle, as though he was about to crack a joke or sneak you a treat. She knew better; he was sneaky and smarmy at best. The Ashgarde family was well-known even outside of the occult for their less-than-scrupulous business practices, mostly thanks to Dirk's own efforts. "I'm disappointed I haven't seen you in quite some time. Were my grandson's attentions so unwelcome to you?"

A memory of Bradley Ashgarde's hands pulling up her shirt flashed through her mind. Charlotte grimaced, steeling herself. "Unfortunately so, Lord Ashgarde. But we're all adults here. Perhaps you can pass Specter back to me and we can be on our way."

Dirk frowned past her, eyes narrowing. "Your little friend behind you seems quite familiar."

"Not my friend," Charlotte snapped.

Hazel made a wounded noise and muttered, "Says you."

Wade floated toward them, distress still all over his face. "Miss Charlotte. These dastardly individuals"—Wade shot a nervous glance over his shoulder—"—apprehended Specter within the house. We were ambushed, I am certain of it, for we were most discreet."

"Not discreet enough, apparently," she whispered harshly.

"That I will agree with, Miss Blythe." Dirk stepped forward, closing the space between them. Hazel dropped into a defensive position beside her as Wade fretted, almost translucent, as though his energy had been spent. Ashgarde gave Hazel a bored, dismissive glance. "I'll tell you what, Miss Blythe. I'm feeling generous today and believe we can come to an arrangement. I'll pass you your cat back, and you stop making your videos. It's just embarrassing for you. Pathetic, even. I don't know how Edith deals with your attitude. We'll deal with the ghost," he said casually, tacking it on as if it were an afterthought.

"They want your spooky buddy," Hazel breathed beside her. "They did something to him, didn't they? He looks wan, even for a haunter."

The Hunter startled Charlotte. She was right—Wade had gone from being passable to a normal person to looking like a poorly rendered CGI character.

"He's a free ghost. He does what he wants. I've got nothing to do with his afterlife." Charlotte shrugged, trying to appear casual even as her heart pounded. She knew acting with bravado was more important than actually being brave. She sauntered forward. "I'm going to grab my cat now and be out of your way."

As she passed Dirk, he whirled around with surprising swiftness and grabbed her, pressing her back to his chest. "I can't let you leave, Miss Blythe," he hissed in her ear. "You have been a reckless disaster for far too long, and the only thing that has saved your skin is Edith's influence. You would have been tried a long time ago if you didn't have her protecting you. Well, she's not here, little Lottie, is she? No one is here for you."

Charlotte let out a cry and struggled against his grip. He may have been her grandmother's age, but he was strong and surprisingly in shape, unlike Charlotte, an unhealthy waif.

"Grab the phylactery from her and get him. We'll take the girl and cat with us and contact her grandmother. I'm sure she'll agree it's time Lottie does something useful—perhaps continuing her family line before there are no Blythes left, instead of being a public nuisance."

A rumble of laughter rolled through the group of cloaked figures. Anger bubbled in her, a rage that she had spent years suppressing by self-medicating and sheer force of will. It began to unravel now like a coiled-up snake, preparing to strike. She'd let it take over after she had spent so long ignoring it, ignoring its potential. She submerged herself in it, letting it build, blocking the sound of the world, letting her mind drift elsewhere.

Before she could unleash those feelings, there was a flash, and she felt herself hurtling through the air. She hit the lawn, the earth solid and dry from the hot summer. Instinctively she rolled, raising her arms to brace herself. An oddly stilted throb ricocheted through her skull as she thudded up against the bottom of the porch steps.

She lay there, stunned, darkness clouding her vision.

"Miss Charlotte, we have to make haste. Please get up."

Wade's anxious voice fluttered by her ear. Charlotte forced her eyes open, gasping as spots filled her vision and nausea overwhelmed her. She blinked back tears and struggled to her feet, wobbly and unsure as her vision blurred.

"It will be alright, I am right here beside you," Wade whispered, hovering as close as he dared. "Your new friend has it handled, but I have to get you away to your vehicle at her behest. Please, Miss Charlotte—Specter and your friend will be joining us soon."

Charlotte shot a glance at the group. Several of them, Dirk Ashgarde included, now lay on the ground, unconscious. Her jaw dropped as she watched Hazel disarm the surrounding group with ease and precision. The one holding Specter's carrier tried to run, but the other woman shot forward and grabbed their arm, twisting the wrist that held the carrier until a stomach-churning snap resounded. With a howl, they dropped Specter's carrier. He hissed as it dropped and popped open, dashing straight toward Charlotte when he was freed.

Hazel risked a glance at them. "I told you to get her moving when I rushed them, ghost! Hurry up, I'll be right behind you. Just get them outta here!"

Without a word, Charlotte scooped up Specter and limped back the way they came, hoping Wade had listened and that Hazel was as competent as she seemed.

CHAPTER TEN

Charlotte's lungs were threatening to explode by the time they reached the RV. She hurtled inside, unsure of how she was going to drive. Even running on adrenaline, she was one shaky step from collapsing. She slid onto the floor near the kitchen, her entire body giving out beneath her.

"Wade, are you able to get the door? I gotta start the RV." Her words came out in bursts as she gasped for air. A stitch in her right side started to tug.

"I'm on it." Hazel vaulted into the RV out of nowhere, jumping over the steps completely as she pulled the door shut behind her in one fluid movement. She slid automatically into the driver's seat, extending her hand to Charlotte. "Keys. I'll drive; get your ass in a seat."

With a shaky hand, Charlotte dug into her pocket and pulled the keys out, tossing them to Hazel awkwardly. Hazel had the RV in gear and on the highway before Charlotte could even crawl into the passenger seat. An anxious Wade hovered behind them as Specter, who had been deposited onto the floor, jumped onto her lap.

"We're going to have to circle back around to get to my car." Hazel furrowed her brow. "I didn't expect it to go like this. I thought they'd be there, but I didn't realize you'd be *so* mixed up in it."

"I wasn't exactly expecting it, either," Charlotte muttered, catching her breath.

"Anyway," Hazel continued. "I'm getting a clearer idea of things. Want to tell me about your friend here?" She jerked her head toward Wade, not taking her eyes off the road. "He seemed pretty important to them."

Charlotte twisted in her seat to look up into Wade's solemn face. His mouth was twisted in concern. "I don't know what he is to them. Specter and I only met him this morning."

"Wait, you met him this morning?" They were speeding far out of Salem now. "As in before or after the B-grade movie slaughter?"

"After. It's so strange—I got an email from my source, so I rushed over. That was, what, half an hour before I got there? But the bodies . . . their spirits only started appearing after Specter and I got inside. And it was still sealed up with some nasty dark magic." She felt disassociated, as if the day had happened to someone else.

Hazel suddenly yanked the vehicle off the highway onto the side of the road. Specter let out a yelp and dug his claws into Charlotte, who also hissed. The other woman paid them no mind and yanked off her seat belt to turn toward them. Charlotte was pleasantly surprised as Hazel leaned forward and a hint of the Hunter's perfume hit her, pumpkin and cinnamon.

"That makes no sense, though. Let's say you were emailed the literal second it happened—there should have been a lot, if not all of them, gone. You're saying you saw them emerge?"

Charlotte nodded. Hazel's dark eyes snapped to Wade. "And what about this one? He doesn't seem like he died today."

Wade muttered something to himself, but Charlotte thought she heard the words "indecent" and "disrespectful." He cleared his throat. "I think I have been there for quite some time, that is true."

"You *think*? Does your ghost have amnesia or some shit?"

Charlotte shrugged. "I don't know much about him. I did only just find him."

"I am not her ghost. I am Wade van Baird," he mumbled snootily.

Charlotte rolled her eyes before returning her attention to Hazel. "Okay, then, what does this all mean? I'm struggling to even wrap my head around *you* being there to find me."

The other woman paused, glancing between the ghost and the ex-socialite, chewing her lip contemplatively.

"Not to be a drama queen . . ." Hazel said slowly. "But I think you were set up to be there when it went down."

An icy chill ran over Charlotte at Hazel's words—not helped by Wade, who leaned into her to stare at Hazel with wide eyes.

"You think someone set me up?" she choked out. Hazel nodded, lips set in a grim slash. Charlotte instinctively pulled Specter up against her chest, as if cuddling the creature could fix everything that felt wrong. Much like she had in the months following the incident, always holding on to a shred of love and normalcy.

"Look." Hazel pulled back onto the highway, speeding. "I'll grab my car, but we have to meet somewhere a lot safer than this and talk this out. I was planning on chasing this lead solo, but it seems to be a lot bigger than we think. Can you think of somewhere safe? You've got some sort of abilities, don't you? That can keep us safe?"

Charlotte remained silent, her thoughts turbulent. Hazel repeated herself again, waiting pointedly for a response.

"My home," she sighed. "Grandmother has it pretty well warded. I—well, we were planning to go back there to talk after gathering info, too. I guess it's fine if we all go. Although . . ." Charlotte narrowed her eyes. "I don't normally associate with Hunters. What's your deal? How do you know about the Society?"

"Years of generational conflict," Hazel said casually. "We've had a lot of issues cleaning up after them for some time. We've tried to counsel with your lot a few times, but they never go for it. So, we take matters into our own hands. They don't take our magic seriously, then have the audacity to not actually deal with issues that don't affect them, leaving us to clean up messes for the defenseless and weak without help."

Charlotte slumped back in her seat, exhaustion rolling over her. She was done with the day, that was certain, but somehow she suspected it was only just beginning. And it wasn't even lunchtime yet.

Charlotte sat in silence the rest of the drive to Hazel's car, her mood souring as she realized how much was presently out of her control. Hazel flicked through the radio a few times, bickering with Wade like old pals about the music; anything she liked affronted him, and she groaned at any station that excited him. The Hunter was peculiar, gabbing at Charlotte as if they were old friends.

What had been a promising morning to find some leads and connections to her parents' death had rapidly led her down a rabbit hole of stress, mystery, and weird new companions. All things that did not agree with Charlotte. She said as much to Wade when they dropped Hazel off on the outskirts of Salem and began the drive back home.

"I blame you entirely for this," she snapped, glowering at the numbers on the dashboard. The last few days of poor eating, sleep, and stress had left her fatigued and cranky. Wade at least had the decency to look abashed.

"I'm sorry," he said with such sincerity that heat flooded her cheeks.

"Yeah, I know." She sighed. "I guess no one could have predicted any of this."

Wade had settled into the passenger seat again. Specter curled up beside him; they must have bonded over their shared trauma, she figured. Charlotte took a hand off the wheel to stroke Specter, vowing silently to never let him near harm's way again.

"I'm glad it did go this way, or else I may have never met you, Miss Charlotte."

"Charlotte," she corrected automatically, surprising herself. "Like I told you before, you can drop the 'miss.'"

"That may be a little difficult. I already find it distressing to not use your family name, if I were to be completely honest. You barely know me."

Charlotte couldn't help the smile that tugged at the corners of her mouth. "That's more than fair, Wade. I'm sure we'll have plenty of time to get acquainted enough."

The remaining drive back to Boston was lighter after that as they fell into comfortable chatter. She talked about Yale; he was aghast. As a Harvard man himself, he told her, he was embarrassed for her. She flipped him the bird, and he pretended to faint. Charlotte laughed and he joined in. Charlotte asked what he had majored in.

"Business, to take over our family's alchemical distribution. In truth, I was terrible at the job, despite father's praise. I am too giving, I am told." Wade's wry smile sent her heart fluttering. She could believe that about him.

Wade asked her what she had studied and why.

"History, but I wish I had studied media, too. It would make my job a lot easier, but I developed a lot of good research skills that I can use to script my work and discern what hauntings are real or not," she explained. He had cocked his head to the side quizzically.

"I'm afraid I have never heard the term 'media,'" he confessed.

"It's all the things. Newspapers, photos, video, music, the internet. Basically, my job is to document things through video—I'm sure even *you've* seen video before. And the internet is like . . . everything is connected, and you can access all the information of the world through a screen. I'll show you later. It's easier than trying to explain it."

"I'll trust your analysis," he said doubtfully before turning to stare out the window in silent wonder.

Edith Blythe was waiting on the porch of Winterbourne. The woman had an uncanny sixth sense at times. Charlotte secretly wondered if she was tracking her GPS. The large iron gates swung open, exposing the manor to the streets just long enough for the RV and Hazel's beat-up Camry to sneak onto the grounds. If her grandmother was surprised at all, she didn't show it.

"I would have liked to have known we were having company," Edith told her as they approached. She smiled at Hazel and Wade; Charlotte knew her grandmother well, and only the slight arch of her brow betrayed her shock. Charlotte's stomach rumbled as they climbed the stairs. Edith scolded her for not eating more, asking if her guests would like lunch. There was a strange normality to the situation, as though she were merely bringing friends home from school. It nearly made her laugh out loud.

They filed into the house behind the matriarch. Edith veered to the left, bringing them to the sitting room. It was usually reserved for Specter's naps and her bridge games, she told the newcomers nonchalantly, but it was the comfiest space in the house. Ringing the crystal bell that sat on the drinks trolley, Edith ushered them to sit.

Hazel immediately draped herself in Charlotte's grandfather's old favorite armchair. Charlotte was none too graceful herself as she collapsed onto a small sofa. Wade was the only one of them with a sense of dignity as he perched himself beside her. Edith settled on the sofa opposite them, Specter jumping up beside her.

"While we wait for lunch, perhaps you can fill me in on what's going on?" Edith's voice was steady, but the way her eyes flicked to Wade said everything. Charlotte glanced at her two new strange companions before sucking in a deep breath, proceeding to give her grandmother a veritable dissertation on the utterly insane day that was unfolding.

⤜⤜⤜ ⤛⤛⤛

Forty minutes later, they were full of tea and sandwiches and Charlotte had given Hazel and Edith a rundown. Charlotte had the maid set up Wade with a sandwich and teacup. To her credit, the maid didn't so much as flinch.

"You were attacked by Lord Ashgarde?" Edith asked sharply, setting her tea down. The trio nodded in unison, Spec letting out a mewl of agreement. Her grandmother was rarely shaken. Right now, her face betrayed her fury.

"What is going *on*?" Edith demanded. Her attention pivoted to Wade. "You, sir, seem to be at the center of a lot of this. I want you to explain yourself. And you, young lady"—her eyes flicked to Charlotte—"need to learn to stay out of trouble."

"My apologies, good madam." Wade bowed his head low, a gloved hand raised to his chest. "I am most assuredly distraught that I seem to have brought untoward attention to your granddaughter."

Edith raised an eyebrow. "You certainly are a peculiar one. What else can you remember?"

"My name is Wade van Baird," he said, straightening. "And I believe that something horrible happened to me and my family."

"You can't remember how you died?" Edith prompted.

"I can remember the sensation, like I was falling. There were others falling, too, but I got dragged back. My memories are vague, more feelings than solid thoughts. I remember little of before then, including my family. There is such a lingering impression of them, in here." He pointed to his chest.

"He had a pretty gnarly death. That could be why he doesn't remember," Charlotte suggested. "Wade, tilt your head back. Let them have a peek."

He gave her a look but complied. Hazel leaned forward in her armchair and whistled loudly. Edith got up to inspect it, asking him to stand and let her see the wound.

"Barbaric," Edith muttered. "If only we could see your corpse and not just your spectral form, we could determine a lot more. I suspect that is long gone, even for one of our kind. Are you aware of where you are buried?"

Wade shook his head and Edith retreated to her sofa, tapping her chin thoughtfully.

"Fascinating," Edith murmured. "To think, the bizarre and mysterious disappearance of this family line, and suddenly the ghost of one of them returns."

"Well, this is a mess," Hazel chimed in. "Does anyone want to know what I think now?"

Their attention snapped to the Hunter, a coy grin on her face.

CHAPTER ELEVEN

"**I**'m certain the Society is behind it." Hazel braced her forearms on her thighs, leaning in, her voluminous hair bobbing with her excitement. "I've been tracking Charlotte's channel for a while, and I know they have been, too."

"They have been sending her letters to stop," Edith added. Charlotte shot her grandmother a look as Hazel nodded eagerly. Hazel reached for a bag Charlotte hadn't seen her bring in, tugging out a notebook.

"I've recorded every time she's uploaded and every encounter I've had with them after a video. And oh, boy, have I had some run-ins. She uploaded once a week, giving her so many days to film, edit, and drive in. Her locations weren't exactly made secret. This summer particularly made it easier to work out her targets based on some basic research and where she was approximately located, and then I got an alert about Umbra Hollow, so . . ."

Charlotte sat in shock, listening to Hazel detail how she had worked out Charlotte's schedule. This was why she had been right behind her at Evermoor House, and how she had been able to get to the Umbra Hollow situation so soon after her. Hazel smiled smugly as she leaned back in the armchair.

"I figured they'd done the same research. For someone who acts so mysterious, you're a pretty open book, especially online. And they have a lot more resources than someone like me. I also did a little research on you as a person. With my family's knowledge, it was easy to work out you were the next head of your family line, and about what happened to your parents—"

"Alright, we get it," Charlotte snapped, rising to her feet. "You're a genius who knows everything. What I want to know is what all of this is to you. Why are you here? Why are you involved? Do you want money? What are you after?" Anger swelled in her chest. It didn't matter that this girl had helped save her and Specter; she was pushing her luck.

Hazel snorted. "Please. This is feud-related, as I told you earlier. The Society has treated my community and defenseless people like trash for far too long. Sure, they *might've* had noble intentions, and keeping the occult under wraps when the country was smaller was definitely easier. But their efforts didn't grow where the supernaturals did, and they left the rest of us to fend for ourselves."

Edith and Wade remained silent during all of this while Charlotte stood, her fists still clenched at Hazel's offhand comment.

"Alright, then. You have a feud, and you've been using me for information to get at them or something. Tell me how you think the Society plays into all of this, then."

"Well, I wasn't entirely sure before. And I'm still not. Today gave me more ideas, though. I reckon it's beyond you trying to expose them. If they'd wanted to take care of you, I suspect they could have. They want something else . . . call it intuition."

"You've been stalking me, knew they also were and didn't think, 'Hey, maybe I should let her know'? Dude. It's not like they were going to hurt the next head of one of their families."

"Did they not attack you today? And did I *not* save your ass?" Hazel shot back.

"True," Charlotte muttered, sinking back down beside Wade. He reached a hand over, pausing midair before retracting it awkwardly. She gave him a questioning look. Wade merely looked away.

"This is what I have. Charlotte has been pissing them off, and she's the next head of a powerful family. She'll be in a position of power to destroy them from within and they don't like that. So, they want her gone. Fair enough; you've kinda tried to expose them constantly. So they've been chasing her down, trying to pick her off when Gran isn't around to protect her. You're welcome, by the way. I've saved your ass from a lot of creepy crawlies."

"Not like I knew!"

"Anyway," Hazel continued, ignoring her. She ticked off her fingers as she listed her points. "There has been an interesting addition to why the Society has been so much shittier than usual. And it has to do with him." Hazel stopped counting to glare pointedly at Wade. "They want him. I bet he's somehow linked to the slaughter today."

"He's just a ghost, and he's been dead for ages." Charlotte gestured to him. "Look at him! He's all weird and old-timey." Wade made an indignant noise, solidifying her point.

"True," Hazel conceded. "He's weird as shit. However, they were pretty eager to have him. Dick was after him. He wasn't exactly careful with his cards."

"Dirk," Edith corrected.

"I said what I said."

Charlotte sat in silence, thinking about the encounter as Edith continued to correct a smart-mouthed Hazel. She ruminated on what Ashgarde had said. Hazel was right; they were definitely sick of her shit and looking to eliminate her. Her heart fluttered at the thought, and she wondered if some small part of her hadn't been goading them so they would. She could call what she'd been doing whatever she wanted—exposing them, acting on noble intentions, whatever. But that didn't change the fact that she had intentionally been trying to provoke them.

She suddenly remembered a few other weird things they had said.

"Dirk told them to get the phylactery," she interrupted the bickering. "I haven't heard of that before. Have any of you?"

They all shook their heads, Wade included.

"Whatever it is, it sounded important to them. Whatever that is, we have Wade at least, right? And I'm not dead, though I would like a shower to get that old man smell off of me."

"What we need is a plan," Hazel said. "And to come up with a plan, we need information. Because this isn't something we're going to be able to just ignore, or else your buddy here might just get a ghost girlfriend."

Hazel cringed as they all started talking at once, telling her how tactless her comment was. "It was just a joke to ease the tension!"

"You aren't wrong, though," Charlotte's shoulders slumped. "I don't think I can leave here without us having a plan in place. Let's rest for a moment and think about it, okay? I've had a long day and I just want a shower for now."

Charlotte stood up and swept out of the room, calling out over her shoulder, "I'll be out in twenty minutes. Don't make any decisions until then!"

⤜⤛ ⤚⤛

Thirty-five minutes later, Charlotte was showered and exceedingly annoyed. Wade had taken her twenty-minute comment as a certainty, and he had popped his head into her room to call her downstairs exactly twenty-one minutes later. Charlotte had been in her bathrobe, pulling out fresh underwear, when the ghost interrupted her. After several choice words and some awkward rushed apologies, he disappeared.

Charlotte may have taken a little longer to come down to spite him, and to hopefully teach him a lesson.

"I would apologize for being late," she announced as she trudged downstairs. "However, some jerk wanted to see my panties."

"I did no such thing! Please, I implore you, it was a reckless infraction and I would never intentionally compromise a young woman in such a way. Miss Hazel suggested I see what had waylaid you." Wade's voice rose in volume as he pleaded, glancing between the three women. Hazel gave him a shit-eating grin; she knew *exactly* what she'd done.

"And yet," Charlotte sighed dramatically, "I *was* compromised, wasn't I, Wade?"

"I beg of you, I did not mean—that is to say, I, well, it was—" As he spluttered, Wade sunk onto a small ottoman, head in his hands.

Edith gave her a sharp look as if to say *Don't break the ghost like that.*

"Ugh, fine, I know you didn't mean to, Wade. But you shouldn't take someone so literally when they say they'll be twenty minutes! And you could have knocked—well, called out, whatever."

"My sincerest apologies," he murmured, still shaking. "I was so swept up in my eagerness, I forgot myself. I hope you'll find it within yourself to forgive me, and if not, I will find some way to make penance."

With a roll of her eyes, all was forgiven.

They were gathered in the foyer now at the bottom of the ornate staircase. She'd interrupted what seemed to be an intense conversation; Edith and Hazel had been looking at a painting on the wall, heads bobbing as they chatted about Winterbourne. Wade had stood to the side, his eyes lit up with interest.

The manor had been built over a century ago in the 1880s when their ancestors had settled in New England and encapsulated the art nouveau style. Wood paneling and intricately patterned wallpaper created the foundation of the home. The staircase and banisters had been carved into intricate ornamental images; vines and flowers wove through them, cherubs and devils interspersed between the images of flora.

A large chandelier hung above. Once lit with candles, it was purely ornamental now with small green glass sconces lining the walls for light instead. Charlotte was sure the hall runner, which extended from the top of the stairs to the front door, was as old as the house itself. Somehow, it never seemed to fade, tear, or stain. Perhaps magic kept it the way it was.

The walls were lined with floor-to-ceiling doors that led to other parts of the house as well as a multitude of artworks, sculptures, and taxidermy. The latter had always made Charlotte uncomfortable; there was nothing like coming down for a glass of water in the middle of the night and finding a shrieking raven glowering at you. It was why she'd stopped eating meat.

Winterbourne felt like a house from an Edgar Allan Poe poem, or a gothic novel. Beautiful, dark, and secretive. In her almost thirty years, she hadn't even scratched the surface of the manor's secrets. She was certain Specter knew more than she did, somehow vanishing just to appear somewhere else.

"I have a question, Gran."

Charlotte glanced at Hazel so fast she cracked her neck. She winced and rubbed it, her fingers brushing against her damp braid. How had they gone from not knowing each other an hour ago to Hazel calling her *Gran?* Had the entire world turned upside down that morning? She was further stunned when Edith merely smiled and told her to ask away.

"I was wondering if this house is haunted. I don't feel anything other than him"—she motioned lazily at Wade—"and whatever weird thing the cat has going on."

"Yes," Edith mused. "It is strange, isn't it? Especially with the magical ties our family and this house has. Quite simply, I don't believe any of them wished to stay between the Veil and here. Even when my daughter and her husband passed the way they did, they didn't have something anchoring them to this side." Edith hastily apologized as Charlotte winced. "I don't mean they had nothing here for them, lovey. They knew you'd be safe, that it was okay to pass."

They had plenty of reason to stay on this side of the Veil. Charlotte needed them; they wouldn't have left her. She was sure of it. Even if she'd never felt them there, she knew that much.

"I've never seen anything here, at any rate. And this has been my home since the day I was born." Edith shrugged lightly. "I guess we Blythes are far too in tune with the ether to feel compelled to stay."

Wade shuddered and Edith smiled sympathetically.

"Weird. It just has the vibes. And you're so involved with the Society and the occult, I just figured it would be." Hazel rolled a shoulder.

"Can we please get back on track?" Charlotte wanted nothing more than a quiet drink alone. "We need to work out what we're doing, don't we? Has anyone got an idea of how we're going to deal with this?"

Hazel winked at Charlotte, who immediately got a bad feeling in her gut. "Yeah, I think I have a plan."

Doubt filled her as Hazel began to lay out her idea.

⠀⠀⠀

The plan was simple, but Charlotte didn't like it. They were splitting up to find out what the Society wanted and why Wade was important, but it made her nervous to trust these two new strangers. Meanwhile, her grandmother had been totally at ease with them both, as if she had known them forever, and they acted the same with the Blythes. Charlotte was far more reserved.

It had been decided, despite her protests, that Charlotte, Wade, and Specter weren't safe outside. They had been targets, and it was highly likely that Ashgarde was still hunting for them.

"They can find us here. It's not like they don't know this is where I live," she argued. That was when Edith stepped in.

"This house is warded and the staff is all highly trained. They wouldn't dare make a move on you here."

Hazel chirped, "Besides, you have an upload schedule and a backlog of footage, don't you? It should be easy enough for you to fake being out still. And Gran is gonna convince them that she hasn't seen you."

Charlotte was aghast at the idea of Edith going anywhere near Ashgarde. Her grandmother stroked her cheek while reassuring her, "My lovey, that'll just make it obvious I know what's going on. I have duties to resume, and I am well and truly capable of holding my own. Besides, it's the best way to keep tabs on everyone and see who is and isn't up to foul play."

"What about her, then?" she pressed, referring to Hazel, who finger-gunned her.

"I have some investigating to do. It's kind of my special skill set to chase leads and take down bad things, y'know? So, I'm going back on the road to see what I can find out and see if I can't corner this Dick guy myself."

"And I'm just meant to sit here and do nothing, dicking around with videos, essentially imprisoned?"

Hazel patted her on the shoulder. "Little bit, babe, little bit. If you get the free time, it wouldn't hurt you to browse the internet and see if you can't find out something about our freaky buddy here, too."

Charlotte sighed to herself as Wade called Hazel uncouth, an argument ensuing between the two. She massaged the throbbing in her temple, wondering how the day had gotten so out of hand.

⟫⟫ ⟪⟪

"I hate this," Charlotte grumbled softly to herself. She had her legs pulled up to her chest, arms wrapped around them. She hadn't spoken since shuffling to the sitting room earlier as though in a trance. She'd been drowning in her thoughts, trying to digest what was happening.

Hazel had left an hour before, intent on following up leads, starting with Umbra Hollow. The Hunter hadn't explained what she planned to do or how, but Charlotte figured that was simply the way Hazel was going to roll. Edith already had plans sorted for the day with some of the family heads. She'd smiled sympathetically at Charlotte, who had nervously pleaded Edith to stay.

Because while she wouldn't say the exact words out loud, Charlotte hated being in the big old house.

Wade remained seated on the small sofa. The gentleman ghost hadn't spoken a word since the others had left either. Specter had wandered off somewhere into the estate, probably to nap, confident that his mom wasn't about to leave him again. Shafts of midafternoon sun danced through the large open windows, a tantalizing breeze wafting through. She knew she was confined to the grounds, not only the house, but that didn't stop the trickle of dread from running down the back of her neck.

She wasn't merely trapped by the wards locking her in. Her life had trapped her, a legacy that she hadn't ever asked for dragging her back down yet again.

CHAPTER TWELVE

hings only got worse.

They were confined to the third floor of the house, much to Charlotte's horror. Specter wasn't happy about it, either, as he was used to being allowed to roam about freely. The reason, Edith explained, was they couldn't risk them being spotted by someone from the Society, and if there *were* issues inside the Society, they would definitely be checking Winterbourne. By the end of their first week being trapped in the lonesome house together, Charlotte, Specter, and Wade had settled into a new, if not somewhat awkward, routine.

Meals were brought up to them on the third floor. They avoided the windows; the curtains were pulled shut at night. Edith would join them for dinner to provide them with updates. During the day, Charlotte's laptop had a dozen or more tabs open while books and notebooks sat scattered across every available surface as they hunted for any scrap of information—on the Van Bairds, the situation at Umbra Hollow, anything. Occasionally Hazel would text, and they were never reassuring messages.

Edith had been right about the Society, of course. In the first three days, Dirk had managed to arrange multiple meetings and drop-ins. Charlotte's name had been brought up almost immediately. He asked her where Charlotte was, and what she was up to. Edith had shrugged and told him she had no clue, that she was probably off making videos. Her RV had been moved to a private parking garage somewhere nearby on the off chance it might be seen.

It killed Charlotte not be able to listen in on their conversations.

The first day of their hiding had been the worst. The third floor, right beneath the low attic, was mostly deserted. It had once been the servant quarters, but with the family so small, Edith had given their small permanent staff their own rooms on the second level. The third floor, while clean and orderly, had a ghostly chill to it, the irony not lost on Charlotte and her own new ghost friend. The overwhelming sense of being alone in the dark of the old house had sent her into an anxiety spiral.

Wade sat with her through it, surprising her. He'd been wandering the floor, curious, when he found her curled on her side of her temporary bedroom floor, unable to breathe. Wade made no comment as he sat beside her, proceeding to ramble about a particularly interesting piece of furniture he had found. His detailed chatter distracted her, allowed her to focus on his voice as she pulled herself out of the yawning abyss deep inside her. When she had been able to breathe properly, she pulled herself upright and carried on like nothing happened. They didn't acknowledge her panic attack; instead, he smiled at her, asking if she wanted to help find him a room to sleep in. She had burst into laughter, surprised he even knew how to joke. She couldn't wipe the smile from her face as she followed him back into the hall of the third floor.

By week three of their banishment, Charlotte was going stir-crazy. It wasn't often that she missed her room downstairs, but now she was desperate for it. One night—she couldn't remember which day, as they had all started to run together—she had just bathed for the night. While the accommodations upstairs were sufficient, they weren't as good as she was used to— unless she was in the RV, anyway. She was drying her hair when Wade knocked hesitantly on her door.

She still hadn't worked out the limitations of his existence, what he could interact with or not. Most of the spirits that could touch and affect things on the living side of the Veil were malevolent or had a nasty buildup of emotions. Wade, however, was like an eager puppy, filled with politeness and smiles. She hadn't seen him even so much as frown as they pored over old tomes and newspapers, outlining what they knew about him. He had been patient and helpful as she scrawled notes, praising her whenever her mood began to sour. It hadn't been long before she forgot that he hadn't always been there with her.

"Come in," she called, dropping her towel on the end of the bed as she made sure her silk dressing gown was tightened. Wade floated through the door.

"I'm sorry to interrupt your evening. I—" Wade's sentence cut short as he emitted an odd strangled noise. "My deepest apologies, I had no—that is to say, I wasn't aware of your current state! I will take my leave and address you when it is appropriate—"

She didn't mean to smirk, seating herself beside the towel as Wade's words jumbled together, tripping over them as they rushed out in one breath. While he'd been more relaxed around her and had even started bantering with her during the day as they worked, he was still a gentleman. And a prude.

"Don't sweat it," she said, crossing a leg, relieved she had shaved them. She flicked her still-damp hair over her shoulder. "Take a seat and chat with me. You aren't going to burst into flames because I have flesh. Your virtue is safe from that."

"It's not my virtue that I worry for," he grumbled. "How dare I *respect* a lady, how ridiculous of me!" He threw his hands into the air as he muttered to himself. He drifted over to the bed and perched on the end of it, keeping his eyes trained upward, as though he had found something interesting on the ceiling. She giggled, surprising not only Wade, whose eyes tore away from the ceiling to look at her, but herself.

"Sorry for laughing, I don't know what came over me." Charlotte sat up, taking a deep breath to compose herself. She was calm and serious; she was not a schoolgirl. "Now, what's up?"

"I'll take it to mean that you are inquiring about my late-night intrusion." She glanced at the clock. It was barely eight in the evening—the sun had only just started to set. "But I wanted to speak to you regarding a thought I had about our research earlier."

Earlier that day, they had finished drafting a rough timeline of Wade's life through newspaper articles, family obituaries, and births. They had placed his birth in 1881 thanks to an announcement in the paper and his death sometime in the early teens.

They'd found nothing else about his family. Not even about their disappearance, despite how widely known it was. Even an extensive academic search online didn't turn up a single trace. When they ran out of newspapers to search, Charlotte had gotten creative with her methods. Desperate to place a rough estimation on when he had died, she had shown him different important events during the Edwardian period, such as pictures of the sister ships *Olympic* and *Titanic*. It worked better than expected. The first, he remembered being finished, but the second, he hadn't. He hadn't heard of Titanic's grisly fate, either, and she regretted being the one to tell him about it.

"I already told you we'll watch the James Cameron movie tomorrow night; it is *way* too long and sad to get into tonight."

"No, it's not about that, although I fear it will wrench my heart thoroughly."

"What is it, then?"

"I think we are looking at this all wrong. We are looking for something that makes me and my death special, but surely if it were, it would be noted. I have quite a prominent family, and to find there is no information about them or myself is disconcerting. Perhaps it is not my death that binds me here."

She cocked her head thoughtfully as Wade rambled on, his brow furrowed as he worked through it.

"We should be looking for things that aren't about me and trying to work out how they would connect to me."

Charlotte frowned. "What do you mean by that?"

"Well, remember how Miss Hazel said there has been a rash of murders in her electronic communication earlier?"

Hazel had texted as much earlier that afternoon. They were smaller group murders, some the normal media hadn't caught up to yet, but the stench of dark magic had been upon them. The other girl was certain they were all connected to the one that had happened the day they all met. Charlotte's stomach clenched as her memories stirred in response.

"What if there had been other deaths through time that we can link to my own death? Ones that have a similar pattern, perhaps? For it feels like for some reason, the death of myself and my family have been purposely obscured, rather than it simply having vanished."

Charlotte's heart raced. She'd wondered why such an important family, the Society aside, hadn't appeared in the papers past 1904, the year his sister Loren had had her cotillion. That was the last scrap on this family that gave them a solid time frame; everything else had been guesswork. Even Wade's approximate age had been mere conjecture, as Charlotte had told him there was no way he was younger than her twenty-eight years, even if it wasn't by much.

Not with eyes as sad as his.

"Your death was horrific, based on your injury. You didn't pass naturally." Charlotte was up now, pacing the stiff wooden floorboards of the old room. "If your death was a typical murder, it would have been reported in the papers. Even the Society's influence couldn't stop that. Also, you haven't been seen in over a century, in ghost form or otherwise, which is another anomaly." The cogs in her head were turning. "So, someone even bigger than your family could have theoretically made sure it wouldn't be known how or when you died . . . but for what purpose?"

Her thoughts and pacing were interrupted by her grandmother's voice floating up the staircase.

"Honestly, Dirk, this is ridiculous. The servants and I haven't seen her in weeks. What is your obsession with Charlotte? I promised you I would let you know when she was home, but you haven't even so much as hinted at what you want to speak to her about."

She froze and stared wide-eyed at Wade. They were about to be cornered by the enemy with nowhere to run.

"What are we going to do?" she mouthed at Wade as the stairs leading to the third-floor landing creaked, a cold wave of fear washing over her.

⌁ ⌁

Time seemed to slow down as Dirk Ashgarde's voice grew closer.

"We have some concerns about her well-being. She clearly hasn't been coping well these past few years, and the Society wants to see if there is anything we can do. For *her* sake. With these recent erratic videos she's making, it is apparent to us that her mental health is on the decline."

She glanced frantically around the room. Her clothes were in a hamper in the bathroom still, and all of her papers were out in one of the small cramped rooms. If he saw any of those, it would be a dead giveaway that she was there. She was about to be murdered in her dressing gown and had nowhere to hide. The antique bed frame had no space to hide underneath, and the small wardrobe was not big enough for her.

"Leave, Wade, you can still get away," she hissed at him. He shook his head emphatically.

"We're in this together," he whispered.

A creak behind Charlotte had her whirling around. The seat at the window bay had propped up ever so slightly.

"Was that you?" Wade shook his head again. She collected Specter from the bed where he had jumped up a moment before, holding him close.

"Miss Charlotte," came a soft whisper. Wade and Charlotte looked around, eyes wide. "Miss Charlotte, over here!" The voice was louder now and the window seat rose higher, revealing the curly blonde hair of one of the housemaids.

"Sylvia, what are you doing? How are you doing that?" She darted over, kneeling before the maid, nervously glancing over her shoulder.

"I've been told to trade places with you. Now, out of the way."

Charlotte scooted back as Sylvia popped out of the bench with unnerving ease. She propped the seat up the reveal a trapdoor in the floor, concealed within.

"You're going to have to climb in and be quiet. It's very cramped, and I'm sorry for that. Take Master Specter with you, and whatever you do, do not make a noise!"

Sylvia scurried around the room, throwing the towel Charlotte had abandoned into the adjacent bathroom, hurriedly hiding evidence as they climbed gingerly into the box. Charlotte's heart began pounding as she stared down into the awaiting darkness.

"Make haste," Sylvia hissed as she hurried back with Specter, thrusting the cat into Charlotte's arms. Trepidation washed over her as she clutched Specter close and slipped down through the dark trapdoor.

⤜⤛ ⤛⤜

Panic rose in Charlotte the second she was ensconced in darkness, chest ready to burst at the gentle click of the window seat shutting.

"I'm going to die entombed in the walls," she whispered hoarsely, eyes straining in the dark. It wasn't like he was going to kill her in there, but her dumb brain didn't care about being rational.

"It's going to be fine, Charlotte. I am beside you," Wade murmured gently to her, his silky voice caressing her in the darkness. She relaxed involuntarily as she felt the subtle press of cool against her side. Thankfully, Specter remained quietly curled up in her arms, as if he, too, knew the direness of their situation.

The thunderous roar of her heart filled the silence as they waited in agony, straining to hear noise above them. A minute passed and she was beginning to wonder if the danger was really there, if her grandmother had convinced him successfully about her whereabouts—

"Mistress Blythe, good evening. How can I help you?"

Sylvia's voice, muted by the floor between them, filled the tiny space. Charlotte's breath quickened despite herself.

"Dirk, this is one of our maids, Sylvia. This is *her* room. While a lot of our staff have moved to the second floor, Sylvia prefers the peace and quiet. Sylvia, this is Dirk Ashgarde. He's insistent on seeing our Charlotte, but I've told him repeatedly that she has yet to visit us. I'm sorry he has decided to . . . *inspect* your accommodations."

"It's a pleasure, Lord Ashgarde."

There was silence as the floors creaked, as though someone was moving around the room. Charlotte shifted her weight uneasily, a shiver running down her spine as she pressed closer to Wade. It might have been her imagination, but she swore she felt him pressing back.

"Seems a bit early for a housemaid to be ready for bed. And the state of the room is one I would reprimand one of *my* servants for," Dirk sniffed.

"We aren't like that here," Edith snapped. "Sylvia chooses to work for us and be a part of this family, and treated like family, she shall be."

"Ah, my dear Edie, you know that attitude won't get you far." The creaking stopped. "This is odd. If this is your maid's room, why is there a suitcase full of her clothing open in the corner and not in the armoire?"

Charlotte cursed silently, sure that Wade's judging eyes were now on her. He'd been harping on her just a few days ago about acting like a lady and hanging her things up. She had waved him off; they had better things to do, and she was more used to living out of the suitcase.

"I just returned from a trip, sir. To see my parents, sir."

"I imagine your parents are ashamed of the slob they raised."

Charlotte's face burned hot with anger. She imagined climbing out of the hiding hole, wrapping her hands around Dirk Ashgarde's neck until his face turned purple. Her thoughts were interrupted by the sounds of opening and closing doors. She froze as Edith cut in. "Now, Dirk, this is beyond ridiculous. It's an invasion of my maid's privacy."

"I have it on good authority that your granddaughter is lurking here. I bet this maid is hiding her for you, isn't she?"

A gasp slipped from between her lips as the top of the window seat opened. Dirk Ashgarde loomed a few scant inches above her.

"It seems odd to me that your maid should have so many perfectly good storage places, and yet she appears to use none."

Charlotte swayed as his knuckles rapped the floor above her head. She had no idea how it opened or closed, but if he found it, she was a sitting duck. She wished she could speak, urge Wade to escape while he had a chance. Maybe she could drop Spec and he could help her kitty escape . . .

It took everything in her not to gasp as she felt a chill wrap around her. The world seemed to stop momentarily as she realized Wade was holding her to him as best he could in his spectral form.

"Excuse me, sir, but I've had a long day and haven't had the chance to unpack."

Sylvia's voice cut through the air and interrupted Ashgarde's rapping. Charlotte's heart pounded as the silk of his suit rustled. She sagged with relief at the click of the seat shutting once again.

"Now that you've thoroughly embarrassed my maid, perhaps I can escort you to the door, Dirk?"

Charlotte, Specter, and Wade waited long after the patter of footsteps disappeared, not daring to make a peep. Wade whispered soothing nonsense placations to her in the darkness, his cool embrace oddly comforting. Her mind drifted, unbidden, wondering what it would have felt to have him embrace her when he was alive. Her skin pricked as she scolded herself. *What on earth are you thinking of that for?*

Her thoughts were broken by the sound of the seat creaking open again. She prepared herself as the door above her popped open, flooding in light. Sylvia's face peered over them.

In the light, Charlotte could see that Wade indeed had his arms around her. Her lips quirked into a smile as she locked eyes with him momentarily before his arms slithered away as he vanished into the wall encasing them.

"Your grandmother has returned and says you can come out now."

She let Specter up first. She tried unsuccessfully to haul herself up until Sylvia pointed out some narrow ridges, built-in steps for getting up.

"I'm so done with today," she moaned when was safely back out. Wade hadn't reappeared yet, but she suspected he wasn't far and was listening in. Edith sat on the end of the bed, Sylvia beside her. "Did . . . did you clean up in here, Sylvia?"

"A little," the maid admitted with a bob of her head. "I couldn't help myself, miss."

"And how did you know about this?" she asked weakly, gesturing to the window seat.

Edith cut in now. "Jacob instructed her. We have a remarkable amount of hidden alcoves like that. One can never be too safe. I know you know a lot of them, but there are always secrets to be discovered in a house such as this."

"Alright, that . . . makes sense. So, what about the evil old miser coming up here?"

Edith and Sylvia exchanged a worried look. "He kept claiming he had it on good authority that you were here, and that he had important business to conduct with you. I told him I was acting Head of the family and he could go through me, but he was—"

"An evil old miser," Charlotte sighed. "Thanks for your help, Sylvia."

"My pleasure." The maid curtsied to Charlotte and Edith. "May I be dismissed, ma'am?"

"Of course. Go have a bath and relax, dear."

Sylvia pulled the door shut behind her and Charlotte sank onto the bed beside her grandmother. "This isn't looking good."

"I'll confess, I feel the same."

They sat in silence for a few moments, alone. Specter had wandered off and Wade remained unseen. She thought about the hidden hole in the bench and wondered if there were more on this level she could learn about, just in case. Maybe she could stash her research in one of them, too. That was when a thought crossed her mind.

"Wade!" she called out excitedly, jumping to her feet. Edith gave her a look as she called out again for him. It took a moment, but he soon popped his head through the door.

"Yes?"

"Wade, the day I met you, when you helped me escape and we realized you didn't have most of your memories." She was pacing now, nervous energy building up. "You took me through a secret tunnel to a caretaker's house to escape. You said you used it the night your family died to get out, right?"

He nodded slowly. Charlotte clapped her hands together.

"Two things come to mind. One, obviously, is that you have to have intimate knowledge of that house to know how to get out. Two, it seems like perhaps some other people might have known about the same passage, right?"

Wade cocked his head. "What are you implying?"

"They died in your home, right? I don't know how I forgot you said that. And whoever killed them *must* have tried to kill you, too, surely. Why did you escape and how? Why not your whole family? What if whoever killed them knew about it? Just like Dirk knew to look for us just now?"

"Maybe it was someone in the Society?" Edith's soft voice was the one to answer. Charlotte nodded.

"I think so, and I think that gives us another lead."

By the time Charlotte sank into bed to sleep, it was nearly two in the morning. They'd come up with a new strategy and she'd called Hazel immediately to fill her in. The Hunter had been keeping tabs on Ashgarde, as well as following the spread of similar murders. She was doubling back to Umbra Hollow now, hoping to find whatever amount of information she could to tie it all together. It had to have some sort of special meaning if they *had* committed mass murder there twice, and maybe they could figure out more about the day Wade died.

Edith's new priority was to attach herself to Dirk. Charlotte hated this, but Edith insisted. He was openly making Charlotte a target now, and Edith would do anything she could to throw him off.

Charlotte and Wade were now tasked with doing everything they could to jolt Wade's memory, to fill in the missing links—to work out why he was so important to them.

As she was drifting off, the effects of one of her loathsome sleeping tablets kicking in, Wade's low voice cut through the still night. "Miss Charlotte?"

"Hmmm?"

"May I speak to you?"

"Yeah," she mumbled, rolling onto her side so she faced the door. Wade had already popped in and was wringing his hands nervously.

"I wanted to apologize for being so forward with you earlier."

"Whatcha mean?"

"I should not have held you with familiarity and intimacy such as I did. I feared the end was naught, and I overstepped, believing you would want comfort should that moment arrive. It was the behavior of a cad. I might as well have taken advantage of you."

"Wade, I'd hardly call that taking advantage of me." Charlotte stifled a yawn and thumped her hand on the edge of the quilt. "Come sit."

He hesitated, then drifted over and delicately sat on the edge of the bed. "This is not what a gentleman should be doing."

"Shhh, 'is okay." Charlotte stretched out a hand toward his, stroking it. Ghosts were a weird sort of matter; they could be completely invisible and able to move through things and be moved through, like a gas, or they could be semisolid, like a heavy wind. Wade was more solid than she was used to, and she was surprised to meet some resistance when she touched him instead of hitting the quilt. He was so different from any ghost she had encountered. He was still as cold as ever, though, and Charlotte shivered.

"Your hand is so cold," she sighed, riding the euphoric side effects of her meds as they tumbled over her like a wave. "You can come into my bed to warm up."

"Miss Blythe!" Wade sounded mortified as she giggled. "I should leave you be; you are in no state for company. I shall speak to you in the morning—"

"No, don't go." Charlotte twisted her hand until she found it wrapped around his. Wade was still as she stroked the top of his hand with her free one.

"So weird your hands can feel so real but not," she mumbled. "I think if I press too hard, it'll just go through."

"Perhaps."

"I haven't held anyone's hand in a long time. Maybe this is just what it's meant to feel like." She giggled again.

"I haven't held someone's hand in an eternity either, Charlotte" was his quiet response.

"It feels so nice, having someone like me around. Someone a little broken." She clung to his hand as she wriggled against her pillow, the siren song of sleep calling to her. "I hope you stay."

Charlotte was almost asleep, but she swore she heard Wade whisper, "Me too," as his voice cracked.

⋙ ⋘

He knew he shouldn't be in her room. It was ghastly behavior from a gentleman, and normally he wouldn't. But he couldn't ignore her any longer. Not when they seemed to be getting worse.

She cried in her sleep often but didn't seem to be aware of it. Nightmares, it would seem. He'd heard her soft cries for help the first night as he wandered the third floor, contemplating his existence.

He had stood vigil by her door every night since, deciding his new purpose was to watch over her, to know that she was safe—if not in her dreams, at least from the rest of the world. Tonight was different, though. She had asked him to stay, after he came to apologize. And so he watched as she fell into a deep, restless slumber, the press of her hand against his own. Something that should have been impossible, and yet . . .

He thought about the before as he watched her. The sentiments were there, though faded and jumbled. He remembered not wanting to suffer anymore before the darkness came for him.

There was a part of him that remembered, and he wasn't sure he wanted it to.

"Please," Charlotte whimpered in her sleep.

This body was an echo of the one he'd had in life. Though muted, it still felt, understood what it was to be human. His mind and soul were the same as they were before.

Chapter Thirteen

"**A**lright, you've been staring at me weirdly since I got here. What's wrong?"

It was lunchtime the next day and Charlotte had surprised herself by *actually* waking up in time for it. She had awoken to the smells of fresh pastry and sugar to find her grandmother and Wade in her temporary office. Her heart fluttered as she saw the mug in front of him.

She listened in on their chatter, sleepily snacking on a flaky tomato and cheese croissant. Edith had managed to find some old family albums from Society events that included the Van Bairds and the twosome were perusing them.

"You look so handsome," Edith crooned, pointing at a photo of him. It was marked 1907; he would have been about Charlotte's age, by their estimates. "I bet the girls were all over you. Don't you agree, Charlotte?"

Wade stared at her, the same peculiar expression etched across his face.

"What are *you* looking at?" Charlotte scowled as she sank into her chair, poking at the remnants of her lunch. Wade glanced away, but she swore his eyes darted back to her. Her brain churned over, seeking a witty, disparaging comment when Edith interrupted her thoughts.

"I've got a meeting with the other Heads today. I've called a meeting to discuss Dirk's unpleasantness yesterday evening. Perhaps it is time one of the younger ones in his family took his place."

"You think Bradley will be any better? Besides, his grandpa can just manipulate him."

"Of course not, lovey. But distrust between Dirk and the other members will be an advantage to us as we get to the bottom of this. I must get ready now."

With that, her grandmother swept out, bidding them a good day. Charlotte stared after her for a moment before turning her attention to the album. "Did Grandmother help you remember anything?"

"Yes," Wade coughed, still not looking at her. "I was pleasantly surprised to remember more of my younger sister, Loren. I had seen the photo from her cotillion, but seeing her in that flurry of white was not the same. This morning, a memory of playing with her in an old nursery came to mind. She always insisted I partake in her tea parties."

"I bet you could remember more if you weren't trapped in here."

Wade sighed. "Perhaps, but we have no choice, not with the unpleasant fellow trying to catch us off guard. I do not imagine he merely wishes to speak to us."

Charlotte pushed back from the seat, running a finger through the crumbling flakes that remained on her plate. "Come on, we're going on an adventure."

"How? Where? Surely we will be noticed if we traipse down the stairs."

Charlotte shrugged. "I don't know all of the house's secrets, but I know some."

Charlotte took Wade down an old servant staircase that ran down between the walls to the two-story atrium at the back of the house. Rarely visited by anyone else, it was one of her favorite places. It was crammed so full of exotic plants and flowers that despite being glass on all sides—save the one attached to the main house—the outside world wasn't visible. Some glass doors led out onto the back patio, but they were covered by plants that she had moved in the way several years before to ensure privacy when she came to weep in her worst moments.

"This is my special place," she told Wade as they crawled out of the three-foot narrow door that popped open in a hidden corner. Wade straightened to his full height, looking around in wonderment.

"I see why this is your favorite place, despite the grandeur of the rest of your home. It fills me with a sense of peace and safety. Is this how you feel here?"

Charlotte tilted her head, watching Wade as he leaned over flowers, sighing contentedly. She wondered if he could somehow smell them. "I guess it's because it doesn't feel like it's part of the house. It feels freer. I can . . . I can let myself have feelings here. I don't owe anyone part of myself in here." She bit down on her lip. She hadn't quite meant to share that. There was something about him that compelled her, that had her speaking truths even when she didn't want to.

Wade straightened back up, glancing at the flowers as he said, "Is that why you have that automobile home? So as to not be in this house?"

She winced at his directness but nodded. "Yeah, I haven't felt right here in a long time."

"That is a sentiment I can most assuredly understand." Wade offered her an arm. "Would you care to escort me for a turn about the garden?"

Charlotte's skin prickled as she shyly reached for his arm. She slipped her arm under his, placing her hand delicately on his forearm. It was like trying to hold cotton candy. It was fine if she was careful, but one wrong move and her hand would fall right through his arm, shattering the illusion.

They wandered through the atrium, silent save for the chirps and croaks of small creatures that had wriggled their way in and lived amongst the plants. It wasn't necessarily an uncomfortable silence, but she found herself struggling to put a name to the peculiar sensation that was gripping her; she felt light as a cloud, but also like she was falling.

"I wasn't looking at you weirdly, just so you know."

Wade's voice cut through her thoughts. They had slowed now, still moving, but it was more of a shuffle. She glanced at him from under her lashes. She realized as she stood beside him that she actually had to look up at him to see his face. Her heart fluttered.

"This morning," he continued. "I didn't intend to look at you oddly. As I do not need rest, I had a lot of time to ruminate on our late-night exchange, and I was pondering what it meant."

Charlotte stopped. Wade paused, too, looking over his shoulder at her. Dappled sunlight hit his auburn hair, highlighting the red, and his pale skin glistened like porcelain as his form wavered between planes of existence. Her grandmother hadn't been wrong; he *was* handsome.

"What 'exchange'? What are you talking about?"

Wade led her over to a raised stone garden bed and gestured her for to sit. Eying him warily, she sat. Sitting beside her, Wade explained that he'd gone to apologize, and they had spoken and she'd behaved oddly.

"You fell asleep with your hand upon mine and it . . . it felt wonderful." Awe filled his voice. "I felt whole, renewed. I confess I sat there for quite a while longer than I should have, but it was as if there were no barrier between us. I am deeply ashamed for invading your privacy in such a way, and pray you will forgive me."

A light-headed feeling threatened to overwhelm her as fragments of the night before returned. She remembered how cold he had been to touch—and how desperately she had wished to warm him up. Her cheeks tingled with warmth.

"Oh my God, I offered for you to get in my bed, didn't I?"

Wade stiffened beside her. "I am a gentleman and was not going to mention that particular comment."

She groaned, placing her head in her hands. "I hate my sleeping meds."

Wade, who had been looking away, no doubt to be polite, suddenly floated away from her to another garden bed. She lifted her head and watched as he bent over it excitedly.

"Blast it," he muttered to himself a minute later. Gathering herself, she rose and joined him, peering over his shoulder.

It was a small tulip garden that had been there much longer than she had been alive. Wade had his fingers around a stem, attempting to pluck it. She watched several more attempts before clearing her throat.

"What are you trying to do?" she asked, out of politeness more than anything. It was pretty obvious how much he was struggling. She winced as he pinched tighter, his fingers bending the stem a fraction of a hair, unable to snap it.

"I wanted to pluck this tulip for you." Wade sighed and let his hand fall away. "I cannot even pluck a flower for a lady. What is even the point of my cursed existence?" He sounded as though he were on the verge of tears, sorrow heavy in his voice. His tone tugged at her heart as Wade hung his head.

"Put your hand back," she told him quietly. He complied. Charlotte leaned over beside him, positioning her fingers right above his, twisting the flower stem and snapping it with a hard yank. Wade's eyes clouded as his gaze followed the flower to her face. She sniffed the tulip, twirling it between her fingers before threading it through a buttonhole in her blouse. She settled down on the low stone wall surrounding the tulips.

"Beautiful," he murmured, a wistful look upon his face. She tapped her long fingers along her thighs, plucking occasionally at pilling on her wool trousers as she waited for him to say something more. The prolonged silence agitated Charlotte. She was about to say something when Wade's eyes widened, his mouth popping open in a silent *oh*.

"What is it?" she demanded, the queer tenderness of the last few minutes forgotten. She shuffled closer to him against the wall. "What are you thinking?"

He grimaced, hands to his temples as though he was in pain. "It is agony; it is all coming in at once. It was so dark, I was drowning in myself. I couldn't go on anymore, Charlotte. I had to end it. I had to make it stop."

"What do you mean?"

Wade sucked in a deep breath. "I *wanted* to die."

⤞⤝

"What on earth are you two doing? You shouldn't be down here, Charlotte!"

Charlotte and Wade barreled past Jacob, her grandmother's right-hand man and butler. Peeling around the corner, she nearly slammed into a vase that cost more than her undergrad tuition. Wade hadn't gotten far into his explanation before Charlotte had hurtled off, an ill sense of foreboding washing over her. She needed to find her grandmother.

"Charlotte, allow me to assist you, for heaven's sake!"

She whirled around to find Jacob had jogged after them. An elderly gentleman, he had been somewhat of a surrogate grandpa to a young Lottie after the passing of her own grandfather. "Jacob, I need to see Grandmother."

"She's already left for a meeting. She'll be back this afternoon."

She cursed and leaned back against the paneling of the wall behind her. "That's great. Just as we're making progress."

"She'll return within a few hours, Charlotte. Allow me to escort you and your guest back upstairs, then I can fix you something to eat, perhaps?"

She sighed at the thought of returning to the gloomy third floor. She thought of the bottle in her second-floor study, weighing if it was worth snatching on her way back upstairs before she remembered they were hurried. "Wait, no, this is serious. Grandmother isn't safe."

Jacob frowned, soft lines puckering around his dark eyes that sparkled with concern. "Edith is not safe?"

Charlotte nodded. "Wade, tell him what happened."

As Wade straightened, as though steeling himself, Jacob raised his index finger to pause him. "Perhaps this is a conversation better had somewhere private. Come along."

⇝ ⇜

The kitchen was colder than the rest of the house. Set down several steps lower than the entrance level of the house, it had retained many of its original qualities. Only a few appliances and small renovations to replace and repair broken things had been undertaken over the course of Winterbourne's life. The walls were tall and drafty, the main long bench along the side of the kitchen studded with many small windows that glanced onto a small section of yard. Jacob had explained to a small Charlotte, who used to sneak into the kitchen for chocolates and pies, that it was so there were fewer distractions for the staff back in the day.

The smell of flour and butter and the heat from the cast-iron stove, inset into its own wall, brought a simple nostalgia to her. It reminded her of a time when the world wasn't hard, wasn't scary. When her only care or responsibility in the world was to be herself.

"Now," Jacob said, pouring three cups of peppermint tea garnished with a wedge of lemon. Her absolute favorite that she used to share with her mom. "Start from the beginning, and we can get a message sent to Edith safely. We have an hour until dinner rotation starts, so let's get through this."

Pulling a small black notebook and a fountain pen from his breast pocket, he waited, pen poised. Wade nestled his hands around his steaming cup as though he could feel its warmth.

"Well, it happened in the atrium. I must preface this by apologizing for breaking the rules of our quarantine. I take the blame for it, as Miss Charlotte was merely trying to help me find a way to recollect more clearly. We were at the tulip garden, where I was trying to procure a blossom." Wade leaned across the table toward Jacob, his voice lowered. "I hope Ms. Edith takes no offense to my actions, and I will request a conference with her later."

Jacob chuckled as he jotted down what Wade said. She couldn't help but feel like she was somehow out of the loop.

"And then?" Jacob prompted.

"It was as though there was a great rush of light coming at me, and it knocked me over. The light, while it didn't chase away all of the shadows, uncovered things I could not spot just moments before. Some of those memories are a little gray still, for which I apologize.

"The day Miss Charlotte and I met, there had been a great loss of life. So much sad, angry energy pulled around me, dragging me in so many directions. I was tumbling in the darkness until this soft red string guided me back out of it like a life rope. And she was on the other end, on this side of the Veil, in all her vulgar, ill-mannered glory."

"Hey, that's a bit rude," she interjected weakly.

"Keep going, Master Wade."

"It was like I had been torn from my body, and I was left untethered until I found her. The dark lingered in the back of my mind as we left there, but there was this instinct within me. On where to go, what to do. It was peculiar. I remember, before she and the feline entered the room— it was cold. There were people all around me. There was this fuzziness around me, as though I was there but also not. They were celebrating something, I believe. Something they had been working hard on was complete, or something near completion. At least, this is what I think.

"There was this oddness to the air, a stifling atmosphere—it was so strange. And then they were in a stupor. I don't quite understand. And then . . . no . . . wait. The black cloaks were everywhere, and I felt full of warmth and light. But then that went away, the cloaks danced between the people. Then a flash of green before they fell, so peacefully, so quickly. I don't truly think they knew what was happening to them, which is merciful, I guess."

Wade paused, frowning into his cup. "I stood there amongst the carnage, invisible, wishing none of it was happening. The cloaks were all around me, as though they were encircling me. And then the man you all know as Dirk Ashgarde lowered his hood and smiled right at me, as though he could see me."

"Gods," Jacob murmured after a pause, a hint of alarm in his voice. "I'll call Edith back immediately."

Jacob hurried from the room, leaving them alone. Wade's hands were still wrapped around his untouched tea. Charlotte sipped her own, hands trembling, wondering what would happen next. If the shaky broken testimony of a ghost would be enough for the Society to open an internal investigation. Her thoughts wandered to the onslaught that had claimed her parents at her debutante ball, the hearings, and the accusations . . .

"Charlotte."

She blinked, her thoughts brought back to the present, back to Wade.

"There is something else."

"What do you mean?" She turned on the bar stool she sat on, leaving her tea on the long island counter to face him. "Did something else come back to you?"

Wade shook his head. "It's more of a feeling." He paused. "I feel like they forgot me there."

"Huh?"

"I think I was meant to go with them, but I don't understand how or why."

"You're probably all muddled up. You're only just remembering things now, after all. You probably got that day all mixed up with the day you died." She frowned. "You didn't actually tell me about how you died. You said you remembered, right?"

With a sigh, Wade slid off the seat. "I don't quite want to talk about that right now. Perhaps, seeing as we are breaking the rules currently, you could give me a tour of your home instead."

The frown remained on her face, but she nodded. "Sure, buddy, whatever you want."

⟫⟫⟫ ⟪⟪⟪

She didn't quite understand the somber expression on Wade's face as they wandered through the house. Sure, he was sad—but he'd already known he was dead, even before recovering his memory, so it wasn't as if it was news. So why the look of despair? She chose not to say anything, figuring he would open up to her when the time was right.

"And this is another hallway lined with a lot of old family portraits, wonky landscapes, and various other pieces." She waved a hand dismissively. Wade, however, was intrigued, stopping to read the plaque under each portrait. They were in a small hallway up on the second floor. This one actually led to her bedroom, which she hadn't been in since the night she returned. She wondered if she should sneak in and grab some things.

"I'm going to be one second—" she started before seeing the painting Wade had stopped at.

It was of her and her parents, Charlotte sitting between them on one of the parlor sofas. She remembered that it took days for them to paint the base; it was the week of her thirteenth birthday, and she had wanted nothing more than to dick around online with her friends at the end of it. Hanging out with your parents hadn't been "cool," according to her peers. And even though they all had to go through the same rigmarole as her, they still teased her for hanging out with her parents so much. She had been so excited to have the painting done. Her mom and dad were staying the entire week with her after a lengthy trip to Europe to chase down a psycho leannán sídhe. It was rare for them to be home that long.

A bunch of the other kids in the Society, who had less hands-on parents who were home more, had been cruel about her wanting to see them. It had gotten to her, their taunts. She resented their comments at first, but then she began to resent her parents. They were the ones that couldn't be normal, couldn't be around more. Even for parents that were involved in a secret occult society, they were extremely absent. She just wanted to feel normal and like the others—to want them to go away for once, instead of missing them all the time.

And now she was always missing them.

"Your eyes are so sad here," Wade said softly, reaching a gloved hand up to the painting. Charlotte averted her eyes, heading further down the hall. "But I guess they're always sad, aren't they?"

She stopped as Wade continued quietly as if he was speaking only to himself. "They're a little less sometimes now. They light up, as if you remember you are allowed to feel good. It fills my soul when they look like that—lighter, more caramel than chocolate. That is how I can tell you are happy."

"Whatever," she muttered. "That's dumb."

"Is it dumb for me to notice how you feel?" Wade drifted over to her, his footfalls silent on the hardwood floor. "Is it dumb for me to care that my closest companion feels safe and content?"

"It's dumb that you notice things like people having sad eyes," she scoffed.

"Only you," he said softly. "I only notice if *your* eyes look sad or not."

Charlotte swallowed, realizing how little space there was between them. Her eyes darted about nervously, looking for a way to break the weird bubble that seemed to contain them, making the rest of the world obsolete.

"Don't you want to look at the rest of the paintings?" She consciously manipulated the lilt of her voice, sounding like a grade-school girl tripping over her words. "There's a lot up here you haven't examined, like an old man lost in a pharmacy."

Wade stepped closer still. Charlotte tried not to make eye contact with him, instead forcing herself to focus on his forehead. On the loose strands of hair that flopped forward into his eyes, on the tendrils that would never be pushed back with the sweep of his dark auburn hair . . .

"Charlotte, are you alright?"

She blinked, stars dancing in front of her eyes. Her head swam as she tried to make sense of what was going on. "Huh?"

"You fainted," Wade informed her, kneeling beside her, lips pursed with worry. "I am so sorry I could not catch you, but I dampened your fall to the best of my abilities. I can see that you are in no well condition. Is there somewhere we can take you to rest this off?"

"My room is down the end of the hall," she mumbled, closing her eyes against the bursts of color. "Gimme a minute and I can get there."

She took several deep breaths, bracing her arms against the wall to hoist herself up. Wade seemed able to help her somewhat—at least, she swore she felt his grip on her upper arm as she stumbled to her feet. Her head clouded with discomfort as she tried to once again understand the parameters of his existence. Carefully, with most of her weight on the hand that carefully moved between paintings on the wall, they shuffled to her room. When they got to the door, she paused, embarrassed.

"Please don't judge it," she murmured. "I didn't exactly clean before I last left it." Her heart fluttered. A boy was going into her room for the first time in a long time. *Not a boy,* she corrected herself, *a man*.

"I could never judge a lady in distress," Wade promised as she pushed the door open. Mercifully, someone had been in and cleaned. It smelled of fresh linens and flowers, despite the curtains being pulled firmly shut. "Allow me to find a light."

Wade floated away as she leaned against the doorjamb, waiting for her eyes to adjust to the low light. She cursed as the stars continued to blot her vision, followed by the yellow glow of her bedside lamp illuminating the room. "Here, Charlotte, come rest."

Her head still spinning, Charlotte stumbled over to her bed, promptly shutting her eyes as her head hit the pillow.

Chapter Fourteen

Charlotte awoke to the sounds of people. Loud voices floated through the door, slightly ajar. She groaned, mouth gritty as though she had swallowed ash. She didn't quite feel sick, but she felt off somehow. Her right palm pulsed and ached as she struggled upright on her bed.

The lamp was still on, bizarre shadows dancing across the walls and floors. She frowned, trying to work out what time it was. She slid her hand into her pocket to find her phone had run out of charge.

"Wade?" she called out tentatively, voice raspy. She coughed and tried a little louder. "Where are you, dude?"

He didn't pop up or answer her, but she swore the voices from outside her room were growing louder. Dread pooled in her stomach as she grabbed the corner of her bed frame and pushed off the mattress. Her lower back twinged in pain from sleeping with her belt still on.

Clumsily, Charlotte shuffled out of her room and down the twisting corridors. Trying to work out where the sounds were coming from, she drifted through the large old house like a wraith. She shivered, wishing she had grabbed some sort of sweater; her thin cotton blouse was not warm enough for the high walls of Winterbourne.

She stopped, feeling for the open buttonhole that her tulip had been in. She realized, with a pang, that it wasn't there. She peeked over her shoulder, wondering when it had fallen out, and debated going back to find it. The swell of voices, growing louder and closer now, quickly brought her back from her thoughts.

Rounding the corner into the east wing, where guests used to stay, Charlotte saw light spilling from one of the rooms out into the hall, followed shortly by Hazel's distinctly perky voice.

She paused, hidden in the shadows. She didn't know Hazel had been planning to return. When did she get back, and why? How long had she been there if she was already in a guest room?

"... someone should go wake Charlotte up." Her grandmother's voice startled her.

She got home safe, then, at least. "I'm here," she croaked, shuffling toward the room. She blinked at the brightness, eyes still heavy from sleep. "What's going on?"

This room was one of the larger ones Edith had used for higher-ranking guests in the past. Hazel sat cross-legged on the bed, her unruly curls bobbing as she bounced, arms crossed and holding her calves. Wade leaned against the bed, *his* arms crossed with a casualness that had her heart skipping a beat. Edith was sitting in a chair by the bed, Specter curled up in her lap as she stroked him.

"What's going on?" Charlotte repeated groggily. Hazel grinned and wriggled over on the bed, cocking her head in invitation. Charlotte obliged, throwing herself on her back. Hazel peered over her shoulder at Charlotte, the mischievous grin still parting her lips.

"It's nice to see you, too, babes. Aren't you going to give me a welcome-back cuddle, after all the weeks I've been on the road for you?"

Charlotte grabbed a pillow from behind her and threw it at the Hunter, who grabbed it with a deft hand and playfully smacked Charlotte back with it.

"Girls," Edith chided, humor in her voice. "There will be plenty of time for horseplay later."

Hazel offered Charlotte a hand, pulling her into a sitting position. Once upright, Charlotte was careful to avoid meeting Wade's eyes. Her heart skipped another beat at the thought of what had happened when they were alone earlier. She was grateful that Hazel was there to be a big oblivious buffer.

"Why are you back, anyway?"

"Well, for one, I would love a hot bath and meal like Gran promised me. Two, after our chat this afternoon, while you were snoring the day away Sleeping Beauty, we decided to brainstorm."

"You haven't missed dinner yet, dear," Edith reassured her granddaughter as she made a face.

"Anyway, I'm struggling. They're being super careful. The closest they got to messing up was when Dick—"

"*Dirk*, young lady."

"Yeah, that old turd. Anyway, he nearly messed up when he stormed in and tried to catch you guys. Other than that, though, I haven't been able to see what they're up to, even with all my tricks. They're warding up like the most paranoid motherfuckers—"

"Language, please," Edith sighed.

"—I have ever seen. They're up to something sketchy, that's for sure. I can't even predict where they're going, so I keep missing them." Hazel frowned, staring at the ceiling. "It's making no sense to me. I *think* a cult has gotten to them. None of the big ones are even registering as possibilities. They're off doing their usual shit. It's making no sense."

"They aren't letting anything on at meetings," Edith added. "I can't even begin to work out who Dirk may have working for him. They all simper so much for him as it is, hoping to take his position within the council." Edith twirled the end of her silver braid in her fingers, looking tired, more fragile, than Charlotte was used to.

"What do we do, then?" she asked softly.

"That's just it. We aren't sure." Hazel let out a frustrated huff. "I'm used to hunting down monsters and squishing them, babes. The Society is meant to be on the same side as me, not be the ones I'm hunting. I mean, they *claim* to be, anyway. I'm out of my depth and need some rest."

Hazel stretched on the bed, her arms out wide. "There are pieces to this puzzle that just aren't making sense to me. I'm sure with a bit of time and sleep, we can crack it."

"Yeah," Charlotte agreed, doubt filling the room like an ominous shadow.

⇝⇜

An hour later, freshly showered and cleaned up, they were seated as a group in the long dining room, a feast spread across the table. Homemade mushroom and steak pie, fresh bread, roasted vegetables, and various types of cold meats sat on silver trays.

"I apologize for the fare, Hazel and Wade. We would have something more planned, but usually only I dine down here now." Edith took her place at the head of the table.

Charlotte slunk down in her seat. Hazel, who sat opposite her on Edith's left-hand side, waved Edith off. "Gran, this is amazing. I've been eating fast food for weeks now and haven't slept in many beds that weren't in a rank, sketchy motel. Don't pretend this isn't a treat."

Hazel winked at Charlotte; the Hunter had sent a few selfies of the cute girls she'd hit on late at night in bars. Charlotte rolled her eyes as Hazel filled up her plate. She was happy for her the other girl, but boy was she *obnoxious* about getting laid.

Edith beamed at Hazel as the Hunter tucked in with fervor. Charlotte, who had Wade sitting to her right, silently loaded up her plate, filling up Wade's plate along with her own. Her eyes trained on her food, she started eating slowly and methodically.

"Charlotte," Wade intoned, her name dancing on his tongue. "May I ask how you are doing?"

"Great," she mumbled around some potato. "Fantastic, even."

"I was worried about you after you fainted this afternoon. I did not mean to frighten you or make you feel uncomfortable. I'm still adjusting to being around people again, it would seem. I pray that you will forgive me."

"Nothing to forgive."

"I hope my offering was not too forward—"

"You're fine, Wade. Let's drop it in front of present company," she hissed, accidentally slamming her fork too hard against the tablecloth. She felt the blood drain from her face as she glanced over at Grandmother and Hazel, the latter eagerly swirling the wine in her glass.

"Oh, babes, don't stop on our account." Mirth filled Hazel's eyes as she drank deeply.

"Yes, I'd like to hear more about this, too." Edith frowned. "You were sleeping because you fainted? Did Mister Van Baird cause you distress, my lovey?"

Charlotte groaned, sinking back in her seat. "It's *fine*, I just got a bit light-headed, and this idiot"—she jerked her head at Wade—"is just getting it into his head that he has some sort of ability to get under my skin."

Wade leaned closer to her. The skin on the back of her neck prickled. "Am I to believe that my presence did not cause the reaction you sustained?"

"Back off, buddy," she snapped, flustered. Hazel smirked at them across the table, smugness radiating from her. "You can quit it with those looks, too." Charlotte glowered.

"Man, he really gets under your skin, doesn't he? Pity we can't take advantage of that." Hazel sipped her wine as Charlotte leaned away in her seat from Wade. "If only he irritated the Society as much as he does you, babes."

"If I could weaponize him, I would in a heartbeat," she assured the Hunter. Wade, the perpetual gentleman, resumed his polite, stiff-backed table manners, his attention trained on Hazel across the table. Hazel stared back at him, appearing to contemplate him.

"What if we could?"

Charlotte snorted, slinking further down in her chair as Edith side-eyed her reproachfully. "Again, I would if I could."

"I reckon we might be able to." Hazel swirled her wine glass again, her expression thoughtful. "Have you considered exploiting your fan base?"

"Huh?"

Edith looked at Hazel like she had grown two heads while Charlotte, still in her post-nap stupor, scrunched up her nose in confusion. Hazel set her glass down.

"What if we played all the cards we had and used your channel to lure them out? I mean, they already know it, right? That's how I found out about you. We don't know what they want, but what if we just throw everything we have at 'em and hope something sticks? And they seemed pretty keen on getting Wade in particular when we last saw them."

"Again, I must reiterate—*huh*?"

Hazel nodded over at Wade. "They want him, and they hate you. Record him. Whatever he can think of, whatever he knows, throw it up on the 'net. We may or may not stumble on whatever use he is to them, but we will sure as hell cause some sort of panic, right? We can pretend to have a plan by doing it, one that they can actively see us acting on."

"You want them to be bait." Edith set her silverware aside. "By getting Charlotte to post content of him, to verify she is with him, you hope to flush them out of hiding to go after them."

Hazel shrugged. "It's the best idea I have. Nothing else is working so far, and the death count around the country is climbing as we speak. I don't know if this is all linked, but I think it's fair to presume it is."

"Death count?" Edith said sharply. Hazel turned her attention to Edith, filling her in on a rash of deaths across the northeast, giant groups of deaths linked in the media as the work of a serial killer cult, seeming to target places of worship. Hazel had forgotten to mention it, too caught up in catching Dirk.

Charlotte stewed on Hazel's words as they hashed out the news. It was risky—they certainly wouldn't be able to remain at Winterbourne if that was the approach they took. Who knew what effort or energy would be redirected at them if they chose to do that? And why was Wade such a point of interest to them? She risked a glance under her eyelashes at him. Wade remained quiet, observant. *What secrets does he have?*

⁓⟫⟫ ⟪⟪⁓

Several days later, Hazel was already back on the road while Wade and Charlotte prepared to get back out again. Edith hurried behind her granddaughter as she haphazardly stuffed things into her suitcase and errant bags.

"You don't have to go to make videos, my lovey. We can work out what they want from Wade without you putting yourself in danger. You're much safer here."

"Burying ourselves in research isn't getting us anywhere. I have to do something; I can't just keep sitting around. And you'd be so much safer if we weren't here. Besides, that way Dirk can't prove you were hiding me and Wade here."

Edith pursed her lips as Charlotte gathered up her toiletries and dumped them into her cosmetics bag. "It's none of his business if my granddaughter is in her *home* or not—"

"Grandmother," she said gently, putting her bag aside to wrap her arms around Edith. She felt tiny in Charlotte's arms. "He's up to something. It might not be his business, but he's *made* it his business. And he's relentless. It's not worth risking it until we know what it is that he wants from Wade."

"I just got you home," Edith croaked. Charlotte held her tighter.

"We'll be home again before you know it. Three kids for the price of one, huh?" Specter meowed impetuously from the floor. "Oops, I was wrong—four kids, I mean. Didn't mean to forget Spec." The feline looked at her with large solemn eyes before slinking back to the adjacent bedroom.

She let go of her grandmother to smile at her reassuringly. "How about we finish getting me packed and then we can have some coffee together before we go? I promise we won't be away for long—just long enough to make the videos, get them up, and convince them we're elsewhere. Then we'll be right back."

Edith wiped her eyes and sniffled, giving Charlotte a reproachful look. "I expect you to keep your promise, young lady." With a sigh, she murmured something about getting coffee ready and needing a minute before shuffling off. She listened to her grandmother go downstairs before returning to the mess she'd accumulated on the third floor. As she grabbed her bathroom bag and wandered back to the bedroom, she wasn't surprised to see Wade sitting at the vanity, offering a hand for Specter to sniff.

"Need me to pack you anything?" she asked casually.

Wade didn't shift his eyes from the cat as he answered, "You know I have no need for things."

"I'm always gonna ask."

"I appreciate it," Wade said softly. "That you treat me like a person still."

She waved a hand, attention turning to the piles of folded laundry that someone had brought up. "You are a person; your form is just a little different right now."

She squealed when Wade suddenly appeared on the bed in front of her. "Dude, the *fuck*?! Announce yourself before doing that shit."

Wade grinned and picked some imaginary lint off her shirt. Her jaw dropped. "Did you just intentionally scare me?"

"One of the benefits of my form is the ability to turn up unexpectedly, correct? I surmised it would be, to be put simply, *hilarious* to take advantage of that."

Charlotte playfully reached out a hand to smack his chest. Whatever he was feeling, whatever magic that made Wade himself, at that moment he was more solid than ever, and she was shocked when she felt the crisp crinkle of his piqué shirt against her fingers. Unthinking, she rubbed the fabric between her fingers in amazement. Wade's eyes widened in surprise as she pressed her fingers down, feeling the firmness of his chest underneath.

"This is incredible," she murmured. "I know noncorporeal beings can exert force upon things in the living world, but I've never heard of anyone being able to touch a ghost. Not like this. It's almost like you aren't one; I can feel the fibers in your clothes."

Excited by the revelation, Charlotte sunk onto the bed beside him, her fingers stroking the length of his chest, reaching up to his shoulders. She let her fingertips dance along the seams of his jacket like someone examining an extant garment, looking for clues.

"I can't believe I can feel you like this," she wondered aloud, scooting closer to examine the stiff collar. "This is fascinating from a historical and occult perspective, you realize. I wonder what makes you so special."

She froze as she felt the cool of Wade's hands wrapping around her waist. Her heartbeat went into a frenzy as she realized what was happening. In her excitement, she leaned over him, close, her hands roaming over him. She gulped hard, forcing herself to look up at his face. He stared at her with an intensity, a hunger that she didn't quite understand, but that a part of her recognized.

Charlotte reached a trembling hand up to his face. Wade sucked in a deep breath, his eyes trained on hers as she swept her fingertips down the curve of his jaw. He shuddered at her touch, and she nearly leaped out of her skin as she felt the slight prickle of facial hair that wasn't quite visible upon his face. He was far colder than her, but she could feel him as real as any person, any man. She pulled her fingers away, unsure. Wade loosened a hand from her waist, snaking it upward to wrap her hand in his and press her fingers back gently against his jaw. He leaned against her hand, closing his eyes and sighing into her touch.

Heat spread through her, a fire she didn't understand. She raised her other hand to stroke his hair, but as she reached for it, he changed again.

One moment, her hand was caressing him, solid beneath her fingertips. The next, he wasn't quite there again. A slight pressure met her fingers, but it was as if a light had gone out in him and he was no longer as real, back to his spectral form.

"What happened?" she whispered, furrowing her brow. Wade's eyes were squeezed shut, their hands blurring together where he had pressed her hand to his jaw. She swallowed hard, the weight of her arm all her own again. A yearning reared its head, an urge to comfort him, sadness and pity a whirling tornado within her.

"I'm sorry, Wade—" she started, but he cut her off by shaking his head vehemently before fading back out of her plane of existence. Dropping her hand to her lap, Charlotte stared at her fingers. She had been able to touch him—really touch him. Her fingertips tingled at the memory of unseen bristles, the feel of icy skin against her own.

With a sigh, she looked around, softly calling out for Wade. When he didn't answer, she pushed off the bed and returned to packing. She had a job to do and she would focus on that, hoping it would stop her heart from crumbling as it threatened to.

CHAPTER FIFTEEN

W hat did it mean?

Though he knew she waited for him, he could not bear to remain in the room with her after whatever had transpired between them. The odd sensation of falling through his own skin but feeling her fingers upon him, his veins on fire from her gentle touch. He had been so close to closing that gap between them. Wade had never wanted to touch someone the way he did with Charlotte. Though she was certainly odd, there was a sweetness and a spark about her that drew him to her, like a moth to a flame.

She'd wanted to touch him, too. He saw it in her eyes as her fingers danced across his chest, leaving a burning, achy trail behind. There was wonder and intrigue, and something else there—he couldn't quite place it, but it felt like longing.

He hid himself away in her room on the second floor. He knew he shouldn't be in there. It wasn't proper. But it smelt like her, and it made him dizzy yet filled him with energy, like he could run a marathon. He paced around the room, taking in the little mementos and trinkets she had scattered around the space.

Charlotte had looked at Wade as though she wanted *him. Wanted him the same way he wanted her, but more than that. She liked his company, he realized. He couldn't remember the last time someone had genuinely wanted him around—had wanted Wade for Wade, not because of what he could offer them.*

With a groan, he sank onto the edge of her bed. It smelt strongly of her, of whiskey and wildflowers and woods. He inhaled deeply, shivering. His thoughts began to wander, traveling down a darker road.

He thought of the memories that had overwhelmed him in the atrium. That piercing, unending darkness that threatened to consume him, haul him back into that place he was in before. He couldn't stop himself as he sank into the memory.

⇒⇒⇒ ⇐⇐⇐

He stood with his back to the wall, hands behind him as he stared out silently into the room. While Wade was not physically chained to this spot, he might as well have been. Though their eyes might slide over him as though he were little more than a piece of furniture, they would be on him if he so much as put a hair out of place.

Dinner was a while ago, and he had gone through the same motions as every other night for the last seventy-three days since they had murdered his family. Seventy-three days since they had used Atticus to bind his magic to them. Seventy-three days since his friend had been able to look him in the eyes.

He was waiting now for them to be done with their idle chatter before the same nightly torment began. Sarah Rochelle and her parents retired to the parlor as they did every evening for drinks and a few rounds of whist, usually joined by Atticus. But tonight was different. They were entertaining, and the Emberleys had partaken more than usual as they laughed merrily with their friends. As if they weren't all gruesome, disgusting, loathsome monsters. Wade caught Atticus's eye, but the demon looked away, something like shame etched across his face.

There was something brewing in the air as he watched them. A languid arrogance of sorts. Their conversation devolved into laughter and excited drunken chitchat about their plans to become the ruling class of both the paranormal and ordinary. Wade stiffened slightly as he watched them all, the hatred that had been slowly building within him the last few months rising to the surface. How dare they get to be so casual, so comfortable—so *alive*? These were the truly privileged and entitled elite, able to not only kill and get away with it, but to have no *shame*.

Though he was a man of honor and integrity, he now resented having saved Sarah Rochelle from falling through the ice all those years ago.

As though she could hear his thoughts, Sarah Rochelle's carefully coiffed dark amber hair bounced as she turned to look at him. She blinked a few times before smiling at him, a wide smirk that had him repressing a shudder. That smirk was a promise to him, a reminder that he was merely a puppet now—not only to her, but to all of them.

His anger grew as her eyes remained trained on him. The salacious things he knew she was thinking roiled his stomach. *The audacity of this girl*. Her gloveless hand stroked the length of her skirts discreetly, where she knew he could see it, as if to say *'not long until you'll be seeing what's under this'*. He suppressed another shudder before glancing away, focusing his attention on a distant cornice. Wade willed himself to drift away in his mind, to be anywhere but there. To be safe.

"And what are you thinkin', handsome?"

Wade jolted at Sarah Rochelle's soft murmur as her hands wrapped around his arm, her sapphire and diamond engagement ring sparkling in the low light. His mother's ring. The one that she had refused to give back and forcefully claimed for herself, like so many other things.

"Nothing," Wade replied curtly. He turned his gaze back toward the cornice he had been focused on. His skin crawled as she grasped his chin in her hand and yanked it back down, forcing his eyes on her.

"That's never true with you. I'm your fiancée, and it's high time you started actin' like it." There was a slight lilt to her voice, one that was most noticeable when she was drunk. And she sure loved to drink.

As Wade stared at her, it was not lost on him that she was beautiful. He had been happy with her once, content to be by her side. The darkness and hunger that drove her and her family, however . . . it was vile. As soon as their true colors had been shown, he knew he could not pretend for a moment longer to have any modicum of pleasant feelings toward her, and he had made that known to her.

His thoughts snapped back to her, to the present.

A dark thought sang to him, whispering tauntingly. He could never be dark the way she was, or how the Order of the New Dawn was. But the thought of making her suffer as she had done to him . . . the idea was tantalizing. He stared at her, wondering if he could truly be so heinous. He imagined his silk gloves wrapping around her neck, of her creamy skin turning blue—

It brought him relief.

His heartbeat soared, his skin thrumming with tangible excitement as he stared at her, at the self-satisfied smile on her face as she waltzed her fingertips up his chest, giggling to herself. They might have bound his magic and beaten his soul down, but they potentially couldn't stop him from ending it. Or exacting some vengeance before he let himself be taken to Hell.

If they could take everything from him, he could take something from them.

"You're right."

Wade swallowed hard as Sarah Rochelle's neck tilted back so fast it audibly cracked, her eyes narrowed in suspicion. She stepped back half a step, gown rustling.

"Oh?" Her voice came out higher than usual. Wade fought the urge to squeeze his eyes shut as he focused on her. A half-baked plan to get her alone—that was all he had. He just had to get her alone, and he could work out a plan from there.

"You're all I have in this world." It wasn't a lie; her family and cult had ensured he had nothing else, had no one that cared enough to even know if he was dead or alive.

"Not the most romantic thing I've heard from you," she murmured bitterly. Wade bit back a retort. He *had* been rather romantic to her when he thought she was good, when he was more than a *possession* or a trinket to her. When he believed that love could happen for him.

"I'm trying my best right now," he whispered. Not a lie, even if his best was deceit.

Sarah Rochelle sighed and stepped close to him again. The others were drunker now, not paying attention. Even Atticus, who kept his magic bound, was paying no attention, too caught up in the debauchery and merrymaking that now echoed through the halls. It would be, should be, easy to entice her away from them.

"I know it can't be easy, my love, but you brought this upon yourself." Wade flinched at the condescending tone, resisting the urge to pull back as she reached a hand up to pat his cheek, harder than called for. "There was a plan, and you and your family didn't want to honor your end of the bargain. Life is about deals, my love, and once a deal is made, it cannot be broken."

"I suppose you're right." He bowed his head, hoping to appear contrite as rage seethed within him. "All I can hope now is to atone for the sins of my actions." *By making them all pay.*

"I have no clue what's come over you tonight, but I must confess I'm delight-ed." Sarah Rochelle swayed slightly, the copious champagne she'd indulged in all evening overwhelming her slight frame. "It's about time you started to get over it."

Don't react, don't react—

Wade smiled tightly, unable to trust himself to say anything as she simpered and adjusted his dinner jacket, prattling to herself about absolute nonsense. About their wedding, what the Order expected of them, about their plans. He only half paid attention, his mind wandering as he started to flesh out his plan. First things first, he had to get her away from the rest of them. Then what? They were on the lower floor of the house. Perhaps he could lure her to an upper level and throw them both off a balcony? *Risky and most assuredly messy. It should do the trick, though.*

He debated getting her to the kitchens and getting her to ingest something lethal instead, but a doctor or someone practiced in the Arts might be able to circumvent their deaths. Even his special skills in potions wouldn't be enough. Wade's head throbbed as half-concocted plans rattled through his brain.

". . . Are you comin'?"

Wade was snapped out of his reverie by Sarah Rochelle tugging on his arm, a coy smile plastered across her face. Panicked, Wade complied, allowing her to lead him away from the gathered party. He wasn't sure, but he could have sworn Atticus glanced at him as he was pulled out into the hallway.

"Come with me," Sarah Rochelle giggled, the beads of her gown clinking together as she wrapped her arms through his, pushed close to him as she dragged him along. Wade's panic rose. He hadn't formulated a real plan, he still needed time to think—

They stumbled through the hallway, through the doors leading to the dining room, and soon he found himself swept outside onto the terrace, the glow of the candles and lamps spilling out onto the stone beneath them. Sarah Rochelle stumbled, a breathy laugh slipping from between her lips as she gripped his forearms to steady herself.

"Isn't it beautiful out tonight, my love?"

The way she spoke to him, her eyes glistening in the low light, was as if she had created the night and its glory herself. The arrogant sweep of her arm as she presented the night sky to him, glittering like celestial diamonds above. A gift she was giving him, the mere privilege of seeing it.

She let go of him to spin in a slow circle. She didn't wear her shawl or gloves out, and the flesh of her upper arms and collarbone were exposed to the night. Goosebumps broke out against her skin. Under the moonlight, she was radiant, exquisite.

The night air had a pleasant bite to it, the crisp promise of the colder season creeping its way toward them. Sarah Rochelle's cheeks flushed pink against her peaches-and-cream skin, her large blue eyes doe-like, faking an innocence that he knew did not exist. Everything about her demeanor—how she dressed, how she presented herself to the world—it was all an act, a way to lure in the truly innocent before utterly draining them.

He swallowed back bile and hateful words. He was a gentleman, and even if he knew he was about to go against all his principles, he could still act the part. He smiled at her, his mask so perfect, she didn't see through the cracks to the pain beneath. She beamed at him, her eyes bright from too many drinks.

"Dance with me, Wade."

It was a command, and he was compelled. He stepped forward, took her in his arms, and they swept across the terrace, away from the streaks of light from the house toward the gardens, where the darkness threatened to engulf them, the waning moon and starlight guiding them.

This was the last time he would hold someone close to him like this, he vowed as they span together, silence enveloping them save for the whispers of the wind and the distant echoes of the others. The couple inhabited their own little world as they locked eyes and whirled through the scattered shadows.

They began to slow, each step somehow both lighter and heavier as they slipped into a dark alcove. Wade was unsure of who had led who there, but it didn't matter, for the dark recess they found themselves in was hidden away from the large open doors they had exited. It was the perfect cover for two lovers who might find themselves on a nighttime stroll, hidden between statues and hedges on the terrace.

This was his chance. He didn't know how he would do it, but this was the only time he would be able to get away—to end it. His pulse quickened as a tipsy, breathy Sarah Rochelle tugged him over to the secluded bench that sat against the wall of the house. Wade obliged, his thoughts scrambling as Sarah Rochelle's hands began to roam all over him.

"Kiss me," she rasped in his ear, drawing strong, steady strokes up his neck with her tongue. "Ravish me the way I know you wanted to, the way I know you used to imagine."

It was as though he was no longer in control of his actions, of his body. He could feel every movement he made, but it wasn't exactly him making those choices. Yes, Wade wrapped his arms around her. Yes, it was he who pressed his lips against the naked swathes of flesh, and it was he who pulled at the fabric of her dress, he whose hands found their way up her back as he pulled her close.

But it also wasn't. This was no Wade he ever wanted to know.

The world melted away and simultaneously rushed about him all at once as he found his hands tangled in her hair, yanking and pulling out the pins and jewelry that swept it up into a formidable hairdo. It was without thought that his hand grasped the long silver-coated metal of her hairpin. The weight of it in his palm turned his senses back on, the sharp prick of its pointed ends pricking through his glove, piercing the skin of his forefinger.

It might not be enough, but it's worth a try.

He pulled them to their feet, readying his arm, the other holding her tight as his mouth claimed hers, his anger feeding her hunger. He had to be sure. There would only be one try, one attempt.

Wade knew Atticus would be busy and tired. He hoped it would be enough to loose enough of his magic to help him in his task. Flipping the pin in his hand so he could hold the ornate top in his fist, he pulled his arm back.

Time seemed to slow as he pushed Sarah Rochelle away from him, back against the wall. Annoyance flickered over her face, then confusion, then finally fear as he drove the hairpin down into her chest with all the force he could muster. He held his hand in place as the blood burst from her comically, an effect suited for a low-budget play. She spluttered and gasped, a trickle of blood emerging from the corner of her rose-colored lips before she slumped back, her grasp on him loosened.

He stood there for a minute, staring dumbly at her limp body. The adrenaline that had driven him was beginning to wane. With one deft yank, he ripped the hairpin from the flesh of her bosom. She slipped down against the wall, falling to the ground.

"I'm sorry," he whispered, though not to Sarah Rochelle, who looked more than ever like a doll as she lay crumpled against the stonework wall, eyes glassy as blood continued to ooze over her shimmering silk and chiffon lilac gown. He looked up at the night sky one last time before running the bloodied steel hairpin as hard as he could across his throat.

He flinched, pulled out of the accursed memory. His entire being was on fire, it burned—

Wade raised himself onto shaky feet from where he had collapsed onto the floor. As his hand grasped the arm of the chair beside him, he gasped when it tilted toward him as it bore the brunt of his weight.

What was going on?

CHAPTER SIXTEEN

"**M**y name is Wade van Baird, and I have been dead for quite some time. My life before is like a distant dream now, like looking at a faded photograph. I am a ghost in many ways."

Wade stared out the RV window pensively, a haunted look in his eyes. He seemed to be remembering something. At least, that's what they wanted the camera to believe. The light dappled and streaked across the tabletop, almost glittering as it hit Wade. The gentle autumn afternoon light was perfect, Wade's opacity waning enough for the camera to see the back of the booth behind him. One could convince themselves it was all smoke and mirrors except for the way he held himself, the countenance of a gentleman from a bygone era, the wistfulness in his eyes—these were little things that would be inexplicable to even the most severe of skeptics. For who could be that good an actor?

"I miss the air on my face, or being able to enjoy the feel of the sun on my skin. Truthfully, I am not certain I quite remember what they feel like. And although my heart does not beat in this form, it still feels. I am a contradiction of existence."

He paused again. "I do not understand why I am still here. I assume it has something to do with how I died." He lifted his chin, angling his jaw so that the vicious scar that marred his throat was visible. Even through the lens of a camera, it was jarring and vivid. "While it eludes me still, I get the sense that it was a death of horror and importance. And not just to myself—it would seem that there is a particular group of individuals whom are most interested in keeping my company, with less than savory methods.

"Hopefully, by talking to this electronic device, I will be able to recollect what it is about me that they are so persistent in gaining contact for. And as I am assured they will be indeed seeking this communication from me, I would like to extend my sincerest apologies, but I fear that I must decline their attempts to 'hang out,' as it were. Did I say that correctly, Charlotte? 'Hang out'?"

Wade's eyes lit up as he gazed past the camera. "My companion assures me that is, indeed, the correct usage. Such a peculiar time to be witnessing." Wade coughed, having caught Charlotte's eye. "I must cut my rambling short. To conclude this rather one-sided conversation, I would like to let the concerned party know that we intend to be a regular hawkshaw and expose whatever nefarious goings-on are transpiring. And with that, I bid you all a good day."

⟫⟩ ⟨⟨

Charlotte plugged her camera into her laptop and got to work. For the last two weeks that they had been on the road together, she had spent countless hours poring over magical volumes and searching the internet, wondering what could have made Wade the way he was. She would read into the early hours of the morning, when she would pass out on her bed, later rousing with the sun to move the RV somewhere new. They never stayed a whole day in one place, and they were careful to be random about where they went. Just in case.

Stifling a yawn, she began uploading the latest video they had made of Wade. They were all short clips, no more than fifteen minutes, all raw, all unedited. One a day, uploaded at the same time right before she delved back into work and sleep. By the time it actually uploaded on her cruddy tethered internet, they were usually back on the road.

Charlotte cracked her neck and leaned back in the booth of her RV kitchenette. The sun would soon set. Specter was curled up asleep in the bed in the back, and Wade had floated off to explore sometime earlier. He wouldn't be back until she'd fallen asleep, she was sure.

They were parked in a national park somewhere in Connecticut. The instant she was done filming him, he had taken off somewhere. Wade, while cooperative for videos and research, chose to spend a lot of time exploring solo. He said it was to help immerse himself in the living and thus would lead him to recollection.

A big part of Charlotte suspected he was just avoiding her. They still hadn't talked about what had happened in that third-floor bedroom. She was unwilling to broach it, and Wade seemed to wish to leave it in the past. Ironic, given how desperately they were searching into *his* past.

"He's just a stupid ghost, isn't he?" Charlotte crooned to Specter, who now yawned as he awoke. The cat blinked slowly at her, his wide yellow eyes seeming to mock her. She huffed and returned to her screen. Maybe she should flick Hazel a text—they hadn't heard from her in a few days. It was isolating to be out there, every noise making her jump. She was in a constant state of worry that Dirk and company were about to nab her or Wade. And it didn't help that he was constantly avoiding her now.

She returned her attention to her screen. It didn't matter; she still had work to do, and a mystery to solve. Pulling up a new tab in her browser, her notebook beside her filled with pages littered with crossed-out theories, she began another deep dive.

Charlotte would figure out what he was and why he was so important to the Society— and what they intended to do with him.

⤖ ⤙

It was the sixth visit since they had left Charlotte's home. She was asleep again, and once again he watched over her. He should leave her be, but he feared for her. What if they found them during the night? What if he were not there to rouse her? It mattered not now if they found him, he had decided, but they would not *be allowed to get near her. He swore it.*

He knew Atticus was there again. He felt the shift in the room. The cat did not stir at his presence; he'd gotten used to the demon. Not once had Charlotte roused during his visitations.

Atticus sighed, a somber expression on his face. He didn't immediately address Wade, nor Wade, he. They spent most of his visits in silence—an odd companionship, unable to breach the divide between them. Wade did not trust, nor care to trust him. Yet, he knew they had an unbreakable bond, a contract that inexplicably sealed his existence and magic to the demon.

Wade sat at the foot of the bed, his back to the wall, one eye on Charlotte, one on Atticus. The demon tutted to himself, sweeping over to the bed to pull a blanket over Charlotte, who was shivering in the chill evening. Wade was surprised but didn't show it. Atticus then spotted the tome she'd been rifling through as she fell asleep. Gingerly, he leaned over her, plucking it from beneath her splayed-out forearm with deft ease.

"And what is she reading about tonight, my dear friend?" Atticus murmured, flipping the heavy book in one hand to survey the cover, his free hand stretching down to stroke Specter. Wade glared as the traitorous cat purred at his touch. "Ryland's Comprehensive Guide to Occult Creatures? *I admit, going back to basics isn't the worst idea she's had, but wouldn't it be best if her companion merely told her the truth, instead of wasting her efforts on this wild goose hunt?"*

Wade glowered at Atticus, then cast an anxious eye over Charlotte. She stirred slightly; she hadn't had a single one of her sleeping aids this trip, nor had she had any liquor to quell her demons. He didn't want Atticus disturbing her meager slumber.

"If I knew what you meant, demon, then I would do as you say. Perhaps you could learn to be less cryptic in your utterings."

"My dearest Wade." Atticus slipped to the floor, a very human-like gesture. He planted his feet against the opposite wall, his back against the entryway to the tiny bedroom. "I am your oldest friend, and it brings me no joy to see you this way. Oh, don't give me that face! I don't relish this position. Do you think I have any choice, either? They bind me much the same way they do you."

"Are you not a demon, an otherworldly being with immense power? Surely you can find some sort of loophole and free yourself." Wade's whispered retort had him glancing once more at Charlotte. His heart, if it could, seemed to skip a beat as he caught sight of her pale face amongst the pillows.

Atticus followed his gaze. "Do you not think, in the last century, that I have tried whatever I am capable of? As their numbers grow, so do their wits, it seems. They were meticulous planners, and remain so. The only hope for someone seeking to destroy them would be from within, someone less on a leash than I."

Wade was aghast. "You're not suggesting I return to them."

"I'm not suggesting anything." The demon boy shrugged a shoulder. His blond hair was loose, falling to his shoulders in a neat curtain. "I am merely here, talking to my friend. A friend, I remind you, I have an equally strong contract with, not just with the Order."

"Fat good that has done me," Wade muttered.

"Not exactly my fault there, Wade. You've your own share of the blame for your present predicament."

Wade sighed, glancing at Charlotte once more. Her angelic sleeping form. For all her bravado, for the angry face she showed the world, she was an open book when she slept. He wasn't ignorant to how hard she was working to help him, to find the truth of it all.

A truth that he was hiding from her.

"Come outside for a bit," Atticus suggested, pushing to his feet. He nodded to the door, slipping out. Wade drifted after him, his soul in turmoil. Atticus had thrown himself on the grass, looking up at the night sky as though he hadn't a care in the world. Wade picked a spot beside him, careful to brush his coat tails back as he sat.

"Why don't you tell her, Wade? I know when you are keeping your cards to your chest. We were inseparable for, what, seventeen years? That's a rather long time for you mortals. You could save her so much stress if you just told her what happened."

Wade said nothing. He only stared at the stars above. Atticus sighed.

"Her parents are dead because of you."

Wade whipped his head toward Atticus. The demon seemed nonchalant, despite what he had just said.

"I couldn't possibly be the reason. I don't even remember the last hundred years!" Wade snapped, hysteria creeping into his voice, into his very soul. Atticus sighed again.

"They did it to get you to come out of your phylactery. We haven't been able to cajole you out, not once. There isn't enough magic in the world, it would seem, to control such a fierce heart. So, they tried feeding your container and its magic, hoping it would be enough for them to be in control."

Wade frowned. "What on earth do you mean?"

"I guess you don't remember," Atticus said softly, *"what happened the night you tried to end it."*

"I remember it," Wade whispered. He unconsciously reached a hand for the scar across his throat. *"I remember . . . I killed Sarah Rochelle. Then myself." It was why his soul was so damned. As if making a demonic contract had not been enough to ensure his eternal suffering.*

"You know they have an ironclad contract with me. I can't get into the specifics; we'll call it a confidentiality clause. I can never reveal the terms of a bargain. But you know they've got me bound up, Wade. I never wanted this to happen to you, for them to seal your power. I never realized making a contract with you would . . . well, I never thought they would work out the terms of our bargain. Of your immense power. I knew . . . I knew how power-hungry they were. And I didn't protect you from that. I think I can now, though."

"How do you propose you do that," Wade snapped, *"considering I am dead and they appear to be chasing me until whatever end?"*

"You could stop running. Perhaps they'd stop trying to feed the phylactery if they thought they had control. If they thought that you were submissive to them. Maybe the massacres would end. Maybe your dear Charlotte would be safe from them if they could assume their status quo."

Wade started. *"She's in danger because of me? I thought they were merely after me . . ."*

"Who's to say, really?"

"You are, you incorrigible demon!" Anger quaked through him. *"I shall just leave, then. If I am no longer with her, then she will no longer be a target— "*

"Do you really think running away is going to stop her being a person of interest to them? If you disappeared again, and she was the last person that knew where you were, that would just make her all the more important to them, don't you think?"

"What am I to do, then?" Wade whispered in despair. It was as though the world was crumbling around him. He had lost so much—he could not lose her too. Not his sweet Charlotte.

"You could come with me. If you come with us, I can keep you safe. And they'll stop chasing you, stop chasing her. My hands are tied while you're actively running away from them. But, if you're close, if you're with me . . . I should be able to keep you from hurting."

"But then I'd have to leave Charlotte."

Atticus said nothing.

"I do not believe I am strong enough to leave her, Atticus." He spoke openly with the demon, slipping back into their old, comfortable friendship despite himself. *"There is something about her that pulls me to her. She is a light in the darkness. She beckons me to her. As though I am strung to her, and she pulls the lead so that I remain near to her. I cannot explain it. It is . . . instinctual, to be by her."*

Atticus remained silent, furrowing his brow. He glanced at Wade, his mouth twisted into a small sad frown.

"Why do you look at me so?"

"Because, my dear friend, you are in love." Atticus let out a huff.

Wade stared at him, wide-eyed. His ears rang as he felt oddly full and hollow all at once. In love? With Charlotte? *No, she was merely a kind rescuer of sorts. For how could someone as wretched as him be worthy of being in love with someone like her? For all her quirks and faults, she was selfless, courageous, caring . . . things that he had not been in the end.*

Atticus got to his feet. "Perhaps it is best not to overthink it. Remember, you can call upon me when you are ready. I fear time is running out for it to be your choice. And I cannot vouch for how safe the path ahead will or won't be. Adieu, dear friend. I hope that next time I call upon you, you will be ready."

Wade sat alone as Atticus vanished into the ether, a heavy burden on his heart. After a time, Wade found himself back in the RV. Charlotte had recently taken to sleeping with the lamp on, which was odd, but it illuminated her. She was curled up not unlike a small child; the blanket Atticus had covered her with was now bundled over her so only her head above her chin was visible. He slid against the wall once more, taking care to sit gently on the bed edge. Even if it wouldn't shift the mattress or disturb her, he didn't want to cause her any discomfort. A pang shot through his heart when she shivered at his presence. He caused her discomfort merely by being near her—he knew as much, and yet, it made his heart ache.

"What am I meant to do?" he whispered. Specter cracked an eye. The cat roused, yawning and stretching, before loping over the bed to nestle beside him. At least the feline liked him enough.

"Perhaps, sir, you would listen to my woes for a while," Wade whispered to the cat. Spec blinked at him, bowing his head as if in understanding. Straightening his back, Wade began to recant his conversation with Atticus, his memories, and the information he had received that evening, all while keeping an eye on Charlotte.

As he spoke to the cat, he came to a decision. No choice he made, whether now or in the past, good or bad, would impact her. She deserved a life free of his mistakes. His heart swelled to gaze upon her, and he knew Atticus was right. He was in love with her, and it was nothing as he had experienced before. Over a hundred years past his death, and he finally knew what it was to love someone beyond the familial, to do whatever it took to keep them safe. And so he would.

Charlotte woke the next morning after the strangest dream. She'd fallen asleep at some point before Wade had returned—that wasn't new—and found herself bundled up in a blanket some strange boy had draped across her as Wade watched in the middle of the night. At least, she had dreamed the boy draped it over her.

As her coffee brewed, she scampered into the shower, mulling over the odd dream. Had it been some sort of sleep paralysis, perhaps? There were connections between the sleep and the Veil; perhaps her mind had wandered into some territory it shouldn't have. As she dressed, she wondered if the tomes she had been combing through were influencing her dreams—creatures of the occult blending together as she tried to understand who and what Wade really was.

At the small booth that served as her dining room, she stared out the window with her coffee in hand, contemplative. The leaves were turning to shades of orange and red, scattering from the trees. It seemed like a lifetime ago that she had met Wade, since she'd gotten caught up in the mystery of who he was and whatever was going on within the Society.

Maybe her jumbled dreams were a result of her body detoxing. She hadn't confessed it to Wade, but she had been finding it difficult to sleep, especially at first. Without the aid of her nightcap, the nightmares had poured in. Sometimes it was her debut; sometimes her parents just faded into darkness, leaving her. Then the nightmares shifted, blurring together into ones like the previous night. Of Wade watching over her as she slept, despite him never seeming to return to the RV.

It occurred to her that maybe, just maybe, she was lonely without him. That she enjoyed his presence and his peculiarities. She glanced at her watch—October twenty-first. It was almost Halloween already.

"Are you ready for me to speak to your camera, Charlotte?"

She jolted as Wade interrupted her thoughts. She hadn't seen him that day yet, as usual. He materialized across from her. *Has he been lurking there the entire time?* Her cheeks heated at the idea.

"For someone so fixated on manners, you've sure gotten lazy at letting your presence, or lack thereof, be known," she scolded him, slumping back against the booth.

Wade furrowed his brow. "I apologize. You're right; I have been showing you unacceptable behavior. I hope you'll forgive me."

Charlotte stared hard at him. There was a soft earnestness across his face. Wade was many things, but a liar, he was not.

"I forgive you," she relented, swigging from her coffee. "I guess."

Wade visibly relaxed. "I know I have been terrible of late, and I will endeavor to make it up to you, I swear it. I will not allow myself to be absent today."

Wade's disposition reminded her again of the odd dream she had. Of him and the blond boy talking. She recalled only pieces of it, hazy snippets of him leaving and eventually returning to the end of her bed. She remembered a part, briefly, where he talked to Specter, how he suggested to the cat that perhaps he was to blame for the death of her parents.

She must have been mixing in her memories with the death of his family, after scouring newspaper articles for weeks and all the research she had been doing. But it made her wonder, would it help him to know her past? Would it help her to finally let it out?

She shuffled over in the booth so she was beside the window, patting the seat next to her, gesturing for Wade to come sit beside her. He obliged immediately, taking care to get up and go around the table rather than through. As he sat next to her, his body angled toward her so that his knee brushed against her and sent a chill down her spine. Charlotte took a deep breath.

"I want to talk to you about something. Something I haven't really spoken about before. But I think it... I hope it might help you, with your own memories.

Or maybe it'll help you piece something together. I'm not sure." She clasped her trembling hands together. "I want to talk to you about the night my parents died."

CHAPTER SEVENTEEN

"**I** don't like this," Charlotte grumbled, tugging at the Chantilly lace neckline. She preferred her cardigans and shawls, to be able to wrap herself up into a cocoon and hide from the world. Her mother had insisted, though. Every girl in the Society had a debutante ball, and no one in generations of the Blythe family had missed one. The last Blythe woman to miss her debut had only missed it because she broke her collarbone and left leg chasing down an errant vampire on a bloodlust rage sometime before the family even had an American branch. She'd gotten the leech but had fallen off a rooftop, taking it down with her. The only thing that had stopped the damage from being worse had been the vampire breaking her fall. Even then, she had fought to make it to her debut.

A time-honored tradition, indeed.

"You look gorgeous," her mother tittered, smoothing a lock of her daughter's hair.

Stephenie Blythe looked like an older version of her daughter. They both had the same long wavy hair, chestnut eyes, and Roman nose, each of them slim and tall in a way that was regal and intimidating to most. They differed in the most subtle ways. Charlotte's dark brows were usually furrowed, dark bags under her eyes from reading late into the night giving her a sallow complexion, while her mother was more porcelain. While Stephenie's lips were usually drawn into a smile, Charlotte preferred her resting bitch face—much to her mother's dismay. It was odd to see their resemblance, as it made their differences all the more pronounced. The only thing she had that was firmly her father's and not her mother's was his attitude. Perhaps that was what made her features so different from the mother she mimicked so.

"Lottie looks like you did the night of your debut," her father said, nodding approvingly. "Like an angel."

Though most debutantes had their own fancy new gown, she wore the same dress her mother had worn at *her* own debutante ball. Her mother's argument had been that this was probably the only time she would see her daughter in a white gown, as Charlotte had been adamant from a young age that she would never marry. She wanted to pass something of her own onto her daughter. There had been a few disagreements about the entire wedding thing, but, as Edith pointed out, no one said the girl had to *marry* to pass on the family legacy. She needed only a daughter of her own that could pass on the bloodline that left them so attuned to the occult. So, her mother had given up on visions swathed in tulle and lace, of her daughter being walked down the aisle by her father, and had focused instead on this night.

"It's only a few hours, Lottie," her father whispered as Stephenie's attention returned to her own reflection. Tall, blond, and broad, Jackson Blythe was like the sun to Stephenie's moon. He was a stoic man, choosing to stay to the sidelines, much like his daughter. He leaned forward and kissed his only daughter on the cheek, his mustache bristling against her smooth skin.

"You're right," she grumbled. She tugged on the lace neckline again. "If I die in those hours, though, don't be surprised, Daddy."

Jackson tilted his head back and laughed. "That's my girl, ever macabre. It won't be so dire as that, I can promise you."

⟫⟩ ⟨⟨

It was, in fact, far direr than her father could have ever imagined.

The first hour or two weren't too terrible, as her father had promised. She snacked on some cakes, had a few flutes of nonalcoholic cider and some champagne, and danced. It was actually a lot of dancing, a whole entourage of parents from other families introducing her to their sons. She'd be swept away onto the ballroom floor with one only to be spun into another. While her poor feet burned and ached, she saw said parents in vibrant conversation with her own parents.

She realized after several dances with their sons that they weren't just chatting. They were negotiating with her parents to secure *her*. She overheard one loathsome man proudly boasting about his son's accolades and skills as she whirled past, asserting how he would be an incredible asset to the bloodline.

It was around then that she decided it wouldn't be the worst idea to dip out, at least for a while. So, with a smile and a polite wave of the hand to the chap whose name she'd already forgotten, she excused herself to go to the powder room. She spied her actual date across the room, Bradley Ashgarde, and fluttered her fingers at him. He caught her eye and grimaced, caught in a swathe of eligible young women. It was all an act; she was pretty sure she'd end with up Bradley.

Only a few more hours until freedom. Until then, she would sneak a few minutes to herself.

Over the years, she had mastered the art of being invisible in a room full of people. She hadn't needed to be seen with how spectacular her mother and grandmother were, especially with their gifts. Thus, she'd practiced a different set of skills whenever there was a large group of people around. As soon as the attention was locked on her family, Lottie would vanish. She would start by dissolving into a crowd, and soon it progressed to seeing if anyone would notice if she slid out of a room entirely.

As it turned out, they didn't.

She snatched a champagne flute from a passing server and slipped around the edge of the room, keeping a careful smile plastered to her face. The more you wanted to blend in, she had discovered, the more you had to look like you wanted to be seen. And appearing happy at a busy party was the easiest way to do to so.

One moment she was smiling, having worked her way to a back wall. The next, she had ducked under the rather sizable round table housing desserts. Its silk tablecloth, she was relieved to find, skirted against the floor on all sides. She could comfortably hide here for a while. She had thought about going to find a quiet room, or even hiding in the powder room as she had told her dance partner, but the risk of her mother coming along to find her was too high. And she felt enough like a prize sow being traded; she didn't need to feel she was being hunted too.

Lottie loosed a few of the bobby pins that dug into her scalp and discarded them on the floor beside her. She scowled and knocked them away before bringing her champagne flute to her lips. It was either her third or fourth of the night—far more than her parents would prohibit, even on special occasions—but she tilted it and swigged as though it were the first. It was the only way she was coping with the evening, her overly eager dance partners bringing them to her between songs.

Leaning back on her elbows, she listened to the revelry around her. Her mother would have noticed her missing by now and would likely have employed her father and grandmother to help find her. She snickered to herself, quite pleased that she had managed to find a hiding place in plain sight. She could get at least a solid twenty minutes of peace under the table, she decided. Then she would go back onto the battlefield.

⟶⟶⟶ ⟵⟵⟵

Twenty minutes of peace turned out to be approximately six and a half minutes before her world began collapsing, and another four before it shattered entirely.

She had been under her table, contemplating reappearing briefly to grab another drink and steer her mother away from a heart attack when it started. The noise of the party dropped first to a near whisper as she reclined under the table, her head tilted curiously. Even the music lowered. Then the shuffling of feet before the room abruptly plunged into darkness. And at last, the screaming.

The only reason Lottie didn't scream herself was because she was simply unable. Her mouth hung open, ready to let out a wail, but she remained paralyzed in the darkness, unable to see even the end of her nose. Her thoughts were jumbled, flashes of images. Of her mother, her father, her grandmother, and her date, Bradley. They were out there, with the screaming folks.

Her mind raced to the worst places as she regained the ability to move. Had it been seconds or minutes? She couldn't see the champagne flute beside her and accidentally crushed it as she shuffled forward, trying to get to the edge of the table. They were in a room full of some of the world's strongest spellcasters—whatever was happening, surely, someone would right things.

Surely, nothing *truly* bad could happen.

Seconds passed and the screaming didn't stop. Flattening herself against the floor, Charlotte commando crawled until she could feel the hem of the tablecloth. With shaking fingers, she raised the hem a whisper, cheek pressed to the floor as she tried to see into the ballroom beyond.

At first, she saw nothing. Then a dull green light filled the space. The exit sign, she thought, but it was moving, and there were multiple splashes of light and color. Then she saw the first body.

She inhaled sharply, a strange fuzzy sensation filling her as though she were about to pop. Her chest burned, sending her into a splutter of coughs. The air was filled with the scent of sulfur, a dark smokiness—of dark magic.

Something evil had invaded, and there was only a matter of time before it killed them all—or worse.

Charlotte dropped the hem of the tablecloth and clapped her hands over her ears, her eyes squeezed shut. She knew she should be brave, that she should go out there and at least be with her parents as the end descended upon them all, but she was too afraid. She would die alone, just as she had always feared.

⇒⇒⇒ ⇐⇐⇐

They found her curled up against her mother, screaming as she sobbed. The world was too harsh, too bright, too loud as they tried to pry her from Stephenie's corpse. She was there and she was not there, her body and flesh still present but her mind somewhere else entirely.

She had vague recollections of the screaming stopping, of silence filling the space. The sulfur left a tinge to the air, but it, too, mostly vanished. Her elbows stung as she crawled out from beneath the table, pulling herself onto trembling legs as she began hunting for her parents. Blood splatter left the floor both sticky and slippery as she dragged her shaking body across it, her eyes aching as they swept across the carnage, her ears ringing.

She stumbled through the congealing blood until she found her mother's broken body and crawled beside it. She was sure she was dead herself, but she wanted to be near her mom when she passed on to the next phase.

She wanted to go together.

"Oh, Charlotte," Wade breathed when she finished. She had brought her legs up to her chest to wrap her arms around them. She hadn't talked about that night since it happened; her grandmother had dealt with official inquiries by the Society, leaving her to grieve, broken. They had tried once to make her use her magic, to prove it didn't have her distinct mark. She had refused, but it wasn't because she didn't want to prove them wrong. No, the truth was that she had been unable to reach that energy deep inside her. It was as if it had erected a wall and barred her out the moment her parents were gone.

She would one day be the last of the Blythe line, and she could no longer use magic. She would be worthless to everyone if they knew. So she hid it, pretending it was a choice. Charlotte was already so scared of being alone. They didn't need to know she had nothing left to offer.

"It's fine." She waved a hand nonchalantly. "It was a long time ago now."

"Time passing does not mean something does not ache any longer." There was a fierce edge to Wade's voice, a passionate rawness. Charlotte, whose chin rested on her knees, turned her head to peek at him. "Something can happen, let's say, oh, a hundred years ago but still leave our hearts bleeding."

He stared at her pointedly as he spoke, the sorrow building up inside her again. He was right—and at least she was alive to show for it.

"I wonder why you're here and they're not," she said dully, unthinking. A strange expression crossed Wade's face, not quite hurt, but something close to it. Then it clicked what she had said, what it had sounded like. How callous she had been.

"I'm glad you're here. I just—they had a violent end, too. So why didn't they stay like this too?" she gestured at him weakly, her inner voice screaming for her to shut up. Any second now he was going to snap and lose it, and she wouldn't blame him.

"I would imagine it is because they were happy when the end came. Not about *how* the end came," he corrected, "but that they had been happy with their lives. And how could they not? They had you for a daughter, Charlotte, and I am sure having someone so precious made their lives unimaginably rich."

A sob slipped from between her lips as she buried her face between her knees. It wasn't an unhappy cry; it wasn't even necessarily because of what Wade just said. It was the way he said it. He was confident that these people, people whom he had never met, would have cherished having someone as messy and broken as her for a daughter. That they loved her, despite her shortcomings. The conviction in his voice ripped open a poorly sutured break in her heart. Though it hurt, she knew it would be better to let this festering wound purge the darkness that had tried to seal it shut.

"Thank you," she mumbled against her knees. "Thank you for saying all of that, Wade. I'm glad I haven't been here alone, and I've had you with me. I'm glad you're my friend."

She choked on the last word. When was the last time she had truly considered someone a friend, let alone said it aloud to them? It had been so long, she wasn't even sure of how to be a friend anymore.

Her oozing broken heart hoped that he thought of her as a friend, too.

A shiver ran down her spine as a shroud of cold wrapped around her. She poked her head up a smidgen to find Wade beside her, arms wrapped around her. Embracing her, despite his spectral arms, their slight shimmer almost passing through her shoulders.

They sat there in silence for a long while, and Charlotte desperately wished she could fall into his open arms for a hug, to feel his warmth wrapped around her like a blanket.

To be kept safe once more.

CHAPTER EIGHTEEN

Charlotte felt as though a great weight had been lifted from her, the burden of that night now shared between her and another soul. Between her and Wade. Her soul felt somehow lighter, her heart like a piece of paper that had been lovingly smoothed back out after being crumpled and tossed to the bottom of a backpack. Wrinkled and messy, but still perfectly functional.

"Sorry for snotting on you," she chuckled through a hiccup. She wiped the back of her hand over her eyes before reaching her hands up to tuck her hair behind her ears. "I mean . . . around you? My brain feels like bees."

"I don't blame you," Wade said softly. "Thank you for opening up to me. I know it could not have been easy for you. Is there anything I can do for you?"

"Nah, it's all good. Just gimme a few minutes to get myself back together."

As she spoke, she felt the telltale vibration of her smartphone in her wool trouser pocket. Gesturing to Wade to give her a minute, she fished it out to see Hazel's name emblazoned across the screen.

"What's up?"

"Hey, I didn't wake ya, did I?"

"Nah, I was up and chatting to Wade already." She slipped from the booth to grab another coffee. It felt like it was going to be one of those days. "What's going on?"

"We need to meet up. Whereabouts are you?"

Coffee in hand, she slid back into the booth beside Wade. Popping Hazel on speakerphone, she placed the phone on the table between them as she pulled her laptop over. Its battery blinked angrily at her; she had forgotten to plug it in after abandoning her web search the night before.

"We're about two hours out of New York right now, at a national park."

"Oh, fuck, I'm down in North Carolina—I came to visit my auntie and see what she could find with some scrying after I lost track of them. They're a slippery bunch, babes. Anyway, to cut a long story short, they're fucking around with something really dark. Auntie reckons they've ripped the Veil open and made contracts with demons and shit. I saw some stuff when we were scrying, though, and I'd rather tell you in person. Where can we meet up?"

Charlotte drummed her fingers on her keyboard. Where even was *safe* anymore? It felt like no matter where she went, she would have the looming worry that somehow, someway, they knew where they were. The fear of the unknown was killing her. It would be one thing if they knew what they were up to, what they wanted. She could plan for that, work around it. But right now, everything was . . . well, it was so far out of her control.

And that terrified her.

"Perhaps I could suggest somewhere if you ladies are amenable?"

"I'd love some ideas. Hazel, are you cool with that?"

The other girl was silent on the phone, and she seemed to be picking her words carefully when she did finally speak. "I suppose you can suggest somewhere, ghost. Dunno how useful your millennia-old knowledge will be, though."

Wade bristled. "You know it has not been that long—"

"It's a joke!" she interrupted him curtly, voice crackling through the speaker. "You know, that thing normal people make. Maybe you should lighten up."

She glanced nervously from the phone to the miffed look on Wade's face. Though he didn't say anything, his lips tugged down at the corners, and his eyes narrowed as he glared at the device. She went to say something, to tell them to cut it out, but the words caught in her throat. She was frozen, dread pooling in her stomach. Why couldn't she say anything? By the time she had found a way to say the words, to do something, Wade had gathered himself.

"My apologies, Hazel. I should learn the humor of the time better—I do hope you will forgive my misunderstanding."

"Yeah, sure, fine." Hazel was flippant, as though she wasn't really listening to him. "What great idea did you have, then?"

"I do not have any notions of it being great, but my family did own a large property outside Philadelphia. It was rather remote, thus ensuring a deal of privacy. I imagine that would suffice for a meeting safe from prying eyes."

"Assuming it's still there. What about its current owners?"

"I doubt that will be an issue, Hazel."

She sighed heavily but agreed with him. Charlotte heaved a sigh of relief. It was okay—they would work it out.

She smiled tightly as they signed off. Wade would give the details to her, who would then forward them to Hazel. She pulled a map up on her browser, the battery blinking until she finally plugged it in. And it was a good thing she did—navigating Wade's pre-internet address was a nightmare. She ended up having to cross-reference some janky hand-drawn maps of the area, which would have been impossible without Wade's knowledge. Apparently, the house still stood, as did the property, turning up in several social media "abandoned house hunting" aesthetic groups. Wade had stared at the screen when she pulled them up, his face an uncharacteristically closed book.

When they were finally on the road after some back-and-forth emails with Hazel, the morning sun well and truly in the sky once more, Wade began expressing his doubts and concerns.

"I simply do not have a good feeling about this any longer, Charlotte. This cannot be safe for you, or Hazel, or your dear grandmother."

"It's going to be fine," she reassured him. "Everything is going to be okay. We'll work it out."

Wade stared out the windshield, his brow furrowed once more. "If you insist."

⟫⟫⟫ ⟪⟪⟪

They didn't speak much as they traveled. She turned on her music—an odd sort of radio controlled by her mobile phone. She had shown him a lot of technology, and as intriguing as it all was, it also exhausted him. So many gadgets to do so many things. Yes, he admitted, there was the ease of communication and information, and he did envy that. But there was never true quiet. No wonder she did not rest easy, for how could one when they were always accessible at the touch of a button?

The cat seemed restless, and they passed through a storm. It didn't bode well for them; he saw it as a bad omen of what was to come. Charlotte enjoyed it, however. Said that it would "clear out the bad vibes" as she wound down the windows to breathe in the storm, the warmth and chaos that came with autumn rain. Even for a witch, she was strange—a stereotype and a contradiction. She felt the energy, and clearly moved with it, and yet he had never seen her affinities or skills. As if she was actively hiding them.

He couldn't talk, though. He was hiding so much—from her, from himself. He was a hypocrite.

But she couldn't know he was a monster. And how was he not? He had killed Sarah Rochelle. His family was gone because of his refusal to go through with his engagement. He had made a deal with a devil, something he had long been warned against. And yet, in his desperate, selfish desire to save a child, to save Sarah Rochelle, he had chosen wrong. He had made a pact with the demon, no matter the cost.

Maybe he would tell her the truth about it all. About how he came to make an agreement with Atticus, about how the Order of the New Dawn had their own pact with him. How Sarah Rochelle's family, upon discovering his power as a warlock after that contract, became obsessed with him, his family, and their place within the occult. How they did anything and everything they could to ensnare him.

Or maybe he wouldn't. He was sure that it would all be revealed to her in a matter of time, as each day they drew nearer to the truth about why they wanted him and what they would get out of him. They would soon learn what they had done in the last hundred years—and how it involved him.

In his heart, he knew that once she knew, whether from his lips or from theirs, she would not look at him the way he did her. That her heart would be frozen to him. And thus he knew he had to tell her how he felt first. So that she would at least know, despite his actions, despite the monster he was, that he cared for her.

He would tell her the truth—at least, the bits of truth that mattered to him. How he felt about her. That was what mattered to him. The rest, he would "figure out," as Charlotte would say.

CHAPTER NINETEEN

They beat Hazel to the Van Baird summer house by an inordinate amount of time, arriving at the property just past lunch. Hazel wasn't expected until nightfall.

After settling the RV in the shade of an old creaking elm toward the front of the drive, Charlotte sprawled restlessly on the bed in the back. She absentmindedly stroked a snoozing Specter as they waited for an update on Hazel's whereabouts. The air was thick and heavy with the promise of an early autumn storm as her very bones ached for excitement and freedom. It was coming from the sea, unlike the smaller storm they had passed through earlier.

Wade leaned against the doorjamb to the bedroom area, his long legs stretched out as he stared out the back window, a distant look in his eyes. Charlotte covertly peered at him from under her lashes several times, wondering what was going through his mind. Her thoughts then turned to Hazel, to what the other girl had for them, to a future where this madness didn't exist. It was wild to her that just a few months ago, she had been touring America in her RV alone, filming content without a care. She should have figured there would eventually be consequences for her actions, but this was a particularly weird way for it to have gone, even for her standards.

She wanted to fidget just looking at his calm, cool demeanor.

Turning her attention back to the bed, she danced her fingers up Specter's tummy as he snoozed on his side, pretending they were spider legs. He didn't even deign to open his eyes. She frowned as he snored away. Even the cat was more at ease than her.

The silence was interrupted abruptly by Wade as he pushed off the wall.

"Would you care to join me for some air, Charlotte?"

His mouth quirked into a smile as he asked—not quite his normal wide one. She paused for a moment. It was subtle, but there almost seemed to be a nervousness to him now. *Odd.* She told him, sure, she was up for it. Wade bowed to her before drifting off out of the RV. She gave Specter a quick kiss on the head before sliding off the bed and traipsing after Wade.

Charlotte slammed out of the RV, catching her foot on the rubber mat at the top of the steps. She cursed, grabbing the door frame to stop herself from falling. She righted herself quickly, nodding to Wade as he started toward her as if to catch her.

"Are you alright, Charlotte?"

"I'm all good, just wasn't paying attention." She tested the ankle that had tried to slip out from under her as Wade stared at the RV forlornly.

"I am sorry I cannot offer you the same accommodations and manners as a regular gentleman," Wade said in a low, wistful voice, bowing his head toward her, his perfect posture slumping just a hint.

Her chest tightened as though all the air had been sucked from her lungs. Biting the inside of her cheek, she forced a smile onto her face. "I'm not the sort of girl people open doors for. Don't stress, buddy."

She cringed as Wade's eyes seemed to grow darker, his silhouette fuzzier. She reached out a hand toward him.

"I'm sorry, self-deprecation is my go-to. I didn't mean to—I didn't think before speaking." She pulled her hand back, stuffing them deep into the pockets of her long linen skirt. She jabbed her nails into the palms of her hands, urging the quelling panic in her to subside. "I'm not worth all of that attention and effort, y'know?"

His edges seemed to sharpen once more, but the dark hue of his eyes continued to deepen. His lips puckered at the corners as if fighting a frown as he drifted toward her.

"I wish you would not say these things, Charlotte." Her heart thundered as his perpetual chill washed over her. He angled his head down to look at her, so close he almost stood over her. "Any man should be so lucky to have the company of a woman such as yourself."

She glanced toward him, heat searing her cheeks at the fierce praise in his tone. "Uh, thanks . . . that was nice of you to say."

"*I* am lucky to be in your company," he whispered emphatically, moving closer still. Her thundering heart roared in her ears, her breath fast and shallow. A peculiar feeling washed over her as though she were underwater, the world muted save for the small bubble ensconcing them. She peered back up at him, his eyes locking with hers as they burned with a dark intensity.

"Would you care for that stroll now? I would like to escort you on a tour of the house." His voice was low and husky. *Hungry.* She bit her lip, nodding with wide eyes. His gaze rooted her to the spot. She let out a sigh of relief when he glanced away toward his old house, breaking the spell that kept her bound.

She took a moment, the blood rushing to her head making her sway. "Sure, sounds like fun," she breathed.

With a solemnness only Wade could muster, he offered her his arm. While Charlotte couldn't actually hold it, she knew what it meant for him—a simple offer of gentlemanly politeness, but also closeness. She thought of how they had walked like that around the atrium. Taking a deep, steadying breath, she pulled all of her concentration together to wrap her arm around his, worried she would go through him as she kept her eyes focused on him. His face lit up with unadulterated happiness as her hand hovered over the chill of his arm.

Wade straightened himself and they began to walk in step up the gentle drive to the house. Charlotte half listened to his chatter as she focused on not breaking the illusion. Despite the effort it took to maintain it, she did find it quite nice. It felt weirdly normal to walk arm in arm—at least, some approximation of normal. For there was and never would be anything normal or conventional about their friendship.

It was nice to see the smile come back to his face, too, she thought to herself.

Wade gave her a comprehensive tour of the place, as promised. Their summering home, as he called it, seemed to have not been touched within the last century. This surprised her, but Wade assured her it would have passed to a trust upon the death of the family. She was dubious about his claims, but didn't question him further; it wasn't as if she were a legal expert.

They entered the home from the basement level. Situated at the back of the house, it was actually at ground level due to the sloping hillside the home sat upon. Built in the Greco-Georgian style, the structure remained relatively sturdy. Charlotte was initially terrified of putting any of her weight on the floors, the image of plummeting to her death repeating like a broken record in her mind. Once she was inside, however, she felt something. Not quite a resistance, but an enveloping of magic. Despite the passing of the home's owners, the place still had a sweet, homely bite of magic to its air—magic, she assumed, that had once run in Wade's veins. She asked him if his family's magic still kept the house intact, and he looked just as bewildered as she felt. It was yet another strange part of the convoluted puzzle she now found herself involved in.

And so Wade showed Charlotte around the old home, a beautiful but strangely horrifying time capsule of Wade's life. He cycled through a veritable smorgasbord of emotions as they poked through the nooks and crannies of the house. He told her excitedly about how their family would come here during the summer, even when it was less fashionable for him and his sister to join their parents. Not uncommon, Wade clarified, it was just that many of his college friends hadn't felt the close bond he felt with his family. That was a sentiment she shared with him, and she thought idly of her own parents as he led her through the rooms.

His father, he told her, would host and attend lavish parties to network. Sometimes they would stay here, too, if they were soon to be traveling abroad. His eyes, back to their normal hue now, sparkled with joy at the memories.

"I was rather fortunate," Wade murmured, running a hand over an end table, sighing as the dust covering the top didn't shift. They had stopped at the landing of the second floor. Though so much time had passed, Wade swore it looked the same as the last time he remembered visiting there. "My sister and I were never too far apart from our parents. We were genuinely close with them. I saw many of my friends scheme and dismiss their parents as mere gatekeepers to their eventual fortunes. But our parents, as awkward as this is to phrase it as such, were my friends. I am certain Loren felt the same."

Charlotte made a sympathetic noise, patting his arm. The solidness she had felt that night in her third-floor room had returned, and she almost shrieked when her fingers caressed real wool. She clenched her jaw, unwilling to startle Wade or draw attention to it. The pieces felt like they were beginning to stick together, and she felt if she could just push a little further, she would figure out how it all worked, how Wade was the way he was—what any of it meant.

Wade, staring wistfully down the hallway once more, hadn't noticed at all. It seemed he was somewhere else entirely when he said quietly, almost as if he didn't realize he was speaking aloud, "I was looking forward to being a father one day, too. Maybe I would have raised them here with my future wife."

She resisted the urge to squeeze his now completely solid arm as he shook his head almost imperceptibly.

"Let's move along. There is still much I would like to show you."

Wade led her to a room at the end of the upper landing. There was a faded quality to the room, the colors muted, whether by the passage of time or merely the eerie sensation she had of stepping into another era. Wallpaper decorated the walls, fluttering and fraying away in some corners. A cavernous fireplace took up the far wall with a bay window to the north, sunlight filtering into the room in patches through the lace curtains. It looked out onto a distant pond, conjuring images of lazy summer afternoons with the windows open, the smell of wildflowers and warmth filling the room.

Toys littered a short squat table in the center of the room, appearing as though their owner had been momentarily interrupted in play and would be back. Marbles fell out of a small leather bag whilst dolls sat around the table with teacups between them. By the window sat a large wooden dollhouse with intricate detailed mini Victorian furniture within it, dolls scattered about. It was a time capsule of sorts, waiting for Wade and his sister to return. It sent a shiver down her spine.

"We did not typically leave our possessions in such a state." Wade coughed, a wry smile on his face. "We were quite organized, usually. In fact, these were played with last as adults, and I suppose Mother didn't want them put away. She cajoled us into it, wanting us to be her little ones just a little longer. At least, that was what she told us. I have no clue why she said that to us on that day. But Mother always got her way, so we played with her then."

A sigh escaped from his lips, his hands slipping into his pockets. "I wish I remembered why she asked that of us, if only to have a complete memory of her and Loren."

Charlotte looked away. There was an intimacy to his memory that she didn't want to intrude upon. Not everything had to be about solving their current predicament, and she felt she owed him this peace and quiet to sink into the past. She let her gaze wander. On the same wall as the door, facing the window, sat a beautiful chaise, its fabric in immaculate condition still, if a little dusty. There was a shawl thrown over the back of it. She briefly imagined Wade's mother, a blurry silhouette, sitting here as she watched Wade and his sister play. Mrs. Van Baird discarding her shawl on the back of the chaise as she swept to her feet to join her children. Heat roared through her, a visceral feeling of envy. She had never had a sibling of her own to bond with, and beyond knowing she was a prized *asset* with all the duties that accompanied that status, she had never given much thought to children of her own. An unsettling hunger, a craving, emerged from deep within her as the woman watching over the children in her imagination morphed into herself. She shook her head vigorously to clear the images from her mind.

Wade's gaze was intense as it landed upon her, rooting her to the spot. "I apologize for drifting away. It is strange, all these memories and sensations, as though I can be transported back to those moments. Whilst I am grateful for that, that is not the purpose of this visit. Would you perhaps like to sit with me for a moment?"

Charlotte regained control of herself as Wade politely gestured to the chaise, bowing his head. She shot him a timid, awkward smile, taking care to pick a path through the toys as he drifted behind her. Her sense of intrusion, of being somewhere she wasn't supposed to be, grew.

Perching on the edge of the chaise, she struggled to keep her hands from fidgeting in her lap. The solemnness from earlier had returned to Wade, an odd formality to him—more so than usual. She straightened her back, caring to remember her manners. She had never felt compelled to be proper around him like this before, but there was something about him in that instant that made it feel right.

Swallowing hard as Wade seated himself next to her, she wondered how ghosts did it. Did he have to hold himself there? Did he feel the furniture beneath him? Her eyes widened as the tails of his dinner jacket crumpled beneath him. She bit her lip to stop herself from calling attention to it. Did Wade realize how solid he was appearing now? How thin the Veil was, how he was interacting with the world? She reminded herself not to fidget, her brain racing a million miles an hour.

"Charlotte." He drew out her name, savoring it. "Thank you for joining me. You cannot comprehend what it means to be able to show you a sliver of my life, of my memories, in such a way." His eyes were lowered, a pause between his words, choosing them carefully as he worried his lip. "It provides me great comfort to be here for this, as it mollifies my anxiety somewhat. For there is something I would like to say to you, Charlotte, if you would allow me."

Wade exhaled softly through his nose before reaching his shaking hands over to clasp one of her own. She gasped softly at the firmness of his hands around her own. Wade, it seemed, still hadn't noticed how much form he had now. She was dimly aware of him speaking as she stared down at their clasped hands. She jolted, tearing her eyes away to look up at him.

"Huh? What did you say, Wade?"

He took a deep, superfluous breath, angling his body closer to her so that their knees almost touched as he gazed into her eyes. The look on his face made her knees weak; she was grateful they were already seated.

"If the circumstances were different, Lottie, I would have considered the time we have spent together to be courting you. Even now, I cannot help but feel I have been, despite the obvious barriers." Her heart began to race as he leaned closer to her, his voice low and hoarse. "If I were alive still, I would want nothing more than to make you my wife. I may not have my body, but I can assure you that everything I feel when I look at you is as real as if I did. I crave the feeling of your hand in mine, of my lips pressed to yours. To be able to slide an errant tendril of hair behind your ear is a bliss I would give everything for."

He moved closer to her as he spoke, his knee skimming hers, leaning toward her in earnest. Her vision swam as his handsome face neared hers.

"There is nothing," he whispered, his breath washing over her, "in this life or the next that I would not give to kiss you in this very moment. I adore you, Lottie, and I love you so completely that it shatters my heart every time I remember I cannot have you."

Her head reeled as he closed the space between them. Her eyes fluttered shut as she felt the press of his lips against her own. It was as though her entire being was exploding with sound, light, color. He tasted bittersweet, like tears, as he wrapped his arms around her. The closest feeling to this sensation, Charlotte thought in a haze, was how it felt to behold brilliant fireworks on a warm summer's night. She wrapped her arms around his neck, pulling him close, her tongue exploring his lips as she opened his mouth to her. Her heart was singing as he raised a hand to her face, cupping her cheek.

The change was slow. First the warmth faded, like nightfall closing in on the day and sapping the heat of sunlight as his lips became a chill against hers once more, his arms like a biting wind surrounding her. She didn't have to open her eyes, to drop the kiss; she already knew whatever magic had brought him so close, so real, was gone.

Sometime during those moments, cold bitter tears began to streak down her cheeks. She shivered. Whether from the cold or her sadness, she could not tell.

Charlotte was the one to pull away first. She gasped as her tears flowed freely upon opening her eyes. The pain in her chest, the feeling of being torn apart from the inside, was mimicked on his face. His hand still cupped her face, as well as it could ever.

"Please don't cry." Wade's voice cracked on his words, as though he, too, would be crying if he could. "I did not wish to sadden you. That was never my intention, Lottie."

Every barrier that Charlotte had put into place for herself crumbled. She had tried to protect her heart for years; she had avoided people, avoided attachments. And now she had unknowingly allowed it to be stolen in the most ridiculous manner. The odd companionship, the friendship that had blossomed with Wade, had felt so natural that she hadn't questioned it. The truth was that she was glad to have made a friend. It had been so long since she'd had anyone like that, save

Specter. And even she knew she couldn't rely on her cat for emotional fulfillment forever.

"Please say something, Lottie." Wade stroked her cheek, goose bumps dancing over her skin. She shivered involuntarily. Despite the early autumn heat, Wade's cold went bone-deep.

"There is nothing I can do right, is there?" Wade's words were the barest whisper, pain lacing them as he stared down at his lap, dropping his hand. "To finally find something to make existence worth it, and I cannot even be near you."

"That's not true," she whispered. Wade's head shot up, eyes wide with hope. The world began to spin as he stood up, a grin spread across his face. He was clearer than ever now, so solid that she couldn't tell where his edges faded.

Almost as though he were alive, and not a man long dead.

Almost as though he could sweep her off her feet into his real, tangible arms and have a happy ever after with her. He leaned over, reaching a hand toward her again, his fingertips brushing against her cheek. Fingers that could never truly hold her, touch her, pleasure her.

She backed away from his touch, her whole body like a live wire as she bolted to her feet. "I think I need to be left alone for a while."

She turned on her heel before the words left her lips and darted from the room. She couldn't be in this house, in this living reminder of what could've been.

Because even if he hadn't died, even if he had been real and alive, he would have passed long before her time. They never would have met, and the sad truth was that words were as good as they could ever get with one another.

Distraught, she fled from the house, tears flowing freely as she ran from her feelings and the blatant truth: that they could never be.

CHAPTER TWENTY

*H*e watched from the window as she tore from the house, not once looking back as she stumbled off across the estate. He wouldn't chase her. He knew her well enough now to know that she needed that space. She'd come back when she wanted to, and he would be waiting there for her when she was ready.

He would always be waiting for her.

Ominous clouds loomed in the distance, toward the back of the Van Baird property. Charlotte was headed toward the overgrown pond that bordered the property edge, and he breathed a sigh of relief. She wasn't leaving without him. He leaned against the window frame, his countenance casual in a way that he was not. The love of his life—it amazed him even still to realize that was what she was—had run away from the profession of love he had so struggled to put into words. He would be a fool not to admit it stung, but he knew her now, knew that she did not mean it as a slight on him. That was just who she was.

And he loved her, flaws and all. That wouldn't change.

Wade didn't look away from Charlotte's retreating form as he felt him *appear. His heart quickened, but he didn't allow himself to react as the demon leaned against the opposite frame, the picture of indifference.*

"That looked like it hurt," Atticus said, his tone sympathetic. Wade didn't allow his eyes to drift from her retreating form at the comment. "I saw the whole thing. I admit, I didn't expect her to flee, but I guess it's a particularly complicated situation—"

"What do you want?" Wade cut Atticus off. Charlotte was no longer in view as the land dipped, so he turned his head toward the demon, shifting his weight to sit upon the windowsill. Atticus adjusted his vest, leveling his azure gaze on Wade, serious. The air in the room seemed to shift with his mood.

"I came to help my friend. To offer some advice."

"A friend wouldn't be trying to trap me the way you have, again and again."

Atticus sighed, his body slackening as he wrapped his arms around himself. "Can't a boy do something because he cares?"

"I would generally say so, but you're a fiendish demon who has done naught to convince me that he cares of anything but his own interests, so I would assume you are once more, to no one's surprise, looking out for yourself."

"You wound me." Atticus frowned, as though actually hurt. "I thought you loved this mortal girl and would like to know how best to keep her safe, but I suppose she'll be joining you soon enough. So what does it matter what I have to say?"

He stiffened at Atticus' words. "What do you mean she'll be joining me?"

Atticus stared out the window, ignoring Wade. "The storm appears to be closing in."

Pushing off the windowsill, Wade got up close to Atticus until all he could see was the demon's face. "Atticus, what do you mean 'she'll be joining me soon'? You must tell me, I beseech you!"

Shaking his head softly, Atticus dragged his gaze from the world beyond to Wade's face. His mouth set in a grimace, it dawned on Wade just how young the demon looked. Not quite a man, not quite a boy. He knew that Atticus aged—he must; it had been over a hundred and twenty years since they first met—and yet he didn't look a day past adolescence.

"They've decided they're going to kill her if you don't come willingly." His pale-blond bangs fell across his eyes, his dark lashes blinking slowly, adding to his cherubic appearance. He straightened so that he and Wade were the same height, eye to eye. "If you truly love this girl, you will come with me willingly. The Order will get what they want in this; they are not afraid to do what it takes to meet those ends."

The world seemed to tilt as a deep cold seeped through Wade, a cold even he could feel. He felt numb, dimly aware of Atticus as he said something vaguely comforting, but he was far away, drifting. He couldn't accept this—that Charlotte should suffer any more than she already had. He thought of her sad chocolate eyes, the slump of her too thin shoulders, how she seemed to hold herself as though she might fall apart any moment. He pictured her kneeling, holding the pieces of her broken heart between her hands. He imagined her stuck like him, or worse—gone from existence forever. His throat caught as he imagined her broken body, the life and color gone from it. To never hear her mock him or curse under her breath, to never again see the prickly brambles she kept herself wrapped in withdrawing, at last, to reveal the softness beneath.

The ringing in his ears faded as he came back into himself. Atticus still had that odd expression on his face.

"You've got until the equinox, dear friend. The stage has been set, so to speak." Atticus pushed away from the window, sauntering toward the door. "I'd probably get to your beloved now, though, or you might not even have to wait until then."

As Atticus spoke, a distant scream tore through the world. Wade glanced toward the window, then back to Atticus, but the demon boy was already gone.

⟫⟫ ⟪⟪

She ran until her lungs ached and her legs were on fire. She'd dashed out of the house, hysteria rising as she took wrong turns, terrified that Wade would follow her and she would have to confront him, confront how she felt. She couldn't, at least not right then. She needed to think.

It shouldn't have taken her by surprise—or perhaps not to the extent that it had. They had been spending so much time together, trapped away from the Society and hunting down information. It was natural that they had become friendly. That was how friendships *worked*.

What she didn't understand was the feeling of *more than* friendship. She hadn't had a lot of patience for people, even before she began purposely secluding herself. Stoic, her father had called her. Bitchy was what other people called her. A prude. She just hadn't felt the bond, the need, to be touched by others, to be intimate with them. Even her entanglement with Bradley had been superficial. Yes, they had been intimate. But it had a looming contract intertwined, something bigger than love. It was *business*.

Or... maybe she had just been scared to let them near her.

Wade was different, though. He was kind, compassionate, and polite. He respected her, and she believed every word he said was sincere. That was what scared her.

Tears still streamed down Charlotte's face as she played their conversation over in her head. She stumbled a few times, her foot snagging on unruly patches of neglected grass and flowers and roots. All she could see was his face as he told her he loved her, the fervent look on his face as everything clicked into place and she realized she felt the exact same way he did.

The sky was darkening above as she raced blindly across the empty acreage of the property. She had no idea where she was headed, but the further away she got, the pain in her chest lessened a little. Charlotte was good at being alone. She knew how to be alone; that was all she had ever been. She was the weird girl that didn't feel the need to have a lot of friends, and they didn't feel a need to be around her, and that was fine. She had been content. And now Wade had to come and ruin everything.

～≫≫ ≪≪～

At the back of the Van Baird's Philadelphia holiday home, so far back that the house was hidden by rolling grassy knolls and trees, sat a pond. It was closer in size to a small lake, in truth; she couldn't see the other side as she finally stopped at its edge. It had gone wild and feral in its years of neglect, with tangles of weeds and flowers up to her knees leading to the water.

Here, away from the house, the world was silent, save the sounds of nature. Frogs and chirping birds filled the space, helping to drown out the pounding of her heart. She must have run for a solid five minutes to get to the back corner of the sprawling estate. She finally collapsed down on the lush tall grass, uncaring that it swallowed her, cocooning her amongst the flora. She could finally breathe.

Charlotte brought her knees up to her chin, wrapping her arms around them as she stared out at the water ahead of her. Her heart finally slowed, and her mind started to clear. Heat seared her cheeks as she thought about how she was going to approach Wade later. She had been insufferably rude, running away from him, but it was too much—it had hurt in a way she didn't know her heart could ever feel again. What was she meant to do when she wanted something so bad, something that she could never have?

It turned out, even the most broken of hearts could still be shattered.

She drew a deep breath, counting as she exhaled, attempting to quell the anxiety that loomed and threatened to resurface. She would figure it out. That was what she did. She was smart, and she was good at solving issues. Maybe not with the same finesse as her grandmother or the brute force of Hazel, but she had a good instinct that led her to the answers. And she could figure out this one.

How to be in love with someone who was already dead.

Typical weird girl, she thought. *Only I could fall for a ghost from a whole other time.* A ghost who, if he had lived, would have been old enough to be her great-grandfather . . . maybe even great-great-grandfather.

She took another deep breath. None of that was the issue—at least, not the most pressing issue. What she had to work out was how she felt, how strong it was, and what she should do about it. Could she really spend her life with Wade, when they would never truly have anything tangible? Knowing it was her job to continue her family line? Could she be selfish enough to keep him around when neither of them could truly offer the other what they needed? What they wanted?

Even if she pushed Wade away—told him that it wasn't possible, that it wasn't worth the heartache and suffering—would he listen to her? He was a ghost. He could just hang around until she died.

Until I die. She had thought about her death a lot since her parents had died. She had thought about ending it so often that she had been living in the shadows of her life, unwilling to commit too much to existence. She had figured something in her travels would end her sooner or later. Who said it couldn't be sooner?

She mulled that over in her head. He could never be alive again, or be with her on this side. But she could join him, surely. She wondered what being a ghost would be like. Could they hold each other on that side of the Veil? Would the thin fabric that existed between them now still be there? Would she be able to feel his hand in her own? Charlotte was doomed on this side of life anyway. She was the failed end of a long lineage. Perhaps there would be more forgiveness for her family, and for her shortcomings, if she was taken early. She thought of her grandmother, all alone, losing both her granddaughter and her daughter. A lump formed in her throat. It would hurt her, but would it hurt more than the life that Charlotte had been only half living?

She plucked a bluebell from the swaying grass and twirled it between her fingers thoughtfully. Contemplating her death, whether naturally or by her own hand, had always given her a melancholic calm. It was a Plan *B* that always needled in the back of her mind, despite how awful it was.

Charlotte frowned. There were some holes in the idea. She would be perpetually held by trauma, assuming she didn't pass straight on like her parents. In all her studies and her probing, she hadn't ever stumbled across someone like Wade. Ghosts usually had their limitations, stuck in their loops, or causing chaos if they were a poltergeist. Wade was so different. He made choices, controlled himself in a way that she didn't realize a spirit could even be capable of. He had full autonomy over himself. It didn't make sense, didn't line up with anything she knew. He was so full of life and charm that truthfully, she forgot he was dead a lot of the time. Forgot how unique he was, how weird.

She brought her arm back behind her head and threw the flower into the distance. The ominous clouds had crept closer, a black-and-purple wall blocking out the sky. Specter hated being alone in thunderstorms, and she didn't care to be caught in them. She could go wait back at the RV for Hazel, regroup, and think of a way to handle Wade. *Hazel will be here very soon*, she told herself. *We won't have enough time alone together to deal with it yet.*

She brushed her legs and made to stand, a sigh of relief on her lips now that she had a plan. But before she could stand, a hand snaked out from between the grass, snatching her ankle and yanking her through the wildflowers as a scream tore through her throat.

⋙ ⋘

Charlotte's screams were cut short as her body was dragged through the reeds into the pond. The crisp fall air and the approaching storm had chilled the water, causing her to feel prickles all over her body like tiny knives as she clawed at the muddy shore, desperate to gain purchase.

Whatever had taken hold of her was tenacious. Though she kicked out as hard as she could, her foot connecting with something firm yet squishy, she couldn't break its hold. She was going under, whether she liked it or not.

"Help!" she screamed, quickly sucking in a deep breath before her head went under.

It was dark beneath the water's surface. Not murky, exactly; it might have actually been pretty clear on a bright summer day, but the storm had finally arrived. The water rippled above her head, raindrops pelting the pond as she thrashed, trying to hit whatever was holding her captive. One of her blows landed, and though being underwater softened it, it was solid enough to knock her assailant away.

She swam for the surface, kicking her legs with all the force she could muster. As her head broke through, she gasped, lungs on fire as she sucked in air. The rain was coming down on Charlotte in buckets. Her hair was a film across her cheeks as her entire body seemed to be weighed down. Glancing about wildly, she spotted the shore a few yards away. As she sucked in another breath, ready to break for the shore, a monster emerged from the water before her.

It was humanoid—at least, it might have once been human. Its eyes were milky, the flesh of its face pulled taut. Patches of dark-blond hair clung to its skull, its wide mouth open as it seemed to stare at her with unseeing eyes.

Charlotte let out another scream before it pulled her back under. Its fingers clamped around her wrists, holding her in place as it yanked her underwater. Panic overwhelmed her as she tried to get away, her hands clasped together as she struggled against the monster's viselike grip. Already lightheaded, she began to drift, and she knew then she'd lost.

She closed her eyes, not wanting the image of the creature's horrid face to be her last thought. She thought of her parents, of Specter, of Grandmother and Hazel. She chose to think of Wade last, his handsome face cracked into a smile, his stormy eyes soft as he gazed upon her.

As she thought of him, she felt something. The dimmest crackle in the dark, dancing between her fingertips. Her heart lurched; she hadn't felt anything like it for the longest time. She squeezed her eyes shut and tried to calm herself even as her lungs tightened. It was her only shot. She thought of Wade, of the way he looked at her, the way his voice had been filled with wonder and bewilderment when he told her he was in love with her.

The crackling grew stronger and wrapped around her already encased wrists like a gentle caress. Her power, though faint, still resided deep within her, and was now her only chance for salvation. Charlotte held on to the warm feeling in her heart, the one that had it thudding and filling her with light and hope.

And then she sent that feeling outward.

Magic had always been a strange, inexplicable thing to her. It had never been a learning process like school; it was raw, innate. It was as much a part of her as anything else, but something that she had to learn to hone. There were some things people could already do, but they had to learn how to identify them, how to coax them out. In fact, she'd often said that her magic was just like her feelings, a whole new set of them that sat beside the other ones. That was how she had learned her magic's pulses and whims, tentatively testing them and learning them until they were as easy to identify as happiness or sadness.

Her magic was tethered to her, unfurling from her body like a coil in the way she directed it. It was tautness that sprang from her, metallic and tightly wound. She could feel it as it lashed out, wrapping itself around the darkness she felt from the being that had captured her. Its dark malevolence was an audible *thud* in the world beneath the water, a heartbeat of its own. Her power curled around the darkness, and she squeezed it.

Charlotte's eyes were still firmly shut when the grip on her loosened suddenly, as though in surprise. She seized her chance and began kicking upward toward the surface again. She could make it. She was going to make it.

It was one of those moments when time seemed to slow down. Her magic was like a rubber band, growing tauter as she pulled away from the creature, but she didn't want it to let go. It would hurt when it finally snapped back to her, especially after so long without it, but this was a risk she was willing to take to keep her life. She waited until she could see the swells of the surface before letting go.

Charlotte's magic shuddered and snapped back to her, its tension hitting her body like a sack of bricks as she broke the surface. She gasped, her head and body heavy from the exertion on her lungs as well as her magic. Despite this, she broke into a breaststroke, heading straight for the shore. She could use her power again. She could keep herself safe. If she could get on land, she would have the upper hand. The desperate desire to live, to give it everything she had, bloomed within her.

A feral snarl, something like a broken scream, resounded behind her as she hit the water's edge. The rain had turned the mud into a thick sludge that enveloped her feet, drawing her into the earth. Her drenched clothes weighed her down further as she dragged her fatigued body through it, too tired to call for help. This was her make-or-break moment.

Charlotte heard the thing as it caught up. The mud squelched behind her, a sickening noise that sent her heart into a flurry. It would catch her soon, and she would be forced to fight or be dragged under again. She squeezed her eyes shut and sent a weary probe down, seeking the already drained well for a scrap of power.

"Babes, we've got you!"

<hr />

Charlotte shuddered violently from the stress and cold as Wade knelt beside her, his face contorted into worry. He raised a hand as if to comfort her before pulling it back. Though she was frozen through and her brain still raced a million miles an hour, she forced herself to turn back and watch as Hazel dealt with the being that had almost killed her.

She had never seen the Hunter at work before—besides beating up Dirk and company—and it was absolutely mesmerizing. Hazel moved like a badass ballerina, performing intricate choreography. She danced out of the monster's reach as it lunged for her, skillfully ducking and weaving despite the sludge-like mud.

Hazel was moving so quickly that Charlotte didn't see the steel wire she had been wrapping around it until the monster fell into the mud with a sickening wet squelch. She raised her eyebrows in awe as Hazel hogtied it with a practiced hand.

"Dead things 101, babes: if you don't want to kill it, you incapacitate it. Never use rope, as the undead have endless strength to break through. Any sort of thin, flexible wire works. I like picture frame wire, personally. She's more likely to slice herself than to actually snap through it."

As Hazel explained her process, Charlotte got her first good look at the creature that had grabbed her. It did appear to be female, but it also seemed like it had been dead for quite some time. She saw chunks of rotten flesh now, and its clothes were bedraggled and moldy, tattered flowy fabrics weighed down with muck and water.

She saw that one of her blows must have connected with its head, as there was a rather impressive indent of her boot sole across the upper half of its forehead.

Now that it was tied up, Hazel kicked the creature a few times to make sure it was secure. It snapped at the Hunter, who merely grinned and danced around it.

"Fucking try me, I dare you," she taunted it.

Wade, who sat beside Charlotte, stiffened. She glanced over to him. Hazel must have noticed the change in his demeanor, too, as she looked over at him with a frown. "What's up, ghost boy?"

"I . . ." he began, trailing off as he furrowed his brow in concentration, his eyes pinned on the creature. "I believe I know her."

Chapter Twenty-One

"What do you mean, you *know* her?"

Hazel's shrill outburst cut through the whistle of the wind and rain, even as the body tied up beside her thrashed and snapped its teeth. Hazel whirled around and kicked it hard in the jaw. Her back turned to them, fists clenched, the Hunter stared down at the creature.

"How the *fuck* does an amnesiac ghost that's been dead for a century know some random corpse?" Her tone was low and menacing, carrying over to them on the wind.

"I said I *think* I know her, not that I actually do," Wade snapped back. Charlotte flinched. This was probably the rudest he had ever been.

Hazel was over to him in a flash. Charlotte blinked a few times, unable to comprehend how she moved so lithely despite the storm and the mud that she kept sinking into.

"Tell you what, ghost. I can get rid of mine and Charlotte's problem right here, right now, if you want." Hazel glowered at him, inches away from his face.

"Oh, really?" he said hotly. "And how would you propose getting us out of this, then?"

"Not *us*," Hazel hissed. "I suspect if I got rid of *you*, a lot of this would just 'poof' and disappear." She made a wriggling motion with her hands. "How about I exorcise you right here and now and send you on to where the hell you're meant to be?"

"I doubt that would help," Wade said, but there was an uncertain waver in his voice.

Hazel's voice lowered with intimidation. "We can't trust you. You're fucking hiding something, and I know it."

Despite her exhaustion and how slick she was with mud and rain, Charlotte struggled to her feet, crying out, "Stop fighting, you two! This isn't going to help us!"

As she called out, she slipped forward, heading face-first for the mud. Hazel had her arm around her in a flash, pulling her up gently.

"We need to get you inside and clean, babes, before you get sick."

Hazel's words reminded her of how cold she was in her thin cardigan. Charlotte shuddered, teeth chattering.

"How long have you been out here? What happened? Ugh, never mind, tell me once you're clean. You smell like corpse."

Hazel managed to keep an arm under Charlotte and haul her along while simultaneously dragging the corpse by a hard rod that wouldn't let it get too close to them. Wade floated somewhere behind them, silent through the long trek back to the RV. Charlotte didn't have the energy to talk to him, to see if he was okay. It was hard enough for her to stay conscious.

Specter hissed when she pushed her way inside, dripping mud and pond scum. She limped to the bathroom, twisting the shower knobs on and sinking into the blistering hot water. She would deal with everything after she was clean and warm again, she thought drearily.

She was used to weird. She could handle it.

⟫ ⟪

Charlotte didn't emerge for almost a full hour. By that time, the storm had subsided, though the menacing dark clouds still lingered.

Specter had joined Wade and Hazel outside, the latter still mud-splattered herself. She offered a shower to the other girl. Hazel shook her head, saying she'd deal with it later.

On the ground between the trio, a few short yards from where Charlotte stood on the RV steps, the corpse lay on the ground. Wade crouched beside it, tilting his head as he examined it. Specter's hackles were raised as he sniffed the thing and Hazel stood watching over them, a cigarette between her lips and a hand on her hip.

"Don't come too close, babes. I haven't killed her yet, and she's pretty hell-bent on getting at you," Hazel warned. Dazed, Charlotte nodded, hovering on the steps.

Hazel flicked the butt of her cigarette away. Wade shot her a look but kept his mouth shut. Apparently, her threats had been enough to temper even his sensibilities.

"Wade reckons this was someone from before he died. Impressive for a corpse, especially one this old. We had a little play with her, got some ideas. You can come a little closer for this."

Charlotte climbed down from the steps and crept closer. The creature had its eyes shut, but it still twitched. It was hard to think of it as a human body, as someone who had once been alive. She had dealt with the gross and the undead, but she had never grappled with death quite so literally.

Hazel crouched down beside Wade. Black gloves adorned her hands as she rolled the corpse over.

"Now, this is going to be a bit gross, but we played a little surgery. Don't give me that look, ghost," Hazel warned sharply as Wade blanched. "You can't vomit. You can't even smell this shit, so get over yourself.

"Anyway," Hazel continued, returning her attention to the body, "I made a few incisions and peeled the flesh back a bit, to get an idea of how our crusty friend here has been managing to keep from decomposing too badly." Charlotte felt her own stomach twitch with disgust. "She's pretty interesting. The internal organs are weirdly preserved. I'd guess this pretty lady here was embalmed before she died. Which is super fucked up, honestly. I can't imagine this was a thing she volunteered for."

Hazel showed Lottie the incisions, pointing out the organs. They were squishy and pink, so fresh that Lottie's eyebrows shot up. She noted the fresh cut Hazel had made in the chest, right by a sharp rough scar. *Maybe they'd botched the embalming?*

"How is that possible, though?"

"I have some theories, but Wade did find something that was pretty compelling."

Beside Hazel's bag lay a small toolkit spread out. Charlotte's stomach turned, a bad feeling creeping over her as Hazel snatched a scalpel. With a practiced hand, Hazel peeled back a hunk of scalp she had already cut into.

"Getting to the brain was a bit messy," Hazel admitted. "I used a portable hand drill to get through the skull and oh, boy, our gal did *not* like that." She patted the shoulder of the corpse in a jovial, familiar manner. "But when I did get in there, I found sulfur. Like, shit came pouring out of her, and she calmed down a lot when it did."

Charlotte finally noticed the small pile of fine golden powder beside the corpse. Then the smell hit her.

"Sulfur, baby," Hazel said softly. "Now, how did that get in there, I wondered?" She ran a gloved finger through the sulfur thoughtfully. "I couldn't come up with a reasonable explanation. Zombies don't work like this; they're usually missing a few of their wires, so to speak. Definitely not a vampire. She isn't *changed*, just . . . dead. And there are no others of her around, from what I can see.

"So, we have this 'sentient' being"—she curved her fingers in air quotes—"who doesn't seem like part of a pack of any kind, with preserved insides and sulfur coming out of her. It didn't seem like any voodoo that I am personally familiar with, and quite honestly, I can't think of anyone or any practice disgusting enough to desecrate a corpse like this. Or, as I suspect is the case, anyone psycho enough to do this on someone who's alive."

Wade stood up and turned to face Charlotte solemnly. "And that is when I had a theory."

Hazel muttered under her breath, "Oh, boy, can't wait for you to hear this."

"One, while I cannot quite place her, I am certain now that we were acquainted in the lead-up to my own departure. Two, I . . . I confess, I have seen this practice before."

Charlotte's breath caught in her throat as Wade crossed himself. She'd never seen him do that.

"You have to understand, when I was alive, it was a different time. There were a lot of things done that were not yet considered poor taste."

Hazel muttered something that sounded suspiciously like "You're telling me," but Charlotte chose to ignore her, trying to maintain focus on Wade's words as dread built in her.

"The occult and practices from all over the world were considered fashionable through my youth and in the years of my parent's youth. There was a lot of experimentation with text and lore, and a lot of research into curses. Especially after some incidents occurring with artifacts that were . . . *obtained* from other cultures."

Hazel swore, her eyes flashing angrily at Wade. He merely nodded absentmindedly in agreement.

"There were a lot of boundaries blurred during this time. I never participated in anything myself, but I know of people who had through our social circle. And one practice, obtained by examining a rather well-preserved body—several thousand years old, in fact—became in vogue. This body could be controlled through certain speech patterns and sulfur imbued in the brain—"

"Essentially," Hazel interrupted, "this motherfucker is telling me they used dark magic and created a new type of necromancy that keeps their corpses nice and toasty. Whatever his deal was, this guy here knew some shady-ass people."

Hazel narrowed her eyes before stepping sideways, coming between him and Charlotte.

The hurt on Wade's face tore at her heart as Hazel hovered protectively by her, positioned between them. The Hunter was back to seeing him as a threat, the enemy—*other*. But he was Wade, and she needed him, and she would make it right again.

"So what did you learn?" Charlotte asked, desperate to break the tension. They immediately began talking over each other, reiterating what they had just told her. Her head throbbed as Hazel and Wade overloaded her with information. New types of dark magic and necromancy. A corpse, one that was over a hundred years old, being sent after them. It had to be a message. What was the message, though?

"Alright." Charlotte rubbed her temples. "Wade knows the—the body. And the body is being moved with some dark magic we don't know about. Alright, so that means someone is controlling it, right?"

"Fuck yeah, they are." Hazel wandered back over and probed the body again. "I'm trying to find any other identifiers, but I haven't seen anything."

"What kind of message are they trying to send by doing this? Is it just to kill me?"

"Nah, I'd say it's a lot more than that. Especially given the reason I asked you guys to meet with me."

Charlotte had completely forgotten about Hazel's urgent call, the reason they were there in the first place. Between Wade's confession and her near-death experience, it felt like a lifetime had passed since then.

"Now, I'm not gonna say my info is infallible, but I'm pretty confident the call is coming from inside the house."

"What do you mean by that?" Wade asked, arms crossed.

Hazel took in a deep breath before continuing. "Alright, your Society isn't all that good, but it's not as bad as it is. As in, it was serving its purpose pretty well and things have been kept running pretty smoothly. Well, I saw some shit. Only glances, mind you, because there is a lot of fog around all this"—Hazel gestured widely—"—but I *think* that the Society has been infiltrated and is being remodeled silently from the inside."

Lottie looked at Hazel, dumbstruck. "Infiltrated? What? The Society takes up the entire North American branch. How bad is it? Isn't Dirk the only one behind all of this?"

Hazel knotted her brows together. "Pretty bad if they're using this sort of magic and your friend, the cartoon villain, is trying to wipe you out."

"What do we do?" Charlotte clenched her fists together. It was all clicking into place. It would have been much easier to engineer the massacre that claimed her parents, as well as the rash of recent deaths, if it was an inside job.

"We return to your home and warn your grandmother, and find a way to confront the fiends that are at its core."

It was Wade who answered her. He rose from the ground. "Let us put this one out of its misery and make haste. I believe that is our best course of action. Would you not agree?" He looked away from the creature on the ground, his brow creased.

"Yeah, I do," Hazel said begrudgingly. She dug into her bag and pulled out a lighter and some fluids. "Let's get this done, then."

As Charlotte climbed into the RV, night well and truly fallen, the familiar message tone sounded. The one that had started this all. She slipped her trembling hand into her pocket and pulled out her smartphone. She tugged down the notification, not even needing to open the email to see its short simple message.

Don't trust them. It's a trap.

Chapter Twenty-Two

The drive to Winterbourne was silent and long. Charlotte didn't even turn on the radio. She was waiting for the right words, the right moment, to talk to Wade. She tried to focus on how she could tell him she felt things for him, too. How, if he were alive, she would want to be with him, to have him hold her and whisper her love for him. Her face flushed warm when she thought of him, daydreaming as she followed the road back to Boston. Imagining him warm and alive, his hands tangled in her hair, the feeling of his breath on her face as he leaned in to kiss her.

Every time she went to speak, she imagined what might happen if those inappropriate thoughts came out instead and clamped her mouth shut tight. The horror of the afternoon was already fading, another unpleasant memory on the ever-growing list.

They'd reached the outskirts of Boston, the city lights blinking warmly like the stars above, when Wade finally broke the several-hour silence.

"Lottie." His voice was hoarse, emotion twisting through the syllables of her name. "I did not mean to burden you with my affections. I had thought we were on the same page, and I worry now that I have the wrong book entirely. If it would please you, we can act as though today did not happen, and return to being friends. I wish for nothing more than your friendship and companionship, and I hope not to lose it."

Charlotte drew in a deep breath as Wade slumped back against his seat. Specter snoozed beside him. It was now or never.

"I didn't run off because we weren't on the same page." Wade straightened up in his seat as she gripped the steering wheel tighter. "It was more because we were writing the same sentence and I hadn't realized it before then. I just needed to calm down a bit. It's . . . it's a new feeling for me. And this situation would be just as frightening and confusing to me, even if we didn't have the barriers we do now."

"Ah," he said quietly. "My death."

"It fucking sucks, Wade. I mean, you're going to watch me grow old and I might die and be with you. Or I can die young and *might* be with you, but . . . it wouldn't be what we wanted. Not . . ."

"Not real." His mouth quirked into a sad smile. "I am not sure how I would feel watching you marry and be with someone else, either, even if I could be your constant companion."

"Imagine if I had to explain you to a husband. 'Oh, don't mind him, that's just my ghost lover.'" She laughed bitterly. "And I'm sure you're aware I have to carry on my family line. I wouldn't have much of a choice, or the Blythes would die out with me."

"And that would be unacceptable to me," Wade whispered, "for a world without a piece of you always in it would be like the night without the stars. Dark and empty, even if it continued existing."

If her heart hadn't already been breaking, that did it.

"Let's just savor whatever time we can get with each other," Charlotte said finally, reaching a hand out toward Wade, the other on the wheel. When he went to grasp her hand back, instead of the usual feeling like the press of a strong wind, she swore his hand felt warmer and solid again.

Hazel beat them back to Winterbourne. As Charlotte navigated the RV up the drive, she spotted Hazel standing with her grandmother on the front porch, concern etched across both their faces. Her stomach dropped.

She was getting used to things being bad.

"What's happened now?" Charlotte asked as she clambered out of the vehicle. Specter had woken up and crawled onto her shoulder during the drive, leaping down as her feet hit the ground. Edith's mouth was pulled into a grimace as she hurried forward to meet Charlotte, a letter in hand.

"Another letter from them? Seriously? You'd think they get the message by now—"

Charlotte cut herself off as Edith handed her the envelope. On the front, written in a neat, beautiful hand, were three names.

To Miss Charlotte Blythe, Master Wade van Baird, and Miss Hazel Williams.

"This can't be good," she and Wade muttered in unison. She flipped it over, forcing her hands to remain steady as she tore it open sloppily. Hazel strode toward her, peering over Charlotte's shoulder as she pulled an invitation out and read it aloud.

"Dear Miss Blythe, Miss Williams, and Master Van Baird, you are cordially invited to attend a masquerade ball in honor of the Society on Saturday the thirty-first . . ."

Lottie trailed off as they looked up, staring at one another with stunned expressions.

"This is a trap, isn't it, Gran?" Hazel asked. Edith nodded, her mouth set in a grim line.

"It would appear so. The question is, what makes them think you'll come?"

"I would say this is the reason why."

A piece of paper had fluttered out of the envelope, unbeknownst to Charlotte. Hazel scooped it up, holding it up beside her face. It was a photograph of Wade and a short smiling young woman beside him. A hand written note beneath it said "Wade and Sarah Rochelle, February 28, 1910."

Charlotte glanced at Wade. Could a ghost pale?

Hazel was in Wade's face in a flash. "Who the fuck is Sarah Rochelle?"

Charlotte frowned, mulling over the image. The dark amber hair, the shape of her face. They had seen Sarah Rochelle recently.

"She's the body they sent after us."

⤞⤝

The next few days passed with no hints on who Sarah Rochelle was or how she was connected to Wade. Charlotte and Hazel scoured the internet, a familiar pattern, while Edith looked through a detailed history of the Society. The closest hint any of them found was an article from 1893 about a five-year-old Sarah Rochelle Emberly, who fell through the winter ice and almost died. The only reason it made headlines was because she was the heiress to one of the richest American families of the time, steel tycoons who'd risen into the upper echelons of society. They found nothing else on them, the information on them dying out as suddenly as the Van Bairds. The photo of the girl did not seem to spark Wade's memory.

"I am sorry, but I do not know what you expect. I cannot remember what I cannot remember." He was flippant, distant in his responses when prodded, fading away more often than not.

It was midafternoon on the equinox when Charlotte threw in the towel.

"I'm out of ideas. This is clearly some sort of taunt, but I guess it hasn't worked the way they intended. I guess the only way we can find out is if we go to this stupid party."

"The party is an obvious trap, though, babes." Hazel's cheek was pressed to the table, reminiscent of a petulant child. "You know we'd be heading straight into the belly of the beast."

"Then we just need to be smarter than them. We just need a plan to get our info and get out."

Edith frowned at the girls from where she sat at the head of the table. "It is far too dangerous to play into their hands."

"What else do we have, Grandmother? Personally, I can't stomach running forever or waiting for Ashgarde to get Wade and me. And what about Hazel's lead about a cult infiltrating the Society? If we don't get to the bottom of that, it's only going to get worse. We can't afford to let that happen. We can't trust anyone as it is."

"We can still just give them Wade," Hazel suggested half-heartedly. Charlotte glared at her.

Edith sighed. "I guess it can't be helped," she said softly. "What is your plan, then?"

Charlotte cracked her knuckles, how she imagined Hazel would if they swapped places. "I say we play stupid. We don't act cagey; we just go like we're having fun. Hazel and I will, anyway. We'll be decoys. We know that Wade's memories can be triggered, and he *can* remain unseen, so we'll use that. Hazel and I'll lure out the big bads and get their attention. When Wade gets enough info, or if it gets too dangerous, we skedaddle."

"And what if they want to get into a physical altercation?" Hazel asked.

"That's what you're for. And I may have a few tricks up my sleeve yet."

A devilish smile curled Hazel's lips. "I take this as permission to do whatever I need to do, then."

‑‑⟫⟫ ⟪⟪‑

Wade waited alone in Lottie's former room. He wasn't surprised at Atticus's appearance.

"My, my. You've been quite the liar lately." The demon tsked at him. "It was one thing to tell white lies, dear friend, but this is going too far."

"I know." Wade dropped his face to his hands, wishing he could cry. They sat on the edge of the bed, the third floor of the house eerily silent around them. "I'm a wretched creature."

Atticus shrugged. "Perhaps. But humans are flawed, especially when emotion is involved." The demon grimaced, seemingly disgusted. "The female ones cause such affliction."

"What is your point?"

"Perhaps it is best to be honest, friend. There could still be hope. You could come with me."

Wade said nothing.

‑‑⟫⟫ ⟪⟪‑

One of the nice things about having a rich family was the access to ridiculous things that you just *had*. For instance, they had a room full of lavish gowns and masks from decades of balls and the like ready to go. Hazel had complained, warning Charlotte she wouldn't be as effective in a dress. She told Hazel to wear her jeans underneath and destroy the dress if she had to; it didn't really matter.

Hazel asked Charlotte if she was aware of the insane amount of privilege she had.

"I'll let you wear a tiara" was her response. Hazel had narrowed her eyes and gave a single nod as if it say *'fair enough'*.

It was already five o'clock. The party was meant to start in two hours. Hazel had argued they take her Camry for a swift exit, but Edith had answered with a hard no; they would take the family car, an upscale sedan, and its driver. It was bad enough that they were being lured there, but there would be unaware members at this party, and they needed to blend in.

"Why aren't you invited, Gran?" Hazel had asked as Edith zipped up a long sage-green gown for her, then grabbed several pairs of ivory gloves, debating which pair for her to wear.

"We'll be having our own meeting tonight. Dirk will be there. At least, he should be. I don't doubt he's scheduled this to give himself an alibi. They'll know something is up if I don't go. And before either of you girls give me gaff, I am more than capable of defending myself still."

"That's comforting," Hazel muttered, securing a golden fox mask to her face.

Charlotte sat at her vanity, coiling her hair as she listened to their conversation. A big part of her suspected that tonight was going to go poorly for them. She reasoned to herself that at least her grandmother would be safe, and that Hazel was extremely capable of taking care of herself. And Wade would be hidden.

The plan she'd come up with for Wade had been selfish. She didn't truly think he would find anything out; she just knew he'd be safest if he was out of the way, invisible. She had suspected her own time was meant to be up long ago; she'd made peace that tonight might be it for her. As she went to tie a gem-speckled ivory swan mask to her face, Specter mewled and pawed at the bottom of the gown she wore.

"I'm sorry, kitty, you can't come," she told him, scooping him up. She laid a kiss on his head, her heart aching at the idea of never holding him again. "I promise there will be plenty of cuddles for you after tonight." *Just not necessarily my own cuddles.*

"Whatcha got there, darling?" Something glinted in his mouth, a comb of sorts. She pulled it gently from between his teeth. It was a silver hairpin, a delicate flower with two long prongs. Small diamonds made up the flower with a single extravagant topaz in its center. She tested it against her fingers, surprised by its sharpness.

"Oh, you must have found this in with the other stuff. I'll wear this, just for you," she told him, slipping it into the coiled bun on her head. She smiled at him before returning to her mask. When she was done, she barely recognized the person staring back at her.

In the mirror, Charlotte was composed, carrying herself with the same confidence her mother had. Instead of her skin looking sallow, she glowed, her skin sparkling thanks to makeup and glitter. This was how she thought her mother had wanted her to look for her debut; she figured, if the end was coming, she could at least give it to her now. She was *Lottie*.

She rose from the chair, spinning dramatically for effect. "How do I look? I'm surprised Mom's dress still fits me."

Hazel, who had just strapped knives to her thighs beneath her gown, dropped the hem and whistled. "You look ready to infiltrate an evil society and take them down from the inside."

Chapter Twenty-Three

"This feels like a really fucking bad idea, dude."

"I've had worse ideas."

The two young women stood side by side staring up at the open doors of Meadowsweet House, named for the perennials that surrounded it. Wade, presumably, was invisible somewhere near them.

The fall air nipped at the exposed flesh of their arms, electricity coursing in the air—a promise of what was to come. All Hallows' Eve, the night where the Veil was thinnest, was usually a contemplative night for people like Charlotte. The magic that made her a Blythe, the very essence of who she was, made possible by the shadows and darkness that lurked in the everyday, came out full force on this night. Her heart skipped as she felt the tendrils of the unknown beckon to her, heard the rustle and whisper of the unseen call.

"Alright, guys," Charlotte whispered, "you remember the plan?"

"I seek information, hidden, and try to remember who Sarah Rochelle is and how I am important to them. You two keep their attention trained on you and run at any sign of trouble."

She swallowed and nodded curtly. "That's the one." Quietly, so that she hoped Hazel wouldn't hear, she whispered, "Please stay safe for me."

There was a moment of silence before the chill caressed her neck. "And you for me, my darling Lottie."

She shivered, staring up at the golden light that spilled out of the open doors. Reaching a hand out to Hazel, she stepped forward. "Let's do this."

﹥﹥﹥ ﹤﹤﹤

His heart sank as he watched her receding back. Even after she was swallowed by the crowd, he stood invisible, waiting, hoping she would return and they would leave. That maybe he could find another way to keep her safe and with him.

Wade knew it wasn't possible. There were far too many people wanting too many different things, many of which would end with her hurting.

So, he faded into darkness. He felt two tethers, as he had for a while—the red one that lured him to her, and the tether that bound him, dark and cold, to Atticus.

He followed the cold tether.

"It's good to see you." Atticus waited on the upstairs landing, surveying the party beneath. They had an inseverable connection, binding them through space and time, it seemed.

"You knew you would see me again tonight. That I would come to you, regardless."

"Doesn't make it any less nice." Atticus was dressed the same as ever—a delicate brocade vest, trousers, and a poet shirt. He didn't wear a mask like the others downstairs, and for a moment Wade wondered why. Then he decided he didn't care; none of it mattered. The important thing was that he was here now. He could keep Lottie safe.

﹥﹥﹥ ﹤﹤﹤

This is anticlimactic.

Several hours had passed since she and Hazel had split up to eavesdrop and look for anything out of place. The entire house was filled with Society members drinking and enjoying themselves. Charlotte deliberately stuck to the more open rooms, lingering near doors. The fingers of her left hand fluttered near the opening of her handbag often, ready to throw down a potion or to grasp a piece of silver as she needed. The memories of her last visit to an old home linked to the Society were still raw.

The lighting was orchestrated by magic, candles floating through the air in a flamboyant disregard for secrecy. Invisible servants flittered through the rooms, the occasional blur in her peripheral vision. *Odd.* No expense was spared, opulence seeping through the grand old house. She had never been here before, but there was an ache in her, a familiarity.

Charlotte slipped into the main ballroom area again, catching sight of Hazel across the room. The other girl jerked her head to the left and began weaving her way in the same direction. Careful to keep an eye on the top of Hazel's head, she skirted around the edge of the room, trying to imagine what the Hunter was up to. As she passed an alcove, a hand wrapped around her upper arm, tugging her into the dark corner.

"Miss Blythe, it's wonderful to see you came after all."

Her heart thundered at the sound of Dirk Ashgarde's voice. The corner he had tugged her into had a small love seat shoved into it—a tiny corner of reprieve for lovers, perhaps, once upon a time.

"Come, sit with me," he purred, blocking the path out into the room. Charlotte glanced desperately around him, unable to catch sight of Hazel through the throng. Dressed in deep-gray brocade, the silver thread of his outfit complimented his wolf mask. Fitting, as he bared his teeth at her in a threatening smile. He slipped closer to her and Charlotte stepped back automatically, her calf smacking against the seat. Unwillingly, she sank into the seat as he stood over her.

She gripped her handbag tighter as he took a seat beside her. "Come now, girl, you don't need any of that around me," he scoffed. She glowered at him.

"Aren't you meant to be at a meeting this evening?" she asked tightly. A menacing smile spread across his face.

"Oh, yes, of course your grandmother let you know. I would be remiss to not at least see the party I put so much effort into organizing, however."

"You have a panache for decoration, that is certain."

He chuckled. "Well, yes, it is a special night after all." His eyes glittered behind his mask as he leaned closer to her. "The autumn equinox has always been such a treat for us. When our power is the strongest, when the worlds between connect with ease. This one is very special for us. So much tragic energy has gathered these last few months, after all. This is the best time for all that sadness to redistribute itself."

Charlotte's eyes widened. "What are you saying? What have you done?"

Dirk leaned over to pat her cheek fondly, as a grandfather might. She recoiled, banging her head against the wall, eliciting another chuckle from him. "We are revolutionizing the world tonight, girl. With great power comes great responsibility, or something akin to that. Thank you for bringing the star of the show with you. Such a beautiful, brash girl you are. It would have been lovely to have joined our families."

With a sigh, he pushed off his seat. "You look so much like Edie and Stephenie in that dress," he said, almost wistfully. *Ew.* "Good evening, and goodbye, Miss Blythe. I have matters to attend to now."

Dirk blended into the crowd, leaving a shocked Charlotte alone in the corner. Her heart hammered, her thoughts a wild, jumbled mess. She had to find Wade and get him away, but he could be anywhere. She had to find Hazel, too. What had Ashgarde planned? What did he mean by telling her goodbye? What was going to happen to them?

It was as though she was moving through water, the world slowing around her as she pushed to her feet and stumbled through the crowded ballroom. The electricity in the air crackled, thicker than before, as though in warning. She spun on her tiptoes, searching for Hazel. She had to find her, and then they find Wade. She *needed* to find him.

The lights above her blew out as she scanned the room, plunging everything into darkness. Shafts of moonlight illuminated the room, bouncing off the glittering jewelry and finery of those around her. Charlotte's skin prickled as she listened to the confused murmur of those around her. For one sickening moment, she was back at her debutante ball, in darkness much like this—

"Babes, I got you," Hazel's voice hissed beside her, jerking her back into the present. "We gotta get out of here; I can feel something *awful* is about to go down."

She let Hazel tug her through the crowd, back toward the entrance. People milled around, nonresponsive as Hazel shoved past them. As they neared their escape route, the silence was broken by none other than Dirk Ashgarde's voice booming out across the room.

"Good evening, esteemed friends and members." The girls slowly turned back to the room. In the center, where they had been moments before, the crowd parted, revealing a circle around Dirk. He still wore his wolf mask as he addressed the world.

"I thank you all for coming. A full moon on the Eve of Saints—what a blessing that it is. I am sure you can feel the energy positively coursing around us this evening as we draw nearer to the Witching Hour"—a murmur of laughter at the colloquial term tittered through the room—"and the highlight of our evening comes to head.

"Though the American branch of our Society is still fledgling in the grand scheme of things, it's still full of tradition, of sentiment. These things can lead to stagnation. We have seen this in the past. This is why we stick to the shadows, lurking, cleaning up what the normals, the unblessed, cannot deal with. We keep them safe from something that they cannot tolerate, instead of reveling in the world that was made for us. We hide for the sake of their sensibilities and create a status quo that serves them, not us."

"I do *not* like where this is going," Hazel muttered beside her. Charlotte squeezed her hand.

"It is time that we emerge from the shadows and take our place. As the Order of the New Dawn, we will pave a new path where we rule as one with those that are partial to our lives."

"The cult," Hazel whispered in horror. "They're installing themselves as some sort of magical dictator."

"I don't understand. If they wanted to overthrow the Society charter, he could have done this silently, surely." Dread pooled in Charlotte's stomach as she scanned the room for Wade.

"He's got something else up his sleeve." Hazel frowned, trigger hand twitching at her side. "But what?"

The shadow servants that had been serving drinks and food earlier flickered in Charlotte's peripheral vision. She backed up, her fingernails digging into Hazel's arm. "We gotta get out of here and get Wade, *now*."

As she spoke, chaos broke loose. The shadow servants snatched the people around them, screams breaking out across the room. Charlotte felt their claws scrape her arms as she shrieked. She dug into her bag blindly, pulling out a small sachet of sage and salt. She loosed the tie and threw it high above her, letting it shower down over them.

They snarled as the blessed sachet contents touched them, recoiling. Hazel took no time to turn on her heel and dart from the ballroom, shoving past people to escape out into the house. Charlotte elbowed her way past people, following Hazel, her arms stinging.

"Wait for me!" she yelled, the crowd pressing in around her, suffocating her. The familiar crackle of her magic welled within her, whispering as it begged to be unleashed. She ignored it, instead shouldering her way through the terrified throng.

One moment, Charlotte was upright, the curved archway that lead out of the ballroom in sight. The next she was thrown about violently, being tugged in every which direction. The talons of the shadow servants raked down her arms and face, pulling her, shoving her. They tore at her hair, ripping it loose from its coiled bun. She let out a snarl, magic dancing on her fingertips. She shoved her hand into her handbag once more, feeling for a salt vial. Fumbling with the cork, she spilled it in her bag. She curled her fingers in it, grabbing a small handful.

She tore her hand free, slamming it into the torso of the shade grasping her arm. Her fingers tingled as blue light engulfed it and the creature squealed in pain, slowly burning away.

Now free, Charlotte cursed and shoved through the crowd again, calling for Hazel and Wade. "If you can hear me, Wade, get out of here!" She gasped as something slammed hard against her back. Charlotte was thrown to the floor, her temple slamming against the parquet.

⤜⤛ ⤜⤛

Something was deeply wrong. He was waiting upstairs, but then he heard the screams. He had to go find her, keep her safe—

"She's fine," Atticus said softly. In the soft candlelight, he appeared more youthful than ever, as though he would never age out of adolescence. Such an old soul in such a young body. "My pets are just reclaiming your phylactery. They aren't going to harm her to get it. If you're just patient a few more minutes, Wade, you'll get to see her again, as you. Not as the shadow you are right now."

Wade waited impatiently in silence, his mind racing. Had he made the right choice? Was he always going to be doomed to this path? Had he merely tried to outrun the inevitable? He thought, for just a moment, that maybe he could go back to her and they could simply run far away.

Then the shadows returned, and it was time for Wade to return to himself. He saw the glint of silver in the dark and felt its pull.

⤜⤛ ⤜⤛

The cacophony of noises turned into a high-pitched hum as Charlotte's vision blurred. Her lower back twisted as she slumped forward, gasping for air. Struggling to push herself upright, something violently pulled her head back by the hair.

"Get off of her!"

Hazel's muffled words floated to her ears slowly as though there was a thick fog between them. She blinked away tears, wincing from the pain in her scalp. Then the pain, though it lingered, was replaced by Hazel's cool hands on her cheeks, gently slapping them.

"Come on, babes, time to get up and get out! I've got you." Hazel slipped an arm under Charlotte like she had done mere days ago, hoisting the slim girl so she held most of Charlotte's weight. The world seemed so distant and murky to her, her head swimming. "You sure do like to get the shit beat out of you for a girl who works better with books, huh?"

"No, you," she slurred. She shook her head, willing the stars and pain to disappear. "I'm fine. Lemme go, I can do this."

"Fuck off with the heroics. We gotta get out of here."

As Hazel spoke, the energy in the room shifted. The screams quieted, and Charlotte could feel the pulse of something dark and wrong as it weaved its way through the room, a living heartbeat of darkness and evil. She peeked over her shoulder, back at where Dirk had been standing in the center of the room.

The shadow servants had gathered there, creating a dense dark circle. She nudged Hazel, who turned them around to see properly.

"What's going on?" Hazel hissed. "Fuck, it doesn't matter, we gotta *go*."

"And now, for the main event!"

Dirk Ashgarde stepped forward, a path opening between him and where the two of them stood, frozen. The girls exchanged a horrified glance. Dirk laughed, a booming guffaw that seemed to fill the room. "No need for the look, girls. No, you've been annoying, but you aren't the important thing here, I assure you. In fact, you're very privileged guests that will see the birth of a new era for the occult."

Dirk bowed and slipped to the side, revealing a large-claw foot tub in the circle. They shared another look, stepping back a step. Their backs bounced against the chests of two men much bigger than them. Charlotte clung desperately to Hazel as a group of hooded acolytes, in the same robes as the day they met, emerged from behind the shadow servants, chanting something in a low tone. A blond boy hung to the side of them, watching on curiously. Distracted, Charlotte thought she had seen him somewhere before. The crowd around them began to murmur and hum in excitement, expectant for what was to come, apparently having already forgotten their fearful screams.

"It has taken us a long time to get the phylactery and our sacrificial lamb in the same space. He's been quite the escape artist these many decades." Dirk smirked as the crowd snickered in quiet laughter. "Tonight, we finish the work of our forefathers. For a long time, we wished to have a way to establish ourselves as the strongest, the most remarkable, to make mere mortals quake before us and obey us—nay, to serve us!

"This is much harder to do when under the control of the monarchy and the archaic rules they've imposed. Even in independence, we have no freedom." He sneered. "Thankfully, that particular power has weakened and diluted. It has given us time to collect valuable resources and assets and find the path forward."

"*Fuck*," Hazel whispered, looking scared for the first time since they met.

"Alas, it is not time for me to prattle on. Let the show begin." Dirk swiftly stepped aside.

The claw-foot tub stood beneath the opulent chandelier and the domed skylight above it, moonlight glancing off its crystals, cascading the floor beneath it in shimmery waterfalls of light. Even from thirty or so feet away, Charlotte could see the obsidian liquid within, sparkling flecks dancing across its surface like starlight. The substance lapped at the edges of the tub like waves, as though it was breathing. She was transfixed as one of the acolytes, murmuring still, stepped forward. His hood fell back to reveal a face puckered from a multitude of scars. As he spoke, his hands weaving above the tub, some of the other acolytes began moving around him in a circle, pouring something out of small sacks in a neat curve.

"Is that grave dirt?"

Charlotte glanced at Hazel, who had a hand clasped over her mouth, before returning her attention back to the nightmare unfolding before them. As the two acolytes reached behind the one in the center, they paused their tracing. They waited as the one in the center fished in a large pocket of his robe for something that flashed silver in the moonlight, dropping it into the tub. He bowed his head for a moment before backing out of the circle. They finished the circle of dirt and the hooded acolytes fanned out, creating a second circle around it.

"They're invoking something awful," Charlotte whispered, the world falling away. She didn't have to be familiar with the spell to know that much. The smell of sulfur and decay wafted through the night air, the energy in the air now whipping at them, tearing at the clothes and skin of everyone gathered. The voices of those chanting grew louder and frenzied as Charlotte, still nestled against Hazel, watched on in mesmerized terror.

Dirk Ashgarde's voice, muffled by the magic-fueled wind that whirled around them, yelled out ecstatically. "The revolution is coming! All the magic we have spent so long harnessing has not been for naught! Our subservient being, our conduit, is truly working at last! The labor of the last century is finally coming to fruition!"

Growing up a witch and a member of a Society designed to protect people from the occult and the insidious things that lurked under its umbrella, Charlotte Blythe's youth had a few rules.

One, you did not use magic for gain in a way that would be unfair to those that were not magically gifted; it was, indeed, a gift and had to be treated as such. Two, there always had to be an exchange, especially with alchemy and spells. You don't get something for nothing. The third and final rule: you do not do dumb shit with magic. No dark magic, no demon summonings, no necromancy, no murder with magic. In short, don't be a fucking idiot.

Whatever the fuck Dirk and his motley crowd had done that night seemed to certifiably fall under the "don't do dumb shit with magic" category.

The liquid in the bath began to bubble, a makeshift cauldron for the dark magic they were working. Their chants rose as the crowd began to join in, repeating the same phrase that she could not quite place. As their voices grew, the storm within Charlotte matched it, a whirling vortex of emotions and slumbering magic, threatening to overwhelm her.

"Babes, tell me you don't see what I see." The Hunter's voice was raspy. She said nothing, transfixed as the same horror-fueled fever dream played out in front of her.

The vile contents of the bathtub continued to roil as the surface began to stretch and change, becoming taut but flexible. Hazel let out an audible gasp as the liquid starlight began to rise from the tub, contorting to the curve of a skull, and soon, the vague shape of a male torso. Like a monster emerging from the dark depths, the shrouded figure rose until it was standing upright. Despite having no features, nothing to it besides its cloak of midnight and starlight, Charlotte swore it *looked* at her, stared directly into her soul. It called out to her, sung her name in an unspoken voice—

It lifted one leg from within the claw-foot tub, then the other, laughter and cheers sounding out through the room. Glee and wonder stretched Dirk Ashgarde's lips into a smile as he broke out in delighted applause. Everyone but Charlotte and Hazel were thrilled at the sight of this thing, of this monstrosity.

"What have you *done*?" Charlotte screamed, finally finding her voice. The happy noises died off, fading into confused low tones. Despite her throbbing head, she pushed off of Hazel and staggered forward, looking around, bewildered, at the gathered crowd. "What have you played with? This thing isn't right—can't you feel it?! You're all Society members, aren't you? You should know better." She turned to Dirk, voice cracking as she asked, "Why did you do this?"

The shrouded monster cocked its head, seeming to listen to her. Charlotte took another step forward, no plan for her safety, just anger. Hazel called for her to come back, but she ignored her. "Answer me, *Dick*."

The acolyte with his hood down looked to Dirk, who nodded. He stepped forward and scooped something from the tub behind the monster, which stood still, dripping liquid night. Charlotte raised her voice again, demanding to be heard.

Ashgarde scowled at her. "Stupid girl. You're just a child. You have no idea what it's like, forced to use our abilities for the good of those that treat us like garbage. For the untalented of the world. We are no longer the Society for Paranormal Secrecy. This is the Order of the New Dawn, all of us here, no longer just a supernatural-worshiping cult of ordinary, non-magical peasants. Well, look at us now as we enter a new age!"

As Dirk ranted, Charlotte's anger coiled in her chest like a viper waiting to strike. She stumbled toward him, planning to shove him, slap him, to hurt him *somehow*, when she stopped in her tracks.

The monster was changing. No, it wasn't that the monster was changing—the second skin it wore, the darkness from the tub, was beginning to peel away from its form. It fell away cleanly, dissolving as it hit the floor. Parts of a man became visible. Soft pale hands, black slacks, a hint of a silk vest. A hint of mussed auburn hair.

Soon, it fell away to reveal stormy gray eyes, a throat with an unforgettable slash, and a pair of lips that had whispered her name many times.

Chapter Twenty-Four

The world fell away as Charlotte stood rooted to the spot, the cheers and murmurs a distant din. Her eyes remained locked on Wade as the rest of the starlit darkness fell away from him.

He was so different from just a few short hours before, when she had whispered for him to stay safe. His clothes were changed from the evening wear she was so accustomed to seeing him in, yes, but it was more than that—he was more alive than she had ever seen him. Though he was still pale, his cheeks were tinged pink and his eyes sparkled with mischief, the corner of his mouth lifted in a smirk.

As Charlotte watched him, it was as if a spell had been cast on her, and she could see nothing but him. The remnants of noise disappeared as he approached her with a loping gait, his coat pushed back by his right hand in his trouser pocket, a confident saunter that seemed so at odds with his usual self. As he closed the space between them, she was sure her heart would burst.

"Charlotte." He rasped her name, sending tingles down her spine as he stopped mere inches from her. "I'm glad you get to be here for this."

He reached his left hand up and caressed her cheek, his fingertips gently stroking her cheek. His hand was warm for the first time, solid in a way it had never been before. She was dumbfounded as he grinned widely at her.

"How are you here?" she whispered, tears pricking at the corners of her eyes. "I don't get what's going on, what magic they used—"

"Hush. You don't need to know the how or the why, darling Charlotte. All that matters is that it is." Smiling still, he pulled his other hand free of his pocket, reaching for her gloved hand and bringing it to his lips. Goosebumps flared across her skin as she felt the warmth of his breath even through the silk.

Her head swam as though she were inebriated, her thoughts a broken collection of started questions that each trailed off as Wade pulled her close to him. She was dimly aware of Dirk contemplating them thoughtfully in the distance, whispering to the robed figure who'd performed the ritual that brought Wade back to life. He was alive, and here with her. *But how? Why?*

She frowned as he scooped her left hand and slid it onto his shoulder, gathering her right hand delicately into his left as he tugged her close.

"Why did they want you alive, Wade? Why did they do all of this just for you? Why are you acting so . . . so nonchalant?"

He didn't answer her. Instead, he hummed a tune as he swung her in a gentle waltz in the silent dark room. The people around them seemed to fade into the shadows as they danced. "I've wanted to hold you in my arms and dance with you from the moment I saw you, Charlotte."

Her heartbeat sped up once more as his eyes locked on hers, the spell capturing her again. He spun her across the ballroom, through the starlight that twinkled from the domed glass roof above, as though they had all the time in the world. There was no reservation in how he held her, their bodies pressed together as he brushed his lips against her ear. "Is this not what you've been longing for all these long weeks we've spent together, separated by the Veil?"

Every coherent thought left her as his lips trailed down her jaw, leaving a path of butterfly kisses down toward her clavicle. Her eyes fluttered shut as she melted in his arms, caught in pure, unadulterated bliss.

⟫⟩⟩ ⟨⟨⟨

He danced as though in a fog, in a daze. He tried to speak, to move, but it was as though he was locked away. He could see through his eyes, could feel the softness of Lottie's skin, hear the cadence of her breath. But he was not in control. As if a part of his soul didn't belong to him anymore. He tried to speak, to tell Lottie it wasn't safe for her.

He couldn't do anything. But he needed to try.

⤜⤜➤➤ ⫷⫷⫷

Wade swept her around the room, the pair in a world of their own. He didn't take his eyes off her. And for a few moments, she let herself buy into the lie. To ignore the obvious problems—the dark magic, the necromancy and deaths, the scheming.

Tears welling in the corners of her eyes, Charlotte pressed her cheek against his chest, holding him close as she listened to the steady beat of his heart. A heart she never thought she would get to hear. His arms curled around her, and despite the niggling feeling, she felt like she was *home.*

"Look at me," Wade commanded. Without thinking, she glanced up. His mouth was quirked in a smile, but the sparkle in his eyes was gone. She could have sworn they were worried. "See what I have done to be here, to be with you? Look at it all."

Blinking, Charlotte pushed back from him, but not out of his grasp. She glanced toward the bathtub he had been reborn from, to the group still gathered. Dirk was there, frowning at them with a puzzled expression, the hooded figures clustered together. He didn't seem happy now. What had been his plan? And what was going wrong now? She continued to scan the room, and her heart nearly stopped at the figure that stood a little ways behind Dirk.

It was the boy, and all at once she remembered why he seemed familiar. She had seen him in her dreams. His pale gold hair, his glittering brocade vest, and billowing sleeves. She had thought nothing of him; he was merely a figment of her imagination, she had thought. But he was there, and he, too, was real.

"Wade." Charlotte kept her voice low and calm, anger pulsing under the surface. "You need to tell me the truth about all of this. *Now*. I've seen that boy. Do you know him? What do you know?"

He didn't answer her. The magic of the moment—him warm and alive, them drifting in the silent darkness like a ship on a starless night—was beginning to wane, and her senses were returning. Charlotte pushed, asking again, "Wade, you have to tell me what's going on."

Wade scooped her close again, gently, as though she was very fragile. He cupped the nape of her neck, so tenderly, so softly. He was vibrating, his entire body a live current against hers.

"I wish," Wade whispered in her ear, "that all of this was real. But I am afraid it is not. I thought this would keep you safe, but I fear I cannot. You need to run, and you need to do it now. Please."

"What?" she gasped as he pulled back away from her.

His eyes, so terribly sad, remained locked on hers as he yelled out, "Hazel, grab her, now!"

The world came alive again as he said it, and it was a loud, angry, unkind place.

Chapter Twenty-Five

C harlotte was lost in the confusion. Not physically—Wade still gripped her upper arms as Hazel rushed forward and the rest of the room came to life. Everything and everyone had become unbearably loud all at once, but she couldn't focus on anything but Wade's face as it slowly shifted from the kind, gentle one she knew to a blank slate.

She stepped back half a step. Bile rose in her throat, sour and sweet all at once. Her legs began to shake, and the only thing keeping her upright was Wade.

"Please let me go," she whispered into the stranger's face. The beautiful face that looked so much like the man she was in love with, carved now, it seemed, of unfeeling marble. "You have to let me go, Wade."

"No," he rasped. Anger flitted across his face, dark and ugly, his mouth a twisted slash across his face, eyes deepening to dark gray once more. She could see the Wade she loved deep in there, fighting for control. Control that he was clearly losing. "Come with me."

"Let *go* of her, Wade," Hazel snarled. The crowd was pressing in now, yelling. As Hazel pulled her free, Charlotte caught sight of Dirk and the mysterious boy once more. Dirk was yelling at the acolyte who had performed the ritual earlier, his disfigured face twisted in concentration as he stared at Wade, a glint of silver in his hand. The blond boy, the one she had seen in her dreams, seemed almost . . . worried.

Why?

Her thoughts were interrupted as a flash of light blinded her. Fluorescent specks appeared before her eyes as she struggled to find the source of the commotion and light. Blinking furiously, she reached out a hand for where Hazel had been. As her eyes adjusted, she saw her friend in a heap on the floor, Wade standing over her.

"*Stop*! she screamed as he pulled a hand back, a glowing orb bouncing in his palm. Distracted, he glanced toward her. Hazel rolled out of the way, sweeping a leg out toward Wade. He caught sight of the Hunter, dodging out the way, but not fast enough. Her leg glanced off of his and he stumbled. Dirk cursed in the distance, urging Wade to stop them.

All at once, everything became messier. Hazel and Wade lunged for her at the same time, but Wade was faster. He encircled her, pulling her back against his chest, locking her tight against him as the robed strangers prowled, grasping at her, tugging and pulling the Hunter away. Charlotte screamed for her friend as they tore at the gown Hazel wore, attempting to pin her down.

"No you fucking *don't*," Hazel growled. She started slamming into them, unsheathing the blades from her thighs with impressive speed despite their numbers, lodging them into the chests of her assailants with a steady hand.

As she watched Hazel try and break through them, she realized that Wade had lifted her up. He still held her close, but he was walking backward, pulling her away from the fray.

"Wade, this isn't you—you have to let go of me," she pleaded, desperation saturating her words. He didn't answer her as he dragged her toward Dirk, further into the house. "I don't know what they've done to you, but you have to listen to me. Remember me? Your friend. Lottie. The girl you love? The one that picks on you and you secretly enjoy it. You gotta answer me, *please*."

As he continued to pull her along, heat began to build in her. She dug her fingertips into his arms as though she could rip his very skin off. Her whole body was heavy, ostensibly made of lead, her muscles tensed and quivering all at once. She focused on that feeling, of the sensation of falling even though she was held in place, as she reached deep inside herself. She concentrated on her jagged breathing, on evening it out. She had to be in control of herself to even have a chance against him.

"Wade," she said in a low, deathly quiet voice. "I'm going to ask you. One. Last. Time. *Let me go.*"

"Or what?" Dirk chuckled nearby. "You're going to go run to your grandmother and hope that doddy old fool will help you? Oh, we're so scared of the faltering Blythe family! We could slit your throat now and be done with your family line in an instant."

"Then do it, you massive pussy!" she snapped, unthinking, as red-hot anger pulsed through her.

"Vulgar, filthy girl," Dirk hissed. Wade's grip on her tightened, constricting her. She gasped for breath as she heard a rib crack.

"Good." Dirk was seething as he came into her line of sight, prowling around Wade whilst he held her captive. "Nasty little bitch that you are. Couldn't have been more like your poor dead mother, could you? There was a good girl if I ever saw one. She obeyed and minded her own business. Too bad she's dead and we're left with her failure of a daughter."

She clawed Wade's arm harder; she knew she must have been bruising him beneath the fabric. She didn't care. Her control was slipping as Dirk continued to hammer at her, hitting her deepest insecurities. She could tell from the slimy smirk that crept across his face that he knew he had met his mark.

"Oh, does that upset the little princess?" He leaned close to her face. The broken capillaries of his nose were distracting as he leered at her. "Don't like hearing how you're garbage, masquerading as being better than others? Prancing around with your camera, exposing our secrets from that high horse of yours, like you have any clue how the world works. This is why you and your kind will be left behind after tonight, for Miss Blythe, you are absolutely worthless. Perhaps it's best your parents died before they could see just how much of a waste you've become."

"At least I'm not a fucking monster." She spat at the man, hitting him in the face. His eye twitched. Dirk wiped it away, letting out a low, menacing laugh.

"Oh, but how are you not? Your parents are dead, and you let them die. You let your poor friend here sacrifice himself tonight because he thought it would keep you safe. Your other friend is about to learn what scum Hunters get when they get in the way. So, my dear, I would say you're a bigger monster than I, who only seeks the betterment of society and our people."

Charlotte fell silent, ribs aching as Wade continued to restrain her. The smirk returned to Dirk's face. "That is exactly what I thought."

"I think that's enough, Ashgarde. The girl has nothing to do with what you're after, and neither does her friend. Let them go now, and leave them be. They have nothing to do with what you're trying to accomplish."

Charlotte twisted in Wade's death grip, trying to spot the owner of the new voice, soft and calm, but with an undercurrent of power to it. Wade's body turned as if in response to the voice and her eyes fell on the strange boy, who seemed to command not only Wade's attention but also that of Dirk and the remaining robed figures.

He looked at her—or did he look at Wade?—with sad eyes, an apologetic tilt to his head. "You can see she'll be of no harm. She's just a girl." He repeated it, his eyes snapping to Dirk, who choked on his words in his fluster.

"Atticus, surely you cannot truly mean to suggest that. Look at the trouble she has caused, taking away the soul jar, and trying to deceive and mock us! Her mere internet video channel alone has done sufficient damage, not to mention that she led this foul Hunter to us—"

"I said what I said." He was firm, quietly confident. "We've got everything you wanted here. I would recommend pulling your people out before it gets any rowdier. Leave the mortal girls be, and let's go."

Dirk scrunched his face, the red of the capillaries in his nose deepening as his face slowly transformed into a motley shade of purple. His mouth twisted into a sneer.

"You aren't the one that calls the shots here, demon, and it's best you remember that. You made a pact with *us* and are in servitude to the Order. It would be a shame if you were banished now that Mister van Baird is back in our grasp."

Charlotte slumped against Wade, dropping her arms. A fucking *demon*? Not only had these demented idiots performed necromancy, along with whatever other utter nonsense they had done, but they made a fucking contract with a demon? A huge Society no-no—a massive transgression.

Her blood ran cold as she gazed at Atticus. He was young, quiet, unassuming. There was almost a sweetness, a naivety to him. That was probably why he hadn't seemed like anything more in those twilight hours she had seen him with Wade, and why she'd brushed him off—a byproduct of exhaustion and sleep. He hadn't felt *wrong* like so much other dark magic did.

It was all beginning to make terrible, dreadful sense to her.

The demon, Atticus, was how they were managing so many things. It was his dark, untraceable magic that had been present when she found Wade—maybe even when her parents died. The connections, the way these people had managed to remain so distant and unnoticed despite getting their sticky little hands everywhere . . . it was all making sense.

She and Hazel had to get out of there, and fast.

Charlotte glanced around the room covertly, trying to catch sight of the Hunter. She had disappeared from the crowd of hooded figures. Thankfully, it seemed they were hunting for her amongst the crowd of partygoers. It then occurred to Charlotte that many of these masked guests were not only Society members—they would be cult members, much like Dirk. People that she had grown up knowing, betraying everything she knew to be true.

Her stomach roiled.

Dirk continued blustering as she zoned out, and she snapped back to hear him say, ". . . I don't care how they are disposed of. Get rid of them now. The other one has slipped off, but I'm sure you can catch her. Atticus, seal the doors off. Wade. Get rid of Miss Blythe for us."

Without warning, Wade's arms tightened around her chest. Well, *one* arm did; the other found its way to her throat, swift and unflinching as it snaked around her esophagus. Lottie let out a gasp as his forearm crushed against her windpipe. Panicking, she reached up her arms, grasping desperately at Wade, clawing to get him off of her. She wheezed, spots dancing across her vision as she swayed where he held her. He was going to kill her if she didn't think of *something*.

She had to use her magic. It was her only chance. But what if it failed her?

Her head lolled against Wade as he pressed harder. Dirk's face swam in front of her as he bent close to her choking face.

"I'll be sure to console your grandmother, just for you, little Lottie."

⋙⋘

What was he doing? Why couldn't he let go of her? He didn't want to be doing this. His body wasn't his own. He tried to fight it, but it was like trying to swim against rapids. He was floundering, unable to gain purchase.

He shouldn't have gone back to Atticus. He should have realized he would suffocate in the darkness. He had done the opposite of what he wanted—instead of saving Lottie, he had doomed her.

All of it was his own fault, once again.

⋙⋘

Death was meant to be quiet, soothing. For most people, they would go in their sleep, surrounded by loved ones—and hopefully with an IV in their arm pumping them full of sweet, sweet drugs.

In Charlotte's field, you were pretty likely to die caught up in something supernatural. Something heroic, hopefully. Or trapped in something super fucked up, like her parents had been.

She had never thought she would die at the hands of someone as virtuous as Wade.

Death was also loud and messy, it turned out. She could feel herself slipping. Splotches of gray between the flashing of white and color as her vision began to distort, her limbs turning from jelly to nothing at all. Her body was aflame but also numb as his arm continued to press on her throat, tighter, harder. It was worse than the corpse that had tried to drown her—at least then only her lungs had been on fire. Now everything burned like hot steel.

*Maybe I should just accept i*t, she thought as her body fell limp. *It has to be close to the end, surely.*

She wondered if she would see her parents on the other side of the Veil. She could at least finally apologize to them. Because while she might have started to accept that she hadn't killed them—that it hadn't been her fault, despite efforts to pin it on her—she was still sorry she wasn't with them when it happened. Sorry for hiding away, like the pathetic child she was.

Then the burning began to lessen. She shuddered, drawing a full breath. Her entire body was wracked with pins and needles, but the pressure was gone. His arms were still around her but they were loosened, shaking, as though he was struggling. Her Wade was in there somewhere, deep down. He was fighting whatever this was.

Charlotte's arms were still heavy. She wracked her brain, fighting against the discomfort that lanced her skull. He could lose control again at any moment. With great difficulty, she lolled her head to glance at her purse, still hooked over her body. She wouldn't be able to reach anything in there to ward him off; it was going to have to be pure Charlotte to get out of this. She closed her eyes and reached down deep.

There it was. A kernel, not more than a flicker, really. Like a spark of flame on kindling, and yet her power was still inside her, hiding. She coaxed it out, mentally calling out for it. *There*. It sang back to her, an echo of herself.

She lunged for it, seizing it in her grip.

Her magic pulsed like a weakened heartbeat. She soothed it, tugging its edges gently as she persuaded it to embrace her again. They'd been able to work together recently—surely they could do it again. *Please help me*, she pleaded it. *Just get us out of here*. It sang again and this time, when she sang back, it truly answered.

In an instant, she found herself flung from Wade's arms onto the floor. Her magic had exploded—wild, erratic, *chaotic*. She'd had no control over how it manifested. Too tired, too long out of practice. It had worked, though, and that was all that mattered.

Coughing, Charlotte rolled away from where she was thrown on instinct, desperate to create space between them. She gasped for air between coughs, the spots and dancing lights clouding her sight. The flesh of her thigh met the parquet floor, a splash of cold against her skin. Her dress had been ripped at some point, exposing her legs beneath. She braced herself before shoving off the floor, stumbling to unsteady feet.

Pain threaded through her body, her veins a hot wire of electricity. But she was upright. Her vision was beginning to clear and she could see where she had sent Wade flying backward, crumpled in a heap on the floor. A pang shot through her heart at the sight of him, like a puppet that had been tossed to the side. She made as if to step toward him when she caught sight of Dirk Ashgarde in the corner of her eye, racing toward her, his arms outstretched to seize her. Despite the pressing pain in her entire body, she turned on her heel and raced in the opposite direction, screaming out for Hazel as she ran.

"Grab the girl!" Dirk snarled from somewhere behind her. "Look at that magic. It subdued the lich! We can use that. Move, you oafs, and grab her *now!*"

The room swam before her eyes as she pumped her legs, rushing to where she thought the entrance was. She shrieked as someone grabbed her arm, and on instinct, she stretched her free arm to slam them back with her power only to hear, "Babes, it's me, *don't you fucking dare!* I've got you. We're getting out of here."

They ran together through the confusion and chaos, now two when before they were three.

CHAPTER TWENTY-SIX

"What the *fuck*."

Charlotte sprawled out on the floor runner in the foyer. She had fallen in a heap as Hazel dragged her inside the safe confines of Winterbourne. Edith had yet to return, and the sight of a bruised and violently shaking Charlotte had sent the help into panic mode. Her entire being had given out—burnt out from magic, burnt out from stress. Burnt out from the sheer trauma.

She let out a sob as she curled up in the fetal position, wrapping her arms around herself, trying to hold in the pain. Her heart had been shattered into a million pieces once again, and this time she wasn't sure she was going to be able to put it back together.

⋙ ⋘

"You have to eat something, babes. We can't work out what's going on if you won't take care of yourself."

No. She couldn't. She wouldn't. Nothing mattered anymore. Surely they had to know that. So why were they bothering her?

Hazel pushed the plate at her again. "It's been three days. You haven't eaten yet. Eat the goddamn sandwich or I'll shove it down your throat myself! And when you're done moping about, you can come find me, and we can start to work out how to save Wade. Or have you given up on him as much as yourself?"

She didn't have an answer for that.

⤜⤜ ⤛⤛

Lottie.

I know this email has come too late. I'm sorry. I couldn't do anything about it. They were already cottoning on to me before the ritual. The last one I sent you was already so risky. I can't stress this enough— I'm sorry, so very sorry.

Things are messy here. Wade hasn't been as compliant as they wanted, as they expected. The demon, Atticus, told them all before that he'd come willingly at last. I don't think that's true, honestly. There are moments where he says your name, you know. And you just know he's lurking in there, under the spells they have.

They've turned him into a lich. He was the most powerful warlock that the Society had seen in centuries, Lottie. They wanted that power as a weapon. And now they have it. There's nothing I can do from here. That demon has control over Wade, and the Order, over him.

I know you can save him, save us.

I'm sorry, too, that I didn't tell you it was me sooner. This was the only way I've been able to help keep you safe these last years. Between what happened with our parents, and the way you became after, and all this shit Pop has been involved in with this cult—well, I'm just making excuses, really. I care about you, and want you to be safe. No matter what. I'm sorry they swept me up in there with them. I'm not as strong as you.

Or as strong as them. They have plans now—plans to eradicate the Society. To get rid of those that don't join them, including you and your grandmother. This is the last time I'll be able to reach you, I think. I hope I've made it count.

Be careful. Be safe.

I loved you.

Bradley

⤙⤙⤙ ⤚⤚⤚

Edith and Hazel read the email at the same time, their lips moving silently as they mouthed Bradley's words. In a weird way, it made sense to her that it was her ex-sort-of-boyfriend who'd been feeding her information. Had been keeping an eye out for her. It also made sense that he had been able to message her about things before, it seemed, they happened.

Edith had returned from a meeting earlier that day. Grandmother had been tight-lipped to Charlotte about the one she attended the night of the masquerade. She'd only overheard one, brief comment made in hushed tones to Jacob and Hazel about spineless weasels and traitors in their midst. The Order had already fully instilled itself, it seemed. Hazel had gone with Edith, protection in case Dirk pulled anything again. There had been one message given: get on board, or get eliminated. Bradley's email made a lot of sense, then. The others suspected that they weren't actually going to be given a choice to go with the flow—not after Dirk had decided he wanted Lottie's power.

She hadn't felt the tendrils of her power again since. Much like after the massacre at her debut, the spark had puffed out, like a candle in a storm. Also like then, she hadn't tried to call it back out. Charlotte was fine if she never had magic again. All it did was cause her pain.

⤙⤙⤙ ⤚⤚⤚

They stopped talking to her after two weeks. Maybe they had sooner; she hadn't really been paying attention. It was too hard to think, too hard to exist. *They were trying to fix things*, she thought. Why wasn't she? Why had she given up so soon?

She slept a lot, drifting off to the memories she had of Wade. Memories that were tainted now by the truth.

He'd gone with bad people—in the present, and in the past.

~~>>> <<<~~

He needs your help. We all do. Please.

No one is strong enough against him, besides you. I saw the magic you have. They're killing people. You need to stop them.

Bradley

CHAPTER TWENTY-SEVEN

He had already lost track of time in the hellish imprisonment of his own mind. He had been in the dark for countless hours—or was it days? Nothing made sense to him. He pushed tentatively against it at times, but they had a tighter hold of him now. They were running him. Wade was, for all intents and purposes, trapped in the phylactery once more.

The darkness was numbing after a time, and he found himself floating in the pool of night, utterly alone. His heart ached, wondering over and over how Lottie was. He swelled with shame at the memory of his arms wrapped around her, not intimately, but to hurt her. His arms, but not his intentions. He had harmed her.

He wished he could cease to exist.

⟫⟫ ⟪⟪

Wade was catapulted from the darkness.

He hadn't realized he still existed when it happened. It had been a strange, weightless feeling—perhaps he had been sleeping? It felt like how he had always imagined death was supposed to feel.

He blinked against the brightness, nausea rolling through him as he regained control of his senses for the first time in what seemed like forever. He steadied himself, regaining his sea legs, in a way. When the noise in his head and the assault on his senses began to quiet, he finally looked around.

He was in a strange place. Above him was a large vaulted ceiling, arched stained glass windows letting in weak light. Was it the sun or the moon? He felt as though he couldn't tell anymore.

Unused to moving himself, he lolled his head. The silhouettes of people filled his vision, milling about. He made to raise a hand and it jerked behind him awkwardly.

"You're tied up," a voice he didn't recognize whispered nearby.

Male—who?

"They wouldn't drop control of you any other way. The necromancer controlling you does it after he puts you to sleep usually so he can rest, but I woke you up. No, don't react to me, Jesus! Keep calm."

Wade bit back his words. His mouth felt vile, coated and heavy, as though he had consumed laudanum. Perhaps he had. It wasn't as if he would know. Perhaps the man that had spoken to him would. He made to open his mouth and was cut short once more.

"I said don't react to me, or they'll notice. Now, nod if you understand."

A flicker of annoyance shot through Wade, but he tilted his chin slightly.

"Alright, good. I'm trying to help you here. I know it might not look it, but I'm doing my best. Pops would kill me in an instant if he thought I was screwing his plans up."

The voice sighed. They bent over Wade, and he realized he was sitting in a chair. His entire body ached. What had they been doing to him?

"I've been trying to tell Charlotte what's going on, but I can't send many emails without being caught. Now they have one of their deranged cultists following me about like a simpering fool. It's not easy trying to do the right thing, so don't make it any harder, please."

He stopped speaking as one of the other robed figures shuffled past. What was going on? Wade shut his eyes and let his head roll forward, pretending to be asleep. He strained his ears, listening out. Where were they? And what were they doing?

"This was a Cathedral in South End," the man muttered, *"but Pops and the Order used Atticus's weird little shadow underlings and killed off the congregation. The Cardinal and Reverend had no chance to set their protocols up—Pops kinda used you against them. I'm sorry."*

Wade winced. *They had used him for murder. Of course they had—just like before, when they first tried to use fear and the death of his family to keep him in line. When they had tried to get him to help them "change the world." Now, with the cursed phylactery, they could just force him. And in a holy place, no less. Despite being a man of the occult, Wade had no doubts that the Universe provided higher powers, and that they would be judging him.*

"I'm sorry. I thought you'd rather know what's going on, 'cause you need to try fighting it. I know that won't be easy. But . . . it'll make it easier for Charlotte to come and end this. Pops is scared of her. Her mother and grandmother are wicked talented, and much better at magic and understanding their power than Pops. He kinda wields it like a kid learning to write, you know? Rudimentary. They get it, though, and he thinks that she'll come end you just to let you rest."

Lottie. *His darling Lottie. Wade fought the urge to ask him how she was, what had happened to her. He took deep, steady breaths to feign sleep. The shuffling of robes was now accompanied by frantic, excited whispers.*

"Look, I can't hang around here much longer. They're using this holy place to summon more demons for an army. The next stage is to coerce Society families to join the Order, or they perish. Pops plans to wipe out entire family lines if he has to, including the Blythes. He's already sent them missives to meet him. If they agree to join . . ." The voice gulped. *"Grandpa plans to . . . it's gross. She'll be used to make strong babies, let's put it that way. One way or another. Jesus fuck, dude, you gotta keep it together, I can see you shaking,"* he hissed at Wade. *He sighed, waiting for a few robed figures to shuffle past.*

"We're going to stop that all happening, dude. I promise. I don't particularly want to live in a world where either I'm a monster or living in fear of the monsters getting me. I'd kill you myself right now, but I know I can't get your stupid hairpin.

Just . . . I'm sorry. I just wanted you to know what's going on. To tell you it isn't your fault, and I don't blame you for what you did. You thought it'd keep her safe. I know I've messed up trying to keep her safe, too."

Wade's heart hammered in his chest, in his body. His body. What had been traded for him to have it again, just to be used for evil? He rued the day he met Atticus, and yet, if he had not, he would not know Lottie. The curse of existence and its truths was that there was always a price to pay for rewards.

"Tell me your name at least, please," Wade murmured, keeping his lips from moving as much as he could. "I would like to know who is trying to keep my Lottie safe whilst I have been a monster."

He felt the man stiffen by him. "Bradley Ashgarde," the voice muttered. "Dirk is my grandpa."

Wade felt Bradley make to leave, but then heard the shuffle of his robes as they slid back toward them. There was a tug at his hands, then pins and needles.

"I loosened it a bit. Not enough for them to notice, but I thought you should at least get to have feeling. They're treating you like a machine, a monster. Not a person. It isn't much, but it's my best right now."

And with that, Bradley Ashgarde, the grandson of his enemy turned into a most unlikely ally, swept away, leaving Wade alone with his thoughts.

***

He awoke to the harsh, acrid scent of charcoal and sulfur. Wade stirred, head fuzzy, his eyes burning against the smoke. He was momentarily dazed, unable to gain his bearings.

He became dimly aware of the sounds of screams and of delighted, deranged cackles. He blinked against the smoke, its dark haze blotting out his vision. Then he saw what was making the putrid smell.

A twisted, smoldering pile of people. Their bodies were tangled together, charring before his very eyes. With a yelp, Wade made to spring forward, but he found *himself met with resistance. Thick, heavy metal chains encircled his wrists and ankles.*

"Unhand me! We must save these people!" he called out, glancing wildly about, looking for anyone. Was he, too, doomed to burn along with these people? "Please, won't someone answer me?"

"Save them!" came a guffaw. "You're the one that burned them, boy."

An icy shiver shot down his spine as the owner of the voice came into view. Ashgarde. Wade struggled to keep his face from contorting in rage. Dirk looked appreciatively at the burning bodies.

"The Lynalls wouldn't be persuaded. We had no choice but to send a message to other families. This insubordination cannot be tolerated. We have an empire to build, and we can't have people getting in the way of that."

"What did you make me do?" Wade gasped in horror. As he looked at the pile once more, his stomach heaved. Two adults, scantly older than Lottie, and three smaller child-sized bodies were identifiable amongst the blackened flesh. He fell to his knees, heaving bile as he shook from the sobs wrenching from his body.

Dirk stared at him with disdain. "Pathetic. The most powerful warlock in existence, and you act like a sniveling child."

"They're people, and you have murdered them!" Wade gasped between heaves.

"They were given a choice, and they chose poorly. That is on them and no one else. Except," Dirk chuckled, "you, that is. I mean, they did die at your hand, after all."

Wade looked up again, surveying the carnage in front of them. They were in a room, the entirety of which was scorched, the aftermath of a raging house fire. It was recognizable, but only in the way after a fire that one can make out the distorted shapes of what things had been. A sofa, a bookcase. The charred remains of a teddy bear, perhaps. In a room of death and decay, only he remained unscathed.

"I have done this," he echoed weakly. Dirk smiled.

"Yes. See the power you have. See what you could accomplish. And this was with your chains! Pity we had to resort to such old, tacky magic and seal off your power, but we can't afford to just unleash you." Dirk scowled. "Not after the other day."

A dull, throbbing memory came back to Wade. After Bradley had left, and his stupor had worn off. Yes, that was right. He had broken free of his rope confines in the chair. He had almost made it out. He hadn't wanted to hurt anyone, but they had encircled him . . .

"I can see from the look on your face that you remember what you did," Dirk said severely. "Lost your temper, didn't you? Took out seven of our own and almost took your keeper with you. This is why you're chained now. It's your own fault."

"I am neither an animal nor an object," Wade said through gritted teeth. "And certainly not for you to control. I demand you release me."

Dirk tutted. "Foolish boy. You put yourself in this predicament. Imagine—if you hadn't asked for the power to save that one stupid little girl, you wouldn't be here now. Pathetic."

"Why don't you just use Atticus?" Wade snapped. "My power is his power, after all. Why can't you just get him to plow through the world and conquer it for you?"

Dirk fell silent for a beat before turning back to the voices Wade had heard earlier, setting out orders. "We've made him see. Subdue him again. Maybe one day he'll learn what is best for him and cooperate, but today is not that day."

"Atticus won't do it," Wade realized aloud. "You can't get him to loan you his power, can you?"

"Shut up!" Dirk snarled. He drew back a hand and slapped Wade soundly across the face. "The demon is fickle, yes. But we don't need him to do that if we can control you, do we? I can't wait to see your face after you wipe out that stupid little Blythe bitch. That will teach you to be quiet."

Wade's head snapped up. "What do you mean? No, you cannot intend to harm Lottie—"

And with that, Wade's head grew heavy as he once again faded into the lull of the darkness, his final thoughts a panicked wish for someone, anyone, to save Lottie from a fate most cruel.

For how could he exist, in any form, if he were to be the one to make her suffer?

Chapter Twenty-Eight

C harlotte was on her third drink of the day when Hazel finally snapped. Storming into her room, the Hunter slammed the door open with enough force that the door handle lodged itself in the wall. Charlotte didn't look up from the scotch she was nursing, wrapped up in a musty blanket in what was essentially a nest on her bed. No one had been in to clean for weeks. She had barely even gotten off the bed to do anything but pour the next drink. It had been so long since she showered that her hair had simply stopped getting greasy—it was lank, yes, and it hung limply around her face, but it physically could not get any oilier.

"This is fucking disgusting, babes. It's not even ten in the morning yet." Hazel stopped a foot into the doorway. "Jesus *Christ*, what is that smell? Oh, God, it's you, isn't it? When the fuck did you last get in the shower? It's bad enough you haven't been eating, I didn't realize you were this rank, too."

"I've used talcum powder," Charlotte replied stiffly.

"That is *very* much not the same, and you know it."

She groaned and slammed back her drink. "Can you just fuck off, Hazel? I don't need your condescending shit right now."

"No, you need a shower, that's what you need."

Charlotte tossed the glass onto the end of the bed, pulling the mucid rugs up around her, cocooning herself once more. She couldn't smell anything—what was Hazel even on about?

"I'm going to sleep now, bye." She yanked the blankets tight against her and rolled onto her side, buried somewhere on the bed. She was sure the other girl would slam the door shut behind her, just like every other time she had tried to get Charlotte's attention.

"Oh no, you don't."

Charlotte squealed as the rugs were yanked from her body, tearing the protective layers away. She was being stripped naked, at least mentally, as Hazel discarded each blanket, layer by layer.

"Leave me *alone*. Don't you have something constructive to do, or are you just going to be an annoying pain in my ass forever?"

"The second, especially if you don't stop being a dumb bitch!"

The two squabbled as Hazel roughly pawed at Charlotte's nest, tearing it down, exposing her to the world. She screamed as Hazel reached the final frontier—a pastel-blue blanket that was now a peculiar shade of green. With a revolted groan, she tore the blanket from around Charlotte. She was still in her mother's old dress, stains visible around the armpits and chest.

"This is unacceptable," Hazel hissed. Leaping onto the bed, Hazel snatched at Charlotte as the other tried to grapple away. The two girls wrestled momentarily, but Hazel won. She twisted the gangly, awkward Charlotte and flipped her over her shoulder. Screaming like a banshee, Charlotte swung her limbs with surprising force. Hazel pinched the back of Charlotte's thigh, yelling back at her to calm the hell down.

They struggled through the doorway to the bathroom down the hall. One of the maids who happened to be changing the sheets in Edith's room popped her head out into the hallway at the sounds of their scuffle. The two of them crashed through the bathroom, knocking various toiletries off the bathroom counter. Charlotte managed to knock Hazel's glasses off and they fell against the wall, bashing against it with a deafening thud. She gasped in pain as Hazel grunted, stumbling against the weight of Charlotte on her shoulder.

"Sorry, babes, but this needs to be done." With a groan, Hazel flipped Charlotte into the tub onto her back. Slipping against the ceramic, Charlotte flung her hands out, seeking purchase as Hazel climbed in, holding the other girl under her.

Hazel had more energy and muscle, leaving Charlotte fatigued fast, her efforts to slide out futile.

"Get *off* of me, Hazel!"

"Nah, don't think I will." Hazel straddled her and snatched for something on the edge of the tub. Both girls still fully dressed, Hazel began squirting the contents of a bottle all over Charlotte, also covering herself in the process. The scent of flowers filled the air as Charlotte's artisanal body wash was poured over them.

She let out a shriek. "What the fuck do you think you're doing?!"

Hazel dropped the bottle, reaching up to yank down the detachable showerhead. She looked Charlotte in the eye as she said, "Doing the bare minimum because apparently, you're too useless to care about yourself." Then she turned the cold tap on.

Charlotte gasped as a stream of freezing water slammed against her, the pressure like a thousand icy pinpricks all over her body. If she hadn't been awake before, she definitely was as Hazel moved the stream over her, her free hand massaging body wash into Charlotte's hair. Flailing her hands, Lottie tried to smack the showerhead away, blinking against the water and the soap running in her eyes.

"I'm clean, *I'm clean*," she wailed.

"You're not clean, you liar! You're filthy, and I'm sick of you sitting in your room, crying like some sort of broken thing and not letting us even try to help you. You're better than this, babes, and I refuse to let you do this any longer!"

Hazel was yelling by the end of her rant, both girls gasping from exertion as they wrestled in the tub. Hazel's knees slipped and she tumbled onto Charlotte, the showerhead dropping from her hand. It began to dance around like a wild serpent, soaking the bathroom as they both yelped and struggled to get ahold of it.

Both girls were well and truly drenched by the time Hazel managed to stop the water flow. They lay in the tub, curled up beside one another, panting. They stayed like that for several minutes before Hazel broke the silence.

"I shouldn't have been such a bitch and thrown you in the bath like that. I mean, you're really gross and need, like, a proper scrub. But it wasn't cool of me. I'm sorry, babes. It wasn't cool."

Charlotte sighed, gazing up at the ceiling above. The exhaust hadn't been turned on, and the shower had sprayed all over the ceiling. Fat droplets were pooling, smacking her on the nose as they landed.

"No, you were trying to help. I know I'm . . . I'm not coping. And I haven't let you or Grandmother help me. You were frustrated. I get it. I am, too. I've sucked. It's just—everything is wrong now. And I can't fix it."

Her voice quavered as she spoke, a sob catching in her throat as she finally admitted aloud what she hadn't been able to say to herself. Everything had gone terribly wrong, and there wasn't anything she could do about it.

"Aww, no, babes, don't cry," Hazel soothed her as she wrapped her arms around her friend, pulling her close into an embrace as they sprawled awkwardly in the bath. The dam broke, and the tears Charlotte had been numbing with alcohol finally began to flow freely. She convulsed with the force of them as they racked her body.

"I couldn't save him. I lost him, and they're doing bad things to him, and I'm useless."

"Oh, babes, you're not useless."

Charlotte's sobs came out harder, stuttering over her words as she struggled to speak between the cries. "I am. I let him down. He loves me, and I let them hurt him. It's all my fault. It's always my fault people get hurt. I can't do anything right. I'm so, so sorry. I just want my heart to stop hurting. Please make it stop, Hazel."

Hazel hushed her, stroking Charlotte's greasy, lotion-filled hair and reassuring her. "We *will* save him, and take out the pieces of shit that have done that to him,

I swear it," she whispered in her ear fiercely. "They're going to suffer for every second they've hurt you and that weird ghost boy, I promise you."

They held each other tight, two unlikely friends united again. As she cried, she released the pain she had thought she had to hold in alone.

She loved Wade, and it was up to her to make sure he wasn't suffering. No matter what, she had to make sure that he couldn't be in pain any longer. Even if she had to crush her own heart to do so. *I am going to find a way*, she told herself. *No matter what the consequences are.*

⫸ ⫷

Charlotte pored over the tomes that lay spread out in front of her. Several missives sat crumpled up between the various books, tossed there as soon as they were glanced at. Dirk's messages were getting more frequent, more aggressive. *Good*, she'd told Edith and Hazel. *He's anxious. It means they probably can't control Wade as well as they thought.* Hazel agreed—now they just had to come up with a plan.

Unfortunately, so far they had squat.

Specter jumped up onto the dining room table, carefully stepping between the stacks of books haphazardly strewn about as he mewled and sidled up to Charlotte. Without taking her eyes off the page, she reached a hand over and began scratching behind his ear. In the weeks she had remained essentially catatonic, he had spent his time at her grandmother's side. The older woman had told her that he probably felt her broken heart and couldn't handle it.

"I wish you could talk," she murmured to Specter as her eyes continued to scan the pages of a grimoire. "Then you might be able to read some of these with me and we could get through these faster."

Specter yawned, rubbing up against her. With a sigh she leaned back, dragging her eyes away. She had been there for hours that day already before the sun had even risen. The coffee pot sat beside her, already empty. She wondered when the others would finally turn up. Hazel and her grandmother had been going over whatever book or reference they could find on liches and necromancy the last few days, as well as demon contracts. They'd also found a bunch of information on spiritualism in the Victorian era. Charlotte briefly recalled Wade talking about some of the less savory things he had seen and heard people do during his youth when they had disposed of the corpse.

"Perhaps it's time to get ready for the day," she told Specter as he nuzzled up against her. "I can't keep reading with my brain going to mush. I won't be useful to anyone like this."

⟫⟫ ⟪⟪

Charlotte heard Hazel call out a lazy "good morning" to her from the bathroom as she pushed the door to her room open. She hollered one back, shutting the door behind her with a gentle click. The last few days, she had slowly gotten into some better habits. Her curtains and windows were open, and a chill breeze that reminded her of Wade's touch wafted through the air. The scents of autumn were beginning to give way to winter, the rain drops beginning to get heavier and more slush-like. She had also made her own bed that morning when she had gotten up, and the room was absent of any of her usual vices.

Small steps.

Wandering over to her wardrobe, her thoughts were lost on Wade, on how it had felt to have him hold her on Samhain. How he had looked at her. She shivered, a cardigan in hand as she rifled through her clothing. She had longed to be able to feel him, to feel his arms around her . . . but that wasn't a price she had ever wanted him to pay. And yet he had. He had paid high prices many times, it seemed.

Taking her clothes over to the bed, she dumped them in a pile and sighed. Wade. *Stupid, sweet, naive Wade.* Her gaze roamed and she caught sight of the tulip he had given her in the atrium. When she'd first begun to open up to him. Her throat bobbed as she reached for it, delicately grasping it between her fingers, twisting it. It was flatter now, more battered as it pressed itself, infused with the magic that roamed Winterbourne and the wards that protected it. But it was still beautiful all the same despite its rough edges, despite not looking the way it used to. *Kinda like Wade.*

He'd made so many stupid choices, it seemed, and she couldn't make them add up with the kind soul she knew. The reveal that he had made a contract with a demon, the very same that the Order and Dirk had been involved with—how and why had he done such a thing? She couldn't even ask him, for she was sure there was a *reason* for it.

She froze. She might not have been able to ask Wade about it, but there was someone she could try asking. Turning on her heel, Charlotte bolted from her room, calling for her grandmother and Hazel at the top of her lungs.

CHAPTER TWENTY-NINE

"**T**his kinda seems like another bad idea, babes."

Charlotte sighed as Edith and Hazel shared worried glances, her grandmother's words laced with anxiety. They had gathered in the kitchen, talking out her plan over a pot of peppermint tea. It was still early, scant rays of sunlight making their way through the smaller windows of the kitchen.

"I don't see any better ideas," Charlotte persisted. "You've seen me reading from dawn till dusk. Every possible idea I've had involves dark magic with potentially fatal consequences. Short of marching up to wherever they're keeping him and politely asking for them to give Wade back, I have no other plans. And I'm sure they'd be *super* amenable to that."

"She's really grumpy when pumped with caffeine, isn't she?" Hazel murmured, shooting Edith a glance.

She glared as her grandmother whispered back, "Why do you think we're drinking tea instead?"

"I am not *grumpy*, I am just a little . . . frustrated." She inhaled deeply. She had to get herself under control. "Look, there is a risk to it. Sure. But life is a risk. Everything we've done since finding Wade and discovering literally everything we know is a goddamn lie has been a risk, but risk comes with reward! I think we could pull this off." Charlotte gave them a pleading look.

Hazel glanced between them. "Ugh, she has a point," she conceded, her shoulders slumping. "It irks me to rely on the same dirty tactics as them, though. Plus, you know, the potential ramifications or whatever."

Sipping her tea, Edith surveyed each girl slowly, her wise, gentle gaze taking them in fully. There was something in the way her grandmother observed her that gave Charlotte chills. After several tense moments, Edith finally spoke.

"Charlotte is the official head of the family. It is not my place to tell her what to do. If this is what she sees a fit act of service to save our family, then it is my job to facilitate." She placed her teacup on the table. "Tell me what you need me to do, my lovey."

Charlotte drew in a deep breath. "I guess we have to go summon a demon."

⁓⋙ ⋘⁓

As with most things, it turned out that Charlotte had no idea what she was actually doing.

She sat at her computer, a hefty ritual book her grandmother had dug up beside her. Despite feeling like she was in some cheesy *B-Grade* movie, using the internet to research something that a viewer would find ridiculous, she wasn't actually sure where to look for information. She figured using her browser to search "how to summon a specific demon" was as good a starting point as any, really.

"It's all pagan rituals and cleansing," she groaned to Hazel, who was poised nearby with pen and paper, ready to make notes. Edith had taken the servants to survey and reinforce the wards on Winterbourne. They figured they would have to find a spot that was well enough enforced to drop the wards to try and summon within. They didn't want to risk the demon, Atticus, being able to break through; they had to find a way to contain him first, lest he destroy their barriers completely or help the Order work out how to. As much as Dirk would never admit it, Edith was a superior witch, and her magic was uncontested in terms of skill. Charlotte had tried to break the wards once to sneak out to a party as a preteen and learned the hard way.

"I heard that if you have the demon's real name you just, like, ask it to pop up," Hazel suggested, making a popping noise with her mouth. Charlotte glared at her.

"Yeah, let me go ask Dirk. I'll give him a quick call now, shall I? 'Hello, Mr. Ashgarde? May I have the real name of your demon? Thanks, man!' Maybe I'll ask if he wants to pop over for a cup of coffee with us and a donut while I'm at it."

"You're a bitch sometimes, babes."

"Not like you aren't one, either."

Hazel grinned, spinning the pen in her hand. "You could email his grandson and ask. I bet he'd know and spill it to you."

"I thought about that." Charlotte grimaced. "I don't exactly want Bradley being potentially murdered, though, for helping me. I don't think it's a good idea. Plus, if we asked and someone saw, it would definitely tip them off. We can't even leave here without fear of them snatching us. Grandmother says they've definitely got a bunch of their creepy followers watching us constantly, just waiting for us to fuck up."

With a groan, Hazel leaned back in her seat, staring up at the ceiling, her curls bouncing with the exaggerated movement. "Let's just take what we have, then, and give it a go. What's the worst that can happen?"

Charlotte didn't want to say it aloud, but a *fuck ton* of bad things could happen. As she gathered up her things, she had to admit they were out of options and, if Bradley's emails were true, out of time.

~>>>>> <<<<<~

Charlotte felt dubious at best about their configuration. They had set up in a small room in the attic of the house. Edith had drawn sigils and runes all about the walls in dark red, though Charlotte wasn't entirely sure if it was blood or paint.

The room was barely ten feet by ten feet—just large enough to draw what appeared to be an alchemical symbol they'd found in a book that morning on the hardwood floors. The book reiterated several times that it was a generic summoning circle and would suffice for their purposes. Candles were evenly dispersed along its outer circle, flickering in the darkness. Every article and page they had read suggested darkness to entice a contractor—a fancy word for "demon"—and this particular little room didn't even have a window in it. Hazel had commented on the fire hazard jokingly, nudging a candle with her foot.

Charlotte's heart raced as she used a funnel to carefully spread salt in a wider circle around the other one. They were taking whatever protections they could, as they had no idea what this Atticus was capable of. Hazel hung bags stuffed with herbs that the servants had pulled together less than an hour before to aid them while Edith placed symbols of Christ around the room.

"Gran, you don't believe in all that, do you?" Hazel asked dubiously as Edith placed down several silver crosses.

"What I do or do not believe does not matter, as long as it may stop evil," Edith replied simply.

Hazel shrugged but crouched down to examine one thoughtfully.

"I think I'm done," Charlotte announced, stretching as she stood upright. Her back twinged uncomfortably as she glanced about. They had done everything they could think of, it seemed. *Now it's time for the hard part.*

Edith bowed her head, floating to one of the far corners. Jacob, her most loyal servant and a talented occultist in his own right, stood opposite her. Hazel took the farthest corner, between Jacob and Edith, leaving the one diagonal to Hazel for Charlotte. All four directions were covered this way, with four people to help keep the demon in check. Three, really, given that no one knew Charlotte's magic was nonexistent once more.

"I guess we should do this." Her voice quavered as she took the northmost position of the circle. Her hands shook as she rotated her palms up. "I have no fucking clue what I'm doing."

"You got this, babes," Hazel whooped as Edith whispered, "Language!"

Taking a deep breath, Charlotte tried to follow her gut. She hoped that it would come to her instinctively. How else had people summoned demonic creatures before it was written, or before they had peers to assist them? They had to have worked it out somehow. And so would she.

"Alright, Atticus." She stared at the circle. "I don't know your real name, but I'm sure that you'll know how to listen out. You're a demon, after all. Your kind is good at listening in where they aren't wanted. So come on, show yourself. I have an offering for you, and I'll hope you'll take it."

Charlotte slipped her hand into her pocket and pulled out a small blade. With a wince, she ran it along the top of her finger. A droplet formed and before she could hesitate, she reached a hand over and quickly spilled her blood, yanking her hand back as the drop fell.

⟫⟫ ⟪⟪

Charlotte had barely snatched her hand back from the threshold of the circle when the room filled with crackles and light, a prelude to heat so fierce, it had her gasping. The salt circle began to burn on the inner edges. Charlotte shot her grandmother a panicked glance. Had they done something horribly wrong?

A wind filled the room, a thrashing cacophony that threatened to deafen them in the confined space. She could see Hazel's lips moving but heard nothing as they all braced themselves against the walls nearest them. The candles blew out, leaving them in darkness, a howling storm suffocating them. She had fucked up, big-time. Charlotte pushed against the wind. She would throw herself in the circle—maybe she could placate or at least distract whatever they had conjured long enough for the others to stop it, send it back. However, she had barely managed forward a step when the raging storm in the room suddenly stopped. She stumbled over her own feet at the sudden lack of resistance, tumbling to her knees.

The lights reignited, casting a soft golden glow across the room again. Blinking against the sudden shift, Charlotte's jaw dropped when her eyes adjusted. The golden-haired boy sat opposite her, legs crossed, head cocked to the side as he examined her curiously. She heard her grandmother and Jacob gasp as Hazel let out another whoop.

"You called?" The demon raised a fine eyebrow at her, speaking as though she had merely caught his attention—not as if she had summoned him in a cobbled-together, slapdash ritual.

"Atticus?" His name came out broken, unsure. She coughed, pushing herself to her feet. She tried again, focusing on her breath, keeping her tone even and calm. "You are the demon Atticus, right?"

He continued to gaze thoughtfully at Charlotte. "Yes, that is what Wade named me," he conceded. "I normally wouldn't answer to anything but my true name, but you're rather lucky I am quite attached to this human one."

Atticus's gaze began to roam. His eyebrows shot up and he scrambled to his feet, spinning in a circle as a look of disgust crossed his face. He swept an arm around the summoning circle. "And what exactly do you call *this*?"

"A . . . a summoning ritual?"

"Oh, maybe if you were an ape or a Neanderthal, perhaps you would. Are you one of those, mortal? This is positively barbaric. I would *never* have answered to this if I weren't listening out. I can feel the shame from my family all the way from this realm. What kind of offering is this? A *droplet* of blood? No incense? No sacrifice? Where is the fanfare, the art? This is the most rudimentary and frankly *insulting* set up I have ever seen from your kind."

Atticus fanned himself delicately with his hand, sleeve sweeping in an arc. He was unnervingly beautiful, his blue eyes sparkling in the low light. He looked somewhere between youth and adult—definitely not a man, certainly not a child. He was dressed like a poet of bygone years melded with a page boy, suspenders holding his puffy shirt in place. Almost like he was cosplaying as a human. *In a way, he is,* Charlotte thought.

"Well, human," the demon's voice broke through her thoughts. "How about we get this over with, shall we? Perhaps one of your people could find me a cup of tea or some sweet water. I'm not used to such homely quarters for my meetings." He scowled before muttering under his breath, "I thought you people had *money*."

"Like we were going to summon a demon into the heavily warded parts of our home," Charlotte retorted hotly. Atticus merely raised his eyebrows in response. She clenched her fists, letting her nails dig into her palms. She couldn't let this little jerk get under her skin, immortal demon or not. "Also, we aren't your servants!"

"Apparently you're not very good hosts, either," he replied coolly. He pushed his sleeves up his forearms, wandering the circle perimeter to examine them individually. "Ah, yes, this must be Edie. Exquisite, truly. And you, sir, I do not know, but that matters not. Oh, you're the loud one." He clapped loudly and gleefully as he stopped in front of Hazel. "I hear you're a Hunter. You're quite a mouthy girl, you know. Delightful, though. You get under the old man's skin. He can't fathom someone of your position having any power in life, and it absolutely boils him. He's delicious to feed on when you do that." He leaned toward Hazel. "You and I could make a wonderful contract, if you desire."

"I'd rather eat shit," Hazel replied with a blank face. He clapped again.

"De-*light*-ful. You and I will reconvene later. I'll listen out for you; we could be something great." He winked at her before sauntering back toward Charlotte.

"Now, for our meeting. Would you like to begin now that the pleasantries are over with? Or shall I get straight to consuming your soul, mortal?" He snickered as Charlotte balked. "Oh, come now, child. Like I would eat a soul as bitter and charred as your own. I'm what you people may call a sommelier of human emotions. I prefer the taste of human feelings, rather than eating a big meal like your soul. You all have such individual flavors because of your emotions, and I can't get enough of them. Plus, this way, you last so much longer."

"Want me to knock him out?" Hazel called out cheerfully across the room. Atticus blew her a kiss over his shoulder.

"Are you done monologuing?" Charlotte asked through gritted teeth. "Or do you prefer the sound of your own voice even over the taste of human emotions?"

Atticus let out a tinkling laugh. "Oh, you're funny, too. I think I can see why Wade likes you. I mean, I've only ever really seen you asleep before, you know. He wouldn't let me wake you up to play." Atticus sighed as her heart began pounding at the mention of Wade. "That's alright, though. At least he let me pat the cat. Where is Specter, by the way? I don't see him. We haven't spoken in a while."

"Leave my cat out of this," Charlotte snapped. She was close to losing control.

Hazel bounced on the balls of her feet excitedly across the room. She'd shirked her leather jacket, her brown eyes glittering in the low light as she hyped herself up. She skipped over to Charlotte, grabbing the other girl's hand and giving it a quick squeeze. "Tap out for a minute, babes. I reckon I've got this."

Charlotte sighed gratefully and stepped back, gulping in deep breaths as Atticus's mischievous gaze shifted to Hazel. "Oooh, are we making a bargain now?"

"Yeah. You shut up and only answer questions, and I'll consider not shoving your head up your own ass. How's that for a deal?"

Atticus smirked. "I love that you use your *scary girl* words. I can feel the tendrils of fear on you. You've never dealt with one like me before, and that bothers you. You're used to the lowlings, the corrupt spirits—not actual demons. They act on instinct and therefore you can, too. I alarm you with my . . . *soft* appearance."

Edith shot them a sharp glance across the room. Charlotte couldn't see Hazel's face from where she stood behind the other girl, but she guessed that Atticus had hit a nerve.

"I just don't like beating on kids," Hazel replied casually. "Maybe you could show me your real form and make this a fair fight."

Chuckling again, Atticus said, "Oh, sweetheart. You couldn't cope with my true form. Besides, this one is far more pleasing, no?" He gestured to himself arrogantly.

"Cut to it, girls," Edith warned from across the room. "The longer he is here, the more he can do."

"Oh, hush, I'm not going to do anything to any of you. Can't a boy have a bit of fun with new friends? Judging by that face, I would say not." With a sigh, Atticus wrapped his arms around himself. "I loathe being so serious, but I suppose I must. I was waiting for your call. I find myself in a . . . bind, shall we say. I can't help Wade. Not with the pact I have forged with the Order. But that doesn't mean if someone made their own pact with me that I couldn't also honor *that*."

"No deals!" they sang in unison. Atticus rolled his eyes dramatically.

"Ugh, no fun. Fine, no deals. But maybe you could chat with me, ask some questions, and see what happens."

Charlotte stepped forward again, eyeing the demon suspiciously. "What's in it for you without a bargain to feed from? Why do you want us to ask about Wade? What does it do for you?"

Atticus gave her a hard stare. Then, looking away, his eyes softened as he muttered, "Maybe I don't want my only friend getting hurt. Who can say, really?"

Her stomach plummeted as Atticus shifted, arms wrapped around himself still. Was he speaking the truth? That he just wanted Wade to be safe? How was it that he and Wade came to be friends, anyway?

"Demon," Charlotte started slowly. "What can you tell us about your relationships with the Order and Wade? What do they want?"

Atticus's eyes snapped back to her. "I can't tell you what they wanted. I can only tell you my end of things, given freely."

"Fine. Atticus, why did *you* forge relationships with them?"

Dropping his arms, he started pacing the circle again. The old wood creaked beneath his light feet, the candle flames flickering. "The Order offered me a stable food source in exchange for my power to influence and create an army. They assured me that as long as an Order member still stood in this realm, I would have the freedom to roam as I chose. I have been with them for centuries now, and it wasn't until some time ago that they learned how to actually utilize me. A pity, as I was enjoying my me time.

"As for Wade . . ." he trailed off, staring into the darkness. He swallowed. "There are a lot of things one can have with freedom and time. Friendship is one of those I sought. I saw a boy in need. He was kind, his energy so wholesome it made me almost sick, honestly. I couldn't look away from the cleanliness of his soul. So, I offered him all of my power, to be a part of my own soul. In exchange for his undying friendship. I bound us."

Atticus stopped, his brow furrowed. He tapped his foot for a moment, staring up at the ceiling as though deep in thought. He clicked his fingers, twisting his head back toward the girls. "He ended up betrothed to the girl he saved. Sarah Rochelle. He was too kind to say no, after the trauma they went through. He almost didn't make it when she fell through some thin ice on a skating pond. He wished so desperately to save this girl he didn't even know. You could say the brightness of his soul would have been attractive to someone that happened to be around, due to their own involvement with the girl."

He stared at them again, wiggling his eyebrows. Charlotte cocked her head, confused. Atticus rolled his eyes.

"The idiotic thing is, I could have just pulled her out if she had asked, but five-year-old humans are monstrously stupid." Atticus shook his head.

"What can we do to help Wade?" Charlotte asked, urgency lacing her words. Atticus tapped his chin thoughtfully.

"I mean, if *I* were going to destroy a lich, I would destroy their container. That's just me, though. You'd need some powerful magic, demon or otherwise, to do that. If you know anyone like that, they could do it. I'd hate for the Order to capture them also and use me to make another deal to contain that person, too."

Charlotte's heart sped up again. It was going to be up to her, wasn't it?

"Soul jars are pretty peculiar things, though. Sometimes they're actual jars; sometimes they're, say, a jewel attached to a hairpin. As I said, humans are odd creatures."

Charlotte stared at the demon. He was being *oddly* specific.

"*Now*, if you'll excuse me, I have matters to attend to." Atticus gave them a sweeping mock bow. "Next time you deign to call me, it wouldn't kill you to at least get me a comfortable chair and a refreshing beverage, maybe some scented candles. Put *some* effort in."

With a crack, sulfur filled the small room and Atticus vanished.

CHAPTER THIRTY

They stood in silence for several long minutes after Atticus vanished, the smell of sulfur mixing with the sweet tang of sage and rosemary. Tension filled the air—a knowledge that no matter how they proceeded from here, things were going to be bad. There could be no winning for Charlotte, truly. In the end, she was the first to break the silence.

"Well," she rasped, "I guess we have to kill Wade."

Hazel wrapped her arms around Charlotte, embracing her tightly. "I'm sure we can find another way around it, babes."

Edith and Jacob shared a look, and Charlotte knew that Hazel's words, while meant to soothe, were meaningless. There could be no other way.

"We can just take out the Order," Hazel continued, squeezing tighter. "We destroy every last one of them and we get him out safely. Easy peasy."

"I don't think it'll work that way," Charlotte choked. "They're controlling him. Either way, they will burn him up and make him suffer until the bitter end. If we do it, at least it's a mercy."

An awful wail filled her ears. She was crying—the wail was emanating from her, she realized. She felt another set of hands wrap around her and knew her grandmother had joined the fray.

"We will do what we can, to whatever end that may come," Edith whispered, stroking Charlotte's hair. "I will not let my little Lottie suffer for the wretchedness of others any longer. We will stand, and we will fight."

"Yeah," Hazel murmured. "We'll give it our all. For Wade. Because as annoying as he is, he doesn't deserve any of this."

"For Wade," she all but whispered. "We'll put an end to this for Wade, no matter what happens."

They stood there in silence for several more long minutes, the trio holding one another tightly as Jacob slipped from the room. An odd, eclectic family dearly missing one of their own.

⤜⤜ ⤛⤛

There was an air of dread and acceptance as they gathered in the upstairs armory. It was actually an old library that housed trinkets and relics, items that could aid against possession or magnify magic. Supplies that Charlotte used in lieu of her own missing power for some time. They had slept on Atticus's information and roused that next morning with the finality that a reckoning had arrived.

Charlotte paced through the old library, glancing at the glass cases housing centuries of Blythe tools and charms—alchemical potions concocted to conceal, iron blades that had been infused with the very blood of her foremothers in order to strengthen the user. She touched her hands to some of them. What could she possibly use to destroy a relic as powerful as a phylactery? She knew, deep down, it would not be an item but the very strength of her own magic, still dormant within her.

Edith had gathered the three of them and the entire Blythe staff in the library. She had warned them of what was to come; they could leave, and there would be no grudge bared. But a battle was brewing, and any hands that were offered freely would be accepted with eternal gratitude.

All of their staff remained with them. They, too, were part of the Society, they agreed, and had their own parts to play in being on the right side of history.

"What's the plan?" Hazel asked, dragging Charlotte from her thoughts. Charlotte paused, her hand running over the Winchester her mother had used to stop a slew of angry spirits one dreadful spring in New Orleans.

"Well . . . I hadn't thought it through too much," she admitted. "I was planning to contact Dirk, tell him I accept his missives, and hope to get close enough to Wade to break his phylactery."

"That's, like, one part of a multistep plan, babes. What about the rest of us?"

Charlotte looked at their eager faces. Edith nodded encouragingly, and it struck her that this was what it was like to be the family head. To be in charge, to make change happen. A spot her mother and her father had taken, and her grandmother and grandfather before them, in times of crisis. A dull ache in her heart reminded her that the person that should have been by her side was not only missing, but soon to be gone completely.

Charlotte straightened up.

"I want to be remembered for doing the right thing." She gulped, fighting back the urge to panic, to run. "Because that is the point of the Society. To keep the occult in check, and to keep people safe. We've failed Wade, but we can try to make it up to him, to stop the carnage. We can never bring back the people lost, but we can make sure others don't suffer the way they have, too. It is time for a new chapter—for the secrets of the Society to be laid bare, instead of hiding selfishly in the shadows. The lack of candor from our people is what has caused this to become the monster it is. We end it, one way or another, today."

Hazel, Edith, and the other members of the Blythe household murmured in agreement.

"I don't have a good plan, but we are a team. I know that we can work it out together." She looked to Hazel. "I need you to do whatever you can if I fail. Kill me, kill Wade—do whatever you must. I think your focus should be on Dirk and the Order. Grandmother can assist you, as can Jacob. Hopefully, no one else will need to come. Grandmother, is there anyone left in the Society that we can trust?"

Edith nodded. "A few that I know will be stalwart against Dirk. I have not been blind in these past months; there has been noticeable resentment for him. Come, Jacob, we have people to contact if this is to work. Hazel will fill me in."

With that, her grandmother swept off, Jacob in tow. Charlotte gulped, taking a moment before addressing the group once more. "Now, we have to load up and prepare ourselves however we can. We're going to rush the enemy and go headfirst into battle. We can't give them any more time to prepare against us or hurt any more families."

⇒⟫ ⟪⇐

Charlotte held her smart phone in her hand. With how heavy it felt, one would have thought it was the ball at the end of a chain tying her to her fate. She took a deep, steadying breath, her family surrounding her as she dialed the number her grandmother had slipped to her on a piece of paper.

"Yes?" came the familiar curt voice of Dirk Ashgarde. She steeled herself.

"It's Charlotte Blythe."

"Ah." There was a pause. "I see you're responding to our missives at last."

She drew in another deep breath. "Yeah, well, there are only so many hints a gal can get before she notices them."

"And how do you respond?"

"I thought long and hard about this." She sighed, as if resigned. "I can't risk Grandmother's health, or that of our servants. I know what you've been doing to families that say no. And I know you want me pretty badly. Fine. I'll join you, in exchange for the safety of everyone within Winterbourne."

"Lofty demands for a girl who's cornered," Dirk responded dryly. "But fine. If you yield yourself to us, we will ensure they aren't harmed. I can't say as much for yourself, however."

"I don't care. Now call off your minions from our home."

He tsked. "No, I don't think so. I'll tell you what: let them escort you here, and I'll call them off later. We can't be having you pull any tricks on us, can we?"

Charlotte paled. Her plan would collapse if the others weren't able to help her. She looked worriedly at her grandmother. They were in too deep for her to pull out—he would know. There would no longer be an advantage.

"Fine, whatever. I don't care." Her heart raced. She was cornered. She'd fucked up. She had to hang up so she could come up with Plan *B*—

"Go outside now and they'll bring you to us."

Her heart skipped a beat. "What?"

"Right now, Miss Blythe. I don't have all day; there is work to be done. You have two minutes." With that, the phone clicked and the call ended.

They all exploded at once. Hazel cursed loudly and Charlotte shrieked, throwing her phone, while her grandmother immediately began issuing commands to strengthen Winterbourne so they could siege it out. Red spots appeared before Charlotte's eyes as she swelled with fury, anger threatening to overwhelm her as she swayed.

"*Shit*, I've got you." Hazel's arms wrapped underneath Charlotte's once more, keeping her upright. "Gran, what the hell are we gonna do?"

"We'll fortify and hold it down until we can think of something else—"

"No," Charlotte interrupted. Her head swam. "We can't. I have to go. They're killing people. I don't have a choice." She paused. "They're hurting Wade."

Her voice cracked on his name, and she knew her fate was sealed. She had to go to him. Charlotte pushed away from Hazel, stripping herself free of the carefully placed tools and potions she had strapped to herself, shaking as she removed them as fast as she could. She didn't doubt they would act if she wasn't out there at the end of the two minutes.

"You don't have to do this! We can figure it out," Edith begged.

Charlotte leaned down to kiss Specter before striding to the front door, adjusting the mask of false bravado that had served her so well in the past. Pausing with her hand on the doorknob, she turned back to face the others.

"You're going to have to figure it out without me, and fast. I'm sorry." Without another word, Charlotte pushed the door open and stepped out to meet her fate.

⤞⤟ ⤝⤜

The fog was heavy, but not as heavy as the darkness had been. Like an odd sort of twilight, Wade found himself between the planes of here and there, of being himself and being shuttered down deep inside. Something was happening—he could hear it in the daze, even if he wasn't really aware. Something big, important.

It didn't matter, though. The hazy little bits of him that held on still—they had given up. He had been doomed from the day he met Atticus and Sarah Rochelle, doomed to endure a twisted, sick fate. It was better, he reasoned, if he wasn't cognizant for it.

"She's surrendered? How can she have done that? I thought she would make a bargain with me, but no, of course she has to be entirely melodramatic. Humans are disgusting creatures. Oh, hush; you're my servant, not theirs. I merely loan you to them."

Atticus. He could hear Atticus somewhere out there in the fog.

"Wade? Are you there, or is your brain still necromancy slush?"

He pried his eyes open. A watery image of Atticus filled his vision.

"Not entirely there, I see, but good enough. Your ridiculous excuse of a soulmate has gone and sacrificed herself instead of doing the smart thing and contacting me again—did you know that? I told you, you humans are deplorably stupid. I wish you were all half as smart as her cat."

Atticus sighed, stomping his foot like a frustrated child. "I can't circumvent my contract with them to help her. I could if she'd made a deal, but alas, no! I can't help you, either, so I need you to try for me, dear friend. Try and fight them off. I need to think and find a way out of this jam. I fear I may have woven a web and gotten myself stuck."

Wade tried to speak, but Atticus hushed him. "No, save your strength, friend. You'll need it, for things are about to get a bit rough, I fear. I'll do what I can to give you clarity and time, but I fear it's the end of our time here. I'll keep you safe, I promise you. No matter where that may lead us."

Atticus paused before resting his forehead against Wade's. "I am glad to have made a friend of you, despite my own failings. I will see you on the other side of this. Now, rest."

⋙ ⋘

They ensconced her the moment she stepped off the porch and out of the main wards.

The shades from the masquerade wrapped around her, blocking the sun from her sight. She drew a sharp breath, a scream rising in her throat as they wrapped her in a black tattered shroud—or was it their forms she was wrapped in? Before she could make a sound, she felt herself hurtling through the air, then suddenly, she plummeted.

Charlotte gasped as her body slammed against solid flooring, her very bones vibrating with pain. She rolled, instinctively, curling into a fetal position. She was getting thrown around a lot recently. She took mental stock of herself—nothing seemed broken, merely bruised and painful.

"Always the epitome of elegance and grace, aren't we?"

She raised her head to see Dirk standing over her. She pushed to her feet, gritting her teeth as her legs shook under her. Dirk tutted.

"Always with the bravado, Charlotte. It'll do you no good in the end. Come, now, don't look at me like that. You're here now, and that means the hard part is done."

"Why do I not believe you?"

Dirk shrugged. "Believe what you will. But for now, you'll come with me."

With that, he snapped his fingers and the shadowy servants encircled her once more. Unlike earlier when she was sure they had dragged her through a hell portal, they merely wrapped their spindly, inhuman hands around her upper arms to drag her behind Dirk.

As they tugged her along a corridor, Charlotte realized they were in Umbra Hollow, where it had all started. They yanked her through the library to the room where the massacre had taken place.

To where she had first met Wade.

It had changed since she had last been there. Besides a notable lack of dead bodies, for one, it was darker now, an air of hostility to it. The curtains remained drawn, the furniture shoved to the far wall. She started when she realized that the flooring had been gouged, ancient runes carved into the hardwood floors. A sophisticated version of the summoning circle she and the others had created.

"What the hell is all of that?" she gasped, struggling against her captors. They held her with unshakable strength, their long fingers squeezing tight enough to bruise. "I'll fuck you up, I swear," she hissed at them, wishing she were Hazel.

"It is many things, Miss Blythe, but most importantly, it's part of our revolution."

Her stomach dropped. She should have realized that he was going to do *something* to her if she came. She began struggling harder, every fiber of her screaming in regret. Cold beads of sweat broke out on her forehead and neck as Dirk began ordering the shadow servants to secure her.

She screamed as they carried her into the center of the circle, rasping at each other in a tongue from another world—one that still clearly implied, as they stared at her hungrily with eyes black as coal, that they'd like to devour her.

One moment, she was struggling; the next, she found herself clamped in iron chains mounted to the middle of the circle. She jerked to her feet, lunging for Dirk, but they snapped taut, yanking her back to the ground.

"I agreed to come, so what the fuck is all of this for?" Charlotte twisted the chains, searching for a weakness in the links. The familiar robed acolytes began to file into the room.

"It's a contingency plan. You may have been coerced into coming here, that is true, but that doesn't bode well for longevity. We felt it prudent that perhaps we build some loyalty directly into you, for the sake of our prosperity."

She huddled down at the disgusting leer Dirk shot her as he looked her up and down.

"You and your absolutely batshit cult can eat a dick!" she snarled. "I'm not a possession."

"Funny, your boyfriend said something similar, and yet here we are." Dirk shrugged. "I would prefer you not use such foul, common language. We'll get that out of you before you have my great-grandchildren, *that* is certain."

"You can try," she replied cheerfully, trying to channel Hazel's energy. "Let's see who would win one-on-one."

"Don't be stupid," he chastised. "Now, are we almost ready to begin?"

The robed figures had brought in the same tub as the night they resurrected Wade. She saw the one with the scarred face, the necromancer. He glared at Lottie, his pale milky eyes full of hate. She flipped him off, the chains clinking as she did so.

Dread pooled in her stomach as the familiar scent of sulfur began to fill the room, mixed with the unmistakable aroma of rotten meat. She struggled against the chains, desperately casting her gaze around the room. Maybe she could get the demon to help her if she could catch its eye. Unfortunately, she saw only robed figures, Dirk a solitary figure amongst the sea of them as they began chanting. The shadowy servants flitted around the circle, surrounding her.

She was, as they said, up a shit creek without a paddle.

She yelped as the rotting carcass of some animal—a lamb, perhaps? She hadn't eaten meat in years—was tossed at her feet. Dirk chuckled darkly as the shadows seemed to devour the light in the room, muting it.

Her breath came out in short, shallow bursts. There had been many times after the first moment she had tricked death that she was sure her number was up. And this time, she was sure that fate was determined to get its dues. While it might not outright kill her, it seemed there was something worse planned for her.

She closed her eyes tightly, heart pounding and tears pricking her eyes as she whispered a quiet goodbye.

CHAPTER THIRTY-ONE

Charlotte's quiet internal goodbyes were interrupted by Wade's smooth, familiar tenor asking, "And what do you need of me?"

Gasping, her eyes flew open as she searched the cavernous darkened room for him. Her blood ran cold when she finally locked eyes on him. In the weeks since she had last seen him—both in spectral form and as a newly resurrected person—he had changed. He had a pallor that had not existed in either form, purple smudges under his deep gray eyes prominent enough to rival her own. His cheekbones had hollowed out a bit, creating a gauntness to his face. His full lips were thinner, sadder—though that could have been purely her imagination as, despite his morose moments, Wade's face had usually lit up with a wide smile upon seeing her.

He was dressed similarly to the night he had been resurrected, in dark brocades with a large wool cloak swallowing his tall, lean frame. Wade's auburn hair, usually slicked back, now fell across his forehead in an untamed sweep. There was a vulnerability to his countenance, an odd exhaustion that permeated the air around him.

"Wade," she cried out to him. She cringed when he fixed that hard stare on her. She'd forgotten that he hadn't been himself, possessed and controlled by another. His hands clenched at his sides and she flinched, remembering his arm against her throat, crushing it.

That wasn't him. This isn't the real him, she reminded herself. He must have been deep inside of there, surely. She had felt it, seen it in those moments when he held her, twirled her, before it all fell apart. As she sat there, chained to the floor, she thought how cruel it had been for them to be allowed that single moment of rapture before Dirk and the Order had torn it all apart.

Atticus swept in after him. There was a jitteriness to him that hadn't been there when she last saw him, completely at odds with his cocky nature. It was subtle, but the way his eyes snapped from Wade's back over to her, then back again, was enough to tell her that the demon did not feel in control. That maybe he was even a little worried.

She felt like a young girl again, trapped under the table, begging not to die. She wanted to be anywhere else. This time, however, there was no one to help her, nowhere to hide. Dirk's voice echoed across the room, interrupting her thoughts.

"This won't take long. Between the power loaned to you and the sigils, we should be able to bind her will with minimal interference. We've learned a lot since the incident with you, and Atticus's followers assure me initiating her will be a simple matter." There was a tittering through the room as Charlotte looked at Wade and Atticus. The demon was acting aloof now, his gaze wandering lazily over the room, disinterested. Wade's stare remained fixed on her. Heat pricked her cheeks. It was the wrong kind of stare, hateful and scary.

"Let's get this over with, then," Dirk urged the necromancer.

They stepped forward, a steel dagger in hand. Charlotte backed up as much as she could, the chains pulling her short. "It'll barely tingle," the scar-mottled necromancer rasped at her. "And you won't remember a thing. You'll get to be with the Chosen this way."

"I've decided I'm not too eager to do that, so on second thought, let's not."

The necromancer chuckled, a throaty sound, as though he smoked a forty-pack a day. He raised the dagger over her. Resigning herself, she looked to Wade, mouthing "I love you" as the dagger came plunging down.

As it neared her chest, a bright light filled the room, followed by a deafening roar of thunder.

Charlotte threw her hands over her head as she fell to the floor. The world exploded around her, smoke and searing bright light blinding her. She coughed, waiting for the burst of pain, but none came. She blinked furiously, scrambling to her feet, struggling to see anything through the smoke and chaos. A wind swept through—rough, blustering, and most certainly magical—and swept a path clear before her eyes. She blinked in disbelief.

Where moments before the Order, Wade, and Atticus had watched her world beginning to end was now an entirely different scene. They had dispersed through the room, clanging and yelling filling the space. She watched wide-eyed as robed figures scattered from the room, the shadowy servants taking advantage of the confusion to latch on to some of them in a bid to feed. Dirk screamed at them to stay, hurling sweeping arcs of magical wind. She saw now what had happened as she followed the sweep of his hands.

Somehow her grandmother, Hazel, and a handful of Society members were storming the room, throwing spells and ducking and weaving in a beautiful but disorganized choreography of movements and magic. She watched as Hazel side-kicked a robed figure in the gut, twisting flawlessly as another came behind her, flipping them over her shoulder into the one she had just kicked. She was a weapon unto herself.

Charlotte began to panic as a figure sidled up beside her, instinctively dropping to a crouch. She couldn't move much, but she could maybe wrap the chains around them, choke them. Curling her hands, she got ready to lunge, when the robed figure backed up and said, "Charlotte, it's *me.*"

She gasped as Bradley Ashgarde lifted his head just enough for her to see his pale-blue eyes and mop of black hair beneath the hood. He quickly dropped his face again and hurried to her. "Pretend to be hurt—fall over. Make them think I've knocked you down."

Charlotte complied, gritting her teeth as she let her body fall again. She'd already been hurt so much, she supposed it didn't matter. Bradley crouched over her, his brow furrowed with worry and fear.

"We have to be quick, while Pops and Leo are distracted. Oh." He paused. "Leo's the necromancer. He'll be a problem, but we can deal with him. Move your butt over a bit, I have the keys—Pops is going to literally murder me, but you need to be free. You have to destroy the phylactery."

He spoke fast, tripping over his words as he worked on the shackles that bound her.

"I can't," she whispered near his ear as he worked on the shackles around her wrist. "My magic is gone."

Bradley scoffed.

"I doubt that after the way you nearly tore apart Meadowsweet. I was there, you know. You have to trust yourself, Charlotte. I don't think even your grandmother is as strong as you. Taking out the jar might actually kill her. *You* have to do it. Now." He paused, moving to her ankles. "When you're free, I'll blend into the fighting, and you wait a moment and then *run*. Go through the house. The demon has it. I'm sure Pops will send him after you, but you can do it. Let the others and me deal with the fighting down here. Just . . . lure them out. Good luck, and I'm sorry."

With that, Bradley pushed to his feet and dissolved into the chaos. She wondered how nothing had hit her, how no one had stepped on her. The fighting seemed to have flitted through the house, scared cult members dispersing, running for their lives. Dirk was mingled somewhere in there; she couldn't see Wade or Atticus either. Now was her chance.

Taking a deep breath, Charlotte dragged herself to her feet and ran to the closest door, barreling through the house as fast as her bruised and battered body could take her.

─✦◆✦─

It was like he was watching himself in a dream he had no control over. Chaos reigned around him; people lay dead or dying, mostly the robed, unnamed and unknown Order members, it seemed. He was dimly aware of Hazel, of Edith—he could see them. He tried to raise a hand, to yell them a warning, but he was not in control. He was merely an observer. Too strong to be kept in the dark, too weak to take himself back. Wade wanted to do something, to help, but he was motionless, his captor too distracted to order him as he dodged flame and foe, but not weak enough to let go.

He was still trapped within himself.

Dirk was there, screaming. He loathed *the man. He hoped, fervently, that Hazel would bite his head off, that Edith would smite him with rage. He blinked as a pillar of smoke rushed at him and stepped out of the way. Surprised, he opened his mouth in a single silent "Oh." Had* he *done that?*

He twisted his head, body wincing from the way they had pushed him, used him, to commit unspeakable sins. Yes, yes! *That was all him. His gaze darted about and he saw what had happened. The necromancer lay splayed on the floor, having taken a blow of green light to the back of the head. Not arcana magic. He searched for Atticus—he was nowhere to be found, and Dirk was distracted. He remembered vaguely seeing Charlotte. His heart raced. Yes, they had shackled her like a wild, feral animal, her chocolate eyes sparkling with fear and defiance. He moved through the crowd in a haze, searching for the transmutation circle they had carved into the floor of his home, a brief spark of indignation rustling through him.*

He wove through the crowd and caught sight of Charlotte as she sprinted away, her back turned to him, freed from the shackles. He had to follow her, warn her, before they subdued him again. A flicker flashed before his eyes, and he wasn't entirely sure he was imagining it as a red string fluttered through the air after her.

Wade followed it, running.

⤙⤙⤙ ⤚⤚⤚

Umbra Hollow was a maze of corridors and signs. Some museum signs, some remainders from the crime scene it had been a few short months earlier. Charlotte hurtled around corners, urging herself to remember what she could from the brief tour she had taken there as a preteen.

Charlotte heard the rustle of someone, something, trailing behind her as she urged her aching body to keep going, slipping and sliding as she skidded around corners, through doors. She burst through another one, falling back in horror as she realized she had ended up in a bedroom, cornering herself. Scurrying to her feet, she slammed it shut, clicking the lock. She glanced furtively about for somewhere to hide. She needed a way to recover, to get to Atticus and destroy the phylactery. What was she meant to do?

Just as she thought about diving across the dark covers of the canopied bed to put space between her and her assailant, the door clicked behind her.

⤙⤙⤙ ⤚⤚⤚

She was lying in wait in his bedroom as he opened the door cautiously.

Charlotte was like a snarling cornered animal, ready to fight to the death. Despite the anger, despite the raw, primal instinct, he saw her falter, her shoulders hunching in that silent, hesitant way they did when she was thrown off.

"Of course they'd send you to make it harder for me." He could hear the resignation in her voice even as her body stiffened and shifted defensively. She was deflated, exhausted. His heart ached as her eyes drooped with sadness. "He might be buried deep in that shell, but I know you're not him, not really. So, fine. Let's do this."

"Lottie," he said softly, calmly. He could do this. He reached toward her, palm facing down, as if approaching a startled horse. "It is me, truly."

She eyed him warily. "Like they couldn't just pretend to be you. People know how to play pretend."

"People, yes," he agreed. "I wouldn't go so far as to accuse these exemplary examples of human waste to be people, however." He dropped his hands to his sides, sliding them into his pockets. Every movement ached.

Though his traitorous heart thundered loudly in his chest and he wished for nothing more than to sweep his darling, ridiculous Lottie into his arms, he wandered away from her, around the room.

"This is my bedroom, you know," he said casually. In another time, another place, there would be other, far better, implications. "They've made some garish changes, for certain, but it still feels like my own."

She was still guarded. He needed to reassure her, to make her feel at ease. He turned his back to her, knowing that she would likely strike. He strode to his writing desk. In his foolish youth, he had chronicled his naïveté. Perhaps some pages were still here, some part of him he could gift Lottie.

"There is a hidden compartment that my father built into this desk, but it is obscenely uncomfortable to reach. I would wager that no one in the time since I used it last has found the mechanism." He dropped to his knees and pushed the chair aside. He prayed this was enough. This would be proof he was himself, he was sure.

He shifted onto his back when he was underneath so that he could face the odd little board underneath. His father had attached it to the desk and varnished it so that it matched—it looked intentional, like a part of the original design. Unless one was looking very closely and knew what they were after, they would not see the small fingertip-shaped impression that, if pressed upon, would open a secret compartment. Wade did just that, sliding it open and retrieving the journal within.

"This is one of the more delicate journals that a younger me found prudent to stow away," Wade admitted wryly, popping the compartment back into place before crawling back out. He used the desk to pull himself to his feet, keeping his voice light, casual. Surely they would notice he was gone soon, would find a way to tear him apart once more. He had so little time left with her.

"I want you to have this," he urged. He stepped toward her. Her eyes flickered to the door. She didn't believe it was him. He drew a deep breath. "I will be forever *plagued, in this life and the next, that I did not get to know you back when . . . that I did not get more time with you when I found you. There is so much I want to say to you, darling Lottie, to show you. But this will endure on, even after I am not here, and I hope that you will be able to feel closer to me, even if we physically cannot be so."*

He stepped toward her, but as he did so, a searing heat lashed through his veins. The darkness crept inside him, seeking a way to regain control. He wouldn't let it. He braced himself even as his Lottie watched him, wide-eyed. He hissed as the Order sought to regain control. His faculties waned, and he felt himself begin to drift again. No, he growled. He shook from the effort, but the spell soon passed. Heaving a sigh of relief, he flexed his free hand. He was still in control.

Wade's attention returned to Lottie, who had backed up. He held the journal out to her, mustering all his strength to stay upright. His body was not able to endure the strain they had been putting upon it. Despite his best efforts, he stumbled forward, off-balance. He closed his eyes as his vision danced, waiting for the floor to meet him.

⇒⟫ ⟪⇐

She darted forward when he began to sway and sag. Wade—or this form of him, at least—seemed to have lost the last of his energy. His appearance had been proof of that. She couldn't help herself; whether it was actually him speaking to her or a cruel trick, she could not bear to see him suffer.

She ran for him as he collapsed.

She got to him before he fell to his knees, wrapping her arms under his, taking on the brunt of his weight despite the discomfort and pain in her own body. They staggered, and for one horrifying moment, Charlotte was sure they would twist and fall onto the hardwood floors, and maybe that time, they would never get up again. He gathered himself slowly, the moment seeming to pass as she bore his burden.

She held him for a moment, waiting for his hands to come up around her neck, for him to crush her. She flinched as his arms did move, but around her waist, pulling her to him with gentle firmness. Hesitant, Charlotte leaned into the warmth of his embrace. He nestled his face against her hair, and for a heartbeat there was nothing else in the world but the two of them, standing in his old bedroom, holding one another as lovers should.

The silence was broken by Wade, his voice thick with tears as he whispered, "I'm so sorry, my love. I am wretched. I should never have thought they were telling the truth. I was thinking of naught but your safety—"

Charlotte cut him off, twisting until her face found his, until her lips sought his. His mouth met hers, soft and questioning at first. They pulled back briefly, gazing at one another in the eyes before their lips crashed together again and they found themselves wrapped up in one another. The journals dropped from his hand with a dull thud as his hands twisted in her hair. She grabbed fistfuls of his vest, pulling him closer, a burning urgency in their impassioned kiss.

She lost track of time and reason as they seemed to melt together into one. For a moment, a battle was not waging a few rooms away, Wade was just Wade, and the things that made their lives impossible ceased to exist. They were simply Wade and Lottie, and they were in love.

All good moments come to an end, however, this one was broken by the screams of the world below as the walls of their daydream collapsed around them, exposing the cruel pain of reality once more.

⟫⟫ ⟪⟪

Lottie pulled away from him with a gasp, her pale cheeks flushed a tantalizing pink. Her hands—so delicate, so perfect against his chest—clutched at his silk shirt and vest still. There was a brightness to her eyes; she was energized by their kiss, but also by the chaos that surrounded them. He could read her now like one might a book.

"We can figure this out," she breathed hurriedly. "We'll get you out of here, and we'll work it out. I promise you." She grabbed his hand, pulling him toward the door. "Grandmother and Hazel will be able to work out a way—"

"My love," he interrupted her softly, pulling her back to him gently, his thumb tracing the back of her hand. How extraordinary. *He had never felt her flesh before, gloves removed. She was cool to the touch, despite the flush on her face. "I'm sorry."*

"Don't you dare," she croaked, searching his face. "Don't you dare say you're sorry like you've given up."

He lifted her hand to his lips and kissed her knuckles, his eyes never leaving hers. He savored her delicate touch, memorizing the chocolate hue of her eyes, how flecks of gold danced in them. He did not know what awaited him beyond, but he would do his damnedest to cling to the memory of her laughter, her face, the scent of flowers and whiskey that followed her.

She started to cry now. Tears pooled at the corners of her eyes and he could see her eyelids fluttering, fighting against them. "No, darling Lottie. You don't need to pretend to be brave around me. Please. It's alright to be sad."

"Don't leave me."

His heart shattered at her whispered words, so quiet he almost didn't hear them, the most vulnerable and dew-eyed he had ever heard her. He embraced her again, stroking her head, planting kisses in her long braided hair.

"I will always be with you in your heart," he breathed in her ear. "But I must make up for my transgressions now, if I wish for you to have a chance." He pulled back from her, delicately wiping the tears from her eyes with his fingertips. "Shall we go together?"

"Together," she repeated quietly, her eyes searching his. "Always together."

Chapter Thirty-Two

A new kind of madness reigned as Wade and Lottie descended back down into Umbra Hollow. They paused on the halfway landing of the main staircase, observing the worst of it. Most of the fighting had spilled outdoors. Through the imposing windows, they could see bodies littering the ground, people weaving their hands into intricate symbols as they casted, and more running with magic-imbued weaponry at one another, clashing in the intricate dance of battle. Charlotte was unsure how the entire town, the entire country, hadn't noticed this.

"Jesus," she muttered, eyes widening. Shadowy demons flitted over the bodies of the dying, eating hungrily at both flesh and soul. *Barbaric.*

"We don't have time," Wade urged, his fingers intertwined with hers. "We must locate my phylactery. If they should regain control of me before then, I fear for what will happen to you." He closed his eyes for a moment, paling.

"It'll be fine," she assured him. She didn't believe it, though. She had been standing at the precipice for too long now, and now the moment to jump had arrived, whether she was ready or not. "We go together, no matter what." She raised his hand, still locked with her own, and brushed a kiss to his knuckles.

⤜⤛ ⤜⤛

As they reached the bottom of the stairs, a cheerful, piercing whistle called out of a dark corner at them. Hands still entwined, they turned toward the sound as

Atticus emerged from the darkness, the hairpin they were after dangling from his hand.

"The phylactery," Wade breathed. "You have it. Please, I urge you to pass it to me, Atticus."

"Oh, this thing?" the demon asked casually, twirling the hairpin between his fingers. "I can't just hand it over to you, you know. That's against the rules of my contract."

"Atticus, please," Wade's voice was soft and low, gentle but with an urgent edge to it. "Are we not friends? Were we not like brothers? Please, I cannot fall back into their grasp, and you do not wish for me to—I know it."

"I want many things, Wade. Unfortunately, we are creatures with obligations. Perhaps, if we were something else, there would be a way. My instructions have been made clear: to let no human near your phylactery."

The golden-haired demon dropped his hand to his side again as he contemplated the couple. Charlotte glanced at the hairpin dangling in his fingers, taunting them, as though he wanted them to come take it. As she made to dart toward the demon, a black blur lunged at Atticus's hand, snatching the hairpin. Atticus barely looked down as Specter dashed toward her with the phylactery in his mouth.

"Oh, how clumsy of me," Atticus intoned flatly, raising his eyebrows. "How could that have happened? Oh, well, I didn't let any *humans* touch it, I guess."

They stood frozen as Atticus made to turn away. *What is happening?*

A voice broke Charlotte from her reverie.

"You fool!" came a hiss from the darkness. The necromancer who had been controlling Wade lay in a crumpled mess nearby, his legs crushed under a knocked-over bookcase. He raised a hand to Wade and began whispering in a harsh, unfamiliar tongue.

Atticus was by them one moment. The next, he was at the necromancer.

"Poor creature, you must be suffering so," Atticus tutted. "Allow me to assist you."

Charlotte flinched as Atticus slammed his foot down on the necromancer's neck. A sickening crack resounded. The demon glanced over at them as he removed his foot. "I have some payments to go collect, so I don't have time to intercede and deal with you two currently. I'll be back for you before you know it, Wade."

Atticus disappeared into the darkness again, leaving them alone in Umbra Hollow. The distant din of battle outside faded as Specter mewled and climbed up Lottie's legs, the hairpin in his mouth.

"Now to destroy it," Wade breathed.

Charlotte's gut wrenched. *Destroy the soul jar. Destroy* him.

"We have it now," she said uncertainly. "We could just leave—"

"This phylactery was forged with dark, unimaginably cruel magic. As long as it remains, they remain, and they will be able to use it against me." He reached for Specter, taking it carefully from the cat's mouth. "I somehow doubt he is just a mere cat. He is a whole other creature entirely."

Her stomach twisted in knots as Wade bent down, his eyes locked with the cat, as if they were sharing some unspoken conversation. Specter blinked slowly, placing a paw on Wade's hand that now clutched the hairpin. *Is he* comforting *Wade? Can a cat look sorrowful?* Their moment ended as Specter lowered his paw, glancing once to Charlotte, before slinking away into the darkness of the house.

"I think you're right," she agreed softly. Hairpin still in his grip, Wade reached for her hands, bringing them up to his chest. His heart fluttered under her hand, alive and well and whole—

"I see that look, my love, and I cannot bear to think of the pain it will cause you. But it must be done. I cannot go back into the dark, and I cannot hurt you like that. Never again. And the time will come. I have blood on my hands that I can never clean, and a soul that has never rested. It is time for rest and judgment for me, Lottie. So, I ask one last thing of you. You have given me so much by giving me your heart. Now, I must ask that you take mine and cast aside its shadows and pains."

He wrapped his hands around hers with certainty, pressing the hairpin against his chest, angling it up between the rib bones. She felt its pressure. "Just as it has once before, allow this hairpin to end my torment, finally."

"I can't do it." She tried to pull away, but he held her hands firmly in place.

"You can, and must," he urged. "Now, before we falter. *Now*."

He crushed his lips to hers as he pressed her hands with force against his chest. She didn't mean for it to happen, but the flicker inside of her, the tendril of magic, ignited. As though slicing through butter, she felt the hairpin, propelled by her magic, slice through the fabric of his clothes and into the flesh beneath. He gasped against her mouth as her fingers found the wetness of his bleeding heart, the phylactery melting and burning into him all at once as it buried itself all the way in. As she stared down at his chest in horror, the unforgettable dark electricity she had felt the day she met Wade roared around her, fading to nothing. She said his name, quiet, questioning.

He raised his eyes to hers before collapsing to the floor.

⤜⤜⤜ ⤛⤛⤛

Time itself stopped as Lottie whispered his name, as though if she said it louder, the world would shatter. One moment, he was heavy. The next, he was light, as though made of clouds. He didn't realize he had slipped until he felt her arms around him, catching him, pulling him close. He was barely cognizant of her sobs as she tugged at him, laying kisses across his face. How queer and far away she was.

"I love you, Lottie," he whispered once more, reaching a hand upward to caress her cheek. There was a deep, aching pain within him, worse than any other he had experienced. For it was the pain of knowing he was going somewhere she could not follow, that he was leaving her behind.

But then the fog came. It called to him, and he was too weary to fight it. So he smiled at her, every part of him heavy, until he could not fight the slumber that called for him any longer.

A sob wrenched from Charlotte's throat as she held his still, broken body.

There was a peace on his face, like he was merely sleeping. She knew better. Even as a ghost, there had never been the finality of his death. She wrapped her arms around his chest, pulling his upper body into her lap, cradling him. Her tears splashed against his face as she shook silently. She stroked his face with her free hand, fingers trembling as she tried to smooth his mussed hair. It was the most intimately she had ever held him. And it would be the last time for as long as she lived.

She stroked his face tenderly, memorizing its planes, running her fingers over his lips, still damp with their kiss. "I love you," she whispered. "So very much, Wade. I didn't know I could."

As she spoke, something happened. He began to shimmer, to change at the edges. He was losing opacity, fading away. She felt him become lighter in her arms as she pulled him close to her, burying her face in the crook of his neck as she bent over him. She breathed in his scent one last time, the lingering remains of apple and cedar. He wasn't just dead—he was now leaving her in both body and soul.

"I am tied to you, forever and always," she whispered, choking on her words. Her heart crumbled into dust, much like Wade, as he slowly faded from existence, as though he had never been, leaving nothing behind but her broken heart. Wade's journal, stuffed into the waistband of her pants, pressed against her back, the only remainder of him.

She sat there for a moment, dazed, her tears flowing freely. She had been broken down to her rawest and most vulnerable once more, her very soul laid bare. This time, she told herself as she pushed herself to her feet, would be different. This time, she would make sure that those who had done this would pay for it.

The night her parents died had been much, much different. There had been silence after the screams ended. Stillness when she lay with their bodies, waiting for the end to come for her too. She did not have that moment with Wade. They had left bodies; he did not. Death had taken nearly everything that night, leaving her like a broken doll. Now it ran rampant around her, a symphony of pain and suffering instead of broken silence.

This time, she would not wait for death to come find her. She would find it, make it bend for her, make it pay the pain it had wrought.

She rose to her feet, floating, moving as though she were no longer in control of herself. Lottie left the foyer where she had said goodbye to Wade, where she had left her life and soul behind, and slipped through the open front doors.

It was surreal to pass by like none of it mattered, like none of it could touch her. She was a wraith as she passed by people, past demons, onto its lawns where Dirk now stood over her grandmother, goading her.

Her magic was waiting now, and she no longer had to even think to touch it. She had felt it the moment Wade had passed—a hot burning coal within her, her grief transmuted into something tangible. Now, she would use it. She raised a hand, flinging out an arrow of ice and piercing Dirk's shoulder from behind. He screamed in pain, a dark splash of blood beginning to pool on the back of his suit. She threw another, and another, knocking him to the ground.

She had to end it all. One person at a time, if that was what it took. Neither anger nor grief powered her; it was love, lost but still lingering. For Wade. For her parents. For Grandmother, Specter, and Hazel. And she would use every ounce to tear it all asunder.

The coal inside began to grow hotter, a fiery haze consuming her from within. Her magic pushed past the limit she had once known, and for a terrifying moment, Charlotte was brought back to herself—a scared little girl who was never in control of herself or her fate. But her fear melted away in an instant as she pounced on the embers of that feeling and fed fuel to the truth within herself.

She unleashed hellfire and fury. It burned in her, so hot, so bright, and she was afraid there was not enough oxygen, that it would burn her out, too. But it didn't. It kept burning, luminescent as it surrounded her.

It burned out from her like wildfire, beautiful, dangerous, cleansing. It swept past her toward Umbra Hollow, encasing it in its magnificent splendor. It began to burn, dark ash and cinder as it crumbled bit by bit, unable to resist the lick of her flames.

She turned on the lawn, taking it in as though she had all the time in the world. She saw Hazel, face slicked with tears, slicing a blade through one of the few that remained. Grandmother limped away, assisted by one of their own now that Dirk lay crumpled on the ground.

And there Dirk was, a feeble old man calling out for Atticus to help him, calling for the demons. He thrashed and tried to crawl away as he caught sight of Charlotte loping toward him. She stopped her march only to yank a sword free, lodged in a robed figure's back. She was dimly aware of Atticus wandering between the bodies nearby, his head cocked as though contemplating something.

She could see the hatred on Dirk's face, attempting to hide his fear behind contempt as she neared him. He continued crawling away from her, his fingers digging into the lawn amongst the cinders and ashes, coughing. *Weak, pathetic.*

"We had a deal," he snarled at Atticus between coughs. The boyish demon stopped his survey of the lawns and shrugged.

"We had a deal for me to help you build an army. A single girl is not an entire collective and thus isn't truly worth my time and energy. Speaking of which, you've lost my food source. How am I to uphold the end of my bargain if you've failed yours?"

"Kill her, then!" Dirk shrieked as she sauntered toward him with precise, measured steps. "Kill her! Consume her soul, her power!"

"Well, that's not really our deal, is it, Ashgarde? Besides"—Atticus eyed Charlotte—"I would hate to get in her way and be taken down myself."

Dirk started pleading with her then, broken, gibberish promises to change, to help rebuild them for the better. His last moments were spent sniveling, pathetic, with no shred of honor or dignity. He yelled at her to stop, to hear him out, as he told her what he could do for her.

She heard none of them as she speared the sword she had collected right through his throat, right where Wade's own death gash had been. Charlotte glanced over to Atticus. She felt nothing. No vindication, no pain. Just emptiness.

"I'm done here now," he called out over the sounds of Dirk's final gurgling breaths. "I have no more contracts to uphold in this realm. They have all gone to other places. And thus, I cannot remain. I hope that you will make the correct decision and call on me." He nodded curtly, walked away, and vanished into thin air as though he had passed through a door just out of her sight.

She heard a roar of cheers and cries, Hazel and Grandmother calling out to her as she sank to her knees and stared out at the broken, bleeding world around her.

Chapter Thirty-Three

Winter had well and truly arrived as Charlotte buttoned up her black coat with trembling hands. There was a briskness in the air that hadn't been there even a week before, and the leaves were beginning to brown and fall away mournfully as if shedding tears of their own.

It had been a week since her world had crumbled apart. Lottie stared at herself in the mirror, wondering if she was the same person she had been just three short months before. The truth was, she wasn't, and never would be. She had changed. Her life and the world as she'd known it had changed. While the same purple bags rested under her eyes, while she still doubted the world had any justice, she had changed in irrevocable ways. Her heart had found, and lost, love. It had new scars that nestled beside the old ones, but it had also grown bigger, made room for new people, new kinds of love.

Her gaze wandered in the reflection, to the bottle that resided by her bed. She hadn't touched it since she got home. The pull was still there, to seek solace in its easy comfort. But it would be hollow, she told herself. She could no longer numb or run from her feelings. She had to learn to sit with them, the good and the bad.

She was startled by a rap on the door.

"Babes, you ready to come out now? Gran says they're ready to start."

"Coming," Charlotte called, glancing at herself one last time in the mirror. Something was missing. Right in front of her on her dressing table, as if it had been waiting for her all along, was a dried tulip. A soft smile flickered across her lips as she gently threaded the flower through the buttonhole at the top of her coat.

They were her favorite flower now, funnily enough.

⚬⚬⚬⚬⚬

The rain had begun falling, a faint mist that felt more like a chill wind. The procession from the house had gathered at the back of the atrium—Edith, Specter, and a few servants. Hazel held Lottie's hand tightly as they made their way down the back steps to join them. They were, for all intents and purposes, sisters now. The bond they had forged over the last few months together was unbreakable.

When they reached the group, Edith stepped forward, quickly embracing Hazel before pulling Charlotte into her arms.

"I'm here for you, my lovey," Edith whispered against her granddaughter's ear, rocking her slightly as they embraced. "I'm always here for my little girl. You're not alone."

She sniffled as she nodded against Edith's shoulder. "I know, Grandmother."

When they pulled apart, the little group began their winding procession through the grounds of Winterbourne.

Touches of magic were sprinkled through the estate, warm and comforting. Despite the drizzle and dreary weather, flowers that should have been dormant were in full bloom, lining the path that wove through the property. Lottie and Hazel lingered at the back of the line as they all meandered forward, Specter padding along beside them.

"I know I haven't said it, but he was alright." Hazel shoved her hands into her pockets. She wore one of Stephenie's coats, her own wardrobe too sparse for the cooler weather. She left it undone, a black sweater and jeans peeking out from underneath. Charlotte had listened to her argue with Edith that Wade would have expected her to look like this, cleaned up. Hazel had argued that Wade would have also told her that she should have been in a full Victorian mourning garb if he'd had it his way.

"Yeah, he wasn't half bad," she agreed softly. Leaves crunched beneath their boots.

"I was doing some research," Hazel said casually, quieter now. "I'm not quite so savvy at it as you, and I'd appreciate your help."

"Oh?"

"Well, Gran loaned me some books. Did you know there are apparently layers, different worlds that our souls or whatever can go to?"

Charlotte chewed the inside of her mouth, saying nothing.

"Anyway, I was curious about how they worked, and if there was a way to prove they exist."

"They do exist. That's how demon summonings work—that's how ghosts exist. You know that."

Hazel waved a hand dismissively. "Yeah, yeah, I get that. I just . . . maybe there's a way. To go see people that are gone."

"Maybe."

They fell back into silence. The path beneath them began to give away to grass, meaning they were close. Sure enough, she saw the familiar glint of marble in the distance—the resting place of the Blythe family for generations. She stopped, looking around her. Some wildflowers danced in the misty rain and wind a little off the path. Hurrying over, she plucked two small bouquets, one in each hand.

The Blythe family was not a religious sort; even without the occult so interwoven in their lives, they were not the sort of people that could or would commit to organized religion. A small building was nestled next to where the family lay, something of a chapel. A place amongst nature and loved ones to contemplate, to have a quiet moment and talk to those that have gone on, even if they couldn't talk back. This is where their procession stopped, a male servant holding the door open as they filed in.

They didn't have a body for this ceremony, seeing as it had been lost to time and magic. Instead, Hazel had gone back to the Philadelphia property and taken a token from there. In place of a casket, instead of ashes, they had a teddy bear, with "Loren" embroidered on one foot and "Wade" on the other. This memento of him would rest on a little marble pedestal in her family tomb. A plaque had been made beneath it to commemorate not just his life, but the lives of Loren and his parents as well. To help him say goodbye to them, too, wherever he went.

It was not a lot, but it was a reminder for the world that they had existed, especially now that Umbra Hollow was no longer. His family home, hidden under a century of pain and lies, had been cleansed from the earth.

The teddy bear sat on an altar at the head of the chapel on a raised platform. This was where they usually set the deceased so they could face them before they entered the next world, offer words of comfort and love to their wandering souls. There were no seats, no pews. It was not a traditional place, as they were not traditional people. They formed a line, the servants each bowing to the bear and wishing him good luck in the next life. They filed out as quickly as they came in, heading back to their chores. Only Edith, Hazel, Charlotte, and Specter remained.

Edith approached the bench first, her silver hair bound only by a ribbon. She touched a hand to the bear, her back turned to the two girls.

"You were a good soul, no matter what bad things they made you do and did to you," Edith said softly. "You were kind, and warm, and did a lot of good for my girls, especially my Charlotte. I am thankful we knew you. Until we see you in the next realm, Master Van Baird."

She glimpsed her grandmother wiping the corner of her eye as she hurried out. Hazel approached the bench next, having scooped Specter up in her arms at some point. The Hunter was a little more awkward, shuffling from foot to foot as she stared down at the bear.

"Look, man, this feels a little weird, but I guess that's a pretty good summary of our time with you, huh? I'm sorry for picking on you so much and threatening to exorcise you. I never would have, really. If I had a way to bring you back here, I would." She paused. "Speckles also says you were alright. We'll miss you. I hope to see you again sometime, ghost." Hazel dropped Specter on the bench, letting the cat rub against the teddy bear, before collecting him up. She nodded at Charlotte before striding out, leaving her all alone in the small chapel.

The silence was deafening as Charlotte edged toward the dais. She felt like a teenager again, afraid to approach her parents' bodies, scared to admit that they were truly gone.

"I feel robbed, you know," she whispered. She placed both bouquets of flowers on either side of the bear; Grandmother would realize who the others were for. She knelt down on the raised platform so that she was eye-to-eye with the keepsake. "You were hanging around here for a hundred years as a ghost, and I only got to know you for a few months. That's so unfair of you. You shouldn't have gotten to leave me so soon." Her eyes burned, pinpricks of tears forming.

"I know we never really talked about . . . all the stuff you said to me. I'm sorry . . . if I could go back, I would. I was stupid to think about all the bad stuff when I should have focused on the good. I might not have gotten what others would have wanted, but at least I had you around. And now you've left me with nothing. That's not fair, Wade. You left, and you took another part of my heart with you. I don't have much of it left."

Charlotte reached for the teddy bear, wrapping it up tight in her arms as she started sobbing.

"I love you," she whispered against the bear. "I love you and I want you to come back so badly. I never even got to hold you properly." She pressed a kiss against the forehead of the teddy bear, burying her face against it. "Please come back, Wade. I miss you."

⟫⟫ ⟪⟪

When she finally emerged from the small chapel, the rain had picked up. Hazel waited for her under the shade of a tree, a cigarette between her lips, Specter perched on her shoulder. Spotting her, Hazel dropped the smoke and stubbed it out, striding out into the rain to meet her.

"He's really gone, isn't he?" Charlotte said dully. The wind picked up, whipping her plait. Hazel reached for her, gently tugging the tulip from her buttonhole and dropping it into Lottie's coat pocket.

"Keep it safe. You'd be sad if it got hurt." Hazel attempted a smile before sighing. "Yeah, babes, he's gone. But not completely. He's still here." She pointed at her heart, then Charlotte's.

"I miss him," Charlotte whimpered. "He was my friend."

"I know. He was all of our friend. But he was most special to you, wasn't he?"

She nodded, choking on a sob. Hazel spread her arms wide, drawing Charlotte into an embrace as the rain hammered down. Specter squeezed between them, cramming himself between their faces to keep safe from the rain. They stood there for a few minutes, silent save for the rain and wind whipping at them as Hazel held the other girl. A friend, one of the first she'd had in a long time—the other one gone, on to whatever lay beyond.

"Come on, babes. Let's get you inside and warm," Hazel whispered. "We have a lot of adventures ahead of us, and I can't let you get too sick or you'll never get to tell him about everything we get to do together. And you can't let him down like that."

"No, we can't," Charlotte agreed hoarsely, squeezing Hazel tight. "I'm glad you're my family now."

"Me too. Now let's get in before we get wetter and soak the house too much, yeah?"

Arm in arm, with Specter balanced on Lottie's shoulder, the girls made their way back up the property in the storm, Winterbourne's lights beckoning them home.

CHAPTER THIRTY-FOUR

Lottie awoke to the pale grey of predawn and the fresh breeze of a new day. Specter was still curled up beside her, his small black body rising and falling steadily with the deep hum of sleep. She smiled as she scratched him behind the ear, whispering good morning to him before she slipped out from the covers.

She was as silent as a ghost as she dressed and prepared for the day, taking time to brush her hair carefully. Automatically, she went to plait it. She thought on it for a moment, instead reaching for two hair combs that Hazel had gotten her for Christmas. She pulled two sections of hair back and twisted them into place, popping the combs in. Her long tresses flowed over her shoulders and down her back. She smiled at herself in the mirror, confident and cheerful.

She slipped from her room, leaving her door ajar for Spec to slip out later. She was startled to see her grandmother standing at the door of Charlotte's study. Edith caught her eye, motioning for her to come over.

"Have a look inside." Edith's mouth was curved into a mischievous grin. Perplexed, she shot her grandmother a look before pattering into her study.

She had finally moved all her stuff in some weeks ago and had redecorated somewhat, at her grandmother's request. A new chaise sat along one of the book-lined walls, a pile of history books on Victorian and Edwardian New England beside it—for research into future projects. Atop the pile was a neatly placed leather journal. On the drinks cart sat a large water bottle and some tea cups, the bottles of whiskey stowed away with the rest of the alcohol in the kitchen. It was tidy and organized, exactly as she'd had left it the night before. She glanced back at her grandmother.

"What am I meant to be looking at?"

"On your desk, lovey."

She didn't know how she didn't spot them before. A large bouquet in an understated yet elegant vase sat on the edge of the old desk. She drifted over to it, her eyes blurring with tears when she saw what they were. Tulips—dozens of them, in a multitude of colors. A little tag was tied delicately to the front.

He would have wanted you to have these. Good luck with today. I'll see you soon.
–Hazel

She smiled at the little note, scrawled in Hazel's looping script. Her friend certainly didn't mince words, but it warmed her heart—this small reminder of him, as well as a little signifier of their own deepening friendship.

"She had them delivered before the sun was even up." She hadn't heard Edith come up behind her. "And she's right. I think he would be quite proud of you today."

"Yeah," Lottie said softly. "I think so, too."

She leaned into the flowers, inhaling deeply, letting herself be lost in the past for just a moment. To remember the feel of his chill, of his smile, the crinkles at the corners of his stormy eyes. She missed him dearly, but it didn't hurt like her other pains used to. She had grown grateful just to have those warm memories.

"Let's eat breakfast," Charlotte suggested, plucking a single red tulip to tuck into her hair. She wrapped her grandmother's arm in her own, the pair chatting softly as they wandered from the room.

⤞ ⤝

Winterbourne was a hive of activity that morning. Charlotte and Edith were barely seated for breakfast when Hazel barged into the dining room, scooping up a bite of Charlotte's eggs as she plopped into the seat beside her.

"There's so much food right there! Get your own," she scolded, smacking the other girl's hand. Hazel grinned as Edith rose from the table, telling them to stay put as she made a plate for the Hunter.

"Thanks, Gran," Hazel beamed, immediately shoveling a scone into her mouth. She moaned. "How do they get these so fluffy? I'm going to get fat living here."

"Then you'll match your mouth," Charlotte teased. Hazel shoved her, grinning as Edith scowled at them.

"No roughhousing at the table. And goodness, Hazel, your clothes are a fright. You go change after you finish eating. I bought you so many nice new blouses and hung them up. And I thought you were going to be here later today?"

Hazel groaned. "But I like my jacket. And *maybe* I look like this because I chose to rush here and be here for my bestie on her big day!"

"Young lady, it is positively splattered with black gunk. You'll go to your room and get changed after eating. I don't want to know *what* you've been rolling around in."

"Zombie entrails," Hazel whispered conspiratorially to Charlotte. Gagging around her eggs, she shot Hazel a look.

"That's *feral*—I'm trying to eat!"

"I'll help," Hazel offered, pilfering from Charlotte's breakfast again despite her own full plate. Lottie scowled and jabbed her fork at Hazel's arm, who let out a fake shriek of pain. Edith merely shook her head at their antics.

"I think I am done for the morning," Edith sighed. "Hazel, I hope you'll stay here for a while this time before running off again. It would be nice to have both my girls here, where I can keep an eye on you."

"I'll try, Gran," Hazel promised before stabbing one of Charlotte's veggie sausages. Edith swept out of the room, muttering to herself as the two girls bickered over breakfast.

Hazel cleaned her plate in record time and was bouncing upstairs to change, leaving Charlotte alone in the vast dining room. Once upon a time, being in that room even with company had made her uneasy. It was as though all the demons that had been in her were now exorcised, the space cleansed, safe, once more.

The servants emptied the room, leaving Charlotte with a cup of coffee in hand as she leaned against a windowpane, contemplating the day. She had a lot ahead of her, and she was grateful for the few moments of silence she was able to steal for herself.

A movement on the table caught her attention. Specter had finally risen and now sat on the middle of the table runner, his large yellow eyes focused on her. Charlotte pushed off against the window, drifting over to pat him.

"You're going to get fur all over the nice clean table," she told him. "And a lot of important people are going to be eating and drinking off of it soon. But I guess they know you're special, too, huh, buddy?"

He purred in response, content. She scratched his ears, letting her eyes roam absentmindedly. Her attention snagged on the line of portraits on the opposite wall, as it often did in this particular room.

Once, there had been an empty frame beside a shrouded one, ruining the line of striking paintings. Now her mother's portrait was uncovered, her fantastic smile seeming to light up the space. The day Charlotte had returned home from losing him was the day she had ripped the crepe down and left her wallowing in the past. Now, she said good morning to her mother every day with a soft smile.

Beside her mother, where Lottie's empty frame had been, now sat a portrait. This one was so similar yet so different from its predecessors. For in this frame was a smiling Lottie, yes, but also some other familiar faces. Specter sat curled on her lap, and Hazel was perched on the armchair beside her, arm slung over the back of the chair, her head leaning toward her friend. And behind them both, exuding propriety even in this portrait, stood Wade, gazing down at Charlotte, a tulip tucked into his breast pocket.

"Good morning, Wade," she whispered, her chest tightening in a warm, tender, familiar way—with love. "I have a big day today, and I'm glad you'll be in here with me. Make sure to keep me in check, okay?"

As she spoke, the bubble of silence around her seemed to break, and the house filled with life again. The brass knocker of the front door rang through the house, and the sounds of Edith shooing Hazel down the stairs brought Charlotte back to the present. She straightened up as they poked their heads back into the dining room.

"I hope you're ready for your first meeting as head of the family," Edith said. Hazel grinned beside her as she held two thumbs up.

"Yeah, you better be, babes. I have a lot of ideas to throw at you, and I'm not sure how these old geezers will take them."

She laughed as Edith chided the other girl. She glanced at the portrait, at him, one last time.

"Yeah . . . let's do this."

CHAPTER THIRTY-FIVE

*D*arkness permeated the space. It wasn't total darkness like the night—merely muted. There seemed to be no direct source of light in the deep gray fog that encompassed him, but trickles of light somehow stole their way into this space. Even if he could afford the strength to keep his eyes open, he doubted he could see beyond this. Not only was it dark—it was also excruciatingly cold. There was a fire in his veins, even as numbness threatened to consume his flesh.

He was feeling *things*. Things he hadn't felt since he was alive. He was heavy, held down by an invisible weight. Every breath seemed to steal whatever strength he may have found in this dreary place. Slowly but surely, it came back to him.

He had died again. Permanently this time, it seemed. An image of Lottie, her desperate and fierce face, flashed in his mind. She had done it to free him, he knew. The cost for her to do it would have been astronomical.

This meant he was gone from the world that she remained in. Thus, he concluded, whilst lying in the dark, that he must be in hell. For it felt hellish, shivering on the gritty freezing floor, feeling as though some illness overcame him. Perhaps this was the eternal damnation he had been assigned—alone forever felt fitting.

"Ah, I was wondering when you would awaken, my dear friend."

Wade's eyes finally snapped open at the familiar voice.

ACKNOWLEDGMENTS

Wraiths and Wanderings was a dream that has turned into a reality. A literal dream, I mean. I dreamt of a lanky, weird girl and her video camera, and a handsome ghost who had no idea why she was recording him— or what she was even doing, because he didn't understand what a video camera was. I wrote this book in giant slabs (thank you, NaNoWriMo), and cried over fragments at my little desk, wanting my weird children to find their place in the world.

I have a lot of people to thank for getting Charlotte, Wade, Hazel, Spectre, and Atticus here. First, my husband Sean. Without your endless encouragement and pushing me toward my goals, without you reading over my drafts and being so involved, I wouldn't have gotten here. I love you.

Winter and Latte — mama can never get work done when you dig, but I adore your weird form of support when I'm writing.

Mummy, without your unwavering support, I never would have pursued my dreams. I know this isn't the story you were after from me, but I promise I have other weird little blooms in my heart for you.

Adara, my best friend and cover designer, for taking my vision and putting them together. You're the best, and I cannot express how thankful I am for you

Cleo, my wonderful editor. You worked wonders, despite my *bristling* at the American spelling. You are an angel.

My darling Lottie model, Julia — you smashed it, babes. Thanks for bringing my gal to life.

And Lauren. Oh, you thought I wasn't going to mention you because I did everyone else first. I got you, though, didn't I? You have been my confidant, my rock, my support. Not only have you critiqued my work and helped me build a whole new structure for it, you've sat with me. Whether that was during our writing sessions, my anxiety, or my imposter syndrome — you've been there for me, through thick and thin. I love and appreciate you. Thank you for sharing every aspect of this journey with me. I can't wait to do more together!

And to you, who has picked up my weird little book and gotten this far. Thank you, from the depths of my heart. There is so much fear when you put bits of yourself into something, hoping to share it with others. I hope you found some comfort in these pages with me and my kids.

Secrets and Summonings
PREVIEW

It was dark in the old farmhouse, but that was nothing new to her.

The shadows skirted their feet, shying away from the pan of their flashlights across the hardwood floor. There were no noises save for their footfalls—the heavier crunch of one pair of boots, the other a more cautious, light-footed step. No scampering of mice, not even the chirp of a cicada in the space surrounding them. The flashlight beams bounced over an assortment of eclectic knickknacks in the kitchen: a Victorian-era wood-fire stove, a fifties blender, tins from before the war. Altogether, an odd mishmash of different lives and different stories.

"If I was going to be murdered anywhere, this would be the place."

Hazel broke the silence as well as the concentration of her companion, who flashed her a scowl.

Charlotte Blythe was wan, even by the pale glow of their flashlights in the shuttered house. Her long chestnut-brown hair was held in place by a braid that swung behind her as she pivoted, returning her attention to their investigation.

"Is this *really* the place to make those sorts of jokes?" Charlotte whispered with an audible eye roll, glancing about. Hazel shrugged a shoulder nonchalantly, the black leather of her favorite jacket squeaking as she did. Charlotte might have been an amazing witch and an expert ghost vlogger, but she wasn't nearly as collected as the Hunter—at least not yet. Hazel reasoned she could train her up in due time.

"If the set of one of my favorite movie franchises isn't the place for me to haunt," the Hunter grinned, "then where is?"

Charlotte pinched the bridge of her nose, drawing in a deep breath. "We have a job to do. Maybe we should focus on that instead of, I don't know, becoming a crime scene?"

"Sure, babes." Hazel moved past Charlotte, heading toward the main hall. "It's not like I'd go down without a fight, anyway."

They were currently in a Hollywood studio on the set of one of the newest releases in a supernatural horror franchise. It had always been one of Hazel's dreams to be here, to see how the magic was made. Unfortunately, the circumstances in which they'd been asked to come were less than ideal. The director had contacted Charlotte directly through her channel, Wraiths and Wanderings, asking for their help. Something weird was going on here—creepy things that made the cast feel like they were genuinely in a horror film.

Everyone on set denied playing pranks, claiming they weren't the ones making the creepy laughter, slamming doors in an invisible wind, or breaking things that had been nowhere near the edge of a table or what have you. It hadn't seemed legit at first; there was a whole establishment he could have contacted her through, after all, and even Charlotte's channel email would have been more credible. And yet here they were, skulking around a creepy set at two in the morning, hunting for the source of the dread filling the cast and crew.

"I bet we aren't the only channel they asked to come," Hazel commented, pointing her flashlight around the thin hallway and noting the peeling wallpaper. The set design was on point. "I bet the Ghoul Boys are gonna come in after us."

"That means if something is here," Charlotte sighed, "then we'd better find it. I can't stand the idea of a single precious hair on their heads being harmed."

"My boy could take it," Hazel argued as Charlotte followed her out. "He's a demon unto himself. I bet he could vanquish them with a single word or some shit."

Charlotte rolled her eyes. "That's just a meme, Hazel! He's still a normal human, you know. He isn't like us. And he has *way* less common sense about ghosts than my boy. 'Come fight me, demons,'" Charlotte deepened her voice, mocking Hazel. "He'd get sideswiped by something and be down for the count, while my boy would be outta there, safe and sound."

Hazel spun to face Charlotte, hands planted on her hips. "You're lucky Gran doesn't like us betting, or I'd crush you! I would totally wait for them to get here and see who comes out still standing."

Charlotte muttered something she couldn't hear that sounded suspiciously like 'Whatever you think, dummy.' Hazel ignored her friend as she took another glance around, looking for anything out of place. She wished she'd brought her Polaroid camera with her; she could have gotten some cool shots for her journal.

"Hey, babes, could I grab a cam and a mic? I think I could get some pretty sick shots."

Charlotte clutched her video camera protectively, shrinking back. "We have a strict NDA. Plus, I don't trust you not to break it. Sorry, not sorry." Hazel let out a huff at the other woman's words but didn't press the matter.

The hum of the Exit sign and the shuffling of the crew in the distance become audible once more as they approached the front of the house. They'd done a full sweep of the set and had found nothing thus far—nothing that screamed super-natural or occult, anyway. Hazel cocked her head toward the door and Charlotte nodded in response. As they slipped out onto the concrete floor of the studio surrounding the set, Hazel remarked, "At least we're the coolest ghost-hunting duo in existence, right?"

Charlotte laughed, a breathy and easy sound that reverberated around them. Hazel joined in, warmed by the naturalness of Charlotte's joy. It had taken time, but she was getting there, slowly becoming whole again.

"Did you find anything?" Their bonding moment was cut short by the director scurrying over to them. He was slightly shorter than Charlotte with a thick Australian accent that sometimes sent Hazel into fits of laughter, especially with some of the nonsensical colloquialisms he used. The number of times he'd said he was "keen as" that evening had utterly bewildered the girls.

Charlotte immediately entered "head of the Blythe family" mode, answering his questions with a detailed rundown. Hazel's attention drifted as the twosome spoke; she wasn't the details person, after all. Her eyes quickly snagged on one particular sign: Dressing Rooms.

"See you in a bit, babes," Hazel murmured before slipping away.

ABOUT E.K

E.K lives with her husband and two rabbits, Winter and Latte. She has a BA in History and mentors young writers between writing, video games, and collecting Twilight memorabilia.